CATACLYSM

THE MYST CLIPPER SHICAINE

KERRY A. FORRESTAL
AND
JOHN FRACCHIA

First published worldwide in 2016
by Bedlam Boys Publishing
an imprint of
Kerry A. Forrestal and John R. Fracchia

ISBN (978-0-9973232-0-7) – Hardcover Edition
ISBN (978-0-9973232-1-4) – Paperback Edition
ISBN (978-0-9973232-2-1) – eBook Edition
First Print Edition

www.cataclysmbook.info
www.bedlamboys.info

Cover Design by Mirela Barbu

World map by Cornelia Yoder
www.corneliayoder.com

Formatting by BB eBooks
bbebooksthailand.com
All Rights Reserved

DEDICATION

Kerry Forrestal

I wish to dedicate this book to three extraordinary women in my life, my wife Shannon, and daughters Sarah and Riley. You inspire me in so many ways every day. Thank you for the time, support, laughter and love to make this book possible.

And to my Mom and Dad, Jeannine and Richard. No matter how unlikely the prospects of success of anything I've ever tried, you never failed to be encouraging. Your endless support for everything from medical school to writing has helped to make these things possible. I would not be the person I am without your love and guidance. (Yes, I'm putting the blame on you.)

John Fracchia

I wish to dedicate this book to the love of my life – my wife, Nancy Kane. You knew way back in 1978 that we were supposed to be together, and though it took us 28 years to get there, each day has been a joyous adventure. Without your love, belief and encouragement this would have not been possible.

And to my parents, John and Barbara Fracchia. From an early age, you instilled in me the joy of the written word and the endless worlds that could be experienced through it. Without your love and encouragement, this book would not be possible (And for that matter, neither would I).

ACKNOWLEDGEMENTS

This book has been a labor of love but we couldn't have done it without the encouragement, guidance and support of many family and friends. To you we are incredibly grateful.

We would like to especially thank our friend and mentor Elizabeth Haydon whose love, support and guidance has made all the difference. This day would not have come without you.

Thank you, also, to Judith Pratt and Becky Mayr who at different times served as our copy editors and helped tame our wild early drafts.

A giant thank you to Terry McGarry for final editing of the work. Her immense patience with first time novelists, who at times possessed a tenuous grip on punctuation and point of view, was greatly appreciated. The work is stronger for your support and efforts.

We would be remiss in not thanking the many folks who read the work over the years and offered support, feedback and insight. These include Theodore Agnew Jr, Lynne Albuquerque, Beth Brunelle, Jason Caggiano, Zoe Epstein, Sue Fondy, John F. Fracchia (John's Dad), Mark Gutis, Claire Kingham, John Kirkman, Tracy Kirkman, Dawn Kline, Dee Levine, Tammy Longabaugh, Lisa Ludovico, Darren Mahoney, Karen Martin, Janis Moore Campbell, Sean O'Leary, Rick Olshak, Kevin Panke-Buisse, Marc Phillips, David Prunty, Holly Reycroft, Leslie Roman, Chelsea Sanders, Kerry Schwenker, Lorraine Sinclaire, Cat Spurway, Tom Tarantelli, Kayla Vaughan, Gretchen Van Valen, Wiley Vaughan, Evie Weinstein, Chloe Wilson, Ron Wismer. We hope that we haven't forgotten anyone, but if we did, please know that we appreciate you as well.

Finally, thank you to you, our readers, for joining us on these new adventures. If you enjoyed the work, we hope you'll recommend it to your friends. If you did not enjoy the work we hope, of course, you'll have the good taste not to mention that we spoke to you.

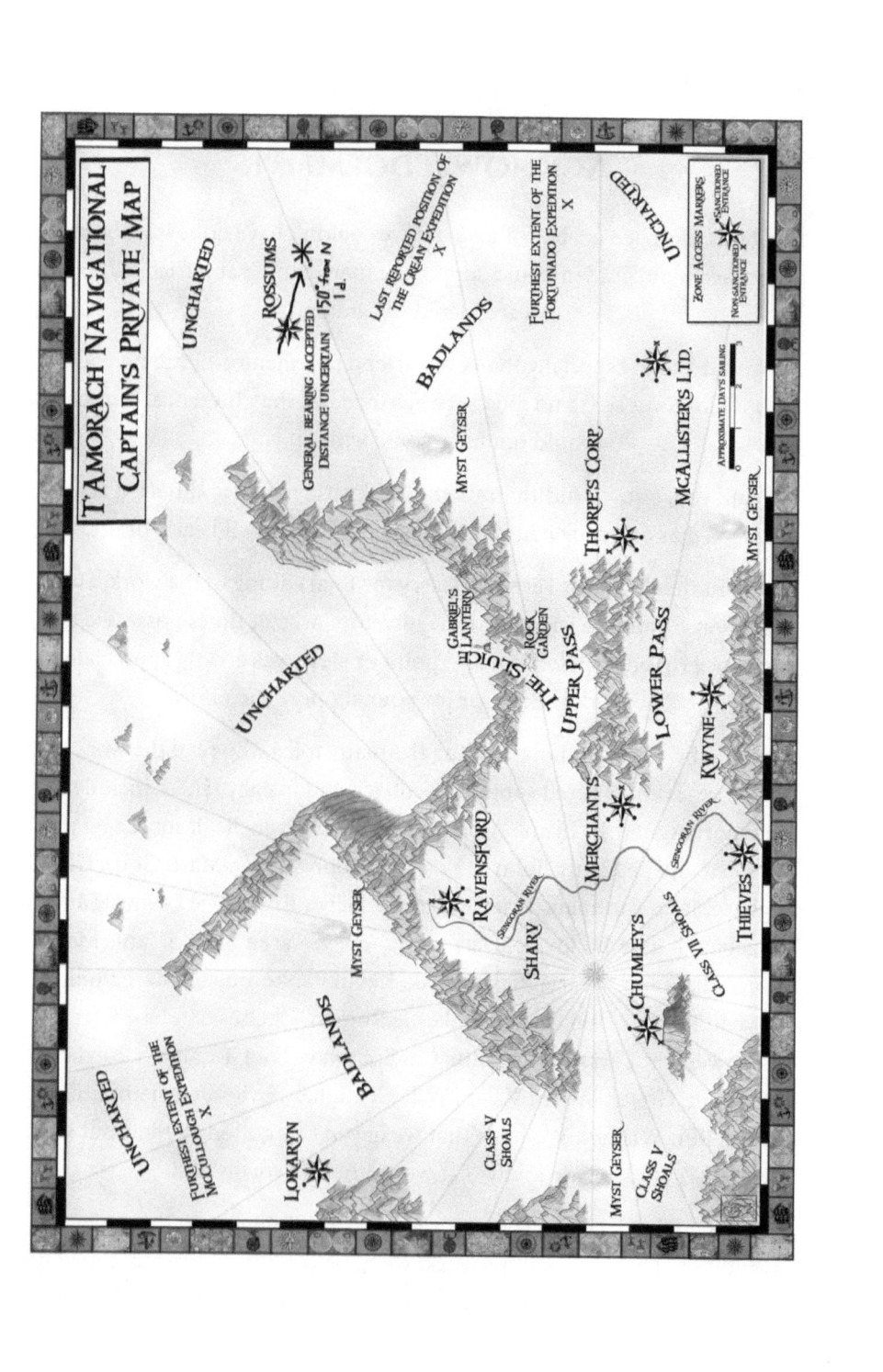

T'AMORACH NAVIGATIONAL
CAPTAIN'S PRIVATE MAP

UNCHARTED

ROSSUMS

GENERAL BEARING ACCEPTED
DISTANCE UNCERTAIN 150' from N
1 d.

BADLANDS

MYST GEYSER

LAST REPORTED POSITION OF
THE CREAN EXPEDITION
X

FURTHEST EXTENT OF THE
FORTUNADO EXPEDITION
X

UNCHARTED

THORPE'S CORP.

MCALLISTER'S LTD.

MYST GEYSER

ZONE ACCESS MARKERS
SANCTIONED
ENTRANCE
NON-SANCTIONED
ENTRANCE X

APPROXIMATE DAYS SAILING

UNCHARTED

GABRIEL'S
LANTERN

ROCK
GARDEN

THE SLUICE

UPPER PASS

LOWER PASS

KWYNE

MERCHANTS

RAVENSFORD

SHARV

SPENCORIAN RIVER

SPENCORIAN RIVER

THIEVES

CLASS VII SHOALS

CHUMLEYS

MYST GEYSER

FURTHEST EXTENT OF THE
MCCULLOUGH EXPEDITION
X

UNCHARTED

BADLANDS

LOKARYN

CLASS V
SHOALS

MYST GEYSER

CLASS V
SHOALS

The truth, while interesting, is irrelevant.

—Tomanus Jugar, two hundred and sixty fifth rohnin of Kwyne

PRELUDE

Aboard the *Wiscott*
Myst clipper of the Merchant House Kebonia
Captain Harlin Rahn, commanding
Ship's Position: SSW of the Sluice
Badlands

SEARCHLIGHTS FROM THE MYST CLIPPER ship *Wiscott* reached out across the expanse of caustic myst that lay before her. The reflection of the intense beams scattered and shimmered along the gentle ripples of the surface as the forward lookouts searched for wreckage, reefs, or outcroppings that could pose a threat to the ship. The sleek craft was buoyed above the myst by a series of sweeping wing like foils that stretched out from her sides so that the deadly miasma passed harmlessly inches below her keel. Each captain had his or her own "witches' brew" for doping the graphene/graphyne-alloy foils so as to capture as much energy as possible from the highly charged myst, giving each ship's foils a distinctive color.

If not for the foils, the craft would look very much like the clipper ships that sailed the oceans before the Cataclysm covered the waters and the low-lying lands with myst. There was an enclosed bridge riding the quarterdeck for protection in rough myst, and an afterdeck astern. In front of the bridge was a small watch overlooking the work deck below. Midships, the work deck around the mainmast was clean and efficiently laid out. The forecastle again had protected areas for lookouts when the myst was roughest. The ship's three masts—main, mizzen, and fore—

could support all traditional sails, including moonrakers.

But she wasn't purely a sailing ship. She had powerful engines belowdecks for propulsion, and antigravity projectors built into her hull to augment the ground-effect-like lift of the foils. The need for the oldest known sailing technology to coexist with the newest was a testament to the enormous energy requirements necessary to sail a ship out on the mysts. And survive.

Outside of the bridge stood First Officer Francis Hurley, his hands tightly gripping the forward rail that overlooked the work deck. Though he had full confidence in the lookouts, he scanned the darkness, alert and watchful.

"We do have crew for that, Mr. Hurley," Captain Harlin Rahn said as he came out of the bridge and joined his first officer at the rail. He handed Hurley a cup of coffee, the steam from which rose into the heat of the night.

"I know, Captain," Hurley said.

"That railing has survived grade-five myst storms, but I'm not sure it's going to take another ten minutes of your emphatic hold on it. Is there a problem?" The captain slowly drank some coffee. Hurley's grip loosened.

"No sir, no immediate problems. We set the ion skimmers to standby about thirty minutes ago. We have a full charge on the main and reserve power."

"Good, so why the death grip?" Rahn asked.

"The sailing is smooth enough, but it's still far too dark for my liking." Hurley motioned with the mug, and added, "Thanks."

"We knew it would be dark. The new moon makes it harder to be detected."

"I'm still not sure why detection is an issue, Captain. We're a cargo clipper, and so far as I can tell the only people who will be interested in detecting us will be curtain salesmen and housewives in Merchants' Zone."

Rahn said nothing in reply.

"Another one of your mysteries, Captain?"

"If I told you, it wouldn't be much of mystery, now, would it?" Rahn said.

"At the captain's pleasure." Hurley took a sip of the coffee. "The worse things seem to get in the world, the more of these strange little jobs we find ourselves on. In the nine months since I signed on, I've yet to see rhyme or reason."

"But you have seen profit," Rahn said.

"True. Whatever the job is that brings us here, I hope it's worth the risk." He took another sip of the coffee. "I've never much liked the northern routes through the Sluice. Faster, to be certain, but just too close to…" He paused for a moment. "Yes I know, fewer ships traveling down here, harder to be detected."

Rahn took a sip of his own coffee. His eyes, like Hurley's, never left the surface of the myst.

"First Officer, if any such thing were going on, how much would you really want to know?"

The question hung for a moment, then another.

"Besides," Rahn said, having taken the first officer's measure, "I've never heard of a sailor complaining about a calm myst."

"I like calm myst with a fair breeze as much as the next man, but on a night like tonight, we can't see anything in front of us. Usually the chop from the myst will flash on the rocks and give us some sort of warning, but I'm telling you it is dead calm out there. It's actually black."

"So it is. Odd to see it like that."

"I don't suppose a few navigational flares would be possible?" Hurley asked.

"No, not a good idea. The myst may be low-energy tonight, but that doesn't mean it won't ignite."

"Aye, Captain. It's a shame those sailors from Ravensford Zone have such an aversion to technology. It would be handy to have one of their crystalsmyths aboard. I've heard that they can forge a crystal that would turn the night sky to day and you wouldn't feel a bit of heat if you held the crystal in your hand until dawn."

"Is that so?" Rahn replied with a small smile. "We'll have to make do without. We have a good amount of time left before dawn. Use it. The searchlights will show any immediate danger to the ship. The radar will show the distant threats above and the sonar below. Signal efficiency should be way up without as much ionization. We should be on the far side of the Sluice before sunrise even at a cautious pace and half sails."

Hurley looked over the port side of the ship into the distance. "It's dark enough that you can see the light from the firefall at the end of the Sluice."

"It's amazing that all we have out here is a light rip current," Rahn said. "It will get worse as we pass in front of the main channel, but we should be safe enough here. I would imagine the main fall is less than a mile away. We should be able to see most of Gabriel's Lantern when we're along the main channel."

"Would the captain care to alter course to take a closer look?" Hurley asked with a slight smile on his face.

"I'll pass. If Gabriel's Lantern warns to steer clear, this is as close as I get." Rahn shook his head and mused, "A flame that big sticking up that high above the main channel, cut from the rock and fueled by the myst itself? Someone meant business."

"Amazing thing, the lantern. It must have been built before the Cataclysm, before myst was everywhere. I can't imagine how anyone could have built it with the main stream on fire all the time."

"And yet the channel narrows, concentrates the myst till it ignites, and then funnels it upward to light the lantern. It had to be designed for that purpose. Quite the riddle." Rahn lifted the mug of coffee to his lips again, but stopped as the rim touched his lower lip. "What the hell?"

For the first time, the two men looked directly at each other. The constant reassuring hum of the engines had ceased.

Rahn spun to the bridge. "Report!" he said, as he moved inside.

"Not sure yet, sir! Working on it," said bridge engineer Rem Halyard, who was furiously checking the consoles.

The main lights flickered out. Backup batteries kicked in with a shrill alarm to announce the action, and emergency lighting snapped on.

Hurley rang the watch deck's bell furiously, shouting, "Wake up, action stations." He then went down to the work deck to begin directing the crew.

Inside the bridge, the captain looked over the consoles and saw the power steadily draining as the ship began sliding sideways, taken by the current.

"Isolate all power sources, cut them all!" Rahn ordered.

"Aye, sir." Halyard reacted instantly, flipping up protective covers and quickly snapping down toggle switch after toggle switch.

"Shut those damned alarms off," Rahn ordered. "There's a problem. We get it." He pressed the comm link button on the console and called, "Engine room, what's happening?"

There was no response.

Second Officer Teague Chapman arrived on the bridge in only his underwear. Noting the bridge crew's confused expressions, he explained, "I was in the head."

"Go to the engine room, find out what's happening. There's no response and we're dead in the myst," Rahn ordered.

"How far from the Sluice?" Chapman asked.

"We're in it. Go!"

"Bloody hell," Chapman cursed as he tore down the companionway with little regard for the fact that he was still in his underwear.

Off-duty emergency crewmembers quickly assembled at bridge stations to serve as extra sets of eyes and ears for the on-duty crew. On the work deck Hurley began issuing orders, and sails rose into the night sky in response.

"We can't sail our way out of here," a "landman" new to the myst shouted as he stood with a sheet in his hands. Hurley looked at him and thought that he was probably no more than a teen. It took the first officer only a moment to determine which approach would work best.

"Pull, damn you!" Hurley shouted. "Or I *will* shoot you dead where you stand."

The young man's eyes opened wide and he pulled the sheet with all his might.

The more experienced crew suppressed smiles despite their dire circumstances. They knew that Hurley's threat was made for effect, but they had no illusions. If it really came to it, those who were a liability to the ship were to be rendered inert as quickly as possible. Most were merely put ashore at the next port to find their own way, but those who threatened the ship more immediately were dealt with more immediately. They doubted Hurley would waste a bullet, but rather toss the offender over the side of the ship and let the myst take him. If their captain felt the person was a threat to the ship, it would take only a nod and the crew would comply.

It didn't take long with the combined efforts of the crew before the sail caught the breezes.

A cheer went up and Hurley stood to face the deck crews.

"Do your jobs! Able seamen and mates, keep an eye on the ordinaries and the landmen. The longer we can keep the ship under control, the longer the captain has to fix the problem. Do your jobs and we'll live to see the dawn. Now move!"

On the bridge, Helmsman Tiega Koerge was switching from hybrid navigation to full sail.

"Trying to tack, Captain. Our stern is swinging about toward the falls. The current is turning us," Koerge said.

"I'll be damned if my ship is going over the falls, let alone ass-end-first," Rahn said.

The ship charged forward as stronger breezes swelled the sails.

"Yes!" Koerge said to himself.

"Good, but turning is one thing, getting out of here is another," Rahn said over his shoulder as he continued to work the consoles to get some idea of what was happening to his ship. "Pull in the starboard foils! Try to create more drag on that side to help with the turn. Any threat, recover them both."

He pressed the comm link button again.

"Comm!"

"Aye, Captain," came the voice of Atan Lance, the ship's communications officer.

"Atan, can we raise anyone?"

"Already on it. Power to the system is sketchy at best, tying in portable generators. Sir, would you like me to notify Arden Rescue Station first?"

"Yes, get Arden if at all possible, but I'll take what I can get right now. We need a fast rescue portal, and the farther down the channel we are, the less chance they'll have."

"Aye, sir."

First Officer Hurley entered the bridge. "Full sail is nearly out, but the wind isn't enough to carry us."

"Then we make some of our own. Fire your aft navigational flares into the far channel; it should ignite the myst and the heat will drive some wind for us. The fire should mostly follow the current down the Sluice, but the wind will spread it out."

"Aye, Captain." Hurley spun and headed back onto the work deck.

"Atan?" Rahn said.

"Working on it. Most of the stations are asleep. Arden Station monitors twenty-four hours a day, but they're quite distant. I think it's the best shot we have, but I need another generator to boost the signal power."

"Find him a generator," Rahn said to one of the emergency bridge crew, who went scurrying down the companionway. Pressing the comm link button, Rahn said, "Chapman! Are you there yet?"

The sound of the last moment of retching came through the comm link. "They're all dead. Slaughtered." There was a pause. "Chief Engineer Logan has been shot in the head. The rest are…dead as well."

Rahn flipped a small toggle on the console in front of him to carry his voice shipwide, and pressed the comm link button. "Security, intruder protocols. Engineering, all shifts, to the engine room." He toggled the comm again and said, "Weaps."

The ship shuddered as Hurley's rockets screamed forth from the vessel to ignite the volatile myst.

"Aye, Captain," replied the weapons officer of the *Wiscott*, Bowman Long.

"Mr. Long, we have a saboteur on board. I'm establishing contact with the Arden Rescue Station, but…"

"Understood, Captain."

"Arm the crew and then carry out…"

Rahn paused for a moment as he searched for answers in the readouts and switches in front of him, but he found none. A light suddenly rose as fire ignited behind the ship.

"Bowman, carry out Tarrthála-North."

"Understood. Out."

Atan's voice came through the comm.

"Captain, I have Arden Rescue Station. I am transmitting our situation now."

A horrible grinding noise racked the ship, and it lurched to the left.

"Reef!" called a stern portside watch.

"Thank you, a bit late, but thank you. Mr. Halyard, get whatever people we can spare up on deck to spot. Shallow up the foils, we can't go to antigrav with the power we have left for any amount of time. Do you have a damage report for that little bump?"

"No hull breaches showing. Hull shielding and plating are holding. Foils intact. We're lucky it was a light impact," said the engineer.

"Captain," called Chapman through the comm link.

"Go, Teague."

"We've lost most of the main and reserve power, but the day shifts have arrived. They don't think they have enough left to do…whatever the hell it is they do in a situation like this."

"Anyone see who might have done this?"

"No, sir. It looks like the engineers have been dead for a while. The blood is dry."

"Are security teams in place?"

"Almost, sir, and I grabbed a few able bodies I trust on my way down to Engineering to help."

"Good. Get us back online, Mr. Chapman."

"Aye, sir."

The ship suddenly moved forward and the crew felt the heat front pass over them. In the distance the myst burned in a kaleidoscope of colors.

"First Office Hurley has given us some wind to move us. Position, Helm?"

"Sir, we're maybe a quarter mile from the Grantways of the Rock Garden. After that no amount of sailing will clear us, it's power out or nothing."

"Set the swivel and chase guns. Fore and aft, load grappling hooks. How far are we from the main channel of the Sluice?"

"I can't be precise, sir."

"Can you get us there?" Rahn asked.

"*Into* the main channel?" the helmsman asked as First Officer Hurley came back onto the bridge.

"The smaller channels are rockier, and we'll more likely get ripped apart well before we get near the falls. The main channel gives us some room to move when we get the power back on. We head into the main channel, grapple onto one of the Rock Garden spires, and hang on until the rescue station sets up a portal, sends a tug, or we can power our way out."

"The myst is a lot rougher there, but if we can hold position, we can deploy the ion skimmers to recharge power. The current will draw a lot of myst over the foils. Not one, but two possible ways out," Hurley said.

"Very good, sir," the helmsman said.

"Helmsman, make your course three degrees to the north and hold steady until I say otherwise," Rahn ordered.

"Three degrees north and hold steady, aye," the helmsman replied.

"Helm, estimated time to the channel?" Rahn asked.

"Sir, the myst speeds are not constant, I can't give a time without knowing all the speeds along our course. I'm going to have to…guess."

"Very well," Rahn said as the ship lurched forward. He looked at Hurley with a small smile. "He knows how to make a point."

"Bridge? This is Chapman in Engineering. We have some auxiliary propulsion online. You have limited power. The main propulsions systems are heavily damaged, but you should be able to at least steer."

"Rem, with that extra, is there any chance if we diverted everything, we would have enough to switch into volitation?" Rahn asked.

The engineer opened a panel on the engineering station and started looking at a set of readouts.

Hurley gaped at the panel, and then said, "Volitation? Only a handful of ships in the world are capable of that."

"A few more than that, but you're standing on one of them," Rahn replied. "One of the captain's mysteries, as you say."

"No, sir, not nearly enough," said the engineer.

"Steady on, then. Continue to the mesas of the main channel."

"You didn't think I should know the ship had that capability?" Hurley asked.

"The technology is rare and those who can control it are rarer still. If you are capable of doing so, I would have thought you'd have presented that in your credentials when you signed aboard nine months ago."

"I've never had the opportunity to try. How many people ever have? But still, if something happened to you…"

"If something happened to me, you'd be far safer sailing to harbor by normal means than trying to use it."

"Sir?" came the voice of Salizar Grason, a mate in the armory.

"Go," Rahn said.

"Sir, Weapons Officer Bowman just portaled off the ship right in front of me with—" He paused. "—a portal crystal, sir."

"Are you sure?" Hurley asked.

"I have the burned-out crystal in my hand, sir."

"Is there a case there?" Rahn asked.

"Yes, sir. Seven more crystals of different shapes, colors, and sizes."

"Bring it to Mr. Chapman in the engine room," Rahn said, ignoring the stare of his first officer.

"Captain?" Hurley asked.

"I'll explain when the ship is secured, I need you on the watch now," Rahn replied.

"Aye, Captain," Hurley responded as he moved to the watch overlooking the work deck.

"Sentinel mesas dead ahead!" called the stern lookout. The ship still floated at an awkward angle, though its aspect had changed.

"Midships and fore cannons, fire when you have a clear shot," Hurley commanded the deck crews. "Don't leave the lines slack, they'll snap when they go taut. Aim high to help keep the ship out of the myst. Keep her bow pointed out of the channel. When we get power back we want to be pointed in the right direction."

The tension on the deck was palpable until the eruption of cannonfire. More eruptions followed, and a cheer went up from the crew as the first grapples found purchase on the rocks.

"Idle down when we come into position," Rahn directed the engine room. "Conserve energy. Adjust the foils so they don't impact the rock face. Use the antigrav only if absolutely necessary to keep the ship level."

"Aye, Captain."

"Helm, hard to starboard," Rahn commanded.

The ship slowly swung into a stable position as the lines from the aft cannons pulled taut.

"Secure the lines," Rahn called outside to Hurley. "Set out as many grapples as you can to whatever anchoring points you can find."

Minutes passed as the first line groaned and ached under the strain, then finally snapped. New lines were launched and took up the burden of holding the ship against the ever-increasing current. A crewman yelled up to the watch, breathless and bruised.

"The myst is dissolving the lines as fast as we can set new ones," he said. "We can't extend the shields out over the lines with the power we currently have. We're being dragged in meters at a time."

"Keep setting lines, we need more..." Hurley was interrupted by the sound of an explosion as the deck under the forecastle of the ship erupted beneath the feet of the cannon crews, throwing them across the deck. Several lines and deck cannons were destroyed.

"Persistent bastard," Rahn said as he pressed the comm link. "Security teams, find him and kill him."

"Minor structural damage, but the forward cannons are out," the bridge engineer reported.

Hurley reentered the bridge. "The crew is repositioning midships chase cannons forward, but I think it's a matter of time. We can't set lines quickly enough in this myst."

"Sir, don't you think Bowman is the likely saboteur?" the helmsman asked. "He did abandon us, after all, and with a portal crystal no less. Those things are incredibly rare."

"No, his orders to leave the ship were mine and I gave him the crystal."

Hurley stared at his captain. The ship lurched backward, and backward again, as more lines snapped, weakened by the myst.

"Captain. Comm. Arden Rescue Station, patching through to you."

"…Repeating. Please be advised, ionization levels at your present location prevent a rescue portal. Communications microportals of limited duration are possible. Prepare your ship's log for transmission. Also send confirmation of body, correction, crew count to be forty-eight sailors and officers. Sorry, *Wiscott*. May Thecla's protection be with you."

There was silence for a moment. "Engine room, report," Rahn said as the ship lurched again and more deck cannons fired.

"We've salvaged perhaps fifteen percent of what we had. I think that's about all we're going to get without recharging."

"Comm, have Arden set up that communications portal for a burst transmission if they still can."

"Very good, sir."

"First Officer Hurley will be down directly with the logs."

Rahn turned to Hurley and handed him a memory cube and a scrap of paper. "*This*, obviously, is not our ship's logs."

"There seems no end to the mysteries tonight, Captain."

"I understand your confusion, Mr. Hurley. We're not done trying to save the ship, but as you suspected we haven't been delivering goods. Someone is trying to start a war between the zones and we've been carrying information for those trying to figure out who it is."

"Bowman?" Hurley asked.

"Bowman is from Rossums Zone. He is an android. He left on my orders with information that I hope will avert war. He stands the best chance of getting the information out."

"Bowman? Is a sentient? He scratches himself. He belches like a sailor. He can't…"

"I know they can be made to seem human, but he's not, Hurley. Androids are tough, but they're not indestructible. There's no guarantee he'll survive, so I need this cube transmitted to the destination on the paper."

Hurley stood stunned by the revelation.

"Mr. Hurley, I need you to get this through for the sake of us all."

"Aye, sir, I will." Hurley took the cube and paper and sped off the bridge toward the communications shack.

The ship lurched again as another cable gave way.

"The remaining cannon crews are still minutes from firing and they'll only be able to fire light grappling hooks from the chase cannons at first," the helmsman reported.

"Very well then," Rahn responded. "Tiega, plot a course to the middle of the channel.

"Aye, sir," replied the helmsman with a somewhat uneasy look on his face.

"I told you, I'm not going ass-end over the falls."

He pressed the comm link. "Teague, report."

"We have enough power to keep the neutralizers in regeneration mode, so the myst below our keel shouldn't be a big problem. After that and keeping the electrical systems of the ship going, and the deck shields, you have barely any power left for the navigational thrusters. I'm sorry, Captain, that's all that's left."

"We'll deploy the foils fully as soon as we're able. The ion skimmers should still be working. Use what you can from them. Otherwise, keep working on a solution for the propulsion." He pressed the comm link and called, "Weaps."

"This is Grason again."

"Ready some incendiary missiles for firing. Target them north of the ship about two hundred meters. Set detonation depth to ten meters. If we burn out the fuel for the mystfire up here, maybe the myst downstream will burn a little less hot when our shields are weakening."

He thought for a moment.

"Helmsman?"

"I have a course set, Captain, down the main channel. The river will narrow quite a bit, but I can't say exactly where the myst gets compressed enough to ignite. I also have no idea of the vertical drop," Koerge said.

"Gabriel's Lantern is about three hundred meters high, use that as a reference."

The ship lurched aft again as cannonfire rang out, and this time the movement down into the Sluice didn't stop.

"I think it's time," Rahn said as he pressed the comm link button. "Comm, is Mr. Hurley with you?"

"Hurley here," came the first officer's voice. "Message is away, sir. I'm not one hundred percent sure of that routing, it was complex to say the least and we're a bit under the gun here."

Rahn said calmly, "If there is any doubt, send it again and then get back up here." He toggled the comm link to shipwide communication and said, "Crew, prepare for mystfire. Weaps, fire."

Two missiles arched up out of the ship's stern and slammed down into the myst some distance away. Moments passed, and then the surface of the myst seemed to rise.

A slow rumbling could be heard as the ship bobbed in the main channel of the Sluice. The crew looked all around: no one had ever heard the sound of oncoming mystfire when the ship's engines were completely silent.

"Helm?"

"Ready."

"Engineer?"

"Ready."

"Clear the rigging and have the deck crews secure their guns."

The command was shouted down from the bridge to the deck. The cannons fell silent as the remaining lines continued to dissolve in the caustic myst. Men and women clambered down from the three masts like so many spiders on threads.

In the distance, fire fountained up and spread in all directions. Unlike the lower-energy flares that had started a small surface fire that had been swept away from the ship by the currents, these were phosphorous charges that detonated deep in the myst layer and started a conflagration that would burn the myst for miles around. It was an old pirates' trick employed only when capture looked inevitable. Its drawback being that it was just as likely to destroy the prey as it was the predator.

The heated air raced out ahead of the fire front and drove the ship forward down the channel. The crew watched as the burning myst closed in on them. The first officer entered the bridge, his mission complete.

"Done. Twice," he reported with a nod to the captain. Rahn motioned him forward to convey orders down to the work deck and then activated the shipwide comm link.

"This is the captain. We are unable to escape the pull of the current, nor hold ourselves until rescue. We are going to attempt to soft-land beyond the falls. Secure yourselves and be ready for action once we get down. Any hand who must remain on deck, find something and be ready to lash yourselves onto it. Pray, if you do so, for sweet air at the bottom of the falls. Ready on the fore lines," he ordered Hurley, who was now in position to be in direct visual contact with the remaining deck crews who were manning the lines. They had electronic communication still, but they knew it could fail at any moment. The old ways did not require electricity, only steady nerves and a line of vision.

"Ready on the fore lines, aye, sir," Hurley shouted as he raised his hand. The forecastle crew looked up at him.

"Away the fore lines!" Hurley's hand slashed downward through the air.

"Lines clear, Mr. Hurley!" they shouted up.

"Fore lines away, sir," Hurley reported.

"Ready the aft lines."

Hurley looked this time to the aft lines and raised one hand over his head. He looked over to the bridge and motioned their readiness to the captain with the other.

Rahn nodded toward his first officer to indicate his understanding. "Helm, bring her about," he ordered.

"Bow thrusters responding and we're coming about. Forty-five degrees. The current has got us."

"Bow thrusters to off, let the current do the work now."

"Aye sir, thrusters are off, turn is continuing. Ninety degrees, one hundred and thirty degrees…"

"Away aft lines," Rahn ordered.

"Away aft lines," Hurley commanded, slashing the air with his hand. The deck crews instantly responded and reported.

"Aft lines away," Hurley reported seconds later, and then called down to the deck for the crew to clear it. When the deck had cleared, he returned inside the bridge.

"Helm, bring us into the middle of the flow," Rahn ordered.

"Aye, sir," Koerge replied.

The *Wiscott* moved slowly away from the mesas as she came about. The only audible noises now were those of the ship's beams and braces creaking under the strain of the current. It was achingly slow, but the ship responded. The helmsman negotiated the turn, barely missing a mesa wall, and brought the *Wiscott*'s bow across the stream almost elegantly. A grand old lady meeting her fate with pride.

"Mr. Chapman?" Rahn called into the comm link.

"Power reserves down to nine percent. We're trying to connect a fuel reserve directly to the propulsion stream and light it manually."

"Understood," Rahn said. "Helm, how are we doing?"

"Coming into the main channel, picking up speed. Aft fire impact less than a minute," Koerge replied.

The noise from the gaining mystfire intensified as the ship was racked and tossed in the ever more turbulent myst. Swells licked the sides of the vessel unevenly, lifting one side up then the other.

"Fire a navigational probe out ahead of the ship to determine the falls' location," Rahn ordered.

"Navprobe away, sir," Koerge reported.

"Ahead! The Lantern!" cried a crewman.

"The base of Gabriel's Lantern," the helmsman said, "I never thought I'd live to see that up close."

"Focus and you will live to see more than that," Rahn replied.

The sound of the myst compression got louder with each passing second. They were now running from the fire they started into the fire they feared.

"Will the aft fire reach the Sluice's ignition point before we do?" Hurley asked.

"Unsure, sir," Koerge replied.

"Ready the mystfoils for full deployment just after we clear the falls," Rahn ordered.

"Aren't the foils too slender, Captain?" Hurley asked. "They won't support the weight of the ship in free fall."

"They don't have to," Rahn replied. "They just have to change our arc enough to help us soft-land at the bottom. Every second we glide is that much closer to surviving. Those things are tougher than you might imagine. Whatever power we have left we throw into the antigrav system when we near the bottom."

"What if we also angle the bow and stern thrusters downward to slow the descent and take some strain off the foils?" Hurley asked.

"Good idea. Mr. Halyard, can you get that done?" Rahn said to his bridge engineer.

"Very good sir, calculating the vectors for thrusters now."

"Are we absolutely sure there is no one left in the rigging, Mr. Hurley?" Rahn asked.

Hurley paused a moment and looked out over the work deck. "All rigging is clear, sir."

"Pull the shields down to the level of the mainsail. That should save some power. Set robots to deal with any fires that fall to the deck."

"Aye, sir!"

The fire finally overtook them. The exposed masts and sails burst into flame at the first touch of mystfire.

"Engine room to bridge. You have that extra propulsion."

"Thank you, Mr. Chapman. Continue your work."

"Aye, Captain."

"Helmsman?" Rahn motioned with one hand to move forward.

"Yes, sir."

The moonrakers, royals, topgallants, lower and upper topsails all burned brilliantly as the ship rode the river of flame. *Wiscott*'s shields glowed white and blue against the multicolored mystfire.

"Escape launch detected," the helmsman called.

"Our saboteur has effected his getaway, it seems," Rahn said.

"Or a coward has abandoned us," Hurley replied.

"Either way the ship is all the lighter for it. Bridge engineer, jettison the remaining escape vessels."

"Aye, sir," the engineer confirmed. "Sir, the telemetry from the probe puts the falls about one to two minutes downstream from us at this speed," he added.

"Very good then," the captain said. "Helmsman, full-powered descent. I want as shallow a curve as we can after we clear the falls. Engage when you are ready."

"Aye, Captain," the helmsman replied. He smiled a little as he pushed the throttles home and the ship surged forward.

"Very good," Rahn said, and then sat down in the captain's chair, securing himself for the fall to come. "Mr. Hurley, can you think of anything else?"

"No, sir," the first officer replied as he secured himself in his own chair.

"Very good then. Now we wait." The two men sat side by side, looking out the bridge ports as the fire beckoned. A moment passed.

"So the *Wiscott* is a true Garand-Trass myst clipper and it's been under my nose this whole time," Hurley said.

"Don't feel bad, builders have been copying the form since Garand and Trass unveiled the ships. Everything looks like a Garand-Trass nowadays. It took Halyard six months to figure it out and he's crawling around in the systems all the time."

Another few moments passed in the odd wait. "The escape launch, what do you think will happen to him when he gets down there?" Hurley asked.

"Eaten, I should hope, by some local with a rotten disposition and all day to dine."

Hurley smiled. "Hopefully no such fate for us."

"No, Mr. Hurley, so long as we stay together as a crew, no such fate will befall us. Besides, we have a war to prevent. The *Wiscott* has a few surprises left in her."

"Captain, we're there, sir. I can see the falls on the monitors," Helmsman Koerge reported.

Rahn smiled, then said, "Deploy the foils as soon as we clear the Lantern, Mr. Koerge."

"Aye, sir."

"Captain?" Hurley ventured. "You said earlier 'that particular crystal.' Were there more?"

"Yes," Rahn said. "In fact, there are eight in that set, made by a former captain of mine. The captain of the *Shicaine*."

"The *Shicaine* is a myth. More of the captain's mysteries?"

"No, my friend. No more secrets. I'll tell you the whole story when we're down. It's a pretty good tale."

"Foils deploying, sir," Koerge said.

"Very good. Here we go," Rahn said.

The *Wiscott* passed through the twin mesas of Gabriel's Lantern with Captain Harlin Rahn in command and her crew at their stations with eyes clear. They did not waver as she rode down the river of fire, past Gabriel's Lantern with its warning spire lit brightly, and onto the brink of the falls. As they passed the edge of the known world the ship spread her wings and rode on into legend.

The so-called underground railroad is little more than a gang of thieves masquerading as liberators. You can no more liberate an android than you can a field plow. As such, Thorpe's Corporation Androidics Division will continue to design and manufacture the fastest, most capable machines possible.

—Thorpe's Corporation

CHAPTER 1

Kwyne
Third Arc, outer district

MOONBEAMS STREAMED INTO THE SHABBY room, illuminating the elegant but gaunt cheekbones of the Lokaryn, Derring, as she tended to the android. She knelt over him, almost as if in prayer, the hood of her cloak partially obscuring her features. Dust glittered in the rays as if it were confetti celebrating her presence. The elegance of her features was a sharp contrast to the worn walls and threadbare rugs. The building's squalor was part of the reason for its selection as a safe house. Law enforcement was lax in the outer districts and all but abandoned in decrepit areas such as this.

Derring finished scanning the android, verifying that his electro-magnetic emissions were as minimal as possible. Next she rechecked the sensor network that she had deployed to warn of unwanted visitors. She adjusted several of the refractory crystals attached to the windows. They looked like so many suncatchers awaiting the morning light, but their true purpose was to dissipate electromagnetic signals so that they appeared to be no more concentrated in her location than anywhere else. Finally she sent a message to her downstream link, a message that she was almost certain would not be answered. She had repeated this ritual in a continual loop, never cutting a corner or missing a step, but so far there had been no response. Though it had been a long time since she had done a transit such as this, she knew when luck was running against her.

She turned again to the android: her old friend Hemingway, a name she had helped him choose long ago, and one which she believed he deliberately misspelled to annoy her. To think of a machine as a friend did not seem strange to her. They had been through too much together for her to conceive of him as anything else. It had been five years since she had seen him, and now that they were reunited he had to remain "unconscious" lest his electromagnetic signature give them away. How she wished the circumstances could be different. Would that she could turn off the dampers that held his mind in stasis, bring him to life and hear some of the jokes that used to make her roll her eyes as she groaned in mock pain. Just one would do right now. Any one. It would be comforting beyond measure.

In his deactivated state, Hemingway seemed like a large marionette with the strings cut. His inanimate limbs held only the potential of life. Yet three amazing years of companionship and camaraderie between them lived in her memory. Some considered his kind to be tools, maintaining that androids were merely sophisticated machines doing the work biologics shouldn't have to, certainly no more than that. Though many older androids fit this description, an unknown portion of the millions that now existed did not. Many had become self-aware a long time ago, a fact that was an inconvenience to the prevailing world order. Most of the androids being manufactured now could, in theory, gain sentience. Granting them citizen's rights would destroy any efficiency or economic advantage gained by making them.

Derring prepared to start her next round of checks. She had to be vigilant or the harshest of deaths awaited her. It was perhaps the only thing she knew for certain. This certainty arose from two facts. The first was that she was working for an organization whose sole purpose was to liberate the race of beings that Kwyne relied on for its economic survival. She called it liberation; the Kwynians would call it theft. But theft, even of a commodity as valuable as an android, was not in and of itself a severe enough offense to warrant the death she would endure if caught. Thieves bought their way out of serious charges every day; it was part of the cost of doing business. What would get her killed was the second and more central fact: She was a Lokaryn in a zone that was largely populated by religious zealots. If caught, they would execute her in the most terrible way they could conceive of: exposure to sunlight.

Derring had seen Lokaryns die that way. Unlike their fictional cousins, Lokaryns did not quickly burn or fall to ash when touched by the light of day. The event was the release of decades, if not centuries, of captured life energy. One cell at a time exploding, slowly at first, then ever more quickly to a crescendo. Only the most sadistic members of the various lokaric clans could watch the whole thing, although there were plenty of those. It was exponentially painful, too, or so a Lokaryn rescued from a near-fatal exposure once told her. It had cost that Lokaryn most of his sanity, and in his rare lucid intervals he would talk only about the pain.

The thought made her shudder, and she tried to force herself to focus on scanning the android, but again her mind began to wander. She thought back across hundreds of years, to a time before the Cataclysm, and farther: before her unwilling conversion to the undead. She treasured her memory of those few precious years of mortality. She had worked with missionaries then, though she was not one herself. To her, what she was doing right now, and what she did when she first met this android, was an extension of that work. She sighed. In spite of her missionary past and her current work as a liberator, she could not and did not delude herself into thinking that she was in any way pious. She was still a Lokaryn, and in order to survive, she needed to take life.

Early on she had realized that there was no shortage of people the world would be better off without—assassins, murderers, and the like. And so she made these her prey. Though it was true that she took life in order to sustain herself, it was also true that she had given back to society a hundredfold by doing so.

A small sound snapped her back to her current situation, but it was only the fractured attempt of an ancient clock in the corner to muster its three quarter hour chime. The sense of immediate threat was followed by a repeated loss of focus—both a holdover from human times, and a symptom of not having fed in many days. She shook her head, trying to clear the cobwebs. If she didn't stay sharp she would be captured, and the android would be taken back or destroyed. The patrols were never too particular about the condition of their targets when they returned them.

Though she had successfully kept the android inactive, the law of averages would soon catch up. As the patrols conducted their search of the area, eventually they would simply come upon her. The plan had called for her to be in this safe house for no more than thirty minutes. Her next stop was to be Thieves' Zone. She had arrived in Kwyne and set up the sensor grid within minutes. Twenty-five minutes after her arrival, she had expected a burst transmission. Five minutes after that, a portal was supposed to open into Thieves' Zone.

The twenty-five minutes had passed into thirty-five, and then into sixty. Something was terribly wrong. Someone had either trapped or killed her downstream link, who was another Lokaryn. If he were still alive, she would have received a signal to wait or to abandon this line and seek shelter with a host in the zone, but no such signal had come. Moreover, he had a panic button, and he had not pushed it. Whatever happened had happened so quickly that he had not had time to react. This suggested either a devastating accident or a deliberate elimination. If it was the latter, it had been planned. Well planned. A liberator's life expectancy was short, but her downstream link was—or had been— tough to kill.

He was one of the few individuals left in the organization that she knew personally, and the only one she trusted. She had been in positions like this before, but she had never felt so alone.

She had calculated that she would have at most three hours of relative safety here if her stay exceeded the planned thirty minutes. The android had without doubt been reported missing by now, and a net would be cast throughout the zone he had been in. That was a thousand miles away in Chumley's Zone, but if someone had compromised her contacts at the next safe house, they likely knew her escape path and would be looking for her in Kwyne. Before long, even abandoned areas such as this would be teeming with security forces. Sooner or later a sensor ship would pass within four hundred yards of the building, and even with Hemingway's electromagnetic signals dampened, they would be found.

The ancient clock chimed an imperfect note ever so quietly in the corner, signifying the end of the third hour. Time was up.

Two viable options remained. She could attempt to physically carry the android somewhere else within Kwyne—she knew of a place owned by a couple sympathetic to the project—or she could escape with him using the special portal crystal that her organization planted in every safe house for situations like this one. Changing conditions over time made use of preplanted portal crystals risky. Portal crystals opened a conduit of specific distance between two points and worked relative to the point from which they were originally activated. If a crystal was moved three feet to the east, the exit portal also moved three feet to the east. Safe passage could only be guaranteed between stationary locations, when a crystal's intended activation point was known.

This safe house's crystal had been stashed under the floorboards that Derring was kneeling on now. She removed it from its velvet pouch and eyed it warily. Too many things had gone wrong already for her not to wonder whether someone had tampered with it. It looked undamaged, and close examination satisfied her that it wasn't a fake—she had seen more than enough of the genuine article to be sure—but being real and whole didn't mean that it hadn't been modified.

She gathered herself to move on foot. Even if the crystal did work as designed, the safety of the intended destination point might have been compromised. If it was tampered with, she could well find herself ported anywhere; into the Rohnin's Citadel, the Badlands, or in the burning myst fire of the sluice. Additionally, once activated, most portals remained open for only a few seconds. Once closed, a portal could not be reopened. Sticking one's head through to take a look around was generally a bad idea. When a portal closed, things stayed on whichever side of it they were on.

The sensor alarm sounded. They were coming. Of her meager two options, one had just died a quick death. If captured she would not be afforded that kindness.

Always check twice. They'll never believe you're a god with a booger in your nose.

—Tomanus Jungar, recently departed rohnin of Kwyne

CHAPTER 2

Kwyne
Rohnin's Citadel

A HUNDRED MILES AWAY AND perhaps half a mile above the android and the Lokaryn, an acknowledged demigod watched a wall of liquid fire advance toward his position.

He appraised the conflagration as coolly as a child watching the waves from a safe vantage point on the shore of some beach. In perhaps ten seconds it would wash over him. He watched the fire boil over and consume the atmosphere as it raged forward. But his mind was on real problems. Slowly, even absently, he turned away as it struck the force-projected dome that protected the room, illuminating his paper-strewn desk, the floor, and the whole of the room. It was like swimming in fire.

Damien Cairo loved the view from his office, particularly when an organics storm raged around his zone. And make no mistake about it: It was *his* zone. He was, after all, the rohnin of Kwyne. Expensive as the view might be in terms of the energy needed to run the shielding that prevented his immolation, he was entitled to anything he desired. He was rohnin and that was the law of the land. But Cairo was a man not given to pointless self-indulgence. This display sent a message. In a world where "enough" of anything was elusive and "plenty" was a bedtime story told to children, here in Kwyne there was a bounty to be had. The message was simple and clear: If the shields could be used in such a fashion, there was no shortage or want in Kwyne. As the

Nehreton, Kwyne's representative body, continued to deliberate, they would do so in the knowledge that the citizens felt safe and content.

The flames continued to dance around the shield, throwing firelight everywhere.

Cairo walked across the marbled floor and paused at the center of the room. Beneath his feet, inlaid into the rich and polished surface, was the arrow that symbolized the Kwynian Messiah's martyrdom. It overlaid an unclosed circle on which was etched the rohnin's chosen scripture:

God made love, God made hate, man decides which prevails.

The unfinished circle served as a reminder of the never-ending labor of bringing Thecla's teachings to the uninitiated of their world, T'Amorach.

Looking down, he saw his image reflected perfectly in the polished stone. Two rohnins met at this interface: one above that the world could see, one below that only he could see. As he walked, his heel strikes made no perceptible noise at all. A by-product of his service in the Kuhbrik.

Having distracted himself briefly with the display, he returned to his desk to ready himself for yet another session with the Nehreton. There was a saying from pre-Cataclysmic times that politics were the last refuge of the rogue. If so, the Nehreton was the embodiment of this sentiment, and somebody within that body was out for his head. Ironically, had they asked for a resignation he would have written one on the spot with effusive thanks. However, the position he held was not one that could be abdicated. If he were to leave the post, it would be as a much celebrated corpse.

Given the two choices, dealing with the Nehreton or the undertaker, he would take the former. He tapped a button on top of his desk.

"Please have my advisors come in."

"Yes, Rohnin Cairo."

From a side door to his office came a cadre of men and women, seven in all. They were of varying ages and all gifted in their individual fields. Most notably, two were from religious backgrounds other than the Theclian theology subscribed to by ninety-nine percent of the Kwynian populace. It was the first time that a rohnin had allowed this level of access to the minority populace.

Following the seven advisors was one last person, Primare Donovus Ko'Doran, the rohnin's friend and advisor through the years. Whereas some might have the rohnin's ear on one subject or another, Ko'Doran had full access at any time.

"Rohnin Cairo," Ko'Doran began, using his formal title to set the tone for the meeting. "We thank you for receiving us."

"Thank you for coming," the rohnin replied. "It has been a difficult day for all of us. Have you been able to make any headway on pulling the intelligence together?"

"We have," Ko'Doran said, and motioned to a grizzled man. "Colonel Geresh of the Kuhbrik will summarize."

Stocky and bald, Geresh had a reputation for absolute seriousness. "The situation is as follows," he began. "First, we can now confirm through the intelligence section of the Kuhbrik that the initial sighting of the Lokaryn did take place in the Third Arc; specifically in the outer district."

There was a groan around the room.

"The shepherd of the Third Arc can be difficult," noted Falin Goss, one of the advisors from the Nineteenth Arc. Goss was an expert on military matters, as well as a master of understatement.

"If the colonel may continue," Ko'Doran said, and was greeted with immediate silence.

"The source of the information was a young man from the Third Arc who on closer questioning admits to never having seen a Lokaryn. Further, he is an inner district citizen with no good explanation for why he was in the outer districts at such a late hour. It could be surmised that he may be of less than sterling character."

"Is this the only evidence that we have at the moment?" asked Goss.

"Yes," Geresh replied. "Aside from this one man, there is no evidence of a Lokaryn in Kwyne."

"From the reaction of the Nehreton you'd think they were walking the streets in flocks. If there is no concrete evidence, why the alarm?" Goss responded.

"The Nehreton does not need grounds for investigation, only the will to pursue one," offered one of the minority religious leaders, Becoen Thrin. At seventy-six years of age, she had seen her share of Nehreton posturing.

Cairo allowed a tight smile to cross his face. "That's at least true."

Thrin continued, "So it may be that since there is no real threat to contend with, they can posture all they want and make enormous demands knowing there's nothing to be done. They look good and everyone goes home to reelection."

There were general murmurs of agreement around the room.

"I see only one problem with that line of logic, Rohnin Cairo," offered Ko'Doran.

"Go ahead," Cairo instructed.

"While I generally agree with Becoen's argument, the prelates are not well known for their attention span, and thus it could be reasoned that their continued interest in this specter is the result of considerable effort on someone's part."

"He's right," Thrin said, acknowledging the alternative theory. "Is there information that we haven't heard yet, Colonel?"

"We're continuing our investigation, but for right now, no. There is no additional information."

Goss spoke next. "Look at it from another angle. If in fact this report is true, what possible reason could a Lokaryn have for coming into Kwyne without authorization? Our security is formidable. A Lokaryn would have to be insane to attempt to breach it. It would violate any number of treaties." Having negotiated a large number of them, he knew of what he was speaking.

"Assuming that it's one of the Apostatic Lokaryn," said Ko'Doran. "The balance of power between the Apostatic adherents and the Traditionalists is tenuous at best. The Apostatic clans negotiated the current treaty, so it seems unlikely they would violate it."

"Then perhaps it was a Traditionalist Lokaryn," Goss continued.

"Doubtful," said Geresh. "The man indicated that he got a good look at the Lokaryn. If he saw the Lokaryn, then as I understand Lokaryns, it saw him."

"And the man would be dead right now," Cairo finished as he stood up. "Thank you all very much. I would like a moment with Primare Ko'Doran before addressing the Nehreton."

The room cleared quickly. As it did Counselor Goss spoke. "One other thing, Rohnin Cairo."

"Yes, Falin?"

"Prelate Kragen is ex-Kuhbrik."

"Yes, I know," Cairo replied. "We served during the same period of time."

"Yes, sir. Colonel Geresh and I are concerned that he will interpret this incident as a military issue instead of one of interzone diplomacy and civilian law enforcement. There is rumor that the Third Arc armories are requesting release of high-end weaponry."

"This is only rumor, though, correct? No indication that the release has been granted?"

"Not to our knowledge, but the situation seems to be evolving quickly out there."

"Meaning?"

"They are aggressively hunting for the Lokaryn, with all the man-power they can muster. It's as if they fully expect to find the thing still in the Third Arc. With Prelate Kragen and his staff tending to things here, command and control is being left to the precinct commanders. Some are very good, others are a bit too eager to impress. Without a strong central command on a night like tonight, it's a short walk to mob mentality out there."

Cairo nodded in acknowledgment. Goss closed the door as he backed out.

"In here, too," Ko'Doran said, motioning down to the Nehreton Assembly Hall below.

If your enemy is juggling grenades, don't ask why, throw him another.

—Tura Candalla, founder of the Kuhbrik

CHAPTER 3

Kwyne

Third Arc, Inner district

VAR KRAGEN, PRELATE OF THE Third Arc, lit his pipe and sat by the window of his office in a plain wooden chair. Though he was used to, and in fact embraced, his spartan lifestyle, he still allowed himself the small pleasure of a late-night smoke. Though late, the city was brightly lit, as if the stars themselves had descended upon it. It was an extravagant use of precious energy. His own lights were dimmed. From this vantage point, he could see the Rohnin's Citadel, which sat at the highest point in Kwyne. He reflected on the current state of affairs while watching a ring of smoke waft into the night.

The majority of his life had been spent in the service of Kwyne. First and foremost in the Kuhbrik as an officer. A highly decorated officer. Now in the Nehreton as a prelate. Kragen loved the rich history of his land, and bristled when others referred to it as merely a zone. Kragen knew that Kwyne was much more than that. Of all the cultures that had existed before the Cataclysm, only Kwyne had endured. Beautiful Kwyne, intact as it had been since the days of Kuna Latte, the first rohnin. Surely *not* a mistake. Intact, but not as pure. This was the matter that concerned Kragen. A matter that he intended to do something about.

He cast his gaze on the Rohnin's Citadel, and his thoughts intensified. A firestorm was approaching and the shield doors had not been closed around the uppermost part of the citadel, the Rohnin's Perch, meaning that the force of the storm was to be deflected by use of energy-intensive shielding. The citadel and the extravagant practice of shielding it with energy were, combined, the most ostentatious symbol of Kwyne's deviation from its historical and moral center. Symbolic or otherwise, Kragen's Kuhbrikian training taught him to focus directly on the source of a problem. In this case, not the building itself, but its chief occupant. It was the wayward leadership of this man that concerned him. As troubling as the current state of affairs was, it was not likely to change soon. This rohnin was young.

Kragen had opposed Damien Cairo's election to the rohnin's chair. Nominated by his predecessor, Tomanus Jugar, just prior to Jugar's death, Cairo had been serving as the prelate of the Tenth Arc. It was well known within the Nehreton that his service as a prelate had been the result of vigorous coercing by Jugar. It wasn't that Cairo was reluctant to serve Kwyne, but rather that he had hoped to pursue more academic endeavors upon his retirement from the Kuhbrik. It could well be postulated, then, that Cairo had been an equally reluctant candidate for rohnin. Yet there he was, nothing short of an elected god. And despite his youth and reluctance, he had amassed a great deal of power in a relatively short amount of time.

Kragen's reverie was broken by a knock at his door.

"Come," he ordered.

The door opened and his fellow prelates Balazar and N'orin entered, accompanied by a young acolyte named Cal'in.

Kragen rose to greet them, placing his pipe down in its holder for the moment.

"*Ton Jouru*," he said. It was the formal greeting among prelates. From a largely dead language in which the original holy book was written, it was loosely translated as "We meet in honest service of the Maker."

"*Ton Jouru*," they replied in unison.

N'orin spoke first. "We convene again shortly, Prelate Kragen. Have you any news about the Lokaryn?"

"Just what is already known. It was seen in the waning hours of the night in the outlying areas of the Third Arc. The commanders of each precinct are preparing for a thorough search."

"What if Rohnin Cairo dispatches the Kuhbrik to join in the search and they manage to find the thing?"

"Then nothing is lost. We will be seen as having compelled him to do so and if he captures it, well, then he has done little more than fulfill his obligation to the people of Kwyne."

"And in the meantime, law enforcement in the arc will have unprecedented license to search and detain. If nothing else you will ferret out any number of illegal activities," N'orin observed. Though the outer regions of his own arc were well noted for illicit dealings, the squat prelate was never one to miss out on an opportunity to be on the "right" side of an issue.

"Such is not my intention, Prelate N'orin," Kragen said. "However, the benefit has not escaped my notice. When the Lokaryn is apprehended, we will restore the appropriate rights to the citizens."

"And if your forces apprehend the creature? What then?" Balazar asked. Prelate Balazar was a tall figure with receding hair and a hawkish nose that seemed well matched to his disposition.

"Cal'in?" Kragen addressed the young man for the first time.

"Yes, Prelate Kragen?" The young man seemed to be chomping at the bit to impress the group.

"Indulge me in an old exercise from my Kuhbrik training days," Kragen said as he again picked up his pipe and recharged it. N'orin and Balazar hated the smoke, but said nothing.

"Of course, sir," Cal'in said.

"You find out that your commander has allowed an incursion harmful to Kwyne. What do you do? Prelate N'orin?"

"Kill the agent and keep it quiet. Your commander is in your debt, Kwyne is protected, and your career is helped," N'orin said without hesitation.

"Do you agree, Cal'in?" Kragen asked.

"No, sir. I'd kill my commander, then follow the agent and kill anyone else he contacts. Then I'd kill the agent before he could complete his task."

"Very good. Thank you, gentlemen, I believe he will do."

N'orin and Balazar nodded and left the room.

"Cal'in, what is the purpose of the Nehreton?"

"To be the voice of the people in petition before the rohnin."

"What is the purpose of the rohnin?"

"He is the Maker's chosen representative."

"I have watched your career for a long time now. You believe that this rohnin is wrong for Kwyne. But if he is the Maker's chosen representative, how can that be?"

"Because the Maker did not choose him. A political process did. The Maker gives us free will to choose, and in that we can make the wrong choice."

"And you feel that we did in this case."

"Yes, sir."

"Bold words."

"I have watched your career as well, Prelate Kragen, and it is no secret that you were the favored candidate among the Nehreton until Rohnin Jugar selected Damien Cairo…"

"Rohnin Cairo. We will maintain the respect due the office."

"I apologize, sir. Selected Rohnin Cairo as his second. He subverted the selection process of the Nehreton in doing so. Your record has been of adherence to traditional values and interpretation of the holy book. It is also no secret that you oppose this rohnin. Kwyne would do well to return to her traditional roots."

"Very well. N'orin and Balazar have vouched for you. I know your family well, and your service to the Fifteenth Arc has been impeccable. Are you prepared to take the next step?"

Kragen was well aware that this was the opportunity that Cal'in had been working toward for the last two years.

"Yes, sir!"

"And you understand that if you betray this confidence I can easily arrange for you and your family to be outcast?"

"I understand."

"Very well then. Information has come to me through a reliable contact that a Lokaryn has indeed entered Kwyne."

Kragen took a puff on his pipe in order to give the acolyte a moment to ponder the enormity of his words.

"There are those of us who believe that if the rohnin cannot protect the citizenry of Kwyne against such sacrilege, then perhaps he does not deserve to be rohnin at all."

Cal'in nodded. "I agree, sir." His sharpening expression indicated that his pathway to power was becoming clearer. With Rohnin Cairo out of the way, Kragen would be the obvious choice for successor. To assist Kragen now would be to secure his own position in the upper echelons of Kwynian society.

"And where has this Lokaryn appeared?" Cal'in asked.

"In the Third Arc," Kragen replied.

For a moment, Cal'in seemed stunned that the prelate would admit to the presence of an unholy creature in his own arc. The logic, however, became clear. "Can I conclude that this location was not by accident?" he asked.

"Very astute," Kragen said. "No, it was not. My contact was acting as a conduit for the parties arranging the passage. He could not prevent the incursion, but he has been very helpful in influencing where they arrived."

Without asking permission, Cal'in sat down. "This way you can concentrate the search in an area that you know well and protect the remainder of Kwyne at the same time. You are indeed a good shepherd to the whole of Kwyne."

"To the extent that it's possible, yes. They were very clever in how they arranged the transit and we have only a general idea of where they might be."

"And you haven't told the rohnin?"

"Information should be as accurate as possible before bringing it before the rohnin. Besides, he has his vaunted Kuhbrik and their intelligence branch. My resources are far more modest. If I can find out, he already knows."

"How reliable is your contact?" Cal'in asked.

"Not reliable enough to stake my reputation on. Such people are necessary, but never to be wholly trusted."

"And your backup?"

"Don't overstep yourself, Cal'in." Kragen had been deliberately indulgent, but he drew the line at being spoken to as if they were equals.

"Prelate Kragen, if I am to play a part in this, it is my neck as well. I have agreed never to betray your confidences; however, I have not yet agreed to play the part you have in mind for me."

Kragen looked at the young man in an evolving light. He had indeed found a person to be reckoned with.

"Good. Very good. Yes. We managed to gather additional information through the net rogue, who had arranged some of the clearances. We know this Lokaryn entered from Chumley's Zone and will be heading out to Thieves'."

"Interesting, but why the circuitous route? Why not go through their diplomatic mission or portal directly from Chumley's?"

"It is unlikely that their activities are 'officially' sanctioned by their government. A long-range portal is going to require one of the legal stations. All cargo and possessions would be subject to search."

"What would be valuable enough for a Lokaryn to risk coming into Kwyne?"

"The net rogue didn't know."

"Was he being honest?"

"Yes, we believe he was. He was threatened with a second orchidectomy if he didn't tell us all he knew."

"A second…?"

"Yes. Regrettable, but necessary. He did get to keep his reproductive capacity, though."

" 'Woe be to the future generations of the man who commits treason against Kwyne,' " Cal'in said, quoting from the holy book.

"Exactly." Kragen exhaled and extinguished the contents of his pipe. After carefully cleaning the bowl and stem, he replaced it in its velvet pouch. Then he tied the drawstring, a single throw of a knot, right over left, and placed it with the bowl facing forward in his left-hand pocket. Just as he had every time before. It was a testament to his meticulous nature.

"So how may I assist you, Prelate Kragen?" Cal'in asked.

"When the next session of the Nehreton opens, petitions of the people are heard first before the business of the prelates. As an acolyte, you are technically still of the people."

"So you want me to bring the discussion to the floor from the people."

"I want to keep Rohnin Cairo as occupied as possible, until our forces can find the Lokaryn. We *know* the Lokaryn is here. I have heard he is skeptical that it exists at all. The less time he has to meet with his advisors and formulate a plan, the more time our forces have to bring this to a close without the interference of the Kuhbrik."

"And when your people find the Lokaryn?"

"That has not yet been decided."

"Prelate Kragen, a man in your position could only bring this to closure one way. You'd petition for penitence from the rohnin."

"It is a possibility."

"That would be seen by some as condoning assassination. Removing a weak rohnin from office."

"By some."

"If you intend to replace Rohnin Cairo, you need to outlive him. You are twenty years his senior, and since there is no retirement option for a rohnin, that limits the palette of options."

"Let us focus on the near term. Can you provide the service that I ask?" Kragen inquired.

"What would my reward be?"

"What would you ask?"

"My arc's prelate is less than fastidious about his duty to Thecla," Cal'in started.

And your family even less so, Kragen thought but did not say aloud.

"His term expires in a year, but he seeks reelection. I would prefer to be the next prelate from our arc."

"You are indeed bold, but fortune favors those bold enough to reach for it. If you serve me well, I will do what I can to aid you." Truly Thecla was shining on Var Kragen. Even if the rohnin remained in power, the prelate of the Fifteenth Arc, who often stood in opposition to the Third Arc, would be replaced with an ally.

The two men shook hands.

"Go to the Nehreton Assembly Hall," Kragen said. "It would be best if no one saw you leave here…Prelate Cal'in."

"I understand…Rohnin Kragen."

There's always an angle.

—Thieves' Zone adage

CHAPTER 4

PRISON TAKES MANY FORMS.

This particular prison held but one convict, a child by the name of
Chenara, who had just been returned to her cell. The incarceration was
punctuated by the slamming of a door once she was inside.

"This is *so* unfair!" the teen screamed at the door. "Do you hear me?
Unfair!"

The young woman threw herself on the bed, consumed with the
angst of a teen wronged and condemned for sins that she might or might
not have committed.

It was a prison of pink tones and comforters, warded by an odd
variety of stuffed animals and dolls at various stages of development. It
was the room of a child, but it was showing signs of a transition from the
schemes of youth to those of young adulthood. A treacherous time in
the life of children that required many applications of solitary confine-
ment. Or so her parents believed when they took the time to notice her.

The daughter was a particularly bitter convict. She had spent her
entire life confined within these soft walls. Her *entire* life; at least, that is
what she would have anyone who would listen believe. The truth be told,
she rarely stood punishment for her crimes. Her father was a prelate, an
important man within the Kwynian theocracy and far too busy to pay
attention to a child. His efforts were directed at career building and not

at rearing the child he might have brought into this world. These duties he left to his wife, who took more interest in his young aides than in motherhood.

The convict who lay atop the down comforter was sixteen years old and utterly convinced of the futility of life. Her existence was peppered by occasions where she was trotted out like a show dog, cajoled into performing a few tricks before being returned to her kennel. She was well fed, warm, and utterly resentful of the society and the absentee parents who provided it all.

The Lokaryn stood by the window and appraised the young woman. She watched unseen, absently twirling the long hair that cascaded down over her shoulders. She had an athletic build, but her strength had little to do with muscle and bone. Her name was Kell and, as a Lokaryn, she was a perfect predator.

She watched silently as her prey got up abruptly and went into the bathroom to prepare for sleep. The young woman brushed her teeth and combed her hair, then settled back onto the bed to write in her diary.

Not yet, but soon, the Lokaryn decided.

There was nothing out of the ordinary about the young woman that she stalked. She was not a princess, not a prophet, and yet she would change the world, if things were managed properly.

"Good evening, Chenara."

The young woman sat upright in her bed, a new excitement replacing the despair of just a few moments ago as she heard the soothing voice of her newfound friend and benefactor.

"Kell?" Chenara asked breathlessly. "Kell, is it you? Where have you been?"

Kell ignored the question.

"I am here now, child."

"I am not a child!" Chenara protested.

"Of course, I am sorry, Chenara."

"They just don't listen to me! They hate me. They set these horrible rules and won't let me see who I want to see."

"They are trying to protect you. The world can be a harsh place."

"I'm sixteen, Kell. I can take care of myself."

"If it won't interfere with your self-reliance too much, I've a gift for you."

The young woman looked at the table beside her bed. It was here that she always found Kell's gifts, appearing as if by magic. Tonight she found a small container of ice cream, a rare treat and one never afforded her by her parents.

"Oh, thank you, Kell. Thank you." She set about consuming the delicacy with voracious abandon and, for the moment, all wrongs were forgotten. Kell watched, thinking back to the times when her own mother had punished her. She fondly remembered those who offered her comfort during those times.

"Kell, why don't you ever show yourself? You've been visiting me for months now and I've never seen you. I thought I might be imagining you, but the ice cream means you're real."

"How do you know the ice cream isn't imagined as well?"

Chenara stopped eating for a moment and looked up with an exasperated expression. "Because my mother found the container the first time you left some and I got another night in here."

Young, but not stupid, Kell cautioned herself. "Would you like to see me?"

"Yes!" Chenara said, quickly raising herself up from her slouched position against the headboard.

"Over here." The voice no longer came from near the window, but from the other side of the room in a rocking chair that only moments before had been empty. There sat a young woman, not many years older than the one on the bed, the blond hair framing a face with eyes of an otherworldly blue. The Lokaryn sat relaxed with one leg crossed over the other and her hands folded in her lap.

"Kell, you're beautiful. Why have you been hiding all this time? I thought you were scarred or something."

Kell smiled a tight smile at that. Not all scars show.

"Eat your ice cream before it melts," Kell said, changing the subject.

"I'm thinking of leaving, Kell. I'm old enough now to know how to make it on my own."

"Is this because of our last conversation?"

"You weren't much older when you left home," Chenara protested. "You said you knew you were ready, wrote your parents a good-bye letter and never regretted any it."

It was a marginally accurate assessment of the truth.

"So you think it's time for you to leave the nest? And how will you make your living?"

"I can sing. They make me sing in the choir a lot. The choirmaster told me I was good. Well, he said I could be good if I practiced. If I practiced a lot. But he said I would be good and now I have a reason to practice a lot."

"I like to sing, too. Will you practice here for a while and see how it goes?" Kell asked.

The young woman became deflated. "You don't think I can do it?"

"No, no. I didn't say anything of the sort. I'm suggesting that you think about it for a while before you do anything rash. And of course, I'm curious to know if you'll be here the next time I visit."

Chenara looked down into her container of ice cream and said quietly, "I was hoping I could go with you, Kell. I won't be a burden, I'll watch out for myself, but just to get started…"

A breeze blew across the room, interrupting the young woman's train of thought. She glanced at the open window, then back to the chair. Kell was gone.

Operation of the Raal Accelerator Mark VI is simple. Power the unit, point it in the general direction of your intended target, and pull the trigger. The Supreme Being (whatever you perceive him, her, they, or it to be) takes it from there.

—Thorpe's Corporation training tape on the Raal Accelerator weapon series

CHAPTER 5

Kwyne

Third Arc, Outer District

WITH CAPTURE MERE MINUTES AWAY, Derring's options had changed. The portal crystal was the only way out of the room that didn't involve a body count of some kind. She was certain that the troops advancing toward her knew that a runaway android occupied the room and that someone was assisting it. She did not know, however, that they were aware of, if not her identity, at least her race.

She was faced with dire choices. A Lokaryn caught in Kwyne would be executed. She was a clan lord as well, so there would be a large celebration to commemorate the occasion. Equally unacceptable outcomes would result from fighting her way out. If she won, she would have committed an act of war: an incursion into a zone against treaty with ensuing fatalities. If she lost, then not only would there be the issue of a treaty violation, but her clan would be without a clear successor. A power vacuum in a clan is an invitation to vicious ascension struggles. With the loss of her clan's strong voice for moderation at the Lokaric Council, the tide of lokaric politics might easily turn toward a more aggressive stance against the other zones, another setup for war.

As she continued to prepare for their escape, she cursed herself for not giving the situation this much forethought before she left. When she had heard that Hemingway was in danger, she had made arrangements and left within the hour. *Someone knew what button to push,* she thought.

Of the available choices, one was really not a choice at all. She could mist out, transform her body to a vapor and seep through a crack in a wall or ceiling and simply hide. However, they would capture or destroy Hemingway, and that was unacceptable.

In the end, the final choice was simple: the portal crystal. They had faced a thousand difficult situations in their time together and if they were to die, at least they would die together.

THE TROOPS ENTERED THE BUILDING and began their ascent: five stories encumbered by their equipment. More troops descended onto the rooftop from grav ships.

THE WARM-BLOODS WERE CLOSING IN now, and Derring could smell the energy packs in their lasers. She could also smell wood, which meant that some idiot was carrying a stake. Though staking a Lokaryn through the heart was effective, if the Lokaryn was awake it was usually the would-be staker who got staked instead. There was also the odor of bright metal mixed with that of lubricating oil, which meant that someone was carrying a coring device—a twelve-inch cylinder with a handle on one end and a set of razor-sharp blades on the other. Mounted on a mechanized spring, when activated the device would rotate inward as its blades came together to form a cup. It did exactly what its name implied: When held against the chest of a Lokaryn and activated, it very effectively removed the heart. Whereas staking could stun a Lokaryn without killing it, a coring device would destroy it. But a conscious Lokaryn was far too agile a target for either. The energy weapons were the primary threat. Though resilient, Lokaryns were not impervious to physical damage.

Derring listened carefully to the warm-bloods' advance, working the crystal and willing it to activate quickly. The warm-bloods walked cautiously up to the door, as quiet as mice, or so they thought. But to lokaric ears, even mice make quite a racket. Pausing at the door, they readied their weapons as a demolition team packed the doorframe with explosives.

Why wasn't the crystal generating the telltale hum yet? She examined it carefully, but nothing was happening. At least, not with the crystal. Troops on the roof threw ropes down the sides of the building, the tendrils cascading past the windows. Another assault team fired bolts into the roof with cartridge guns. The bolts secured a device that would peel away the roof sections, exposing the room beneath in one movement.

In equal measures of desperation and experience, she took the fragile crystal and rapped it three times on Hemingway's skull, the hardest thing within reach. She then balanced it on end with a delicate touch that only a being able to perceive the infinitesimal could manage. Finally, and very gently, she moved her face close to it and softly sang a musical note. It was a trick she had learned long ago, and her efforts were greeted with a faint glow. She lifted the android and their gear in one hand, careful not to upset the crystal, which balanced on its point. It slowly started to resonate.

The demolition team would be setting the fuses as the breech and gunnery teams loaded and locked. The roof teams would be moving to the edge of the building and leaning out backward with their ropes through carabiners. Grav ships with their noisy engines brought themselves down to the level of her room, shining lights through the windows in a vain attempt to see her.

As the searchlights flooded the room, their beams struck the crystal, sending a shower of colors cascading in all directions.

Derring looked at the inert android. "Time to go, old friend," she said.

There is no greater tool of the would-be despot than unfounded fear. It turns the masses from their better judgment and when the righteous and just have been wiped away there is no genuine threat for the usurper to deal with.

—Serham Bajo, first caitiff of Thieves' Zone

CHAPTER 6

Kwyne
Nehreton Assembly Hall

"WELL, WHAT DO YOU THINK?" Cairo asked his chief of staff after the room had cleared.

"It's not likely to be a sanctioned incursion. The lokaric leadership would have nothing to gain. If it is the Traditionalists, why would they let the man live?" Ko'Doran asked.

"Perhaps to cause trouble for the Apostatic Lokaryns."

"Doesn't make sense," Ko'Doran said. "We wouldn't go to war over something like this. Even if war were to come, they still would gain nothing. If we lost, the Apostatic Lokaryns would still exist. Keeping in mind that lokaric crystals provide the power for the majority of shielding in T'Amorach, let alone Kwyne, if we won and gained their territory, we still wouldn't have the expertise to run their mines. No crystals, no shields. Everyone dies and with it the Lokaryns' food source. Ultimately, all zones would be extinguished with the possible exception of Rossums."

Cairo considered this for a moment.

"Rossums would eventually perish as well. Without humans to imprint on, they couldn't achieve sentience." Cairo paused. "Do you think this is just positioning in the Nehreton?" he asked.

"I wouldn't dismiss it as such just yet," Ko'Doran said.

The two men fell silent for a while, each with his own thoughts.

"Do you know any Lokaryns? Have you ever met one?" Cairo asked.

"No, sir. My diplomatic time was spent in Thieves' Zone. Otherwise I've mostly been in Kwyne."

"My diplomatic service was in Merchants'. I met a Lokaryn during that time."

"This is the one who became a clan lord, yes?"

"Yes, she was on the staff of their consulate. We talked from time to time." He lied about that last part. In truth he had talked with the Lokaryn nightly. She had lifetimes of knowledge. It was as intoxicating and thrilling to his mind as battle had been to his body as a younger man.

"She knew verse from Theclian scripture better than anyone I have ever debated," he continued. He found his mind wandering back to that time. She had challenged his beliefs. As a result he found that his spirituality was strengthened. He never got over the feeling that this had been her intent all along.

Would that he could have that counsel now.

The intercom buzzed and the voice of his assistant came through. "The Nehreton are assembled, sir."

"Thank you," Cairo replied. He turned to Ko'Doran and said, "There is much that remains unclear. We should be prepared for any eventuality—including my name being entered into *The Book of Succession*."

"I will not allow that to happen, Rohnin Cairo," Ko'Doran said sternly. "Since you've been rohnin we've enjoyed unprecedented relations with the other zones and there is less want in Thecla's land than any time on record since the Cataclysm. I enjoy my comforts too much. You are not getting off that easily." The truth was that he feared for his friend's life; assassination was not unheard-of.

Cairo turned to walk down the private stairs that ran to an antechamber of the Nehreton meeting hall. As he did, Ko'Doran turned him back around and looked him over.

"Remember what Rohnin Jugar used to say," Ko'Doran said.

"Always check twice. They'll never believe you're a god if you have a booger in your nose," Cairo answered.

The two men shared a brief laugh, and Ko'Doran walked to the door.

"Thecla's blessing on you, Damien Cairo," he said, and pulled the door shut behind him.

Cairo stood at the top of the stairs, looking down into an abyss.

Damien Cairo, the current rohnin of Kwyne, took one more moment at the top of the stairs.

"There are no answers up here," he said to himself. After taking a deep breath, he descended the stairs to the antechamber of the Nehreton hall, some two floors down.

He walked onto the dais of the great hall and assumed his place on the throne of Kuna Latte, first rohnin of Kwyne. Cairo often found himself wishing that the Cataclysm had occurred a day before they found this particular relic, an intensely uncomfortable chair. Cairo scanned the gilded room, looking for one prelate in particular: Var Kragen. With Kragen firmly in his sights, he motioned to the sergeant at arms, who cleared his throat. The representatives of the various arcs scrambled to their seats. Cairo observed Kragen without seeming obvious. He sensed his adversary doing the same in return. Kragen was far more leisurely than the rest in taking his seat. When the rohnin was satisfied that all were in place and had their heads bowed, he waited for a full minute. It was a small gesture to affirm who was in charge.

At an almost imperceptible nod from the rohnin, a child came forward with a parchment and read a prayer, as was customary at the beginning of a session. After the child was finished, the sergeant at arms stood forward.

"Do the people have petitions for their servant?"

"We do," said Cal'in immediately.

Kragen watched, not entirely pleased at how quickly Cal'in came forward. He leaned toward N'orin. "This young man had best understand the need for a light touch in this matter."

"I have said as much to him," N'orin confirmed.

The acolyte stood and approached the dais, confident in the future that he knew to be unfolding. Rohnin Cairo took his measure and waited.

"Rohnin," he began. "The Fifteenth Arc stands before you in…"

Cairo cut him off. "I do not see an arc before me; I see a person."

Cal'in continued, somewhat haltered by his poor choice of words, "I come before you on *behalf* of my arc—"

"On behalf of your arc? Prelate Graugh, is this true?" Cairo called out. "Does this young man speak on behalf of the people of your arc?"

A few murmurings ensued, but the room was otherwise silent.

The sergeant at arms leaned over. "It would seem that Prelate Graugh was unavoidably detained."

"Convenient," the rohnin noted before again addressing the acolyte. "Your arc is far removed from today's events. What could you have to say on their behalf?"

Cal'in felt a burning anger rise in him. Humility and propriety forgotten, he would not let anyone stand in the way of his goals, perceived god or otherwise.

"Rohnin," he said, "the unholy walk in Kwyne unopposed on *your* watch."

There was now complete silence in the chamber. Kragen looked on without expression.

Cairo responded calmly. "You have been made to do the work of those who would not speak for themselves. Step back now with no further mark against yourself."

"Rohnin," Cal'in said again.

A long moment ensued. More experienced men knew that the only course of action was to step back as directed, but the acolyte continued. "A Lokaryn walks in Kwyne. Why do you not act? The utmost responsibility of the leader of Kwyne lies in the protection of his flock."

Cairo looked at Kragen, who sat with a neutral face, pitying the would-be prelate.

"Being unfamiliar as I am with the teachings of Thecla, I was not aware of my duty. Thank you for clarifying it for me." The rohnin looked directly at Var Kragen as he delivered each word to the young acolyte. Kragen, for his part, never loosed his gaze from the faltering man who stood before the rohnin.

"Forgive me, Rohnin, but I wasn't sure that Thecla's teachings were foremost on your mind."

There was an audible gasp in the chamber.

Cairo shook his head as he appraised the acolyte.

"Young man, you may find divine attention more than you bargained for. While every citizen may speak freely in this chamber, it is granted with the obligation to do so truthfully. I judge you to be false in your intentions and petition."

At a gesture from the rohnin, two guards walked to Cal'in's side. He had not expected this outcome. Rohnin Cairo was not known to embrace some of the more draconian powers at his command, but imprisoning those who disrupted the proceedings of the Nehreton was well within his purview. As Cal'in was escorted away by the guards, he realized how far his arrogance had caused him to overreach.

With Cal'in removed, Cairo again nodded to the sergeant at arms.

"Are there any *other* petitions from the people to their servant?" he asked.

The hall was silent.

He paused to let the lesson sink in. He would not add the acolyte to the tonnage that weighed down his conscience, but they didn't know that. When he was satisfied that his point had been made, he stood and addressed the prelates.

"This body has brought before me a boy to be its voice. And to what end? We have met several times through the day for no perceptible reason other than to make speeches. There will be no more special sessions on this subject. We have no proof of this alleged incursion other than the word of a young man who's never seen a Lokaryn, yet troops are invading their own arc. No one has mysteriously disappeared. No citizen is unaccounted for, and no bodies have shown up in the morgue. This report will be properly investigated. I will send Kuhbrikian and general military search teams into the area and contact the appropriate embassies."

A pall had fallen over the assemblage when suddenly a voice from the back of the chamber announced loudly, "They found it! They're moving in and we have a live feed from the helmet cams if we want it."

The rohnin had no choice. He was in a public forum. To deny them access would be to further fuel the fires of dissent. He nodded to the sergeant at arms, who activated the monitors in the room. All eyes focused on the screen. All but one set:

Damien Cairo's were firmly fixed on Kragen.

The Nehreton watched the troops move down the hallway. Kragen shifted his gaze to the rohnin. Their eyes locked as though the outcome of the events unfolding might somehow be determined by sheer force of will. Had they been watching the monitor, they would have seen the trouble at hand. Other members of the Nehreton had past military experience. Balazar was among them and was the first to recognize the disaster about to occur.

"They've got Accelerator guns! Get them to call off the attack!" Balazar shouted, sending a number of pages scrambling to find a way to communicate with the troops in the field.

Kragen turned to the screen just in time to see the telltale snub nose of an Accelerator. Raal Accelerators were reserved for use in the open Badlands, where unlimited power was required. Yet here were troops wielding immensely powerful weapons in a confined space, about to destroy everything within a thousand meters.

Damien Cairo shook his head. Only fools would assume that they could so precisely direct such power; fools, or zealots intent on the destruction of the unholy.

Var Kragen looked back to the rohnin, intent on continuing their game of visual recrimination. But the rohnin's eyes were closed and his head was bowed. His lips moved silently, as he mouthed a prayer from the ninth book of Thecla.

A moment later the room was enveloped in a brilliant white flash.

Importantly, when deciding to accept or decline the invitation, read closely to see if you are being invited to dinner or for dinner.

—X'goram, clan lord, D'Agosh Clan
A Guide to Dining with Lokaryns

CHAPTER 7

Lokaryn Zone
Clan Lord T'Gareth's offices

KELL LEANED ACROSS HER CLAN lord's desk with both hands on the mahogany finish, seething.

She was careful not to bare her fangs, lest she be perceived as challenging him for his position.

"The name. I want the name."

"No," T'Gareth replied. He was one of the oldest Lokaryns known to exist, immensely powerful and ruthless.

She did not care. He had something that she wanted and she would have it. "I've done all that you have asked. I will have her in place on time. Now give me the name."

"The fact remains that she's still at home and until she's where I need her, you haven't fulfilled your part of the bargain. I will not have you distracted and I will not give you the name until my needs are met."

"Then perhaps your needs will not be met. I am the only one who can lure her away." Kell stood upright and folded her hands across her chest. She held a unique position in whatever T'Gareth was planning, and she had no qualms about using it.

T'Gareth leaned back in his chair. "Very well then. You are of no further use to me. You may go."

Kell considered her options. It was in moments such as these that her *gift* was most useful.

"Patience," the voices counseled.

Kell's aspect visibly changed as she traced the black onyx inlays of T'Gareth's desk with a long fingernail. She smiled and said, "Very well, my lord. The girl will be in the alley as promised. But once you have your incident, I will have my information." Then, defying both protocol and tradition, Kell turned her back on her clan lord and left the room.

She did not wait for acknowledgment from T'Gareth, and she made sure that she flung the door open for proper effect.

The door slowly closed as Barros, an assistant to the clan lord, entered through a side door. Barros was one of the few Lokaryns that T'Gareth trusted as an aide. He generally preferred to use humans, as they were capable and more easily controlled. Assistants to the clan lord were privy to dangerous information. An ambitious Lokaryn with the right information could kill the clan lord and assume his role. Barros had no such ambitions. He had come to the Lokaryn Zone to escape outcasting from Thorpe's. Barros's skill as an administrator was superb, and he quickly rose to senior management. Once his term was done, he was free to leave with a fortune. Instead he requested to become one with the Body. T'Gareth accommodated him, an extremely rare occurrence.

"Clan Lord, respectfully, I think you should reconsider your course of action," Barros said. "You've placed too much time and effort into this to entrust it to someone as chaotic as Kell."

"She may appear chaotic, my friend; however, Kell will deliver the girl to the alley as planned. I have information she wants."

"What information?"

"She's been hunting someone. He crossed her many years ago. She thought he was dead, but apparently he merely had the good sense to change his identity. Now that she's discovered he's alive, she is obsessed with finding him."

"You know where this unfortunate soul is?"

"No. But I know where to find the man who does."

"Unlucky bastard."

"Very unlucky, but no concern of mine. Kell will deliver the girl to get the information. She'll see that the right people get the wrong impression."

"How can you trust her? She's insane."

"You are more correct than you know." T'Gareth reflected for a moment on his decision to make Kell part of the Body. Had he realized then that she was ill, he might have made a different decision. Still, in spite of her affliction, Kell had proven extremely useful.

"How can you know that she'll deliver? She was a Kwynian, you know. She might still have allegiances."

"Yes, I know, though I doubt that she has any ties. Her treatment by Kwynian 'True Believers' has proven our biggest ally. Her mother was a devout woman who read their holy word with an emphasis on the punitive aspects of child rearing."

"What you said before, about Kell's sanity. What did you mean?"

T'Gareth paused for a moment. "Kell has an affliction that she would call a gift: Voices talk to her, torment her, guide her, and keep her company. The Kwynian upbringing that you think could work against us might well be the cause of the problem."

"I don't understand."

"Kell's mother was abusive. She would place her in a closet for weeks with the barest amounts of food and water. That book the Kwynians adore so much prescribes seventeen days of penance and one more night, or some such nonsense. Her mother took it upon herself to decide what 'penance' meant. I'll spare you the less pleasant details."

The younger Lokaryn shuddered.

"Kell believes the voices saved her. She told me once that they told her how to seduce me."

A look of disbelief came over Barros's face.

"That's right. While I am Kell's adra, her maker and mentor, she was the one who initiated it. Her father was serving as the ambassador from Kwyne to the lokaric leadership. Not a coveted position to say the least. Her mother, devout as she was, refused to come here, so as eldest daughter, it was Kell's responsibility to take her mother's place. She was twenty-one, and still at home. After years of her mother's penance, she was so psychologically scarred and socially stunted that her chances of marriage were next to nothing."

"But they didn't mind sending her to us as part of the embassy mission to our zone," Barros observed.

"Interestingly, she blossomed in her two years here. Away from the repression of her home life, she grew by leaps and bounds. She spent hours in our libraries, learning history from a non-Kwynian perspective. She attended our cultural events, learned the etiquette of each zone, languages, art and sciences…It was really quite incredible."

"You said she seduced you."

"When her father's tour of duty ended, he was more than ready to leave. Kell had other plans."

"Or the voices did."

"Perhaps. I was sorry to see her leave, as I had grown quite fond of her. She had a keen mind, and her way of thinking was refreshing. A rare potential that I had not encountered before, but conversion would have started a diplomatic incident, and likely a war."

"I can see where converting the ambassador's daughter might not be looked on favorably," Barros said.

"Kell, on the other hand, was not so encumbered by diplomatic considerations. Her prospects in Kwyne were nil. She came to me that last night. She knew I hadn't fed. She adorned herself with everything a male Lokaryn might desire. She looked beautiful, and fragranced herself with the barest hint of blood. She took my hand and led me into the garden that adjoins this office. She had scented it with animal blood."

"You must have known she was up to something."

"I thought I might taste her, feed upon her as we do those in the chamber. I wanted to keep a small part of her with me after she was gone. She was so enticing and I let myself be led to the edge. But once beyond it…well, I needn't tell you that once in the reverie I was lost.

"As I came to, Kell was in my arms. She hadn't cried out but she was near death. I had intended only to feed, but I had long passed that point."

"So you decided to make her one with the Body?"

"I did. I pulled away from her. She was pale, barely alive. She looked at me with a fading smile and said, 'Please.' I drew her in again and infused her with life force. Hers, my own, and a small part of those lives I had consumed."

"You didn't know about the voices?"

"Once I shared her life force I had that knowledge. But there wasn't time to think about the implications of such things. A few more moments and she would have been gone."

"But in the time since, as her adra, you could have destroyed her."

"True, but Kell has proven to be a reliable agent and an asset to this clan."

"Reliable? She disappeared for some forty years."

"She's never accounted for the time, but I suspect it has something to do with the man she is seeking," the clan lord said. "Kell will deliver the child to the alleyway. The rest is up to us."

"Have you selected someone as the bait?" Barros asked.

A knock came at the door. T'Gareth looked at the time and smiled at Barros.

"Come in, J'Nath," T'Gareth called out, knowing who stood at his door without needing to look. "Your timing is perfect."

While in-zone you may pray to whatever deity you like. While out on the myst, he is called "the captain."

—Myst-clipper adage

CHAPTER 8

Aboard Independent Merchants' Zone Myst-Clipper *Shicaine*
Captain Nathaniel Gedrick, commanding
Ship's location: Grantways of the Cassynthian Region

THE GREAT VESSEL MOVED OVER the myst like a ghost. Though silent, her bow cut the waves, parting it with immense force, while in her wake eddies of vapor swirled and danced briefly in the darkness of the night. The chaotic patterns were illuminated softly by the glow of her ion skimmers. As she sailed on, the light faded and the currents calmed, leaving nothing behind to mark her passing. Such was the passage of a myst-clipper. The enormous weight of the ship, the thrust to move her forward, the lift to keep her from sinking into the caustic myst all balanced precisely, barely disturbing the earthbound clouds on which she rode.

She was, as myst-clippers are, a rare and beautiful ship, but more than that she was a Garand-Trass myst-clipper and therefore unique. She was designed by a madman, and built by another man obsessed with that vision. She was a vessel that, at her full potential, could not be controlled by even the most talented of conventional pilots. Though she was known as the *Manumit* now, she was called the *Shicaine* by her master, a man without allegiance, a man who had lost his identity as well.

The bowsprit sliced through the air in a bobbing motion as the ship was propelled forward. The wind was stiff and the sheets were taut with impulse. Moving over her foredeck, men and women went about the business of sailing. The ship moved as if driven by purpose, but none were privy to what that purpose might be. The crew tending the lines and sails worked without question, though they now traveled a dangerous myst.

At the railing of the Quarterdeck stood the captain. His name was not Gedrick, but it was the name by which he was known. Of average height with dark hair and hazel-grey eyes, he wore no rank or insignia. His authority was born of intangibles and he had yet to be challenged by anyone who had ever served aboard the ship.

The craft coursed forward over the growing swells of myst as the first officer, Neville Chapman, approached the captain and handed him a steaming mug.

"Thank you, Mr. Chapman," the captain said, though not obliged to do so. "Did our esteemed new cook make it stronger this time?"

"He's catching on quickly, though it took him a bit of time to believe that I wasn't pulling his leg about your fondness for strong coffee."

The captain took a sip. "Not bad. Is there any more?"

"Yes, but the chief has laid claim to it. He's going to use it to kill rats in the engine room."

Gedrick smiled at that. "A rat would fare better in the lokaric feeding chambers than it would with the chief."

"I know the captain would not be implying that the chief's hospitality is lacking."

"Why don't you carry a piece of cheese down to the engine room and report back your findings," the captain suggested.

"The myst swells are growing," the first officer noted.

"What's on your mind?" the captain asked as he again raised the mug to his lips. He had expected this conversation for some time now.

"Our sudden change in course," Chapman replied.

"I could tell you it's for a lucrative contract," Gedrick said.

"You could."

"But you'd know I was lying."

"Yes. 'No contract is so lucrative as to risk the ship by sailing dangerous myst at night.' Or so I'm told." Chapman offered the captain's own counsel from a past opportunity not taken. "Besides, we abandoned a lucrative contract to come out here. I doubt the take would have covered our losses from that as well."

The first officer paused for a moment. He did not wish to overstep his bounds.

Placing his elbows on the railing and looking out over the decks, the captain said, "Go on, Mr. Chapman."

"The crew is uneasy sailing these mysts in darkness. They expected to put into port at the Teylau microzone to ride out the night before coming out here."

"Are you saying I have a potential problem with the crew following my orders?"

"No, sir, there is no such potential. The crew remains steadfast. Simply uneasy at what might motivate a man with a reputation for caution to engage in such an activity."

"Did they use just those words?" Gedrick knew the question also came from his first officer. He shared the captain's appreciation for caution while engaged in dangerous activities.

"Yes, sir, they're quite an eloquent bunch when you get to know them."

"No doubt."

"In any event, I also noted that the chief is more irritable than normal, which *is* saying something. Captain…"

Gedrick suddenly tensed. His mug dropped from his hand.

"All hands brace!!" he shouted as Chapman hit the General Alarm and started down the companionway to the work decks below.

A tremendous roaring noise struck the ship. The deck lurched violently to starboard as the ship was knocked over on her beam ends. It was the first, and usually last, harbinger of a rogue wave. Or worse, the leading front of a storm.

Gedrick began issuing orders.

"Mr. Chapman, you have the deck. Make sure we recover all mates. You have ninety seconds."

"Aye, sir!" Chapman replied as he vaulted over debris dislodged by the force of the ship's movement. He began issuing orders to the crew. For some of them, this was the first time they had ever experienced the fury of the myst and the suddenness with which it could manifest. The more veteran crewmembers knew that time was short and they had no room for error if the ship was to survive.

"Helm! Hard right rudder! Steady on 040!" Gedrick ordered. "I'll take control of the helm from the flying bridge directly."

The helmsman was seasoned by years on the mysts and was already moving the ship's wheel to bring her bow toward the wave. Though his face imparted no emotion as he pulled the wheel over, his heart raced with adrenaline and fear.

Gedrick moved over the threshold of the command bridge quickly. Though the loss of his ship was imminent, he was measured in his movements.

"Activate shipwide communications. Ops, prepare for powered sailing. No checklist. Chief, bring us to full power. Emergency circuits to the shields. Communications? Do *not*, I repeat, *do not* radio our position to anyone." He continued to issue instructions as he moved inside to the pilot's chair and strapped himself in. The electronics flared to life the instant he sank into the curved chair.

Out on the deck Chapman noted that the drop continued. The trough was a measure of the wave to come. The deeper the drop, the higher the wave would be. When they finally hit the base of the wave, they might well continue under it. At that point no amount of shielding would save them.

One of the newer deckhands watched in awe as the wall of myst rose up in the distance, barely perceptible. It rose over his head, growing thicker and higher with each passing second. The ominous rumble was pierced by the shrieking discharge of the electricity that illuminated the face of the wave. He stood motionless, holding the ropes to a yardarm. He was stunned by the immensity of the wall of myst that towered above him and the ferocity of the lightning. The ship's shielding protected him from the myst, but not from the debris flying around the deck.

Chapman saw it coming before the man ever knew what hit him.

The rope pulled tight around the young sailor's wrist and yanked him upward into the rigging. Shielding set for myst would deflect the small particles that permeated the environment, but would allow for large objects to pass through. If not arrested, the force would hurl him through the shielding.

"Captain!" Chapman shouted into his comm link as he ran toward the man. He grabbed a machete from a deck workstation.

"I see it. Dropping the yardarm now. Get ready to cut him free."

With a small motion, Gedrick touched his command screen. Explosive bolts blew apart the collar of the topmast and it began to fall to the deck. The young man's flight was arrested. With a sickening impact, he crashed to the deck, tangled in ropes. His shoulder was dislocated and his wrist fractured in several places. The angle of his knee indicated that there was a break there as well. But he would live to sail another myst, if the ship itself survived. He struggled to get free of the ropes as the topmast hit the yardarm below it and began to slide off to the port side of the ship. His eyes went wide as he realized that he'd be pulled overboard with the rigging and burned to death in the myst. Chapman was on him in an instant, slashing at ropes with efficiency and fury.

"Lie still!" he commanded. The speed with which he macheted the ropes did not allow for the mistakes that a thrashing target would cause. The young man was immediately immobile but watched in horror as the sails and yard slid over the side. As they descended into the myst, the rope that ensnared him rapidly disappeared as well.

With no other options, Chapman raised the machete high above his head for a last attempt at freeing the man. Loose rope was everywhere, and aiming seemed impossible. The young man saw what the first officer intended: amputating the hand to save his life. As the blade came down, the crewman yanked his hand out of the way, yelling as the blade traveled through the endless coils of moving rope. His hand came to rest on the deck, and a moment later most of the coils snaked over the side and into the myst.

"Thank you, if you hadn't moved, it would have been too easy,"

Chapman noted. Several crewmembers dragged the shaken man inside a companionway and secured the hatch. As if to provide malevolent orchestration to the action on the deck, the rumble grew into a roar, as a vicious wind preceded the wave. Electricity crackled everywhere around the ship, and the driving rain, rich in acid, sizzled against the shielding.

The looming wall slowed in its rise above them and the ship's motion started to change ever so slightly. The worst was about to come.

Chapman, seeing that the decks were clear, dove into a companionway and sprinted back to the bridge.

On the bridge, Gedrick's task worsened. Sails conserved energy while out on the myst, but were a liability in this situation.

"Helmsman, I have her now. Ops, pin her ears." It was an instruction to lay the masts down to the deck to improve the aerodynamics of the ship.

"Aye, sir. We're not sure if the foremast will seat properly after the collar detonation."

"Understood. Do what you can."

He drove the throttle of the engines forward in a steady fashion, turning the ship out of her dive and up into the wave, completing what the change of course had started. The ship's handling improved dramatically as the yards spun even with the masts and both were dropped to deck level. He brought the shields down close to the surface of the ship. The skimmers acted as airfoils now. Though not as strong as wings, they were substantial. Sails tangled in the bowsprit caught fire as the ship lurched upward. Instead of going up the face of the wave, Gedrick powered the engines and the ship surged forward, cutting diagonally up the behemoth. At this aspect, if the wave crested and struck the ship, it would capsize her.

His left hand remained steady on the yoke while his right moved like a blur over the controls. The ship started to right itself, but the myst had not leveled. The starboard ion skimmer touched the wave front, while the port skimmer hovered meters about it.

Gedrick drove the throttle home as the myst tumbled down the wave face toward the ship. The leading edge of the myst began to strike the shielding, which shimmered and sparked in response. The *Shicaine* began to slide sideways in response to the force of the myst. "Come on, *'Caine*," Gedrick whispered as he willed her over the last few meters.

The starboard side of the ship burst through the wave, and they found themselves riding down the back of the would-be ship killer.

"Chief," Gedrick called down to the engine room. "How are we doing down there?"

"Son of…"

Gedrick cut off his comm link. "He's alive, in any case. Mr. Chapman?"

"Sir."

"Get the damage teams going. It looks to be the leading edge of a storm front, not a single wave."

"Aye, sir."

Through the next two hours the storm roiled around them, though nothing so dangerous as the leading edge. After another two hours the clouds parted and the myst was again tranquil. The masts were raised, as were the sails, with exception of a damaged foremast topsail, and the ship moved on.

Gedrick powered down the pilot's station, and the skimmers recharged power to the ship's reserve. He stood again at the command deck, watching the silver sky begin to form, preceding the sunrise.

Chapman approached his captain and handed him a cup of coffee.

"Thank you, Neville," he said.

"You're welcome, Captain. Try not to lose this one."

Gedrick smiled. "I know this is difficult, but you have to trust that I wouldn't bring us out here unless I absolutely had to."

"I know you try never to miss a sunrise, but after a night like this, shouldn't you be trying to get some sleep, Captain?" the first officer asked.

"I enjoy the sunrises a lot more after a night like this," Gedrick said. "Do you have the operational update?"

"Power is at fifty-three percent. If we encounter another storm…"

"Understood. How is our young crewman?"

"He has a dislocated shoulder, a broken wrist, and he tore the right knee up pretty badly. The doctor's knitting him back together as we speak. He also got a visit from the sailing master."

Gedrick couldn't help but smile. "Brought him flowers?" he asked.

"Not exactly. Sir, will we be sailing again tonight?"

"Possibly. We'll be at our destination by midday. I'll let you know after that."

The first officer did some quick calculations in his head. "Captain, on any heading, that doesn't put us near any major zones. Are we going to an outpost or a microzone?"

"A microzone affiliated with Thieves' Zone."

"I see. Shall I tell the crew to prepare for cargo?"

"No, Mr. Chapman, no cargo."

"No, he's just visiting old friends," came the voice of the chief from behind him. "A bad idea, I might add."

Gedrick sighed and took another draw from his coffee. "Good morning, Chief. How are you?"

"My engine room is a wreck is how I am."

"Then shouldn't you be down there mopping up or something?"

"That little stunt did serious damage," the chief continued.

"We're not so badly off, Chief, unless there's damage you didn't relay to me," the first officer said.

"Just the damage between our captain's ears," the chief answered.

Gedrick turned to his first officer. "I do outrank him, correct?"

"I'll check the ship's roster, but I think so," Chapman answered dryly.

"After all that, you are still dead set on doing this?" the chief said.

"Yes," Gedrick answered. "I have to. I would do the same for any member of my crew."

"Do what exactly, sir?" the first officer said. "A moment ago, you asked for my trust and I gave it to you. Might I expect the same courtesy in return?"

"Without going into detail that you are better off not knowing, a previous associate of mine…"

The chief cleared his throat.

"Excuse me, of ours...sent a message..."

"May have sent a message. You have no way of knowing it was him," the chief corrected.

"Why would it be anyone else?" Gedrick countered.

"Because you have enemies."

"From a lifetime ago."

"*He* is from a lifetime ago, and from that particular life I might add."

Chapman looked confused, but said nothing.

"We're going to check on an old associate who may or may not be in trouble. If he is, we'll fix the problem. If he isn't, then we'll be on our way."

"We just navigated the Grantways in the dark of night, and you'd do this for any crew member?" the first officer asked.

A voice of the bridge officer crackled over the comm link. "Captain, we've received clearance for the Baltan docking facility, bay fourteen."

"Time will tell, Mr. Chapman," Gedrick responded.

There are only three acceptable expressions of assassination. Surprise is most common. Fear if you enjoy that sort of thing, and—in the hands of a master—time for the target to reflect on the inevitability of their impending death.

—D'Artak Olgossen, philosopher-assassin

CHAPTER 9

Thieves' Zone
Terrapin Arc
Club Mutante

HENNIX, OR RATHER HIS MENTAL projection, raced through the electronic ways of the cybernetic ether like a firestorm racing across the myst. His mind twisted and spun through each channel, desperately trying to reunite with his body while eluding his pursuers. Traveling the electronic ether that permeated T'Amorach was intoxicating, like what he imagined flying to be, only better. Usually. Right now, fear drove him forward, as he recklessly surged toward the haven of his physical body. Once there, he could safely unplug from this place. They were gaining on him. Whoever *they* were. They had laid out information to entice him, but he had snatched it away instead of being caught in their trap. His neural networks still held the encoded information. Information worth killing for.

He had managed to set up another snare at the last junction, but it was only a matter of time before his pursuers worked through it. Thirty seconds might mean the difference between life and death. Thirty seconds added on to the hours of this relentless pursuit.

It had started as a simple pickup, though the fact that someone had gone to the trouble of hiring a net rogue belied its simplicity. Net rogues, particularly those with his capabilities, did not come cheap, not least because they often dealt with dangerous information. The sender of the information was unknown to Hennix. That was not unusual—senders often went to the trouble of cloaking their identities—but it was rare that Hennix was unable to defrock them. It made him uneasy.

The recipient of the transmission was not unknown to Hennix, however. He was myst-clipper captain Gedrick, a man for whom he had once conducted deliveries on an exclusive basis. Though Hennix would never admit to having been a member of the *Shicaine* crew, he had lived and worked aboard the ship for years. He knew Gedrick to be a fair man, and this captain had his respect. In the world of a net rogue, that too was unusual.

The delivery had gone smoothly enough, though Gedrick was clearly troubled by the information that he received. After he finished reading the message that Hennix had delivered to him, the captain had looked the net rogue square in the eye and said, "Hennix, I think it would be best if you came aboard *Shicaine*."

"For how long?" the net rogue had asked.

"Indefinitely."

"I can't do that. I have a life here. Even if I wanted to go, the *Shicaine* Pact would prevent me from doing so."

"I think that deal may have been broken. That's what this message is about. I don't have the time to try and convince you, Hennix. I've been here too long already."

"Captain, I appreciate your concern, but I can take care of myself," Hennix had said.

"Then I wish you well, my friend," Gedrick had said. Without another word he was gone.

Curiosity is the hallmark trait, and inevitable downfall of net rogues. It had bothered Hennix that he could not identify the sender. It was both an affront and a challenge to his abilities. This had eaten at him until his only recourse was to jack back in and dig until he found the answers. Someone else, however, was already there looking. Someone very powerful.

He needed to focus now. How he had gotten here was less important that the fact that he had one more junction until he was home free. The landmarks he used and the pathways he traveled began to blur, but he could still see the junction shimmering in the distance. He couldn't disconnect himself until he was at his anchor point; if he did, his consciousness would be set adrift without a physical component. He could not survive in that state. The junction drew closer, and closer, as greyness set in. He was in trouble. They were nearly on him.

Intense pain. Keep moving.

Aim for the corona of the junction. Jump.

There was complete darkness and pain. Was this the afterlife or safety?

Hennix fell back and yanked the access plug from the port into his brain. He was breathing heavily and perspiring. His eyes twitched in a familiar way as he groped for the bottle of tequila that had set down in front of him. It was not the medically recommended treatment for cyber withdrawal, but it worked. He barely noticed the burning sensation as the alcohol crossed his lips and tongue, dry from hours of hanging open. In the ether, simple reflexes like swallowing to keep one's mouth moist were lost. Stimulants and anesthetics, in cartridges beneath the skin, kept the body functioning while the brain explored. As the haze of the electronically induced ether receded, the sensations of the real world set in: the musk and feel of the dull torn leather of the booth in which he sat, the smell of smoke as it wafted around the bar. Faltering neon colors blended into one another, while music from some band droned on. Alcohol, urine, smoke—the first breath was always the hardest.

Then perfume. She had come back to check on him.

"Hen?" The bartender pulled his head around to look at him. "Hennix? You alive?"

Alive? he thought. *Yes, I must still be alive.* His head cleared more slowly than usual as he took another drink. The bartender gave him a doubtful look but moved on as her next table beckoned her. He had information he needed to decode. His movements were clumsy and slow as he took a small cube from a case beside him, set it on the table before him. The device was no larger than his fist. He pulled a slender cable from the thing and attached it to his wetware port. He began to upload the information to a cube to decode as he took another drink. He dared not jack back in without this information.

Facing reality after experiencing the cyber world was…the only word was "disappointing." To leave a world painted in imagination for a world dictated by mundane physics was a hard thing to do. There were blues in this real world, but they were pale compared with the blues of imagination: perfect blues of perfect skies and perfect seas. Reds of pure anger, purples you could breathe in and feel course through your veins. There were continents on clouds, vast cities beneath the waves, and plentiful monsters. It was a world driven by two things: information and imagination.

He blinked hard, trying to clear his vision. The sensations of the real world started to filter in. He realized he was hungry. Very hungry. The scent of food filtered through to his brain. The woman had brought him food and it was still warm. She knew the routine. She was why he came here.

He took a deep breath and a bite of the food. The memories started rushing back: Lucy was her name; she was his lover. He recalled the bar and how he found it. He recalled the life he was leading and farther back to years ago…to…why he was so eager to forget. He wasn't alive by half and hadn't been in five years. For all his bravado to Captain Gedrick, he was living a shadow of the life he'd once led. A net rogue should need no one or no thing, but he had violated that axiom, once, years ago: he had let himself become a part of something. Its absence left a wound that did not heal. He shook his head to clear those thoughts.

Lucy reappeared at his side. He looked up at her. Her brown hair was drawn back from her face with only a few small curls escaping to frame it. She had features most would consider attractive, but years of working in places such as this were recorded in the various scars that she had acquired. Her eyes were an unblemished green and they conveyed more than a little concern. A question formed in his head.

"Twenty hours," she responded without him asking. "I thought I had lost you toward the end. Did you find what you were looking for?"

"I'm not sure," he said hoarsely. He ached. His lips hurt. His throat hurt. The information continued to decode.

"What did they throw at you? It looked painful. You were thrashing around a lot." She placed more food in front of him. He didn't know what he was eating, only that it satisfied his body's craving.

"Not painful," he replied. "Just vicious." Although the mind separated from the body during a jack-in, the tendrils of connection still existed. Expert net rogues used that link to throw programs and viruses at the physical body that were numbingly lethal. In this case they had thrown viral code at him designed to destroy the portion of the brain that made breathing automatic. The result was that so long as you remembered to breathe, you lived. By net rogues' standards, it was perfection: nasty, cruel, and permanent. You would live your last hours desperately trying to find stimulants to keep you awake. He had narrowly averted this fate by reflecting it back at the sender. As much as he admired the craftsmanship of the code, he did not envy the net rogue who had received it back. In a few hours, whoever sent it would fall asleep and cease to breathe.

"Fair's fair," he said to himself. Lucy was staring at him.

Hennix took a long draw on the tequila bottle and hiccupped. Lucy laughed. Hennix laughed too, and was starting to wind down a bit. He was safe now in his own body, and in a place no one would ever think to look for him. Somewhere else another net rogue was running. Trying to preserve his life. Trying to remember to breathe.

He laughed because he was alive, because he had survived a brush with death and had lived to tell the tale. Lucy stood up as he hiccupped again.

"You're OK, Hennix—a little drunk maybe, but you're all right. Hiccups," she said, shaking her head. "Unbelievable."

Hennix looked at Lucy.

"Hey, Lucy, what the hell are hiccups anyway?" he asked, and then took a draw from the nearly empty bottle.

"They're just breathing spasms, baby." She picked up her tray and headed back to the floor. "I get off in an hour. Why don't you relax until then, maybe take a nap."

He slowly swallowed the drink in his mouth and hiccupped again.

Breathing…spasm. Breathing. A badly timed coincidence? Perhaps he hadn't been so successful in turning the attack after all.

He took one last long draw from the bottle and stretched out, drunk.

Only one way to find out.

The concept of "Backer" is simple enough: Important individuals discourage assassination by contracting a backer for retribution if they are killed. Problems can arise, however, as backers frequently contract other backers, which leads to rounds of retribution as contracts are called and fulfilled. Two decades after the establishment of the zones, the killing of a relatively minor, official from McCallister's Zone served as the spark for the "Backers War."

—The Addlebrain's Handbook of T'Amorachian History

CHAPTER 10

Baltan Microzone

Ship's position: Northern Reach, Cassynthian Region

WHAT THE HELL WAS I THINKING? Gedrick berated himself silently as he reloaded his energy pistol. He squatted down in a well-sheltered alley, scanning for snipers.

Have the ship out of here in an hour. Another barrage of gunfire impacted the wall that he was using for cover.

I should make a point of adding this to my captain's credentials: easily swayed by nostalgia into making dumb decisions. He took a deep breath and calculated his next move. He couldn't call to the ship. If he called the *Shicaine*, net rogues would have its position. They already had his.

A volley passed over his head.

"Hey!" he shouted. "Technically, this is Thieves' Zone. Everything has a price, right? So let's talk a deal. I'll triple whatever you're being paid."

"We get your ship after we kill you. You can't triple that," came a disembodied voice.

"Thank you," Gedrick said to himself. The microprocessors layered in his skull went to work analyzing the angle and direction of the voice.

He pulled a microgrenade from inside his flight jacket. Once the firing solution was finalized, the information was relayed to his left eye, a cybernetic device that was implanted after a small disagreement with a former captain. He could see where he needed to place the charge, but it was up to him to do so. The eye and layered computer were the extent of his modifications.

The grenade was set to detonate upon impact, with a wide dispersion. Probably not lethal, but it would still stun a large number of individuals in a broad area.

"Counteroffer!" he shouted as he threw the grenade.

The hunters' confusion about their target's cryptic reply quickly turned into anguished cries as three men were thrown against brick walls. Those closest to the blast fared less well.

Gedrick darted down the alleyway and into the back door of a building that he hoped would bring him to the edge of the warehouses. From there he could get lost amongst the multitude of buildings and catwalks. Perhaps even stow away in a freighter bound for Merchants' Zone.

It was daylight now and warm in the zone. The heat-imaging capacity of his artificial eye was limited. He made as much noise as he could ramming through the door in the hope of drawing his pursuers. He laid down traps to snare those who would follow.

"Thirty minutes," he muttered. "What's wrong with sixty minutes, Gedrick, or even seventy-five? Five more minutes and I could have made it back to the ship."

An explosion at the doorway to the building signaled that someone had followed him in.

Looking for the next exit, he peered over a large crate. A hail of bullets and plasma greeted him.

He ducked down and took a quick inventory of his remaining supplies. While they were not critically low, he had no idea how long he would need to defend himself.

Through the window he could see the edge of the warehouses. The crates of the customs house absorbed another hail of fire.

"Thecla!" he cursed loudly. "Just how many of you are there?"

"We ain't falling for that again." A brief pause ensued, followed by, "Oh damn!"

"Thanks!" he shouted back as he threw a piece of wood where he figured they'd be. He took aim at the doorway and waited for them to scramble out in order to avoid what they assumed was another grenade. As they did, he unleashed a barrage of stun bolts that would incapacitate them until he was long gone. He wasn't sure whether his reluctance to kill came from his upbringing in the order or the practical fact that assassins had backers: people who would come to finish the job. Most had multiple backers. For every one you killed, many more would come in their place.

"It makes a mess," his former captain used to say.

Looking at his handiwork, he realized he had made quite a mess himself.

He sprinted across the street between two warehouses, away from the battle.

He moved quickly to the quay where the *Shicaine* had docked but could not see her masts in the distance. He was glad that his ship was safely away, but his heart sank as well. It was unlikely that he would ever see her again.

"Good man, Neville. The safety of my ship and crew is more important."

"There he is! Shoot him!" came a voice from down the alley. With nowhere else to hide, he sprinted out onto the dock, looking for any cover he could find. Time was short now and he knew how this would end. In the last moments of life left to him he finally allowed *her* to fill, or more accurately put could not prevent *her* from filling, his thoughts.

"There he is, shoot them," he heard a different voice call out. It was the voice of the sergeant at arms from the *Shicaine*.

Gedrick turned and saw a shore party from the *Shicaine* leveling weapons at the men who were chasing him. He dropped to the ground to give them a clear shot. He had caught a glimpse, beyond them, of the sergeant commanding from the captain's gig.

"Fire!" the sergeant shouted. In response to the command, a barrage flew over Gedrick's head, raining havoc around the would-be assassins, who scattered and dove for cover.

The sergeant ordered his team to fall back, knowing better than to prolong the fight once they had bought enough time for Gedrick to escape. Gedrick sprang to his feet and sprinted across the dock as the crewmen boarded, then jumped between the two providing covering fire from the safety of the boat.

"Go!" he shouted.

Gunfire pelted the boat's hull as the pilot turned it from the dock, but in moments they were out of range. Minutes later they were alongside the *Shicaine*, and, once aboard, the captain made his way directly to the bridge.

"Captain on the bridge."

"Report."

"Captain, we are in good sailing condition, though our foremast remains without topsail," Chapman said. "We await course instruction."

"Phira Point Light Station. I'll give more instructions once we're there."

"Very good, sir. Helmsman, steady as she goes."

"Mr. Chapman, I left instructions that the ship be emergency portaled into Merchants' Zone if I didn't return at the appointed time, didn't I?" Gedrick asked.

"I believe so, yes," Chapman answered.

"So, shouldn't this ship be docked in Merchants' Zone right now?"

"I don't think so, sir. We were to have the ship ready to portal if you hadn't returned within thirty minutes."

"That was almost an hour ago."

"Forty-three minutes. We had to navigate the boat to a safe distance from the quay to facilitate the portal."

"It took you almost an hour to position the ship a half a mile outside of the harbor?"

"Forty-three minutes. Yes, sir. You can't be too careful when preparing to portal an entire ship."

"And the shore party?"

"You left no instructions regarding shore leave and these men were due," Chapman said.

"And this is what they do for enjoyment?"

"You recruited them, sir."

"I see," Gedrick replied. Returning to the business of sailing the ship, he called over to the officer monitoring the ship's environment. "Sensors?

"Sir."

"Any pursuit?"

"None, sir."

"Very well, continue on this heading. I'll be in my quarters."

"Very good, sir," the first officer said.

"No, Commander Chapman. Excellent."

Gedrick activated his portable comm link as he walked to his quarters.

"Chief."

"Yes, Captain."

"I think it's time we talk."

"It's about bloody time…"

Gedrick snapped off the comm link.

"I suppose it is at that," he said to no one in particular.

PHIRA POINT LIGHT STATION CAME and went over the coming days. Like so many other guardians of the myst, it was a feat of engineering over reason. Placed in the most inhospitable of places to warn mystfaring ships away, the light station was built upon a rock outcropping that jutted above the myst level by some hundred feet or so. The stone tower was charred nearly three-quarters of the way up its height: a reminder of past organics fires. The beacon spun around endlessly, magnified by the Fresnel lens that served as a low-tech but reliable magnifier.

The navigator was surprised to find that his new plot was taking them to deep myst in an area of the Badlands for which no charts existed.

Out on the command deck, the captain monitored the progress of the repairs to the sails.

"Nearly done," the first officer said. "Perhaps by nightfall."

"Perhaps."

"Another night of sailing, sir?"

"I don't think so."

"I see. Are we close to our destination or a port to put into?"

"Destination, I should think."

"Captain, there is nothing to my knowledge within a several-day sailing radius. Is it possible there has been an error?"

"Sure. I haven't been here in five years and it can be difficult to find."

"We're a long way from anything if something should go wrong."

"Yes, we are."

"Mr. Chapman?"

"Sir?"

"I think we've arrived." Gedrick opened a shipwide comm link and said, "Helm, come about to bearing one-three-five. Sailing master, pull in the top reef."

The crew was stunned to find that they were sailing toward a cliff face that towered a thousand feet above them.

"Decrease the right foil five percent."

The Garand-Trass foil, which was constantly trimmed to afford maximum lift, now worked less efficiently, giving the ship a list to starboard.

"Trim sails and come seven degrees to port."

As the ship traveled with its odd starboard list, the maneuvers caused it to drift slightly to port.

It was an unnatural movement for the ship to be making, and the crew was becoming uneasy as they continued toward the rock face. If the *Shicaine* were to strike the wall or any unseen rocks below the myst surface, they would all be lost.

"Top foils in," Gedrick commanded.

The tempo of the crew's work slowed. Lowering the top foils would cause the *Shicaine* to lose fifty percent of her lift. She would be reliant on thrust and antigravity, two very energy-intensive sources, to keep from sinking into the caustic myst.

"Captain?" Chapman said quietly. "Have I mentioned that we don't carry enough energy to make a safe port if we can't redeploy the foils, and no one can portal us out of here this far away from a salvage base?"

"Yes, I believe you have," the captain of the *Shicaine* said in a controlled voice. "Mr. Chapman, if those top foils aren't down in the next three minutes, this ship will be destroyed."

Chapman had only his gut to go on. With the barest shift of stance, he loomed over the slow-responding crew.

"Your captain gave an order," he said. "Anyone who doesn't feel they can do their job can hop overboard anytime they like. Now *move*."

The crew resumed action smartly.

As they came within two hundred yards of the cliff, Gedrick began snapping out orders in quick succession. "Daggerboard to zero, forward thrusters full power to port! Aft thrusters full power to starboard, right full rudder – steady up on course 270. When the turn is complete, drop the daggerboard to seventy-five percent and the bow thrusters should keep on course."

"Captain, the wall…" the helmsman said.

"Watch."

Their fates now sealed, the crew watched with morbid fascination as the wall grew closer and closer. The crash would be spectacular.

When they were only fifty yards from the wall, a crewman shouted, "A breach in the rock face! I can see a breach! We're heading right for it." Each crewmember strained to see. It was difficult to make out the gap, as the jagged rock face created a near perfect optical illusion.

"Engineering, look sharp," Gedrick said into the comm link. "I take it we've arrived," the coarse voice of the chief replied.

"Remember how to do this, Chief?"

"Like it was yesterday."

"You pick an interesting time to check if the chief can do this," Chapman said.

"Feel free to take your chances with the myst, First Officer, if you have your doubts," the chief replied.

The base of the opening approached and the ship slid backwards into the gap, which the crew now thought was a blind alley. They stood dumbfounded, looking at the narrow walls that towered over their heads. Had the foils remained out, they would have been ripped from the ship.

When a collision astern seemed imminent, Gedrick gave the order. "Helm full ahead. Now, Chief!" The engines roared and the ship abruptly stopped, with its bow rising up. "Helm, cut forward thrust, starboard 45 degrees." The bow thrusters strained to steady the ship as the bow of the *Shicaine* abruptly shifted to the right at the base of a V-shaped canyon. "Ahead slow," Gedrick ordered and the ship moved forward, emerging into a lagoon. They cut the engines and in moments were floating in silence and light myst that gave way to sweet water.

They navigated toward a settlement that bordered the lagoon. Gedrick remembered the beauty of this village set against a waterfall, with gentle waves that lapped at its shores. It had been an idyllic setting from a different time.

Things seemed to have changed now. Thick black smoke rose from the town center and an acrid smell permeated the air.

"Captain, shall we prepare for a quick departure?" Chapman asked.

"Yes. Given our last port of call, we should be ready for anything."

"Another friend of yours?" the first officer asked.

"My former pilot, Seyschell, lives here."

"I see. And the microzone we just visited?"

"Hennix, a net rogue who used to work with me. He's more than likely dead."

"Your past seems to be catching up with you," Chapman observed.

"So it would seem," the captain said.

He began issuing commands to the crew. "Make mooring as quickly as possible. Arm the crew and put the ship on attack status. Prepare the captain's gig. I'm going ashore."

Although he did not order a security detail, there was one aboard the gig when he boarded it. Gedrick looked up at Chapman and nodded. The gig cast off toward the burning port.

The boat came ashore just south of the main village. They proceeded cautiously to the outskirts. Deserted. They moved more quickly toward the village center, and crouched at the corner of a building at the edge of the main square to survey the situation.

"Snipers could be anywhere," one of the crew observed.

"No," said the captain, rising. He walked into the middle of the square transported back in time. He saw the once bright colored doors of houses down the side streets smashed and splintered. The flowers of the square, once buzzing with the activity of bees and butterflies, lay trampled and dead. Shatter glass was everywhere and reflected light in every direction. The small shops on the town square that had been made primarily of wood were largely burned to their foundations, with only their chimneys standing in memoriam. Those made of stone had fared little better, with many missing large sections of wall from where cannon fire had hit them. Worse, the business owners he had supplied with goods over the years, some his friends, were nowhere to be seen.

"What has happened here is over," Gedrick said. He did not bother to conceal his movements.

"Seyschell!" he yelled.

A moment later the villagers materialized from a multitude of hiding spaces. The shore party was outnumbered many times, but Gedrick showed no signs of nervousness.

An elderly man walked up to Gedrick. The captain studied the man's face for a moment before recognizing it.

"Venka?" Gedrick said finally. The years had etched a new identity onto his old friend's face.

"Yes, Gedrick," the older man said.

Gedrick asked the next question at a bare whisper: "Is she dead?"

"We don't think so. At least she didn't die here. She tried to lead the attackers away: took her ship out in full daylight." His eyes welled up. "They were attacking the village. She said that if she died here, the attackers would leave no witnesses. She sailed out to draw them off."

"It worked. They're gone and you're still here."

"The *Gradine-Smalls* had a good head start and it's a bloody fast ship. She might yet be alive."

Gedrick looked at the man.

"Did she tell you where she was going?"

"She said that if anyone came looking for her to tell them that she went *crazy*. That's all she said."

Gedrick knew where his old friend was heading. There was one specific bar, in one specific port. The crew of the *Shicaine* loved the bar, but Seyschell often complained that the music was so bad it was going to drive her absolutely mutant crazy. He had his next port of call. He turned to leave the square when the old man touched his arm.

"Gedrick," the old man said. "Tell her, when it's all over and done, to come back to us. She said she was sorry when she left, but tell her there's nothing to be sorry for and that she is a child of this village. Tell her on the day she returns we will celebrate."

Gedrick looked at the old man. He nodded.

Many miles away, Seyschell stared intently into a bottle of liquor and contemplated her own death.

Some structures in the body are meant to be weight-bearing. Some are not. It is best not to get them confused.

—Keptor Prin, pragmatist to the tarran of Ravensford' Zone

CHAPTER 11

Thieves' Zone
Orlehachs' Arc, Outer District
The Drunken Angry Bitch tavern

"YEAH, BUT SHE HASN'T ACTUALLY killed anyone," the bartender pointed out to his manager, as the second man struck the barroom wall and crumpled to the floor, moaning in pain. The wall reverberated from the impact of his two hundred pounds, but it held. It was a well-built room, in a well-built building—a remnant of a time when structures in the zones were made to last forever.

Or at least until the next apocalypse.

The Drunken Angry Bitch was an outer district bar of considerable reputation, and a favorite of myst-clipper crews. Named after the original owner's mother-in-law, it had everything an outer district bar could need: cheap glassware, cheaper spirits, and a standing arrangement with the local mortician. It was also a product of its location not just in an outer district, where the residents were somewhat less *civilized* than their inner district counterparts, but in the outer district of Thieves' Zone, where the only real law of the land was that if you could not defend what you had, you weren't allowed to keep it—including your life.

Despite its reputation, the Drunken Angry Bitch was in no way a unique bar. The décor was forgettable. A series of nondescript pictures and advertisements hung from the walls, and they had blurred into one brown mass under the onslaught of smoke that wafted in sinewy clouds from the unfiltered cigarettes, cigars, and occasional burning body. No one in this place worried about contracting one of the wasting diseases that these vapors caused, as few ever lived long enough for disease to be an issue. The floors were made of dark planks that were well worn but sturdy. They were swept occasionally but rarely cleaned. Their color was derived from a mixture of spilled drinks, crushed cigarettes, urine, vomit, and blood. Sawdust was laid down as required and replaced with reasonable haste.

The establishment was laid out over three levels. The first floor was for dancing in an area known as the Pit. The Pit was flanked by bars on each wall, and unlike the dance areas in some other establishments it had a bathroom that the patrons were encouraged to use. The basement also contained a dance area, which was designed for those who desired more privacy. Its walled areas and darkened recesses allowed the braver patrons intimate contact with complete strangers. The second floor held a maze of rooms, all encircling a central bar that was tended by one of the greats, a weathered old man named Grizwald.

He'd tended the bar here for a long time, and he knew when to be concerned. Like today. Places like this were magnets for the worst elements of society. Five of those elements had entered a room intending to satisfy themselves on an unwilling petite blonde who had been engaging in a slow motion suicide for the past two days. Only one of them remained in there.

"She hasn't actually killed anyone *yet*," the manager pointed out. He was new; the last manager had been killed in a knife fight between two members of the clientele laying claim to the same barstool. "How many people can actually come flying out of that room, hit the wall, and not get seriously hurt?"

"As many as are dumb enough to go in, I suppose. Her aim has been pretty good," the bartender offered.

"Worse yet," the manager persisted, "how about the two who went out the window?"

"Ah, they'll be fine. Hit the bins in the alley. She hasn't bothered anyone who ain't bothered her first. And after all, there were five what went in there to have their way with her. I say she's been right polite about the whole thing."

"Polite? Two out the window. Two over the bar. You call that polite?" the manager replied incredulously.

"To tell the truth, I'd be most worried about the guy who's still in there. I know these guys. He's a mean one and not too bright."

"I'm not sure where you're going with this…" The manager stopped in midsentence. He looked at the room's doorway, through which five large men had entered swaggering and the two lucky enough not to be tossed out the window had exited flying. Out came a smallish blonde, with the fifth man in tow. Had this not been the case, one would never suspect that she was the beneficiary of a set of genetic mutations that gave her preternatural agility and reflexes, as well as strength many times greater than a man three times her size.

The manager had never actually seen a man dragged by his genitals before. It was both impressive and painful to watch.

"Another bottle, Griz," the woman said. She lifted the man over the bar and shook the money out of his pants, which were now bunched around his ankles. "My new friend here is paying." She had to stand on the barstool to get enough height to do it.

The man shrieked with each bounce as she loosed the coins onto the bar top.

Grizwald, almost out of pity for the man, acknowledged that she had dispensed enough money.

"No, no, old friend," she countered. "You forgot about the tip." With one final shake, the man lost consciousness. She dropped him to the floor.

"Ma'am," the manager began hesitantly, "perhaps another establishment might be more to your liking."

The woman looked up at him. He cringed, imagining the contents of his pockets on the bar, as he stared at the unconscious man who now lay at their feet.

"No, I like it here just fine. Open twenty-four hours, good liquor, and"—she looked down at the man on the floor—"good entertainment. Don't worry. I should be gone soon."

The manager started breathing normally again. It was the first bit of relief he had felt in the two days since the woman had entered the bar and begun drinking.

"So you'll be leaving...soon?"

Seyschell picked up the two bottles of tequila that the bartender had laid out for her. She had a faintly sad look about her.

"I didn't say I'd be leaving. I said I'd be gone. What you do with the remains, if there are any, is up to you."

She turned and went back into the room to await her fate.

The manager looked nervously at the bartender. "Most of the customers cleared out after second guy went out the window, so maybe we should close down for a while."

Grizwald looked back at him, confused. "She hasn't caused *us* any trouble. In fact, those five guys have been a headache for a long time. Maybe you should offer her a job."

"I don't think so," the manager said. "I don't want to be here when whatever she's afraid of shows up."

"I believe I do," Grizwald said. He began to count his shells.

Management reserves the right to liquidate any employee that it determines is less valuable than their insurance policy.

—Thorpe's Corporation employee handbook

CHAPTER 12

Somewhere north of Kwyne
The myst-clipper *Blackthorne*
Captain Loh'l, commanding

TARRO HAD NOTHING LEFT TO do but die.

He hung in a small compartment cuffed to overhead steam pipes aboard the *Blackthorne*, a clipper ship of foul reputation. After enduring beatings and interrogation for days, Tarro had been left here to consider his situation. He might have been in here for hours or even days; he had long since lost track of time.

The heat of the steam pipes worsened the stench from the urine and feces. The constant hiss of the pipes had left him nearly deaf on one side and his breathing was becoming more labored. Yet he was becoming oddly detached from these discomforts. Perhaps his deliverance wasn't so far off.

He was left to think about his situation, and he did just that.

The chain of events that brought him to this dark and lonely place had started with the death of a friend; a man named Harlin Rahn. Rahn had been the captain of a clipper ship by the name of *Wiscott* at the time of his death. In the final moments of his life, Rahn had sent him a simple message.

The pact is broken. It came accompanied by the *Wiscott's* logs, but the transmission was garbled in a great many places. It had been sent from Rahn's ship while she was in an area of tremendous ionization. As such the information was corrupted, offering only a few tantalizing clues and little more.

Tarro shifted uncomfortably as he dangled from the pipes, never able to fully stand, as his feet didn't quite touch the ground. Nor was he able to rest for very long, as the weight of his body made breathing difficult whenever he fell asleep. His captors were precise about the lengths of his bonds, going so far as to use old rope that was already stretched.

He focused his mind on the journey that had led him to this spot with hope that it might offer some insight into his pathway out.

He had met Harlin Rahn aboard a Merchants' Zone ship named the *Sojourner*. Tarro had enlisted as an intelligence officer, and Rahn had already been aboard the ship for months as the weapons officer. The two became fast friends after a drunken brawl during a shore leave. Fortunately, both were too intoxicated to recall who had won the fight.

Sojourner was not an ordinary ship. Though she carried goods from zone to zone, Tarro noticed that they were forever "buying" and "selling" artificials to handle the freight. It didn't take him long to observe that no artificial was ever kept for more than one trip. When he asked his captain about this, she growled a terse reply: "Find me one worth a damn and I'll keep it."

He quickly figured out that the artificials weren't being bought and sold. They were being picked up and dropped off as a part of the underground railroad that permeated T'Amorach.

When he started to ask what he thought were discreet questions, he promptly found himself in front of the captain. He had heard many times throughout his life that he was too smart for his own good. The guns that the security detail leveled at him during the conversation punctuated the point. In the end, Rahn vouched for his friend's fealty to the cause and Tarro found himself inside a world that didn't exist. At least, one that none of the authorities could find. In a short time he came to love the work.

Perhaps a year had passed when Tarro was given what was to be a fateful task. One of the ship's engineers had gone missing. He was in fact the ship's former chief engineer. While he was a very capable man, he had lost his position owing to numerous infractions of the *Sojourner*'s Code of Conduct. After one particular shore leave, the engineer did not return, and Tarro was sent to find him.

He established fairly early on that the man had been in a bar fight and ended up in a dumpster outside. While there was general agreement that the dumpster had been peppered with gunfire after the man was thrown into it, no one could say for sure if he was dead or even hit. Tarro had examined the bullet holes in the container and did indeed find blood, but no body.

His search continued over many months until he located the man, now the chief engineer aboard a ship called the *Shicaine*.

The compartment's hatch opened and Tarro shut his eyes quickly from the pain of the light. A woman walked in and grabbed his face roughly to look it over.

"Still alive?" she said. "You're doing better than many of the others. We're taking bets on who will last the longest. The captain has put some money down on you."

Had he any saliva left he would have spit it in her face, but none would come. Instead, he made a rasping sound that substituted as his voice. "What do you want?" He did not know what else to say.

"The same thing as always, Jayesh. If that is your real name. We want to know why you are on board our ship and what you have to do with the recent trouble we've been having."

The woman stood there framed in the reddish glow of the hatch. Crew from other ships moved past her, in and out, oblivious. The place he was kept in was part of the engine room. The heat vapors distorted her image, making her look hellish. Steam made the ghosts of his memory even more surreal.

He drifted back again to the time aboard *Shicaine*. She was captained by a man named Gedrick, who was young but capable. The chief, as the man Tarro had been hunting liked to be called now, was not inclined to return to the *Sojourner*. He enjoyed reclaiming his old position on this new ship and the fresh start the situation offered.

Tarro saw an opportunity, and with very little effort the *Shicaine* was recruited to the cause of liberating sentient artificials from captivity. Tarro ultimately stayed aboard the *Shicaine* and was joined by his friend Rahn.

The woman had moved to the other side of the hatch while he was lost in the past. She gave a nod to two crewmen, and they hoisted a large bucket and drenched him with freezing salt water. The shock to his system was severe, like a thousand knives slicing him all at once. Salt penetrated his open wounds, causing agony. Water steamed off him, making the air even thicker than it had been before, and making it much harder to breathe.

The woman slammed and dogged the hatch.

Tarro found comfort in the past and now willed his mind to that place.

After five years, the *Shicaine* had become a legend in the railroad. Her exploits were told and retold, growing larger with each telling. Tarro smiled at that. Her crew was a mix of all the zones; they even had a Lokaryn serving aboard. No one had ever kept count of the sentients that they had helped over the years, but the number would have been high. Gedrick was a smart captain who managed to mix the work with commerce, and as a result the crew grew rich. His philosophy was that a happy crew bears no traitors; it was more lucrative to remain loyal.

The heat continued to drive the ice water into steam. Tarro, a great connoisseur of irony, wondered if he would drown while suspended in air.

The end of his time with *Shicaine* was a bitter affair. Gedrick's philosophy had worked well over the five years they were together. To this day Tarro felt that someone had betrayed the crew during a relatively simple pickup, but could not determine whether that betrayal had come from someone aboard the Shicaine itself.

They had often used the Sluice as a pickup point, exchanging artificials for sentients, since it was an extremely dangerous area that few ships ever ventured near for ordinary business. Tarro and Kisner, the First Officer had been aboard a small vessel called the *Wanderer*, making the pickup and paying off the ship's captain, when they suddenly found themselves surrounded by a small army of the *Wanderer*'s crew. All had weapons drawn. An uncounted number of ships portaled simultaneously into the area, and *Shicaine*, too, found herself surrounded. The capture had been well planned. *Shicaine* darted into the relative safety of the labyrinth, and the pursuing ships either turned back or sank, but once she was hidden, there was no escape.

It was a stalemate and Gedrick used it to his advantage. First he petitioned powerful friends in a number of zone governments for assistance. Next, he blackmailed certain prominent Merchants' Zone families who had profited from his activities. Finally he reminded his remaining adversaries of his backers. In the end the *Shicaine* Pact was born. *Shicaine* would be spared but she could never again transport sentients. The crew would be spared, but could never again work together or contact one another, and no individual among them could have any further role in the liberation of sentients. Should any crewmember violate the pact, all would be held accountable. Execution by outcasting, without option of asylum, would be the punishment.

Given their activities, the bargain was a good one. For Tarro, though, it was a hard one to accept. He had found his life's work aboard the *Sojourner*, and now it was to be taken from him.

He determined to continue it. He cashed in his shares from the *Shicaine*, which now amounted to a considerable sum, and set himself up in a friendly trading house in Merchants' Zone. He assumed a new identity and surgically altered his appearance. He became Lucius Martanz. As Martanz he prospered, magnifying his holdings many times. And as Martanz he continued the work without breaking the pact. He could buy and sell any commodity he liked, including artificials. If he chose to sell his artificials at a loss to Rossums no one could fault him for it. It was not the same by far, but at least it was something.

This went on for some years, until the day that Rahn's message was delivered. The few clues it had presented and the message that the pact had been broken left Tarro no choice. Rahn offered no proof that it was broken, only a last-minute suspicion. Tarro knew that reconnecting with any former member of *Shicaine*'s crew would result in severe consequences if discovered, but to do nothing might sacrifice them all anyway.

He carefully crafted a message and sent it using an extremely complicated process called Hajjat's Maneuver, which would cover his trail well. There were very few net rogues, if any, who could untangle the maneuver. He left one clue in case the net rogue he sent the information to was actually alive to receive it. One of the points embedded in the information routing included a bar called, the Drunken Angry Bitch.

There was more. As Tarro began to piece the puzzle together he discovered that the *Wiscott* was not the only ship to have been destroyed in a suspicious manner. He noted that a number of ships had been lost recently, primarily from trading houses that were at odds with other trading houses. War between the trading houses would cripple commerce throughout T'Amorach.

He was now faced with two puzzles and needed to know if one was part of the other.

A man in his position, the head of a prominent trading company, would draw attention if he began looking into things. He was left with one option. He sent his message using Hajjat's Maneuver and readied the next part of his plan.

Lucius Martanz had to die.

It was a good death, Tarro felt. He was out for a leisurely cruise aboard his yacht when he picked up a distress call and responded as any responsible mystfaring ship would. Both ships were destroyed in a freak organics fire. Nothing was ever found of the second ship. As was tradition in Merchants' Zone, Martanz's will transferred the net of his estate to the zone leader: the morgan. It turned out to be a paltry sum. For all his opulent living, Martanz had no assets. At least on paper.

He again changed his identity and appearance, this time to become a man named Jayesh. Free now to pursue his investigation, and with considerable sums of money stashed away, he began. Tarro followed the meager leads that Rahn had left him and found a single name appearing again and again. The *Blackthorne*. When people talked of the ship it was in hushed tones, and a sense of dread laced the air whenever someone spoke about her doings. Tarro never actually met anyone who had served aboard her, though a number of people knew of someone impressed into her service. Stories of crewmen thrown overboard for minor infractions abounded.

He began to suspect that a berth aboard the ship was a terminal one.

Tarro followed the trail to the Thieves' outer districts and found that the ship was not welcome even in the most despicable ports. The trail continued into microzones affiliated with Thieves' Zone and then, finally, to the independent zones, where any ship could find harbor. There he waited.

He knew it when the ship finally came into port. There was a change in the tone of the place. Rough men and women who usually swaggered around the town kept their heads down when *Blackthorne* crew entered the port's only drinking establishment.

Tarro could tell immediately that this was walking evil.

He very deliberately did not look down as the crew entered the bar. In doing so he quickly caught the attention of the woman leading six hulking men. He locked eyes with her. She seemed physically attractive, but something within her burned with an ugliness he had not seen before. She walked over to him.

"Are you a sailor?" she asked.

"Yes," he replied.

"Name?" she asked.

"Jayesh," Tarro responded. "And yours?"

The woman looked at him as if he had insulted her.

"Natrina Ma'Goran, first officer of the *Blackthorne*, and you *will* learn your place," she said.

At a jerk of her head the six men descended on Tarro. Tarro crippled one of the men before he was overcome, but in the end they beat him to unconsciousness.

He awoke on the *Blackthorne*, his body racked with pain from the recruitment process. It did not matter; he was put to work immediately. The crew assembled on deck before the watch began. They said nothing as the man Tarro had disabled was thrown overboard into the myst.

"Any crew that cannot perform their duty will receive the same. Dismissed." Ma'Goran looked up toward the command bridge, where a silhouetted man nodded.

Tarro quickly learned his duties and watched the ship's activities while learning what he could of the *Blackthorne*'s involvement in *Wiscott*'s destruction and the war between the trading houses.

Over time, Tarro, now Jayesh to all, became invisible among the crew: one more kidnapped soul pressed into service and trying not to be thrown into the myst at the whim of the first officer. As for the captain, no one except the seniormost crew ever saw him. None of the common or able-bodied sailors knew his name. It was said that he was the bastard spawn of the most evil creature on all the mysts: the Grendel. The man, whoever he was, kept his identity well hidden.

Tarro continued on in this way for months, gathering answers as best he could. He found that *Blackthorne* was indeed hunting old members of the *Shicaine* crew, from ordinary sailors to her senior staff. The broader picture, though, was still elusive and the *why* of it all still evaded him.

There had been three attempts on *Shicaine* crew since he came aboard. By tapping into the communications system, he had managed to warn each target before the *Blackthorne* arrived. He knew this to be incredibly risky, but on a ship this size it could be done. He also continued to look for a way off the ship. Escape proved to be impossible, however. The ship docked only at tiny microzones, and the common crew was locked belowdecks whenever the ship put in. Even if he could get off the ship, there was nowhere to go.

He continued to warn *Shicaine* crew as best he could. He couldn't stomach the idea of sacrificing any of his old crew, even if it meant his life. The third time a target miraculously escaped, Tarro's luck ran out. There was no warning. Anyone who had started serving since just before the first failed assassination was interrogated and tortured. Tarro had no idea how many crew had been rounded up.

This brought him to his current situation.

The darkness stretched out until the door again snapped open. He was cut down and fell to the floor. Ma'Goran was there again, as were several large crewmen.

"Take him," she ordered. Too weak to fight, Tarro knew the myst awaited him. Though it was a small consolation, at least he could meet his end having been loyal to Gedrick, Kisner, and the rest of the crew of the *Shicaine*.

It is not wise to be the guest of honor at a banquet of a Lokaryn.

—X'goram, clan lord, D'Agosh Clan
A Guide to Dining with Lokaryns

CHAPTER 13

Lokaryn Zone
Lower district
Feeding chamber

IN A SMALL CAGE, IN the center of a hell, bathed in the complete absence of light, there crouched a human.

He could neither stand nor sit comfortably, and his excrement fell, mostly, through the bars at the bottom of the cage. His food fell in a mass on top of the cage. What he could funnel into his mouth or hold in his hands, he could eat; the rest fell through the cage to the cages below him to be recycled for future meals. He could not sleep until exhausted by the perpetual crouch he had to assume. Sleep was no escape, however; his dreams were permeated by the insanity of those around him tormented over years and decades as food for the undead. Awake or asleep his agonies were just the same. Just as the Lokaryn wished it to be.

When the Lokaryn came to feed, a wailing spread across the feeding chamber that was a mixture of anguish, madness, and pleas for death.

It was better than he deserved.

His life had been a litany of affronts to every moral code ever conceived. He was a predator who had hunted for decades, killing not for sustenance but for pleasure. He found little flavor in the momentary sensation of killing, but in torment there were delicacies that could be savored over days, weeks, and months.

Through the decades he traveled from zone to zone, never staying in one place very long. He lived and hunted the outer districts, where the law was less enforced, and he never returned to the same arc within a zone. He was an engine of suffering until the day a security officer burst through his door.

His trial had been brief, the evidence overwhelming: one should never keep souvenirs of ill deeds. He smirked at his victims' families when he engineered asylum in the Lokaryn Zone. He had avoided the death sentence of outcasting. He would live, for a while, among the Lokaryns and then be on his way. They would appreciate his dark talents. He thought he might even be celebrated.

The last face he saw before entering the transport was that of his arresting officer. He smirked again, with the confidence befitting a man who had gotten away with so many murders. The officer laughed as she slammed the hatch of the transport ship shut and he thought about the look on her face all the way to the Lokaryn Zone. The last laugh would be on her. When he arrived in he would find kindred spirits, who undoubtedly would applaud him as a virtuoso in their field. And when he had served his time, he would find her and slowly turn her laughter into screams.

After long weeks on the myst, the motion of the ship stopped and soon it reverberated with the sounds and movements of docking. Then all was silent.

He retrieved the small blade that he had stolen from his last meal and quickly wrapped it in a bit of cloth to minimize the damage to himself. Aware of the likelihood of cavity checks, he instead swallowed it and waited.

Just when he started to believe that he had been forgotten, the lock to his room abruptly activated and the cabin door opened. The light in the companionway was low and it took a moment for his eyes to adjust. Finally he was able to make out a dim red line on the floor that marked the path he was to follow. He held his head high and proceeded down it until he arrived at the ship's hatch. It was open and led into a large inprocessing station.

He stepped through the hatch with great expectation and could not have been more surprised when he was roughly grabbed and shoved into a line.

"Welcome," his assailant said, "I doubt you'll find this place to your tastes, but I'm sure we'll find you to ours." She licked her lips for added effect.

The man ahead of him turned around and extended a pudgy hand in greeting. "My name's Falworth," he said.

"Torvan," he replied, leaving the gesture unanswered. Falworth was undeterred.

"I think this is a lot of high drama so we won't forget our place here. I'm sure we'll be placed anywhere but the feeding pens. I'm an executive...rather, I was an executive in Thorpe's Zone. I got caught with profits that were not entirely my own. Did it for quite a while too. Who knew the Lokaryn Zone was on the other end of my efforts? But this beats outcasting or assassination. *And* if I play my cards right, I can even buy my way back in and get the old career going again. They say when you've finished your service here, the Lokaryns give you a pretty tidy sum of money. My terms of asylum require seven years of service and..."

Torvan finally spoke. "You talk too much."

"Yes, I've been told that, nervous habit I'm afraid. If there's a place to be nervous I would say this is it, wouldn't you? I mean, we're about to be 'inprocessed.' It's either to a new job or..." Falworth pointed down toward the ground with an idiotic look on his face. Torvan thought it a small wonder that this man hadn't been caught much sooner.

"So where are you from?" Falworth persisted. Torvan seriously wondered what the penalty would be in the Lokaryn Zone for killing a fellow refugee. His pondering was interrupted as a heavy metal door opened and the former executive from Thorpe's was ushered by a human into the interview room. The door closed with an ominous sound. At first, Torvan could hear nothing, but as time went on Falworth's increasingly strident voice could be discerned. It continued to rise until he could make out content.

"But I'm an executive, you could use me."

The lokaric interviewer's response remained low and unintelligible.

"No, I don't have engineering skills, I'm an executive!"

Again the Lokaryn's voice was too low to hear through the heavy door.

"No! Of course I've never worked in a mine, I'm an executi…Hey wait!"

Panic now sprang into Falworth's voice.

"No! Wait a minute, no! Oh my god."

Torvan then heard a scream that would have disconcerted most. To him, it was the first familiar thing about this place. He took an odd comfort in it. He next heard an even more frantic scream accompanied by a sizzling sound, like meat cooking. The scream suddenly stopped and he incorrectly assumed that Falworth had passed out.

After a few long minutes, in which he strained to hear more and didn't, the door again opened and the same human beckoned to Torvan. He decided that a strong front was best with these beings and thus walked in with a certain arrogance. He would not be cowed. The human who walked beside him said nothing, and took his place beside a large, dark wood desk.

The Lokaryn behind the desk sat back in his chair and looked Torvan over. "This is the one?" he asked.

"Yes, sir, number three-oh-five—"

The Lokaryn interrupted the human as he read from his clipboard. "This is no number, this is…Mr. Torvan. We heard you were coming, but to be the one on duty when you got here, well, I'm just the luckiest guy I know."

Torvan smiled inside. His gamble had paid off.

"I'm glad you appreciate my talents," he said.

The Lokaryn said nothing, but stood quite abruptly and walked over to the newcomer. He stood close to Torvan, so close that they were touching. The Lokaryn leaned in, brushing past his cheek. Torvan lurched back, startled. As he did, the Lokaryn snatched his hand roughly and, before any other reaction was possible, bit Torvan on the finger, drawing a single bead of crimson red. Torvan wanted to fight, but his hand was held so tightly that his only thoughts were of the pain. He was sure bones would start snapping at any moment.

The Lokaryn inhaled deeply over the blood; then, closing his eyes and with the slow movement of an oenophile about to savor a rare vintage, he brought the hand to his mouth and tasted the blood, which now flowed in a trickle. Torvan watched all of this as though he were an observer. His ears roared at the pain that emanated from his hand. A smile came across the Lokaryn's face, and the crushing sensation in Torvan's hand abated. It was several more moments before the Lokaryn released the hand completely and opened his eyes. Torvan grabbed his hand back, and massaged it with his other hand, away from the Lokaryn. The look in the Lokaryn's eyes conveyed his fate, and for the first time since his capture he felt afraid.

"Four stripes," the Lokaryn said, still apparently lingering in the fading sensations he had experienced from the blood.

Torvan looked around for an avenue of escape. His attention was involuntarily focused on a door that slid open and on a large deformed being that stepped into the room. The little of its face he could see beneath the matted hair was completely without symmetry. Boils both fresh and scarred decorated the flesh of the creature. Certainly not a Lokaryn, but not a human either. It held a long branding poker in its left hand that glowed white. The thing walked as if lame, but was still quick enough to grab Torvan by the neck. Its hand was as coarse as sandpaper, with fingers thick but strong. It was large enough to grab the neck and the collarbone without stretching, its thumb reaching all the way past the frightened man's spine. It had to apply but a little of its strength and Torvan was on his knees in pain.

Torvan struggled for a moment before he felt the heat of the metal near his face. He looked up to find his vile attacker grinning at him. He was amazed as he heard the once comforting screams emanating from his own mouth. He was still conscious through two of the brandings, but as the third began he felt the blackness taking him. Laughter issued forth from the beast that wounded him now, and the still-nameless Lokaryn looked on, expressionless. That utterly impassive face was the last image

Torvan remembered as his agony swallowed him.

He awoke in the cage that had been his home now for days. As each feeding period came and went, and those around him were fed upon, he remained untouched. His neck still hurt from the branding. Four times they had drawn the poker across this neck; it felt as if it burned as much now as it had then. His cage had been moved twice now. He understood neither the purpose nor the pattern of the moves, but each time was an exercise in disgust. Large brutish animals, probably related to the one that had branded him, serviced the cages, sloshing through the vomit and fecal matter that accumulated on the ground. When a cage was to be moved, one of these hulks would physically lift it onto his back and walk it to wherever it was to be, slamming it into place.

Torvan's new location had a continuous metal walkway that ran over the top of all the cages in his view. Cages in this chamber, as best he could tell while being brought here, were laid out in concentric circles. His cage was in what seemed to be the center, and concrete walls blocked the view toward others in the section. He could, however, see the lesser offenders. The chamber was far too dimly illuminated for him to make out much at first, but after days of light deprivation his eyes had adapted. He could see that executive a mere ten feet from where he crouched. The executive's cage allowed for him to at least sit. A small improvement, but one that Torvan would have paid any price for.

He needed information. "Falworth," he whispered.

The executive was looking straight ahead when Torvan called him. He did not turn his head.

"You don't have to whisper, they don't care what we say to each other," Falworth said in a normal tone. "They don't have to. We can't hurt them."

"Have they fed on you?"

"Tonight is supposed to be the first. They say it isn't bad. If I don't fight they'll put me to sleep while they do it."

"And if you fight?" Torvan asked.

"I'll have the most horrifying experience imaginable."

"Why are the cages so small? Where is the door on this thing?"

"We're food. They can't waste space on us. And the Lokaryns can pull the metal apart, they don't use locks. Locks can fail or be picked."

"I can't sit or stand in mine."

Falworth offered a bitter laugh. "Nice to know things aren't as bad as they could be. At least I can sit."

"Why is my cage like this?"

"I don't know. How many times were you branded?"

"Four."

"I got one, maybe it has something to do with that. Maybe they want you to see something that you wish you had the entire time you're here. I don't know and I don't care. This may come as a surprise to you, but I'm really not in the mood to talk right now."

"Listen, if we work together maybe we can get…"

"Out? No one has ever escaped. The others, the few sane ones anyway, talk pretty freely, about the feedings, the cages, the whole thing. No one gets out until they are let out. Besides, where would you go? We're in a cavern who knows how far below ground, and even if you could get out of the chamber, past a lower and upper district filled with Lokaryns, and actually reach the surface, you'd have to cross the Badlands on foot. It would take months to reach any settlement. Anyway, I'm a one-stripe, they let one-stripers move out of the cages if they behave. I have nothing to gain by helping you. I may be a nervous talker, but I'm not an idiot."

Very suddenly, the creatures that walked over the cages tending them started to run for the recesses of the cavern. The other captives became agitated. Most had lost their sanity quickly and were left feral or worse; those grabbed the bars and began shaking their cages like wild animals trying to escape. The sane ones prayed, cried, or sat. They were in the minority. Torvan looked around, trying to figure out what was happening. His eyes picked up a dim light near the top of the chamber. At first it seemed to be a solitary glowing red dot, but soon he saw that it was not alone. There were hundreds of dots flitting around like fireflies on a dark night.

He glanced at Falworth, who seemed to be mesmerized by the lights, as if he'd forgotten both his fear and the cacophony of sounds from the other captives. But a look of terror crossed his pudgy features, which drew Torvan to look up again, following his gaze. The dots had grown even more numerous, and as they circulated high above the cages, they had begun to take on the aspect of a swarm of angry bees. No wonder Falworth looked terrified, Torvan thought. He was starting to feel a little terrified himself.

The swarm grew until the entire roof of the chamber was covered in an eerie red glow. An earsplitting bell rang out, increasing the frenzy of the room. It pealed out again and again, and the lights seemed to vibrate in response, growing ever more menacing. When it seemed that the screaming could be no louder and the bell no more urgent, one of the lights plummeted so quickly that Torvan's eyes could not follow it. There was a thunderous crash in another section, then a sound of twisting metal, and a bloodcurdling scream.

At first it appeared that a man was floating in the air, but soon Torvan was able to make out the eyes and then the shape of a Lokaryn as well. The Lokaryn grasped the hair of her victim, and flew around the chamber for all to see. Four more red lights swarmed down and descended on the floating man. They attacked him savagely, yet miraculously the man did not die. When they were done, he was dropped back into his cage and the sound of steel again twisting could be heard. The screaming was unlike anything that even Torvan had ever heard. For a Lokaryn, he thought, this must be seasoning: fear spiced the soul.

The ceremonial rites now complete, the swarm descended en masse. The feeding frenzy had begun. They flew around the room, landing on cages, taking off again, and finally making their choice for the evening. Broad black feeding capes settled over cages, giving each Lokaryn privacy to feed. The room grew louder and louder from the screams. All attempts to block out the sounds were futile. The smell alone was overwhelming, as victim after victim lost control of their bodily functions.

Torvan saw a glowing light descending on Falworth's cell. Not the frenzied approach he had been witnessing, but more of a floating that was utterly out of place amid the carnage. He heard the clatter of boots on steel, and then another set.

"I asked you to dine with me tonight, J'Nath, to discuss your future with your clan lord missing," the first Lokaryn stated.

"She's been gone only a short while. She's done this before. She'll be back."

"That was a long while ago, and this is different. She is not without her enemies and I fear for her safety. Should anything happen to her, you will have a home in our clan, J'Nath."

Falworth had clearly heard the exchange too, and seemed perplexed, perhaps by the ordinary tone of the conversation; perhaps to him, Torvan thought, it sounded like two Thorpe's executives sitting down over a meal to discuss business.

Torvan perceived weakness.

"THANK YOU, LORD T'GARETH," J'NATH said, determined to hold firm. "I appreciate your offer, but Lord Derring will be back."

"As you wish. Have you dined with us before?"

"No, sir. I have never been invited. I have to say the opportunity to taste something fresh is very appealing. The offerings in our clan's caverns are extensive, but still, after a while it becomes repetitive."

"Really? I understand that Lord Derring stocks a very ample larder, including one of the best samplings of three- and four-stripes available. I've dined on her five-stripes more than once. Her taste is excellent."

"I will have to take your word on it, Lord T'Gareth. I am still relatively new to the Body and have not yet attained those levels."

"I'm sorry. Do you mean to say that after fifty years as a Lokaryn you still haven't tasted a four-stripe?"

J'Nath shifted a little uncomfortably. "No," he said.

"J'Nath, I don't mean to pry, but have you tasted a three-stripe?"

"Once, not long ago. It was felt by Lord Derring's regent, Solipher, that my reaction to the soul warranted caution. I must admit, my behavior was a bit erratic for a few days afterward," J'Nath lamented.

"Caution, J'Nath? This life we lead is not one of cautious attainment. Being one with the Body means that limits placed by others are wrong. You take what you want and make no apology."

"You almost sound like a Traditionalist, Lord T'Gareth," J'Nath said with a small nervous laugh.

"No, my friend, I am firmly Apostatic, but as responsible adherents of the new order, we should embrace the strengths of our forebears and add our own distinctive abilities to them. I only suggest that *you* are the best to decide when you are ready to advance, not someone else. You know best your strength, but enough of that. Let us feed." Rhetorically, T'Gareth added, "Are you ready?"

The two Lokaryns took their positions—J'Nath over the one-stripe he understood to be an ex–Thorpe's executive, and T'Gareth over the four-stripe mass murderer. While protocol would have T'Gareth begin the meal, J'Nath was surprised to see the elder Lokaryn motion for him to proceed.

"I insist," T'Gareth said.

"Thank you, Clan Lord." J'Nath did not know what he had done to deserve such an honor, but he knew he could not decline it.

He reached down and opened the bars to the cage and seized the one-stripe expertly by the throat. He lifted the man out of the cage roughly, and found himself staring into eyes that offered no threat. And no exhilaration. It would be a meal different from what he could attain in his own clan's feeding caverns, but it might as well be the same.

The one-stripe struggled as J'Nath held him dispassionately. "But I'm an executive!" he screamed.

J'Nath looked him over. "Sleep," he sighed. "It is the best way."

The one-stripe fell unconscious still protesting his credentials.

"Not to worry," J'Nath said unenthusiastically to the limp body. "You only have two thousand five hundred and fifty-five nights more to go until you can resume your career in Thorpe's." He pulled the body close, hearing the metal of the second cage give way to the strength of the older Lokaryn, and tilted his head, poised to bite into the carotid.

I AM PREDATOR, NOT PREY, Torvan thought, *and this captive is ready for you.* Unlike his fellow captives, he had come prepared: Earlier in the day he had painfully but triumphantly disgorged a small, plastic-wrapped blade swallowed prior to coming here.

When the Lokaryn pulled the bars apart, Torvan sprang from the cage like a psychotic serpent. He would kill everything that stood between him and his freedom. Soon he would be feasting on the officer that put him here.

One tasty organ at a time while she watched.

He felt the glory of the kill rising in him as his blade came to bear on the Lokaryn's chest. To kill a Lokaryn. How delicious. How infinitely malignant. The dinner had become the diner and…

He heard the snap, but did not feel it. His next awareness was of being suspended above the cage by his neck. His wrist hung at an odd angle from the rest of his arm and it did not respond to any command from his brain to move. He heard the clatter of the blade as it fell between the cages.

He felt pain in his neck from the branding before he actually felt the pressure of the hand that suspended him above the cage. As he focused on the Lokaryn, he realized that he had failed.

"MY, AREN'T WE THE FRISKY kitten?" J'Nath heard T'Gareth say to the four-stripe. J'Nath stood wide-eyed, motionless, still holding the one-stripe.

The human's mouth opened, but he could not speak.

"What's the matter, kitten? Cat got your tongue?" T'Gareth asked with sublime malice. Words stripped from him and actions defeated, the four-stripe struggled pointlessly.

J'Nath found himself embarrassed to even consider partaking of this feeble meal as he stood in the presence of such mastery. J'Nath watched and felt panic, fear, and a host of other flavors rising from the man held aloft in T'Gareth's brutal grip. The elder Lokaryn paused for a moment, visibly savoring the aromas. Then, pulling Torvan close, he said just loud enough for J'Nath to overhear, "I have waited a long time to meet you. Many of my friends want to meet you as well. You are going to be popular here. *Very* popular. We don't like people like you. We were once human, we have descendants that are still human, and when we think that they have to live in a world with people like you, it makes us *crazy*. We watch over them, we cherish them, we guard them and you…killed one of *my* family, S'joren Lis, in McAllister's Zone. Tell me if you remember her."

TORVAN FOUND HIMSELF DOING SOMETHING he had only heard others do: beg. He mouthed the word that he could not speak: *Please…*

He soiled himself; he pleaded and struggled. His identity as the predator molted away from him like a snakeskin with nothing to replace it. He hung there in T'Gareth's grasp naked and destroyed.

The Lokaryn drew his fangs close to Torvan's neck. Torvan felt the pressure of T'Gareth's teeth on his skin. His mind boiled in agony as images began to pour into his mind. They were the visions and the feelings that his victims experienced as he tormented them, all concentrated into a single moment as the Lokaryn bit down. Torvan's mind raced for the safety of insanity, but T'Gareth blocked this exit. Trapped, Torvan shrieked an inaudible dirge as the ghosts of his victims gleefully visited upon him their desire to destroy him.

The Lokaryn drew him in. Torvan kicked like a man dangling by his neck from a rope, to as little avail.

T'GARETH LOOKED UP AND SAID, "Delicious." He oozed satisfaction as he asked, "How is yours, J'Nath?"

The younger Lokaryn had not partaken of his own meal, but stood salivating openmouthed at the display before him. He dropped the one-stripe and moved toward the murderer, whose back arched in tetanic spasm. J'Nath looked down into the exquisite torment in those eyes. Eyes that would burst into flame if given the chance. They reflected decades of horrifying acts replayed again and again with the victimizer as the victim.

The elder Lokaryn said nothing, and with only the smallest of motions offered the murderer's body to J'Nath. The younger Lokaryn, intoxicated from the pollution that reeked from the man, seized him from T'Gareth, and in a single motion plunged his fangs deeply into the exposed neck. Darkness swirled through the younger Lokaryn's vision.

The rapture of malevolence consumed J'Nath entirely.

01011001 01101111 01110101 00100000 01101110 01100101 01100101
01100100 00100000 01101101 01101111 01110010 01100101 00100000
01110100 01101111 00100000 01100100 01101111 00100000 01110111
01101001 01110100 01101000 00100000 01111001 01101111 01110101
01110010 00100000 01110100 01101001 01101101 01100101.

—0130201401.1a, fifth founder of Rossums Zone

Chapter 14

Ravensford Zone
Location unknown

THE FORCE OF THE EXPLOSION blew the Lokaryn and the android through the portal as it began to collapse. The pairing of the two was like the beginning of a bad joke at a Badlands bar, but this was no joke.

They landed amid the tall grass of what under different circumstances would have been an idyllic setting. Derring fought hard to remain conscious. She had been thrown some thirty meters and landed with jarring force while trying to protect the inert android from damage. The pair had landed by the edge of a river with no signs of civilization around it. *My first break,* she thought, and hoped that it would not be her last. Several hundred yards away the river tumbled into a waterfall, something of which she used to be quite fond. But now the sound of the water served only to deaden her normally acute sense of hearing. Her list of disadvantages was growing rapidly.

She looked over toward Hemingway, who did not seem damaged. She was. Her body ached from the concussive force of the blast, and both of her hands were blackened and bloodied. As her adrenaline rush began to subside, her pain was immense. But the groan she heard belonged to neither of them.

Sergeant Peli Domar of the Third Arc Special Operations Group had been part of the assault team that breached the windows. Propelled by the blast, he involuntarily accompanied them through the conduit. At least, most of him had. Derring and Hemingway had been most of the way through when the Accelerator was fired. The Accelerator was not a close-range weapon, and its first shot set in motion the destruction of the entire building. As the room disintegrated around them, the portal quickly destabilized under the intense force, at the moment Sergeant Domar was thrown through. It collapsed around his legs, leaving him a bilateral amputee below the knees.

Bleeding from the stumps of his once-strong legs, Domar assessed his situation. He tried to stand but quickly realized that most of his legs were gone. Cursing, he struggled to bring himself up on his elbows.

It was then that he saw her.

Lit by the moonlight was the fierce countenance of the Lokaryn he had sought to kill.

She looked back at him, showing neither anger nor pain. She seemed strangely preoccupied.

For Derring's part she was indeed preoccupied. Four days without feeding and a man who had tried to kill her lying helpless at her feet. Her hunger screamed, but she did not yield to it; this was not an unjust man. She could see it within him. He was a product of his culture, misguided, but not evil. He cursed at her, but she heard few of the words as she fought the bloodlust welling inside her.

"Go on, do it," Domar rasped, knowing that he could not fight her off. His breaths were becoming shallow and he was in a cold sweat as his heartbeat started to become erratic from the blood loss. The world was failing around him and his time was short. He looked at her with hatred as he had been trained to do. As he prepared himself for her strike, a silent prayer formed on his lips.

Tru' dora, m'unsto, elara, he mouthed.

As she knelt beside him, she looked at him in a way that he had never seen before. He would remember her exact words to his final days.

Three simple words: "Pray with me."

Then she ripped the cloth of his shirt and made tourniquets to stanch the flow of blood. Each crimson drop was pure torment, but she dared not take one lest the bloodlust completely overwhelm her. She prayed aloud, and after several stunned moments Domar joined her, in a rushed and uncertain voice.

Her task completed, she stood away from him. He was unsure about what would happen next. A Lokaryn praying? Even if she were saying grace before finishing him off, it made no sense to bind his wounds.

"I cannot stay near you. I cannot minister to you any further. I cannot contact anyone to come for you."

Domar nodded, understanding, grateful to be alive, though confused to be so. He could not comprehend that a Lokaryn had just saved him from bleeding to death.

"Where are we?" he asked hesitantly.

"I do not know," she replied.

"I am Peli Domar," the soldier said awkwardly, not sure what to do next.

"I do not care," the Lokaryn said, picking up her equipment.

Domar's question finally filtered through her head: Where?

She looked up at the sky and saw the stars. Only one zone had a clear unaltered view of the night sky: Ravensford Zone. It was the zone populated by those commonly referred to in T'Amorach as "technophobes." The zone shielding was clear because it was generated by natural crystals. Derring looked over at the soldier again.

"Do you have any…"

Before the word "electronics" could pass her lips, the first blast from a hand crystal landed ten feet from her. This zone prohibited all technology, and the electronic signature of the soldier's battle gear registered like a flare in the night on the detection grid that permeated the zone. The grid was composed of thousands of crystals that slowly resonated at regular intervals in the pristine, electronics-free environment. Domar's unfortunate arrival had immediately set off alarm after alarm, and law-enforcement teams had set out by cat to intercept the renegades.

The cats were a product of McAllister's Zone, genetically altered felines almost two meters tall at the shoulder. The responding teams were on the other side of a wide river. Powerful though their mounts were, they could not jump the water span. Derring could easily traverse the distance, but killing would be an act of war. Escape was her only sane option. More forces were almost certainly closing in on her position from this side of the river; the water became her only choice.

She grabbed Hemingway's inert form and the duffel bag of gear and ran. Shot after shot piled around her. She was moving too fast to make a clear target, but there was always the danger of a lucky shot.

"Hold your fire!" Peli Domar yelled. "Hold your fire! The electronics are mine. I am a member of the Third Arc Special Operations Group and I landed here through a portal accident."

Domar's statements brought a pause in the assault. Derring slowed and looked at the soldier in confusion. He motioned with his head toward the river. "Go!"

She hit the fast-moving water and in moments was swept over the falls, holding Hemingway and her duffel. She pushed away from the lip of the waterfall and arched out in the manner of a cliff diver. Though she made it look easy, it was a remarkable feat. They hit the water and not the rocks as might otherwise be expected, and she was off. She had an advantage in, or rather under, the water, and she pressed it now. Hemingway was an android and did not need air; as a Lokaryn she could do with very little.

They traveled down the river for a good twenty minutes before she needed to surface. By that time they were far downstream while her attackers still stood at the bluff of the waterfall, scanning the basin for any signs of bodies.

Four times she repeated this, until they were well down the river and seemingly away from danger. Finally, drenched and heavily burdened with the android and her gear, she trudged out of the water. Sensing no immediate threat, she flopped down in the sand of the riverbank. It was quiet here and she'd be able to hear anyone coming, a welcome change from proximity to the waterfall. She couldn't decide if her luck had been good or bad. She had made several mistakes thus far, largely owing to the haste in which she had come after Hemingway. She was ill prepared, and as she reflected on recent events, she began to suspect that she had been set up.

"Set up by a dead man who doesn't know it yet," she swore aloud.

She opened her duffel bag, and gave thanks to Thecla that her equipment was still dry. She removed four rods and crystals from their waterproof wrapping and began to set up a small dampening field. She checked her work many times before pulling out a small keypad. Then, with a deep breath, she keyed in a fourteen-place alphanumeric code. Less than a handful of people knew it; it was Hemingway's activation code.

The android sat up, shaking his head. Derring knelt behind him, and put her hands over his ocular sensors. Hemingway was unable to get a bioreading on her, which could mean only a few things, most of them bad.

"Guess who?" she said softly into his auditory sensor.

The android whipped himself around and threw his arms around her in an enormous hug.

"Hello, Hemingway. It's good to see you," she said, trying to hold back her emotions.

Hemingway put his hands on her shoulders and pushed her back to look at her. He went to speak but spasmed just a little bit with slightly pursed lips. It was the reaction of a man about to speak who suddenly realizes that his mouth is full. The surprised look on his face gave way to one of mild displeasure and a furrowed brow. He pursed his lips again and spit out a long arc of river water. It took him several seconds to finish.

"OK, what the hell is going on?" he asked. "Why are we wet? Why are we sandy? And why are we sitting on the edge of a river in the middle of nowhere? Don't get me wrong, I'm happy to see you, but aren't we *not* supposed to see each other. I mean anyone from the crew?"

"Hemingway?" Derring interrupted.

"Yes?"

"When a Lokaryn tells you to shut up, what's generally the best course of action?"

"Run?"

"Hemingway," she said again, sighing. The part of her that had just narrowly escaped immolation was getting annoyed, but the larger part of her, which had waited five years for this reunion, had to work hard to repress a smile at the 'droid's wiseass answer. She pressed on.

"We're in Phobes' Zone without shelter or contact, and it's a few hours before dawn. You are wet because I just spent the last hour and a half under water trying to save your shiny metal ass from the security forces in a zone where, to put it mildly, you aren't welcome. You are sandy because I decided to get out of the water and drop you here. You can go back under the water any time you like. We are in the middle of nowhere because everyone here wants to kill you. You have been deactivated for the last three months, because apparently someone found out you were in Chumley's Zone working for the network and tried to have you assassinated. They were well on the way to being successful when a guardian angel showed up."

The android said nothing. He had a long list of comebacks for her guardian-angel remark; however, having just heard the words "you," "deactivated," and "assassinated" in the same sentence, he stored them away for another time. Hemingway was a wiseass, not an idiot.

Derring continued, "I still don't know who tried to kill you. However, your protector disrupted the assassination. You were damaged badly enough to shut down during the attack."

"So what are you doing here?" Hemingway asked. "You're not with the underground anymore."

"Someone sent word to me that you were in trouble, and I left within an hour of receiving it."

"Thanks," he said.

"You're welcome. I never stopped to think that someone was using you to bait me."

"So here we are, a Lokaryn and a 'droid alone in Phobes' Zone, just before dawn with very little prayer of finding safe haven. So other than that, how have you been?" Hemingway asked.

" 'Droid, when a Lokaryn tells you to shut up, what's the best thing to do?"

"Order a clean set of underwear?"

Derring smiled in spite herself. "I've missed you, old friend."

"Me, too. We should have never accepted that damn deal."

Her smile faded. "Don't start. There was no other way. Gedrick's deal saved all of our lives, yours included."

"I'll bet he regrets that last part," the android said.

"You're wrong. Maybe he was the guardian angel who saved you?"

"More likely he hired the assassin," Hemingway replied with only the faintest of smiles.

"He loved you like a brother and you know it," Derring shot back.

"Great! That should have his old man spinning in his grave."

Silence ensued. She loved the android, but at this moment was regretting the fact that she couldn't bite him. Hard.

Hemingway was the first to break the silence. He was looking up at the stars, making calculations, but also thinking about what Derring had said.

"I'm sorry," he began, but for what he was apologizing he did not say. "I've pretty well figured out where we are: either the east side of Demminer Arc or the west side of the Winter Arc. Either way you're about thirty minutes' travel from a large settlement in the outer districts."

"You? I think you mean 'we.' I didn't come all this way to drop you off for the phobes to crucify."

"You, Derring. Here's what I think we should do. Dawn is about two hours away. I go back into stasis: you bury me. When did you feed last?"

"Four days ago."

The android paused to look at her. "You've increased your endurance. Used to be four days would have had you gnawing on anything that moved: animate, inanimate, it didn't matter. You don't seem too bad."

"I'm feeling it."

"So once I'm underground and the dampening field is over me, you head into town and see if you can't find a malcontent that T'Amorach would be better off without."

"OK, but let's change our position a bit. We're too close to the river's edge and they may yet search this area. The crystal nearly didn't work and I still have the feeling that we're being set up. I bury you here and you'll likely wake up dead."

"Smart. OK, the plan is move camp, deactivate me, go feed, and wait it out until dark. Then you come back, right?"

"I didn't come all this way to make you a planter."

"Actually I'd be a plantee."

"You know what you do when a Lokaryn tells you to shut up?"

"Remind her that dawn is coming fast?"

They quickly worked to cover any trace that they had been there, and then moved inland from where they had surfaced. It was an area that would not be a logical place for someone on the run to go. It took little time for them to dig the hole. When it was complete, Hemingway climbed in and deactivated. The Lokaryn found the idea of burying the inert 'droid upsetting. Though she knew it wasn't a funeral, still she felt compelled to say a small prayer at the graveside.

The interment done, she memorized the place that she had left him and quickly traveled to the settlement.

"One more day, I need only survive one more day," she reminded herself.

She hid herself in a condemned warehouse, settling in shortly before the sun rose. She hoped that today would not be the day that they tore it down. She slept fitfully, waiting out the day, while hunger poked and prodded her. She could not leave, and by nightfall she was famished.

The settlement had about ten thousand inhabitants. A small fleet of fishing vessels plied the inland sea for the fish that grew plentifully there. Some were horribly mutated, but most were edible and a few even delicious. At the river's edge, small cargo ships dotted the docks and wharves. It was here that the criminal element flourished.

When feeding outside of their zone, Lokaryns often chose a street urchin, an elder, or a solitary citizen. Relatively defenseless, their disappearance rarely caused a stir. With this in mind, however, most Lokaryns were not otherwise choosy about their meal. Derring, on the other hand, preferred to do the community that supported her a service. Over time she came to find that corrupt souls tasted the best. And so she took up vigil in a run-down area of the docks, watching the comings and goings, until she spied her meal for the evening.

He was a seedy-looking middle-aged thief, rail-thin with long stringy hair and mean slits for eyes. She had observed him ply his trade for several hours and was convinced that he would suffice. What this thief lacked in community status, he more than made up for in filth, odor, and cruelty. It was his practice to sit outside the local bars and wait for drunks to stumble out. Then he went about earning his living. He always deprived them of their money and sometimes, depending on his mood, their lives. He liked robbing, and his favorite victims were women, probably because in his mind they were a double payday. Tonight there had not been any.

The man was very deliberate about where he killed. Derring noted that he scouted the river's edge, and she took a moment to appreciate the irony. The thief was smart. A body would be quickly swept beneath the aquifer and beyond the reach of anyone except perhaps an overambitious sanitation worker. It was a brilliant strategy and she would use it against him.

The thief waited for his next victim of the evening, and Derring waited as well. As the hunt continued, the bloodlust swelled within her and any feelings of remorse faded to whispers on the wind. With each moment that she stalked her prey the anticipation of the kill mounted. The more she watched him, the more she knew that he would taste delicious. Especially, if she made the kill last a long while.

He moved in on his next victim, a smallish, well-dressed man. A fool to come to this part of town so well appointed, but likely he was looking for some vice that could not be easily obtained in an inner district. The thief moved in on him quickly, placing a knife to his ribs and hurrying him out of view.

Derring pulled her hood over her head to obscure her face and walked from around the corner seemingly oblivious. Her female form and movement caught the thief's eye immediately. He quickly slid the knife into the drunk's ribs and left him to pursue the more alluring target. Though the drunk would not ultimately die, he would have a rather difficult time explaining to his wife why he was in this particular part of town when he was supposed to be in the Center Arc negotiating a grain deal with Chumley's Zone.

The thief caught up to Derring and said, in a falsely soothing voice, "A pretty lady should not be walking in this area so late at night and alone."

She stopped, allowing him to angle in, watching his approach, and knowing that it would be crude. As she predicted, he drew the knife and held it to her ribs.

"Move, bitch, toward the river, down by the shed."

She quietly complied, but did not feign terror for him. Had the thief been focused on something other than his lust, he might have noticed, but he didn't seem to. Upon reaching the shed, he spun her violently around, which she allowed.

"Strip and don't forget I have a knife. I'll cut you so bad that you'll beg me to finish it."

He started to unbuckle his pants, watching her the whole time, trying to juggle the knife and his belt. She made a point of seeming like she wouldn't give him any trouble. She didn't shake, sob, or cry out. In fact, she risked seeming a little too calm as she reached up and unfastened the hood of her cloak.

"Be gentle with me," she said, in a voice pitched to pass though the thief like a winter chill.

He held the knife out, in a stabbing motion, forgetting his pants, which fell down around his ankles. It was then that his gaze focused on her face. She knew how terrifying she looked, her feminine features blended with a lupine menace. He dropped the knife, tried to back up, and stumbled to the ground, tripped by his pants. He rolled over onto his stomach, and came to his hands and knees trying to scramble away.

She was already in front of him.

"I thought you wanted to sample some of my charms?" she said, grabbing him by the chin and standing him up.

He began to whimper.

Derring looked down at him, making a pointed gesture of examining his groin.

"Not aroused? Or is that the best that you can muster?" she said scornfully.

"Please, let me live," he begged.

He attempted to strike her, but she deflected the blow with such force that one of his wrists was instantly dislocated. Before he could howl in pain she gripped the back of his neck so strongly that no noise would come. His neck began to move in unnatural ways as the muscles collapsed and severed under the pressure of her grip. Yet his spine was still untouched. He would be able to feel searing pain. He would be able to feel her breath on his neck. He mouthed the words "please, no" over and over again.

She looked him deeply in the eyes.

"How many have you killed? You could have taken the coins and let them walk away. How many widows have you made? How many orphans?"

The man stared back at her, begging for his life with his eyes.

"A Lokaryn can kill in an instant, or we can take years. Unfortunately, I only have a few hours. Perhaps I'll leave you as a vegetable. Oh, you'll know everything going on around you, but you won't be able to form a coherent sentence. And every time you close your eyes, you'll remember our little rendezvous. I'll decide later."

The thief struggled feebly as Derring shifted him in order to get a better angle on his neck.

Though he could make no sound, she heard him screaming a silent scream for their many hours together.

It was a meal to remember.

Walking the Prophet's Path is easy! Just step outside of the shielding and head north. Leave it to a Kwynian to make a big deal about something that an eleven-year-old was able to do.

—Otman Norbunder, net-rogue comedian
Last person executed in Kwyne for heresy

CHAPTER 15

Kwyne
Third Arc

KRAGEN SURVEYED THE RUBBLE THAT until recently had composed an entire block of his arc. Though it was not the most affluent of areas, it was usually bustling with the activity of street vendors engaged in local commerce. Now it was eerily still. He appreciated the salt-of-the-earth flavor of the region, perhaps because his father had been born there. He considered it to be the true embodiment of Kwyne. Damage-control teams worked furiously among the smoldering wreckage, engaged in the hopeless task of searching for survivors. Thus far, there were none.

Kragen was followed by N'orin and Balazar, who were busily noting the damage and thanking Thecla that this hadn't happened in their arcs.

"The Lokaryns will pay for this act of terrorism," N'orin said, trying to impress Kragen.

Kragen stopped for a moment and then pointedly asked, "Did you not see with your own eyes, on the floor of the Nehreton itself, that our weapons caused this?"

"Our forces cannot be held to blame. Still, this never would have happened had a Lokaryn not come into the zone."

"How do you propose that we convince our citizenry of this when there are no remains, and not one of the sixty security-force members could give a positive visual confirmation?"

N'orin had no answer. Unfortunately, neither did Kragen, and he knew he would need to provide one soon.

The whole turn of events left Kragen feeling off balance, an unfamiliar feeling for the former officer of the Kuhbrik. Though he could not admit this to the others, he was fairly certain that an act of terrorism had occurred, but could not prove it. Only certain codes could be used to authorize weaponry of the kind that had done this—codes that were closely held. The rohnin would know, but Kragen knew better than to accuse him of sabotage against his own people. On the other hand, the rohnin needed only to intimate that Kragen, in his zealotry to catch a Lokaryn, had acted irresponsibly.

Kragen could go no further with the survey of the damage until the rescue crews cut further into the wreckage. He turned to make the long trek back to his offices. N'orin watched as Kragen started to walk away. "Var? Ground transport will be much faster."

Kragen waved them on. "No, please go on."

"Var," Balazar said, "it will take you some time."

"We could all use some time to consider what happened," Kragen replied, and walked into the night.

Kragen envisioned this as a prelude to walking the Prophet's Path: an outcasting that offered the possibility of redemption and return. Those who chose it left the protection of Kwyne proper to walk the route that Thecla had walked to the ancient Kwynian city of Turin Tan. Leaving the protection of the zone's shielding meant exposure to the elements of the Badlands. It was considered an honorable choice, a choice of true atonement, but a choice from which one did not expect to return.

It took the better part of an hour to reach the office, and his thoughts had distilled down to one: *It was not an accident.* He considered the situation from every angle he could think of and all led to the same conclusion. Someone released the weapons to troops not trained in their use. Given the layers of steps necessary for such an authorization, it could not have been incompetence that caused this.

He stopped in midthought and, suppressing the urge to stiffen, reached into his pocket.

The prelate's famous smoking ritual: right over left, left over right. Or so anyone watching would think. He did not want the assassin in the shadows to know that he was aware of his presence.

Kragen hoped that the assassin had not observed his movements closely enough to recognize that his tobacco and pipe were in the other pocket.

He moved with a nonchalance forged of hard discipline and a lifetime of application in the arts of the Kuhbrik. His hand reached into the pocket, as every hair on his neck prickled, waiting for the impact of a bullet. He listened for the faint report of a silenced hammer falling, or a dart leaving the chamber of a gas-propelled weapon. None came as his fingers found the handle of his weapon.

Now the discipline shifted from one of stealth to one of fury. In a move that blurred in the eyes of the man in the shadows, the prelate's sight painted the assailant's forehead with an eerie blue dot. The weapon had been trained to cleanly part the man's brain down the middle, even before the prelate had turned halfway around. The same motion had caused a small diversionary device to drop from the handle of the gun, obscuring the figure of the prelate in smoke and refracted light.

"Out!" the prelate commanded, using a technique that made his voice sound like it emanated from somewhere other than where he was.

A man of medium build stepped out of the shadows, his own weapon still held in a position to fire. He had black hair tied back and metal-grey eyes that held no joy or mercy. His expression belied no fear or surprise at being uncovered, and his smile betrayed nothing of his thoughts. "Var," the man said by way of greeting.

"I suggest you remember who you are addressing, Captain Loh'l," Kragen replied evenly. "You could be a puddle of smoldering goo."

"Hardly the answer I'd expect from a man about to have victory delivered to his doorstep. Are we going to be putting down our guns?" Loh'l asked.

"Feel free to lower yours, Captain," Kragen said. "I'll keep mine where it is until I've asked you a question."

"Very well then," Loh'l replied, holding his gun out. He seemed little distracted by the laser that still traced his forehead. "Ask your question," he said.

"Scores of my troops lie dead and who knows how many civilians. Why should I trust you?" Kragen seethed.

"I can understand why you would be upset about the loss of your men, but what has that to do with me, Prelate? I delivered the Lokaryn as promised. If you were unable to capitalize on the opportunity, how is that my problem?" Loh'l asked.

Kragen stood silent for a moment, hating that this man was right. The truth was that the release of weapons had to have come from a highly placed source, not a freelance agent such as Loh'l. Kragen lowered his weapon, and finally spoke. "You said something about delivering a victory."

"I may be able to give the Lokaryn to you yet," Loh'l said.

"How?" the prelate asked.

"How is not your concern. You have only two things to consider. First, are you still interested in apprehending a Lokaryn?"

"Not *a* Lokaryn, *the* Lokaryn," Kragen corrected. "I have no desire to see these profane things in Kwyne. When you came to me with information that this incursion was inevitable, you did not offer the option to prevent it, only to influence where it might shelter."

"True. It was not in *my* power to prevent a Lokaryn from coming into *your* zone. But when asked to provide information about a safe house, I came to you. I felt you were one of the only leaders in Kwyne with the courage to confront the problem."

"Please, Captain Loh'l, pandering does not suit you. You are not Kwynian, so why would you care where the Lokaryn went? Your decision was a purely financial one. If the Lokaryn is still in the zone, I will have atonement for the dead. Yes, I am still interested in capturing the Lokaryn."

"Which brings me to the second consideration," Loh'l said. "Are you willing to pay the fee?"

Kragen looked at Loh'l suspiciously. "We've paid you handsomely already."

"And I delivered as we already discussed. If you want the Lokaryn delivered to you a second time, it will be done, but there will be a second charge for doing so."

"Very well, Captain," Kragen said, "we will meet your price. But understand this: If I find that you had any role in trafficking Lokaryns into Kwyne, *you* will make atonement for the lost lives." The prelate was thankful that he had lowered his gun. Had the blue dot still painted the man's forehead at that moment, Loh'l's survival would have been in question.

Forget this single point at your own peril: When your target is in range, so are you.

—Baeless Tremmel, master of assassins

CHAPTER 16

The Badlands
The Drunken Angry Bitch tavern

DEATH LOOKED PRETTY MUCH LIKE what she had expected, and she hadn't had to wait long for it to arrive. But it smelled a lot worse.

It manifested in the form of an ugly giant who had appeared in the Drunken Angry Bitch scant seconds before. So large was the assassin that he had to stoop to enter the bar. When he came to his full height he had some four feet on the mutant and no less than four hundred pounds. His clothing bespoke his profession: dirty, stinking, and stained with the blood of countless victims. As dirty and squalid as the Bitch had seemed just moments before, it was a paradise before this walking filth pile entered it.

Few noticed him as he walked in, which was typical in the Badlands. Fewer still made the effort to take his full measure. It was general practice in regions like this to not "notice" things that one wanted to avoid. The simple act of eye contact in this place had made more widows than the Scutbrew. In all, only three in the bar paid any mind to the man. One was Grizwald. The veteran bartender immediately knew who had walked through the door. The giant walked up to the bar, ordered a bottle of whiskey, and spit on the bar as payment, adding:

"That includes the tip."

He offered a semi-toothless grin at Griz, who looked unimpressed, but harmless. Turning, the colossus walked deliberately toward the back room where his prey awaited him.

As lethal as the giant was, he did not come alone. Behind him followed several smaller but equally dangerous hangers-on. The contract belonged to the large man, but if he were to fail, the others might still be able to make a payday of it.

He stood in the open doorway and bellowed, "Seyschell," in a voice altered years ago by a knife to the throat. "You have been a naughty girl, leading me so far. And for what? Here you sit like a lamb in the slaughterhouse."

"I'll make you a deal, assassin," she replied evenly. "I won't put up a fight, if you leave my people alone."

Though normally he preferred a bloody fight the assassin thought about it for a moment and readily agreed. In spite of the fact that she was seated at a table in the corner of the room and decidedly drunk, all things that gave him the advantage, he had been well informed about his prey's capabilities. Better to accept her capitulation. After she was gone, her village would make easy pickings. He did not like leaving battles unfinished.

For her part, Seyschell said nothing. She could see that he had no intention of dealing, especially from a position of strength. She looked up readied herself.

She turned her gaze directly to the giant and threw back another shot of good whiskey.

"Get on with it. Your breath smells like the ass end of a dead Maldavean dung camel."

"I'm in no hurry," the assassin replied through a rotted smile. He raised his weapon, which was a large one of the energy variety. Most soldiers needed to grav-balance a weapon of this size, which minimized the interaction between the weapon's weight and gravity, essentially allowing them to lift it. The giant, however, did not need such assistance. He stared down the immense barrel, readying his shot, as the sighting laser came on. He was disappointed that her diminutive size put so much of her in the sight. He aimed low to leave her head intact so that he could mount it on the front of his ship as he had done with the many others. He took a satisfied breath and fingered the trigger.

"Wait," she said. This was the part that the assassin liked best: the begging. It would make no difference, of course, but it would at least add to his amusement. He enjoyed killing, the way that some enjoyed a good game of Dranwyene. Thus far, however, this contract not been that much fun.

"I have a large cache of gems that I will trade you for one piece of information: Who?"

"Your fairy godmother, mutant," he said with a malevolent smirk. He did not care for money, of which he had enough to fund himself for several lifetimes. Though his payday for this execution would be handsome, he was in it for the blood and for the glory. He would forever have bragging rights that he had killed one of the vaunted *Shicaine* crew, the copilot no less. A clean kill with no backers to come after him.

"Nighty night…Thrasher."

Seyschell's eyes went wide on hearing her railroad code name spoken. It was a name that few knew. Before she could process how this thing knew it, however, an enormous sound erupted, not from the assassin's gun but from the wall and window to her left. The concussion of the explosion knocked the assassin off balance and caused his weapon to discharge into the ceiling, but he remained standing. The enormous noise shattered most of the glass in the establishment. As she tried to clear her head, she found herself with a stray thought: *Griz will not be amused.* It was then that she noticed the man sprawled on the floor in front of the giant. He swiftly rolled to his knees, brought a shotgun to bear on the assassin, and squeezed off a center shot. The attack would have killed an ordinary man, but the giant was in no way ordinary. The assassin swatted the weapon out of the smaller man's hands before he could fire again.

Though Seyschell couldn't see it, she could imagine the look of surprise on the smaller man's face when the giant grabbed him by the head with one hand and lifted him fully off the ground. The man dangled, his hands grasped around the larger man's wrist. Seyschell knew that the assassin would crush this man's head and finish the job he came for. She jumped to her feet to attack the behemoth.

It was the giant's turn to be surprised as the man dangling in his grasp produced a blade seemingly made of quicksilver. In an instant the weapon severed the assassin's hand and was gone as quickly as it had appeared. The assassin howled in pain as both his hand and the smaller man fell away. The man landed on Seyschell, and together they collapsed on the floor in a huge tangle. The assassin's working hand still held the now-recharged weapon, and he brought it to bear on the wriggling mass at his feet. Another enormous explosion filled the room.

The giant's face took on a blank expression as the blood drained from his head. His heart no longer inhabited his chest and thus was unable to push blood to his brain—or anywhere else for that matter. He fell over face-first, breaking a table in the process. Behind him stood Griz with a similar weapon, though his took advantage of the grav-balancing feature.

Griz looked down at Seyschell and only smiled.

"Lousy tipper."

The others in the group all lay dead from the poisoned whiskey given them by Griz. There would be no payday for any of them.

The bartender walked over to the dead man's body and spat on it. "Your change, sir," he said with a sardonic grin. He leaned down and took the arm of the man who had just disrupted the assassination of Seyschell.

"Your timing, as always, Captain, stinks," he said, pulling him to his feet. The cloak fell back and a still-hurting Gedrick winced.

"The sweet sound of gratitude, I never get tired of listening to that. You might have shot him a bit earlier, you know."

"Couldn't pull out the gun until the weasels were all tucked in, and by then you had gotten in the way. Unless you meant for me to take the shot with you in the sight as well."

Gedrick only nodded. "With your aim? Might have been safer."

Seyschell started to gather her things. "I have to go back to the village. Whoever sent the assassins will go back to my village."

"We're not going back," Gedrick said.

"Fine, then. Thanks for coming, but I have to go."

"No one will be attacking the village," Gedrick said. The mutant continued to pack her duffel. "Shell!" Gedrick shouted, snapping the mutant to attention. She realized that she was reacting as if she were still under his command aboard *Shicaine*, and her eyebrows furrowed in an unpleasant manner.

"What?!" she responded with annoyance. Then her face softened.

"Seyschell," he began gently, "anyone going back to your village, if they can even find the opening again, will be greeted by some very nasty surprises, including a plasma cannon mounted on the entrance wall. Your townsfolk are well armed now. Anyone expecting easy pickings will be fertilizing the lagoon floor before they catch sight of the town steeple."

Seyschell started at him, confused.

"We were at the village. They're all OK. We equipped them so that they can hold off anyone. At least for a while. But we can't defend the village forever against whoever's after you. After us."

"Us?"

"Us. Someone tried to kill me as well. The only thread between you and me is the railroad and the *Shicaine*. We can't defend the village indefinitely, but if we can kill the source…"

"Is anyone from the crew dead?" Seyschell asked.

"Not that I know of. Yet."

"How did you know I was here?"

"Well, Venka, your village elder, gave us a pretty good idea, but it wasn't until Griz sent a message that we knew for sure. We almost missed it."

"You might have responded," Griz noted.

"It would be too dangerous to do anything outgoing from the ship. We got into port last night and started watching the place, looking for traps. When I saw our friend here enter the bar, I came over to your window, and the rest you know."

"So we're back in business?" Seyschell asked.

"No. But we're going to protect our family," Gedrick said, looking down at Seyschell. Then, without turning, "You ready, Grizwald?"

"Aye, Captain," Griz said, hoisting a large bag onto his shoulder and picking up two others with his free hand.

The only real use for peace is to prepare for the next war.

—Merchants' Zone saying

CHAPTER 17

THE MAN CREPT SLOWLY TOWARD the bed where the child lay sleeping. In his hands he held implements that would normally be used to till the soil, but before this dawn they would serve a more sinister purpose. He silently moved forward, his plan well laid out. It was one he had carried out many times before, and he felt assured of success as he encroached on the sleeping form.

The "child" was in fact almost eighteen years old, a woman by her society's standards and an intelligent one by any standard that mattered. The man approached, and threw himself into the attack with purposeful malevolence.

The implements did their noisy work without effect. She made no movement. He soon discovered that there was no body under the blankets at all, only pillows. The young woman had anticipated his attack and had gained the upper hand. She was a worthy adversary, but not for long, he thought. The man looked about quickly. He turned to face the closet, anticipating a counterstrike.

He was right that an attack was forthcoming. However, he miscalculated its direction. His intended victim lunged from under the bed, grabbed his legs, and screamed. Though he had anticipated her attack, it still startled him when it came. She had reacted ably, and though later he would argue mercilessly, he was well pleased. Seconds after her hands were on his calves, he was looking at the floor, his implements now scattered about him. He was well pleased. No one would sneak up on the daughter of Stannis Klemm.

"Dad! Don't you *ever* get tired of this?" Lyrie protested as she crawled out from under the bed.

"No. Why?" Klemm countered.

"I'm almost eighteen, Dad. It's not cute anymore." She offered him a hand up.

"It's not meant to be cute, sweetheart. It's good training for life, you never know when…"

"What, Dad?" she interrupted. "A stray stalk of asparagus is going to attack me in my sleep? We're farmers, for land's sake!"

His faced changed for a moment, and then he broke into a smile. "Asparagus isn't the real threat. Broccoli is the killer."

Lyrie looked at him for a moment. She trusted her father, but there were times when she wondered why a farmer would think such training was necessary.

"Come, breakfast is about ready."

Downstairs Lyrie's mother had a country breakfast prepared that would see them through the work of the morning. As a child Lyrie hated the chores around the farm, but as she grew older she began to feel the connection of time to the things around her. Each animal that she tended had a lineage. She knew each as the child or grandchild of an animal from her own childhood. She cared for them and in return they supported her human family with milk, eggs, and wool. Only rarely was an animal slaughtered for meat. Lyrie often thought the decision was based more on the temperament of the animal than the need for meat.

She ate quickly and went out into the yard to feed the animals their breakfast. That task done, she turned to the rest of her day. She loved it out here, but she also knew that the day was approaching when she would be the one inside preparing the meals and tending to her own family. Her children, once old enough, would tend the farm with their father—her husband. That was the way of things, not only in her arc, but in the whole of Ravensford, or what outsiders referred to as Phobes'

Zone. It had worked for hundreds of years, and it would work for hundreds more in exactly the same way.

And so it was no surprise that not much happened in Ravensford Zone and most especially in Demminer Arc. Her days always proceeded in the same fashion, as did the seasons and the years. Even the father of her children would be no surprise. He was literally the boy next door, Timan, the eldest son of the man who owned the neighboring farm. Their marriage would bond the parcels together and the families would be considered to have joined the wealthy.

Timan and Lyrie had grown up together, but she was a year older. He was tall, strong, and—most important in a future husband, at least according to zone wisdom—he had the knack of the land. They had played together as children, discovered that they were built quite differently as young adolescents, and later found this not as entirely vexing as they first thought. As young adults it would be only a matter of time before their intentions of marriage were announced.

If there was anything that could be considered a surprise in this place, it was that Lyrie's younger brother, Ren, remained alive. Only five years younger than she, he took a constant delight in tormenting his older sister about everything, and Lyrie was not a woman that most men approached lightly. At the moment, Ren was also in the yard mending the fence. As he spied his sister he began to sing one of his standards:

"Is there anything that Lyrie could want MORE
Than to kiss the little boy next DOOR
Live a life pulling weeds
Staying away from electrical leads."

Lyrie looked at him sternly. "Very clever, little man. Try this one.

"My name is Ren
Let me tell you when
I used a verse
that contained a curse

and I got a bona fide
Father-tanned hide!

"And *that*, you little dung heap, is what Dad will do if he hears you using those words," she admonished.

"What's so bad about *tech* anyway?" the younger sibling replied, much put out that her rhyme had been entirely too clever.

"Ren, forget about things of the other zones. You are a farmer and a talented one. If you continue to persist in this fascination, Dad will find out. Do you want to end up like the Heretic?"

Ren made a face at his sister. " 'The Heretic' is a boogeyman tale that parents tell their children to scare them away from technology. There I said a naughty word. What are you going to do? Technology! Technology! Technology! Tech…"

It was in Lyrie's face. Ren knew in an instant that their father was behind him. He turned around to find him standing not more than five feet away. His expression was not one of anger or disdain, but one that could be more accurately described as concern.

"Ren," he began evenly, "all intelligent young people go through this phase of questioning."

Her father glanced at Lyrie as if reading her mind. His look conveyed the acknowledgment that she too had questioned; however, Lyrie's questioning of the tenets of their Ravensford life was somewhat more…vigorous. Her examination called into question many of his own beliefs, and eventually it was an affirmation for them both. He was sure, however, that it would be a decade before he had fully recovered. He expected a somewhat easier time with his son. He looked at Lyrie, winked, and then continued.

"Technology," he said as he looked at his shocked children, who had never heard him use the word before, "is neither sinner nor saint.

"It's only a tool, but one that can make us unwise. It gives power, but removes consideration of that power's use. Using the tools available in other zones, I could clear that whole back field by myself in less than a day. If, on the other hand, I have to hack each weed, cut each tree, pull each stump, I am far more likely to take only what I need. With technology I lose sight of what I am taking. Do you understand?"

"Yes, sir," Ren replied, his head hung now. He was both surprised and grateful that his father was not angry.

"Go on now, finish your chores. And by the way, I think the two of you would do well to whitewash the front fence this afternoon."

"Why me?" Lyrie protested.

"Setting your brother up like that. Really now, Lyrie." Stannis Klemm was no fool.

"And one other thing…" The children cringed. "I want you both in bed early tonight."

The remainder of the day passed without issue. When it came time to whitewash the fence, their father started Lyrie at one end and Ren at the other. The competition between the two had the job finished in one-third the time it would normally have taken.

It is good for a father to know his children.

The evening came and the lamps were lit, burning the pure oils produced from plants that grew on the farm. Lyrie considered the day as she ascended the stairs to her bedroom. The day had progressed much like any other, even with the discipline and early bedtime. Discipline was expected and the mark of a good parent. Yet somehow something was not right. Their mother was quieter than usual and little was said at the dinner table. Lyrie wondered if Mother had somehow caught on to the conversation in the yard. While their father was a little more relaxed about such things, their mother was staunchly conservative.

Lyrie was concerned, and though she knew that she would pay for it when it was time to get up for chores, she endeavored to stay awake. She wrote in her diary in order to stay occupied. An hour had passed when her thoughts were interrupted by a knock on the front door. The door opened quickly and Lyrie listened through her partially opened bedroom door. Her fears were quickly alleviated by the familiar sounds of voices she knew well. Timan's parents and several other old friends of the family had come to visit.

How strange, she thought, that so many friends had visited this evening. More voices. The Woodses and Josphers were there as well. Friends for as long a time as Lyrie could remember. Such an odd collection. She could scarcely understand how it was possible. Timan's parents, the Josphers, were more the upper-crust elitist sort, and the Woodses were just as far in the opposite direction. Rumor had it that Mr. Jospher was still wearing his first set of adult pants, simply patching and mending them over the years. It wasn't true, of course, but so legendary was his frugal nature that some still believed it.

Yet here they all sat. Try as she might Lyrie could not make out the words of their hushed voices. But though the content was hidden from her, the quality of the tones bespoke tension. Then came the knock she would remember until the day she died.

It's strange how a person becomes acclimated to the atmosphere of a house. The sound of the front doorknob turning, the creak of floorboards when someone walks on them, the smell of morning coffee and bacon and eggs on the weekend. It is almost a subconscious understanding. It was for this reason that Lyrie knew something very unfamiliar was happening, in the form of the stranger who now talked to her parents in hushed tones. She knew that her parents were good people, but she also sensed that something was wrong. The voices were rushed, scared even. She crept to the edge of the staircase and strained to hear better, though she could still only make out some of what was being said.

Several times she heard the terms "android" and " 'droid," which in her zone were more profane than the one for which she currently stood punishment. The whole zone actively discouraged the possession and use of all technology, yet here were the heads of families, pillars of her society, using profane words. But even they wouldn't readily use the word "android," the walking talking incarnation of evil against which Ravensford Zone was founded.

She angled closer to hear better.

"They landed here, I tell you, and they need our help, Klemm," said the stranger's voice.

"They can't be here," Lyrie's father said evenly. "The last time someone tried to run an android through Ravensford, they were caught within hours. The electrical signature is like a scream in church."

You tell them, Dad! Lyrie thought. *Now tell that lady that we don't abide technology and throw her out!*

"And with a lokaric conductor?" her father continued.

Lyrie's mind froze, uncomprehending.

"Where would they hide during daylight hours? Even Derring wouldn't attempt to run an android through this zone. I mean how the hell would they get out?"

STANNIS KLEMM LOOKED AT THE young woman. She was from another zone, but her credentials were impeccable. She had the sanction of the railroad, but her story was not to be believed. Unless—Suddenly he understood.

"Derring? Derring came out of retirement for this run?"

"I didn't say that," the young woman immediately replied.

"You don't have to, I can see it in your eyes. Holy…" He interrupted himself in mixed company. "If the Kwynians find out Derring is in the open, they'll have a free-for-all. If our government finds out she's with an android, they will stop at nothing to destroy the thing."

"I understand that," said the young woman, annoyed at being treated like a neophyte.

"No, young lady, you do not. Not entirely. An android in this zone will be destroyed, whatever the cost. And if you happen to be anywhere nearby when they do it, don't make plans for dinner that night."

"All the more reason to get this over with," she responded. She had the air of someone who did not like dealing with people who had lost the fire, but had no choice.

Mr. Woods broke the uncomfortable silence. "They know there is a run on, correct?"

"Yes," the stranger replied.

"A hunter's bounty has been posted?" Mrs. Woods asked.

"Two million," the young woman replied.

"Two million and they know it's a Lokaryn?" Mr. Jospher now chimed in.

"Yes, they portaled here and a soldier from Kwyne inadvertently came with them," the woman said. "He's being debriefed by the Seb-Ichi in an outer district monastery. He was severely injured and Derring apparently saved his life before escaping with the android. Highly unusual."

"Not unusual. You have to know Derring." Klemm paused a moment. The uncharacteristic act of mercy brought back his memories of Derring. He remembered why this had been a worthy endeavor, then. And was now.

"What I don't understand is why the hell she came out for a run. She knows she can never conduct again. She does know that, right?" Mr. Jospher asked.

Klemm pondered the situation while avoiding the obvious question that had not been posed to the group of once, and apparently future, railroad sympathizers.

Mr. Jospher was the first to speak. "I'm in."

Mrs. Jospher did not have a look of approval on her face, but said nothing.

Mrs. Woods was next. "We are, too." Her husband added.

LYRIE WAS FILLED WITH DREAD. She must be dreaming; this couldn't be true. Not her father. *No, Daddy,* her mind screamed.

"Don't get the idea that you have a new safe house, young lady. We are not back in. We're doing this for our own reasons." His voice fell silent, and then he said, "Where do we start looking?"

Lyrie's world had begun to end.

Beware Lokaryns bearing gifts.

—Unknown

CHAPTER 18

Kwyne
Prelate Goli's mansion

"UNFAIR!" THE GIRL SCREAMED AT the door as it slammed shut in her face. She pounded it with a clenched fist for emphasis.

"Unfair," she said more softly, this time to herself. Her fist hovered a few inches short of impact, and then slowly she opened it and rested her palm against the wood. Her forehead touched the cool oak, not in anger, but in defeat. Once again she had managed to get her parents' attention the only way she knew how, by making an enormous scene at an inopportune time. Tonight it had been a dinner party. Although it had worked, she still felt a profound sense of futility. Tomorrow would come and the whole cycle would start over again. There would be another gathering of some insignificant group of local bureaucrats, and once again she would be on display as the dutiful daughter. Whether she obeyed or defied her parents, she would end up in her room at the end of the night.

Kell watched from her covert perch as the girl turned slowly from the door. *So easy,* she thought as the young mark took a knapsack from under her bed and loaded it with fruit that she had secreted away in a fold of her dress. Most of the remaining space was occupied by a beloved teddy bear. The prelate's daughter changed into clothes more suitable for traveling and pulled her hair back into a ponytail.

The packing complete, the young woman sat on her bed with her back to the door and the knapsack at her feet. It was a ritual that she had practiced many times already. Maybe tonight she would find the nerve to follow through. She anxiously watched the open window for any sign of her nocturnal visitor. Kell knew the moment to be ripe. She silently slid away from the window and into the courtyard to finish her preparations, which were quickly and easily completed. Then she ascended back to the window with the confidence of a predator, stealthily moving closer while the prey remained blissfully unaware.

To Chenara, it was as if one moment there was nothing at the door and then Kell was there.

"Looks like you've had a rough night," the Lokaryn said.

"I can't do this anymore, Kell, I can't take another night of parading around like their trained pet. I can't do it. I won't do it…."

"Is it so bad? They feed you, give you a beautiful home in which to live, the best clothes, and send you to the best schools. Isn't that worth a little parading?" Kell was careful not to make the argument too forcefully, lest she actually convince the child.

"You sound like them!" Chenara whined. " 'We give you this, so we own you'! I'm my own person. They don't own me! Why are you taking their side?"

"I'm not taking sides, I'm merely asking a question," Kell countered. "Is it so bad?"

"The beautiful house is surrounded by a wall. I can't go anywhere. There are guards all over the place, who tell my parents everything I do. A few of them even make suggestions…about…stuff."

"Why not tell your father?" Kell asked.

"He never believes anything I say! I have to get out of here, Kell. I have to! Will you help me?"

"Of course, Chenara." Kell's manipulation was simple but effective. "Would you like to know what you should do first?"

The girl snatched up her knapsack breathlessly. "Where are we going, Kell? Merchants' Zone? Thieves'?" Her excitement at seeing the world was overpowering. In a matter of moments she would go from the confines of these four walls to having the whole world laid at her feet.

"We are going nowhere. I am going out this window and you are going to sleep. Think about this carefully before you do something you might regret."

"You said think about it a few nights ago and I did."

"Consequences, not freedom."

"Did *you* regret leaving home?" Chenara said, desperation creeping into her voice.

"No, I didn't," Kell answered. "Chenara, believe me when I say that you should stay here, do your homework, and if your parents want you to do a few tricks, indulge them."

The girl looked bitterly down toward the floor and said nothing.

"It's for the best," Kell said with a flip of her long blond hair. This time, however, she didn't simply vanish. Instead, she allowed herself to be seen moving out onto the terrace and over the railing. Chenara, sixteen years old and with the certainty that comes of inexperience, stood up, placed the knapsack over her shoulders, pulled a carefully crafted letter from her nightstand drawer, and laid it on her pillow. She followed the path that Kell had blazed for her out the window, onto the portico and down the trellising that adorned the house.

It was exhilarating for both women. For Chenara, it was her first steps into the world she had so longed to see. For Kell, it was the culmination of months of subtle work that brought her another step closer to obtaining the whereabouts of a man she would delight in killing: Arles Timmerson.

Chenara could still see Kell and moved quietly, but quickly, to keep up with her. The younger woman stopped and gasped when she saw the first inner-compound guard. Reality set in: The letter on the bed said such horrible things. If she was caught and had to face her parents after they had read it…

A puzzled look came over her face. The guard was not reacting to her presence. Her father's vaunted protection was sleeping! The compound wall still felt impossibly far away. She was hovering between running back to her room and pursing her freedom when a small sound caught her attention. She looked and saw Kell ascending the far wall of the courtyard, mapping her path. If only she had the courage to follow.

Chenara began to move again, avoiding the other guards, not knowing that they would never awaken again. Kell had seen to that.

Kell waited impatiently a short distance away for the young woman to reach the wall.

This is like waiting for a three-legged dog, she thought, standing with her arms crossed. *Wave bye-bye to Mommy and Daddy and get your ass over the wall.* After what seemed an interminable wait, Kell heard the sounds of the girl pulling herself up over the hurdle.

Good dog, Kell thought as she resumed the charade of being followed.

For several hours Kell allowed Chenara to follow her at a distance. As soon as Kell turned a corner, Chenara would sprint to get there and peek around to catch Kell's trail. She followed Kell to a rail station and watched her board the front car. The railway was mostly used to shuttle freight back and forth along a line that spanned the inner and outer districts, but it also carried passengers during the day. Few people traveled at night and even fewer traveled to the outer district at this hour. As civilized as Kwyne was, its outer districts were not for the timid. Chenara snuck aboard the train, hiding from Kell and the conductor. The latter slept during the ride, affording Chenara a free ride to the outer districts and enabling her to conserve the few caryns in her pocket.

Kell had proven fairly easy to follow, but when she hailed a carriage outside of the outer district rail station, Chenara began to panic—until she overheard Kell say to the driver that she wanted to go to the Apostle's Draught.

"You don't have to shout, ma'am," the driver said. "I'm not deaf." At a flick of the reins, the horse pulled the carriage forward. While Kwyne was a society capable of producing both internal-combustion and battery-driven engines, horse-drawn carriages required no fuel except grass for the horse and produced no pollution except for fertilizer—which also had a use. Engines were reserved for military, law-enforcement, and medical uses.

Chenara hopped in the next available carriage. "The Apostle's

Draught," she proclaimed. The carriage driver looked down at her.

"That's a rough place," he observed, doubtfully. "What business would you have at this hour of the night in any bar?" Chenara didn't answer. She simply sat back and clutched her knapsack to her chest.

The driver shrugged and snapped the reins. He had dealt with spoiled rich kids before. It took nearly twenty minutes to reach the Apostle's Draught, a run-down-looking bar complete with a sign that had not seen the touch of a paintbrush in a decade. Chenara audibly gasped at the sight of it as they came around the corner. Kell was already getting out of her carriage, and heading into the bar.

The second carriage pulled up just as the first left the front of the bar. The driver looked down to find that his fare had vanished. He sighed. Getting stiffed by fares was a part of the job, but he had just been stiffed by a child. In his younger years he would have hunted for the girl all night to get his due and had he gotten down, he would have discovered her clinging to the back just out of his line of sight. But age and experience counseled him that it was more profitable, and safer, to use the time seeking another fare. He snapped the reins and headed off into the darkness. Chenara stayed low to the ground in case the carriage driver looked back, but he didn't.

Once confident that he wasn't returning, she stood up and looked around. Every shadow, every nook appeared menacing. Her breathing was rapid and she could feel her heart beat in her ears, seemingly faster with each passing second.

Illumination from the lantern of a passing carriage revealed one nook that had only a few vermin picking over some trash, but nothing worse.

"Thecla be praised," she said without irony.

She spotted a broken broom handle lying near the trash heap and swept it across the ground to rid the recess of its occupants. She cleared the trash as best she could and settled back into the sweet safety of the shadows. From here she could see across the way to the bar entrance and somewhat down its side alley to the side door, but to be discovered herself would practically require someone to trip over her.

She breathed a sigh of relief and settled in to watch the bar. Once

Kell came out, she would make herself known. Kell couldn't say no then! Time passed, with each minute seemingly moving slower than the last. Hours became exercises in cruelty and with each one she became more acutely aware of her surroundings: The movement of rats. The smell of feces and urine. The dirt and the grime. She had always thought of Kwyne as a beautiful place, unlike no other. She mentally counted the stuffed animals in her room to distract herself, imagined morning breakfast, and more than once found herself not praying as she had been taught, but talking directly to Thecla. She received no response for her efforts.

She continued to watch the bar but was distracted on a regular basis as couples left and engaged in back alley behaviors that she and her friends used to speculate about. And lie about. It was mostly a woman and a man, sometimes two men! Her friends weaving their falsehoods, trying to impress one another, could never have invented the things she saw in those few hours. One always went back into the bar later emerging with another partner as if engaged in contest. She found herself naming them based on their attributes: Knees, Mr. Hands, Howler, the Flexible Girl. As the first rays of light forced their rays through the night sky, Howler held onto the lead that at one point had been in danger of being surpassed by the Flexible Girl.

Dawn finally broke through as a grey and rainy day emerged. Patrons still entered and left the bar, as a light rain seemed to wash away the sins of the night.

Still there was no sign of Kell.

Chenara's thoughts turned to the letter she had left for her parents. They would be finding it soon. Perhaps she had been too harsh. Perhaps she shouldn't have said some of the things that she did. But there was no way to undo it now.

Dawn passed, then half the morning, and still there was no sign of Kell. The midmorning bell that called the faithful to prayer rang dimly in the distance. People in this part of the zone used it more as a timepiece than a sacred reminder. Here, it sounded different to Chenara; dull and dirty. She never thought she'd miss *her* bell so much. She had eaten a small meal from the nearest street vendor so that she could keep an eye on the bar, but Kell never emerged.

Gathering her courage, she walked into the bar, only to find an assortment of frightening-looking people and one of the women with yet another man. She felt the eyes of several men on her as she walked the length of the bar. It reminded her of some of the guards, and it was a feeling that she didn't like at all. They openly stared at her chest until she covered it with her knapsack. Not seeing Kell, she approached the bartender.

"Have you seen a woman by the name of Kell?" she asked in a small voice.

The bartender looked her over for a moment.

"People come here for drink, for drugs, or for sex. We don't ask their names. If you're not looking for any of that, then get the hell out of here." He returned to what he was doing.

Chenara stood for a moment unsure of what to do next. Suddenly, a gnarled hand clamped down on her left breast. She let out a scream. Pulling away, she ran from the bar, chased by the laughter of many of its dwellers. Her assailant collapsed in an inebriated heap on the floor.

The young woman headed for the nearest refuge she could find, fleeing in a desperate game of hide-and-seek. She ducked into an alleyway. Checking to see if her assailant had followed her, she tripped and landed in some garbage. She picked herself up and looked at what she had fallen over: an addict. He still had the needle in his arm and his left hand was pawing at the air trying to touch some hallucinated pleasure. She had only heard about such things. Against the outside wall of the bar was one of the women that she had watched walking with different men. Her skirt was hiked up above her waist and a man was violently thrusting himself into her. Across from them was a man urinating on a wall.

Chenara turned and fled back down the alley, running as fast and as far as she could before exhausting herself. Hands on her knees, panting, tears streaming down her face, knowing that she had cut off any road home with that letter, she could only whisper:

"Kell, where are you? You're all I have."

Take.

—Thieves' Zone motto

CHAPTER 19

Thieves' Zone
Aboard the *Shicaine*

GEDRICK LIMPED ABOARD HIS SHIP with an unlikely duo, a ragged grizzled man in his fifties and an attractive young woman.

The first crewman to catch sight of the battle-damaged captain gasped.

"Would you like an aspirin or something, sir?" he asked, not knowing what else to say.

"Only if it's dissolved in a glass of scotch."

The older man was shown to his quarters, but the woman made her way to the bridge as if she owned the ship. Driven by her excitement, Seyschell worked her way through the complicated passageways well ahead of Gedrick. Once on the bridge she caused a stir when she burst through the entryway and made a direct line for the pilot's crib, seating herself at the copilot's station.

Chapman responded instantly. "Bosum," he said.

The Master at Arms had already unslung a plasma rifle and, in response to Chapman's order, painted Seyschell's head with a laser target. "Sir?" he asked, waiting for permission to fire.

"Ma'am, I would recommend that you stand up and accompany this man to the brig," the first officer instructed.

"The brig won't hold her, Nev, and Master at Arms, please don't shoot. Last time that happened it took a month to clean the piloting area," Gedrick said. "I'll explain everything shortly, Nev. For now make ready to sail shorthanded."

Chapman did not take his eyes off of the woman in the copilot's seat. For what reason he could not say. "Why shorthanded, sir? We have nearly full complement, with the exception of Engineering."

"Well, the chief can be hard on new recruits," Gedrick said.

"Old ones too, but to my original point, why would we be sailing shorthanded?" Chapman asked.

"I'm going to make a shipwide announcement that will likely lighten our complement."

"Short of making the chief our morale officer, I don't see that happening."

"I thought I told you this configuration was a bad idea," the woman in the copilot's seat called out while making adjustments to the controls.

"Does she know what she's doing?" Chapman asked.

"She should, she was once the copilot of this ship," the captain replied.

"I see. Does the lady have a name?"

"Seyschell," the mutant answered without looking back.

"I see. Interesting coincidence, that."

"The announcement will start with the fact that I'm revoking the open cash-out of shares on the ship," Gedrick said.

"I've sailed with you four years now and you've never held a crewman to his contracted time if he wanted to leave," Chapman observed.

"Never had to."

"Why would that change now?"

"That's the second part of the announcement."

"Which is?"

Gedrick's finger fell to the comm-link button.

"Attention to crew of the *Manumit*," he began.

"*Manumit*? What the hell is a *Manumit*?" Seyschell asked.

"Shut up," he said to Seyschell quietly.

"This is the captain speaking. Contrary to the terms of your contract, the *Manumit* has always operated on an open-cash-out basis. Shortly we will be leaving Thieves' Zone for…" He paused. "We will be departing for the Lokaryn Zone. While it will not be our final port of call, all those who wish to cash out their shares of the voyage may do so within the next hour. Anyone staying on will have obligated himself or herself to serve for the remainder of their contract. After those who wish to depart have left there will be additional instructions. One further announcement: Chief to the bridge."

The crew was stunned. They had never heard the chief summoned to the bridge, and the cash-out announcement was only slightly less astounding. The open-cash-out policy reflected the fact that it was so profitable to be on the ship that no one ever wanted to leave. The crew was good at their jobs and they were well rewarded. The announcement that the captain intended to go to the Lokaryn Zone, combined with the events of these past months, left the crew bewildered, with little more than fifty-nine minutes to decide their futures.

"The captain has gone mad," many said, though few left.

A brave minority watched as the chief engineer, a man not lightly *summoned* anywhere, stormed forward to the bridge, cursing as only a sailor can.

"So we're going to the damn Lokaryn Zone," he fumed as he burst through the door. "Big deal. What's so blasted important that you had to call me from my engine room?"

"Well?"

The copilot's chair swiveled for the first time in the chief's recent memory. No one sat in that chair now, not even him. Seyschell came into view and the chief's face turned from one of anger to one of elation. She knew that she would have to act quickly if she were to capitalize on the moment. She flew into his arms, knocking him back a couple of steps. He caught her with a resounding hug and spun her around, before he caught himself and quickly put her down.

"Well. Ahem. You. Look remarkably like a young woman I used to know whose only apparent talent was losing to me at Dranwyene."

"Sorry, James, nice try, I got a hug and one full spin out of you. I thought you might even cry. You won't be living that down anytime soon"

"James?" the first officer asked.

"Yeah, I have a first name. What'd you think? My mother named me 'Chief' at birth?

There was a brief pause while Chapman considered his answer.

"Yes," he replied. "I did."

Seyschell continued. "The cards? You still owe me a hundred caryns that I might be willing to let you try and win back tonight if you're not too busy with your girlfriends."

"The chief has girlfriends? Like multiple girlfriends?" Neville asked incredulously.

"First officer, and you don't know about the chief's ladies, Esmerelda, Berta, Yoli, and what was the fourth?" Seyschell said with a sly grin on her face. The chief scowled at her, or at least he tried to scowl at her, but his pleasure at seeing her again was not to be masked.

"Oh yeah, I remember now, Tessa the temperamental!" Seyschell enjoyed tormenting the chief.

"Tonight, your money will be mine, my sweet little mutant," the chief said, as he turned in a huff and left the bridge. As stormy as his exit seemed, his behavior on the way back to the engine room would later be described by those who saw him as positively giddy.

An hour passed and, as Chapman had predicted, the ship was lighter by very few souls. Gedrick ordered her away from her moorings, and once out to myst he again addressed the crew.

"To the crew of the…"

The crew well knew what ship they served on. The merchant vessel *Manumit*.

"*Shicaine*."

Shicaine. The name brought disbelief to the ears of the crew. The legendary wreck *Shicaine*. A myst-clipper, a Garand-Trass myst-clipper, and her crew lost. The legend had grown over the years. Some said they had gone over the falls of the Sluice much in the way that another merchant ship, the *Wiscott*, had. Still others held that they had fallen afoul of powerful people and the ship and her crew yet sailed through hidden from all. The legend had grown, but as with all good legends, no truths, only rumors were ever found.

"My fellow shipmates, you have served ably aboard the *Manumit*, but in truth this vessel's name is and has always been *Shicaine*. Many of you have heard legends about this ship. You are now part of that. The *Shicaine* lives now, resurrected by forces we do not yet understand. As the crew of the *Manumit* you served her proudly as she plied the merchant's trade. But now we angle for deeper fish. Those who still want to stay, welcome. To those who wish they had gone, I am sorry." He released the comm link, then called down to engine room. "Chief, how many do you have left?"

"Eight of eleven stayed and we were short before."

"We'll try to fill in as we can, Chief."

"I'm not worried," the chief replied. "You have a first-class talent for picking up strays."

Seyschell leaned over into the intercom. "True, Captain. You do have a talent for picking up strays. Now, tell me again: You originally found the chief in that dumpster with how many bullet holes in him?"

"Cards start at nine o'clock, you little..." Gedrick hit the comm-link button, severing the connection between the bridge and the engine room.

"OK, that went well. Neville, make ready for the Lokaryn Zone."

"Aye, sir, course laid in, engines report ready, neutralizer and shielding at full charge, sail crews standing by. All remaining crew report ready. Sir, you have full power and capabilities at your command."

"Thank you, Nev."

"Captain."

"Yes, Nev?"

"I would have stayed even if you had told me earlier."

Reborn, the *Shicaine* slipped her moorings and set out to an uncertain shore and an uncertain future.

Contrary to the popular belief of many zone dwellers, tequila is not a food group.

—Thieves' Zone government health bulletin

CHAPTER 20

Thieves' Zone
Terrapin Arc
Hennix's flat

HENNIX ATTEMPTED TO SHAKE OFF the haze of the morning after, or in this case, the days after. It was going to take a while. He wasn't sure how long it had been since he had last jacked in, and the crash afterward was severe. Tequila, though helpful at the time, was taking its toll. The processor implanted in his head signaled that it was done decoding his last job. *Right,* he thought, Gedrick's message. Through the blur of his wakening mind, he could barely remember jacking in. He decided that the message would have to wait. If he played it now, he wouldn't remember it anyway.

Tequila or food? Tequila or food? Tequila or food? his mind kept repeating. He hated infinite loops in the morning.

His dank flat was dark, and he did not yet know if it was night or day.

He searched his mind, trying to reorient and found himself very much relieved to have woken up. It was coming back to him now…searching the ways…the attack…and the desperate flight out. It had been close. Then, the pulsing music of Club Mutante, the tequila, and…Lucy.

Lucy had been right. The post-jack hiccups were a breathing spasm after all, and not a sign that his attackers had been successful in transmitting a virus to him. The rest of the evening was coming back now. He'd fallen asleep in the bar and Lucy had roused him after closing time in her own unique way. It had involved nudity, more tequila, a sturdy Dranwyene table, and vision helmets. The vision helmets were not a necessity, but their ability to target individual nerve clusters within the body certainly enhanced the experience. A skilled practitioner could damn near cause an endorphin overdose in their partner. It was one of the reasons that two net rogues rarely hooked up. His ability with this particular device was one of the reasons that Lucy was with him, but he didn't care. There was genuine affection there too, and even if there hadn't been, for the number of times that she had watched his back he would gladly have returned the favor in this way.

The last thing he remembered before passing out was uploading the data that he had retrieved into his vision helmet for processing. One could never be too careful with rogue code, but he held on to the routing information for further analysis. He accessed the data stream as he lay on his bed and was disappointed to find that the sender's identity was still cloaked. "Son of a bitch," he said. "Hajjat's Maneuver, again."

Hajjat's Maneuver was a routing protocol that sent different parts of a message through the ether at different times and through a large number of different routes. When the code was ultimately reassembled, the sequence of routing stations was impossibly jumbled, and the originating node, while still staring the receiver right in the face, was effectively rendered invisible.

"Why the hell is everybody using Hajjat's Maneuver," he said.

The realization made Hennix sit bolt upright in his bed. His senses heightened now, he was acutely attuned to his environment. The degree of light in the flat, the heaviness of the air, and…the stench.

It was not decaying food, or unwashed clothes, though either could easily be found in a net rogue's flat in ample quantity. It was more pungent. It was the smell of death.

He jumped out of bed and scanned the room. Nothing. He raced into the other room and the odor almost brought him to his knees. He could make out her form sitting in the chair, and he found himself praying to whoever was available that it wasn't her. The decay over-whelmed him, and he fell to his knees vomiting. "No, no." He heaved the words up from an emptied stomach.

She was still sitting in the chair, wearing a vision helmet: his. By the look of things, she had been there the entire three days that he was out. "What have you done, Luce?" he said with tears coming to his eyes. She had often wanted to experience the ether through the recordings of his travels, a practice he had always cautioned her against. She would often ignore those warnings while he was passed out. There was little he could do to stop her and for the most part there was never really a need, just his overabundance of caution with someone he loved too dearly.

This trip had been different, though, and he suspected that he would find something dangerous embedded in the information that he had brought back. He was drunk and exhausted when they had gotten to the apartment; he had warned as he usually did, but that was the problem. There was nothing different in the warning this time, and that had likely cost Lucy her life. Tearing through the junk around the room, he found a cable and plugged one end into a monitor. He approached her gently and plugged the other end into the still-running helmet. It caused her head to drop forward, and he caught it without thinking and placed it back into a comfortable position as the monitor flickered to life.

He turned to the screen and booted up the forensics program, which allowed him to view what she had seen without being neurologically exposed to the experience. He ran the recording back to its beginning, and there he saw imagery forming of thick myst as one might see from the bow of a clipper. "Oh crap," he said aloud.

Through this fog he saw the form of a chess board materialize as the virtual perspective flew over a checkered landscape. The forensics algorithm allowed the program to extrapolate the user's experience into an omniscient view, allowing him to watch the unfolding scene from multiple perspectives. Slowly the pieces materialized, the black side first, with the traditional pieces except for the queen, who was a dark-haired woman with green eyes. The king did not appear at all. The queen had an evil look about her and she grinned a devil's grin. The white team slowly began to appear, all in the form of people that he recognized. Crewmen from the *Shicaine* appeared as pawns followed by the rooks: Harlin Rahn and Tarro. The knights came into view one at a time: the king's knight, Cade, whom he knew as the *Shicaine*'s navigator, followed by queen's knight, the chief. Next came the king's bishop, Seyschell, and the queen's bishop, Hemingway. Finally Derring appeared in the form of the white queen, and Gedrick as king. The last piece that came into view was a grotesque and unflattering representation of Hennix, who held no traditional position on the board.

A thick fog rolled across the board, obscuring the black side as the pieces began to move at once. Suddenly, the black king emerged from the fog, though Hennix could not see him clearly. He moved swiftly across the board in what were neither traditional nor legal maneuvers. Mounted on a massive steed, he charged directly at Rahn and struck him with his lance. Rahn exploded into what seemed like a million fragments, which rained down on the board in a shower of spark and fire. The king's horse began galloping wildly in a sadistic victory lap. The pawns that were visible applauded grotesquely, and Hennix heard cackles of approving laughter from within the fog.

The king brought his horse into a canter, finally stopping in front of Hennix's position. It was now occupied by Lucy, who looked confused and frightened but was unable to move. The king dismounted and approached her position with sword drawn. He paused and stared at her as if conducting a scan, which in fact the program was. "You are not Hennix," he said, "but you will serve as my messenger." He bowed as if approaching her for a dance at the cotillion and bent her backward in a vicious kiss. He remounted his horse and brought it back a step or two as Lucy tried to wipe the memory of the kiss from her lips, spitting and cursing all the while. Suddenly, the stream of profanity stopped. Her eyes became distressed and her mouth opened just a fraction. And out it came. Small at first, but undeniable. A hiccup.

Hennix stared at Lucy's image in disbelief as more hiccups emerged from her mouth, each louder than the last. The violence of her breathing spasms shook the board, and the black king's horse reared triumphantly amid the chaos. More cackling from the fog. The pieces on the white side fought to keep their footing as Lucy's hiccupping increased in both frequency and volume. So did the panic on her face. Tears began to stream down her cheeks as she realized the inevitable. She tried again and again to call out the name of the only one who could save her, but the man was passed out in bed. She looked up at the black knight with pleading eyes, but to no avail. This was a program. Although the figure was real enough to the dying woman, in truth she was pleading for her life to a phantom vision constructed of malevolence and electrons.

Hennix watched helplessly as she began to turn blue, and fell to her knees, one hand on the floor and the other at her throat. When she fell the final inch to the floor, she gave up her life both in the electronic world and the real one.

The black king galloped away shouting, "You can't hide behind the skirts of some trollop forever, Hennix. Send as many as you like, I'll kill them all. I will find you. I will find the rest."

Hennix smashed the monitor with his fist. He should be the one lying dead in the chair three days decomposed, not Lucy.

The black king had missed his target. A poor marksman has his arrow returned, he recalled from a long-dead Thorpe's assassin. He would make arrangements for Lucy and he would send it back.

Of this I am certain: Every good conflict is sowed by power or greed. If done correctly, both.

—Serant Nan, fourth morgan of Merchants' Zone

CHAPTER 21

Lokaryn Zone
Zeninger Arc

THE *BLACKTHORNE* ENTERED THE COVE and slipped into the private docking area in the lower district of Zeninger Arc. Painted an almost gunmetal black, the grand clipper had sailed through the night mysts undetected. And though this had served it well in reaching its destination, upon arrival it found a port that was busy with activity. Unlike the other zones, which were composed of inner and outer districts, here the residents had opted for upper and lower. And for good reason. Little sunlight made it this far down. Such was the way of the Lokaryn Zone.

The first officer directed the crew in short staccato bursts, and to the man they reacted as though her words were lashes from the large bullwhip that she carried on her belt. They were well trained, well paid, and appropriately fearful of her. Their fear of First Officer Natrina Ma'Goran was surpassed only by their fear of their captain. And with good reason: It was his ship and, as such, his legal system. In a land where laws already varied greatly from zone to zone, out on the mysts the captain's whim was the law. The crew well remembered the last man who had failed the captain. The mistake was made by Dergen Hammel, an apprentice navigator who failed to pull the correct chart when requested by Captain Loh'l. For this crime he was myst-hauled: dragged under the ship while it was out on the myst, without the benefit of protective gear. What was left of the man when they pulled him back on board was mostly muscle attached to bone, which twitched or struggled depending on who you listened to. As was ship's law, the entire crew was required to watch.

The ship nestled alongside the dock and the crew quickly secured the lines. They knew that a rare shore leave would follow once they were done. The Lokaryn Zone was one of few places where the captain knew his crew could not slip away into the night. To the uninitiated, Lokaryns' could hardly be considered a good time. The initiated, however, knew differently. The Lokaryns were well aware that giving their visitors an unparalleled good time could only benefit business. So they littered the lower and upper districts with every sort of pleasure and depravity, either real or imagined. Tonight the crew would drink and whore and carouse at a bar called Bloody Pissed. Pissed was a strange place—part tavern, part cabaret, part brothel and amusement park. Best of all, the Lokaryns were smart enough to import their ale from Phobes' Zone.

As was his custom, Captain Loh'l did not leave his ship. Instead, he retreated to his ready room to await a visitor. He would receive a package that would, in turn, net him a small fortune and all it would cost him was a two-dranz flask of his own blood. Fresh blood.

He had no sooner removed the needle from his arm and capped the flask when there was a knock on the door. "Enter," he commanded as he placed the flask inside his jacket.

The door opened and a cloaked figure seemed to materialize in the room. He was impeccably dressed and looked to be about thirty-five. In truth he was many centuries old. T'Gareth had seen much in his day. He predated the Lokaryn Zone and the Cataclysm. He had witnessed the rise and fall of civilizations, surviving through his cunning and secrecy. During the ancient war between Kwyne and Borulsia, a culture long since gone, he had lived handsomely off the dying. A few he had converted, but most he simply consumed, absorbing their essence and growing more powerful with each one. The war had lasted over twenty years and it had been a glorious feast.

But for T'Gareth, things had changed. The Cataclysm had ensured that. Lokaryns now coexisted with mortals out in the open, and his culture no longer needed secrecy or valued the thrill of the hunt. They had their feeding chambers, and with them an endless source of nourishment. It even afforded them some small measure of power, which helped to sustain their culture. But without the hunt, the traditional Venery, something important was lost: the potency of the energy that was transferred when a life was fully consumed. That last moment held surpassing essence: the aura of the death struggle consumed.

Yet here his brethren sat, well fed and gaining only a fraction of the power they might otherwise. Their sworn enemies were still actively engaged in the hunt every night through the long centuries since the Cataclysm. The first war between the Apostatic Lokaryns and the Traditionalists had been a draw. The second would come while his people stayed safely inside: a sitting target growing fat and feeble with each passing day.

But that would soon change.

"Captain Loh'l," T'Gareth said. "Welcome. I did not expect to see you again so soon."

"Thank you, Clan Lord T'Gareth," Loh'l said, nodding to the Lokaryn. "The events in Kwyne were unexpected."

"But the possibility was not unanticipated," T'Gareth responded. "I believe that means you have something for me."

"I've never wagered my own blood before, but yes, I have your winnings. You may have them once my cargo is aboard."

"Your cargo is being loaded as we speak," the Lokaryn said. "Derring can be quite resourceful, so making these arrangements seemed prudent. I must warn you, though: Even in its subdued state, this Lokaryn is still extremely dangerous."

"Understood," Loh'l acknowledged. "Lord T'Gareth, are you sure he will feed when awoken?"

"By the time you get him to Kwyne he will be starved to the point that he will feed from any living creature that you put before him. Why do you care, Captain? You are paid to do your part."

"I have my reasons, sir," Loh'l answered in rare truthfulness.

"Would you care to list them, Captain?" T'Gareth asked, genuinely intrigued by Loh'l's last statement.

The voice of Natrina Ma'Goran interrupted the moment. "Captain, the cargo is on board," she announced through the comm link. Loh'l instantly produced a flask of his own blood from inside his jacket. T'Gareth felt the glass and inwardly smiled at its warmth.

"As we both have what we want, perhaps a toast is in order," Loh'l suggested. He walked over to the small recessed shelves in his cabin and poured himself a glass of red wine. He offered an empty glass to the clan lord, who accepted it with a gracious nod. Loh'l did not yet drink. Instead he gently swirled the contents around, watching the red rivulets trickle down the sides of the crystal.

The Lokaryn poured a small portion of the flask into the snifter. He inhaled deeply. "Excellent," he pronounced.

The pair raised their glasses. "To a profitable association," Loh'l said.

T'Gareth's eyebrow upswept slightly. "A man willing to drink a toast with his own blood," he said, touching his glass to the captain's. The Lokaryn drew a small amount into his mouth. Intoxicating.

"It's not my blood anymore," Loh'l said as he drew deeply from his own glass. The Lokaryn merely nodded as he finished his drink and placed the glass on the captain's desk.

"Good luck, Captain Loh'l. Let us hope you can make better use of this resource than the last."

"By the way," Loh'l said, "which clan?"

"Mal-Drevian," T'Gareth answered, and closed the door behind him.

A smile spread across Loh'l's face. Mal-Drevian: Perfection. Derring's clan.

Time steals from the fearful but barters with the brave.

—General Igor Chumley, founder, Chumley's Zone

CHAPTER 22

Phobes' Zone

THE MAN'S BODY HIT THE ground with a satisfying thud.

Derring breathed heavily several times, opening and closing her mouth to work the muscles. She swayed slightly with her eyes closed as she did. Three hours was a long time to spend latched on to someone's carotid artery.

"Wow! That was good!" she said to herself, holding her abdomen like a gourmand after a gluttonous revelry. "A four-striper, no doubt." She blinked several times and then belched loudly. Slowly, she came out of the bloodlust as she looked at the man lying lifeless at her feet. As always she imagined the person stirring, then rising and running off, none the worse for the encounter. But it never happened. The satiated feeling gave way, as it always did, to the feeling of remorse.

So often in prayer she turned her eyes upward to petition Thecla's grace. In this moment, however, her eyes remained downturned, her head bowed. She could not blame bad luck or circumstance. She had chosen to kill him so that she might live to find that grace. Her most profound instinct was to pray for his soul, but dawn was coming and she needed to find shelter. She would pray for him later.

She found shelter in the form of a water-runoff access tunnel. It was dank and claustrophobic, but it protected her from the sun. Even dissipated by the zone's shielding, the pure sunlight would still be more than enough to kill her.

Unable to sleep, Derring listened to the passersby as they went about their business in the small waterside town. She caught enough from their conversations to know that she could not spend another night in this runoff: rain was scheduled in this region tonight. The storm waters would flood the tunnel and she'd be forced to abandon it or be swept away to the purifiers. Another day to hunt would have been preferable, but havens such as this were rare this far in-zone. Moreover, she told herself, leaving Hemingway unattended for another night was unwise.

The day seemed interminable. It always did when she was forced to see the shadows she could never again cast. She saw the sunlight filtering though the grates only a few meters above. Her blessed sun, forever taken from her. Finally, it began to sink below the horizon, and she watched the walls of her prison as the shadows grew long and finally succumbed to the night.

As she made her way overland, she felt the first drops of rain. The storm intensified and engulfed her as she traveled back to Hemingway's interment site. Once there, she began to unearth the android as fast as she could. She clawed at the soil with a frantic need to see him well. Mud flew everywhere, splattering her. The rain fell fully now, making the earth muddier and more difficult to move. At last her hand struck the hard metal of Hemingway's endoskeleton, causing her to inhale sharply from the pain, and exhale with relief. She paused in her frantic exhumation and let her fingertips rest on the android's skin to confirm its existence. It took her less than three more minutes to remove him from the grave. Her frustration mounted as she worked to set up the electromagnetic signal dampening field in the shallow of the muddy grave, while the furious storm hindered her efforts every step of the way.

Once the dampening field was finally assembled, she attached a small tarp to its generating posts in order to provide them some protection from the rain. Still the rain made its way inside. Satisfied that she had done all she could for their situation, Derring knelt beside the android, sat him up and reactivated him.

Hemingway's eyes opened instantly and he stretched as if waking from a long sleep. He looked at his muddy clothing and said, "Son of a..."

"A trillion ops a second and you can only express yourself in profanities," Derring said in exasperation and relief.

Hemingway began to pluck the larger chunks of reddish soil from his clothing.

"A trillion ops in far less than a second and yes, when it's appropriate, I express myself in profanities. After two hundred and eighty-three years you still haven't learned not to interrupt when people speak."

"Wait a few minutes, the rain will wash it all off," Derring said.

The android looked at Derring with a mildly annoyed smirk, then cocked an eyebrow to fire off a remark.

"Why, thank you, Derring, I was going to head over to the nearest house and grab a shower, but your idea is better."

Derring ignored his comment. "I've been thinking about our next move," she said, as rivulets of rain and mud ran down her face.

"Only one move possible: the Klemms," Hemingway replied as he continued wiping away the soil. "Stannis is a good man. He'll be reliable."

"We can't do it, Hemingway. He got out of the railroad to protect his family. We can't drag him back in. I don't want to risk his life. It's not fair."

"Then you forfeit yours and mine as well. There's nowhere else to go."

The rain felt cold, and the distant rumbling foretold the height of the storm to come.

"It's not about fair, Derring. I didn't ask to be sentient, and you didn't ask for a lokaric life. We never sought to meet nor serve on the *Shicaine*. Yet all of those things came to pass. Klemm did what he thought was right then, and I know he'll do what he feels is right now."

The weather continued to intensify around them.

"Besides, he can always say no, Derring," Hemingway reminded her.

The Lokaryn looked at the android. To anyone more than three feet away from the pair, the two would be barely visible in the darkness and the rain. But with his cybernetic sight and her supernatural vision, the two glared at each other.

"He won't say no, Hemingway, you know that. If we go to the Winter Arc..." Her voice trailed off.

"And they're found out, they'll be killed along with everyone else that can be accused, guilty or not."

Although the rain was an event scheduled months ago by the farming bureau that controlled the weather, Derring felt as if each cold drop bore the sting of judgment. She could remember a time when some rains were warm and gentle, not like these artificially conjured ones.

"You realize the Klemms may already be dead," the android added. "Whoever is doing this knew how to get to you and me." He watched the sky—for what, Derring could not tell.

She looked at Hemingway. "So the fact that it's you and I who were targeted means that this is definitely about the Shicaine," she said. "If they took us out this easily, it stands to reason they will be able to get to the rest of the crew."

"If they haven't already," Hemingway added. "They may have targeted the more vulnerable members first, making sure that we couldn't gather enough of the crew to mount a defense. Not for nothing, though, Der, they haven't gotten us yet."

The storm continued to intensify, with the rain coming down more strongly now as the winds built, driving the cold drops to miniature lances. The lightning drew nearer.

"Come on now, you didn't come all this way just to die and leave me in the one zone where I can't do much to defend myself in the process, did you?"

"What if we're not the last?" she shot back. "What if we're the first? What if we're the thread they started pulling on to unravel the whole thing? What if they're using us to get to the others?" More slowly, she said, "They found you out somehow, and they used you to get to me. What if they use us to get to Klemm..." Her voice trailed off into the storm.

Lightning strikes began to join slowly with the report of the thunder. The body of the storm was tracking toward them, yet still distant. The rain pounded against the tarp and they had to shout to be heard above it.

Hemingway knew who was on Derring's mind. "The only way to protect *him*," he said, "is to get to *him*." The Lokaryn's head snapped up. "The first step in protecting the good captain is getting to Klemm." Derring nodded. "Der," Hemingway continued, "I don't think they're using us to get to the others. OK, they did use me to get you out of the zone, but I was supposed to be dead by the time you got there. And you were to be killed in Kwyne—specifically in Kwyne. You were meant to die in that room."

He paused a moment, straining to see or hear something in the storm, then continued to make his case. "Think about it! Why else would they route us through here? The escape route they provided was a brilliant backup plan. It brought us to the one place where electronics show up like a flare in the night and the purest sunlight to be had in any zone exists. They planned for us to die here if we didn't die there. They aren't using us to get to the others because they don't seem to need to."

Derring looked at the android, but Hemingway still looked to the sky. She kept kneeling beside him in the mud of the grave as he continued to gaze skyward as if willing the next bolt of electricity to fall upon him.

It very nearly did, electrifying the air around them. Derring's skin tingled, and the report of the thunder was like a cannon exploding an arm's length from their ears.

Without a word, Hemingway lifted himself from the mire of the mud and stepped out of the protective cocoon.

"Where are you going?" she shouted.

"They can't read me in this! The lightning blinds the sensor crystals. If we follow the storm to the Winter Arc, they can't track us." He began to pack up their things.

"This is insane!" Derring said.

"Derring, they will eventually get Klemm if we don't get to him first!" he shouted as he loaded gear into duffels. "They'll get to all of them, if they haven't already."

"You can't know that they aren't using us, that we're running right into their trap and taking the rest with us. What about that?" She began to pull him up from his work to face her.

He spun on her viciously, bringing his face to within a centimeter of hers, and in a controlled voice he said with utter conviction, "Then we die running toward something instead of away from it!"

He yanked his arm from Derring's grasp, and she stumbled backward a step or two before regaining her balance and straightening herself.

There, in that moment, she was as a newborn in the world: reincarnated with only the ghost of memories of how she used to be. She had been running until now. The activity of fear. No more. She looked at him, renewed, reborn. She had just been baptized into the now and the possibility of the future. She was resurrected from the slow death of the past she suffered. Not from her lokarynism, though that had cost her dearly, but from a greater deprivation by far.

He turned to leave, knowing that he would not be leaving her behind. As he did, he said in a barely perceptible voice, "It's time to take back what's ours."

Derring, with the exact same thought in mind, turned with him to face the true storm, and in between the flickers of a lightning strike they were gone as if the night had swallowed them whole.

Of greatest importance in the meal is the choice of the wine.
A good red with AB-positive blood type is the standard.

—X'goram, clan lord, D'Agosh Clan
A Lokaryns' Guide to Dining

CHAPTER 23

Kwyne
Center Arc

KELL FELT THE ANTICIPATION GROW within her. Although the kill would not provide her with sustenance, she would prosper from it all the same. Soon she would have the information she needed to kill Arles Timmerson, and all she had to do to get it was sacrifice an innocent girl to a starving Lokaryn.

If there was some dimension of her psyche or soul that rejected such a premise it was completely suborned by her desire to see Timmerson die, a desire that was encouraged by the voices who guided her.

Young Chenara, the prelate's daughter who had eaten at the finest tables in Kwyne, now foraged in the trash cans of the outer districts. The horrors she had suffered in so short a time ensured that she would never be young again. Kell had secretly watched her every night since she left home. More than once a would-be assailant met an untimely end with Chenara never being any the wiser. Kell watched her, studied her routes and patterns, and knew where to set her trap.

When Chenara saw Kell standing at an alleyway smiling at her, there was little in the way of a delay. Chenara raced toward the Lokaryn, just as Kell knew she would.

Kell slipped around the corner, but Chenara was determined to catch her. Around the corner and down the alley she raced, but once again Kell was gone. Chenara tore about the alleyway, uprooting boxes and trash cans, running into every recess, and scanning every high place. She finally screamed in frustration and began to kick the debris scattered around her, flailing in every direction, until her foot struck an object that responded with a nearly foot-breaking thud.

There at her feet lay a body.

She quickly looked around, knowing that the last place in the world she should be was in an alley with a dead body. She knew she should run, but she also had to survive. The body lay inert on its side; its left arm lay limply forward. This gave her easy access to his wallet. She quickly rummaged through the pockets, hoping to find money. Nothing. She rolled the body over. That's when she saw it.

Even in the dim light of the alley, she could see the dagger that protruded from the man's chest. The handle was encrusted with gems of every description. Her eyes widened. This would be her salvation. It would be worth a fortune. She was hungry, she was beaten and bruised, she was many things she wasn't before she had left home. Without a second thought she pulled the dagger from the man's chest and turned to look at the jewels in a better light.

Behind her J'Nath slowly awoke with a writhing hunger and a body that ached with every movement he made. He struggled to focus. Sounds and images blurred with the pain. He did not know when he had last fed. The bloodlust that welled up inside him provided the answer: far too long. Despite his best efforts, he could not subdue it. Predatory instinct consumed him as he sensed warm blood nearby. With a blur of motion, he seized Chenara and plunged his teeth into the soft flesh of her neck. Before she had even a moment to understand what was happening, he began to greedily draw her in.

As the girl's essence infused into him, he slowly became aware of his surroundings. He was in an alley, but where? How had he gotten here? T'Gareth had promised him the opportunity to feed from a four-stripe, something that his own clan would not allow. But things got muddy after that. Now he was here, wherever "here" was.

The alley was narrow and it stank. As he shook off the catatonia of being staked, he saw the young woman on whom he fed. He regretted taking a life, but he needed her essence if he was to sustain himself. He did not know when he would feed again.

Go peacefully, he thought. He was draining her fast. The intense hunger eased, but would not be remotely sated. He would need another, and soon. At least he could think more clearly.

It was at this moment that he sensed a group of warm-bloods. Like a feral animal defending a kill, he turned on them, fangs bared.

It made for a ferocious sight. The troops who had come for him had learned well the lesson of their Third Arc peers.

J'Nath recognized their uniforms: Kwyne. They opened fire.

The first shock hit him. Annoying, painful, but certainly not lethal.

J'Nath exploded into motion as the ensuing shots fell harmlessly around him. He was on the first of them in moments. He could have run, he could have misted away, but the bloodlust had him still and the confusion, anger, and fear of the troops only heightened it.

He tore into the first man's chest.

The man fell to his knees, his hands clutching the empty space. In moments, the blood drained away from his brain and he fell over lifeless.

"Where is he?" a squad member screamed as the troops frantically searched for a target. His answer came in the form of the heart that landed at his feet drained of its blood. Swinging his weapon up, he illuminated J'Nath, whose fangs still dripped with blood from the organ. They fired, but hit nothing as he materialized on a second soldier.

He weighed his options as he continued to kill. He was outnumbered. Eventually someone might get lucky. He then sensed a most reassuring presence. Another Lokaryn was here. Whether she had just arrived or he simply hadn't sensed her, he could not be sure. But he knew now that the battle was won. Many mortals might overcome a single Lokaryn, but two? Never. There would be a feast in this squalid place tonight to rival the best private feeding pens of the Lokaryn Zone.

His ally edged closer. Emboldened, J'Nath moved in on another mortal. Instead of a quick kill, though, he stopped, grabbed the man by the neck, and bit down, drawing him in for a moment.

It was one moment too long.

He felt the stake penetrate the skin of his chest as the other Lokaryn drove the wood perfectly through the gap in his ribs. A flood of confusion filled him, and then he recognized her.

"Sweet dreams, lover," Kell cooed as she drove the stake the last centimeter through his chest and into his heart.

Conversion to the Corpus of the Lokaryn varies.

The willing initiate will endure about seven days of agony as they shed their living shell.

The unwilling initiate takes far longer and suffers much more.

Enjoy.

—Lokaric *Book of Commonality*

CHAPTER 24

Lokaryn Zone
Outer Reef Lighthouse

THE *SHICAINE* CLOSED QUICKLY ON the Outer Reef Lighthouse, heading for the Lokaryn Zone. Lighthouses were deliberately different from one another, often reflecting local customs. These differences helped in their use as navigational aids. This particular lighthouse said welcome in much the same way a rotting carcass on a doorstep did. Despite its unpleasant appearance, its light pierced the night and the myst, offering an odd comfort in the predawn hour.

On the bridge of the *Shicaine*, First Officer Neville Chapman had the watch and the unpleasant duty that falls to many sailors: waking his captain.

"Captain, we're about forty-five minutes from the Lokaryn Zone. Would you care to give any briefing or instructions, or shall I simply wing it when I get there?"

Gedrick lay awake in his bunk, no more rested then when he had lain down two hours ago. He reached up and flipped the intercom. "Wing it."

"Very good, Captain," Chapman replied, and directed the duty mess cook to start a fresh pot of coffee. "The captain will be up in twelve minutes, so have the coffee strong. Make half a pot so he thinks it's been boiling down for a while." The first officer often marveled at his captain's fondness for coffee generally deemed undrinkable even by mutants.

Twelve minutes later Gedrick walked onto the bridge and headed for the coffee. Seeing the swill that remained, he smiled a knowing smile and poured a long cup.

He took a satisfying gulp, and turned to the bridge crew. "Any of you been to the Lokaryn Zone before?"

Only Seyschell raised her hand.

"We enter in the upper district, which is generally reserved for the humans who run the place."

"There are humans working in the Lokaryn Zone?" a newer crewmember asked. "Aren't they just food to the Lokaryns?"

"No," Gedrick answered, "the unlucky ones are, but mostly the humans work like they do in every other zone—as engineers, teachers, and so on. The Lokaryns tend to stay away from the upper district because it has a full day of sunlight. They know that humans do better when they can see the sun."

"Polite for the undead," Chapman remarked.

Gedrick remembered something Derring once told him, that of all the sacrifices necessary to live the life of power that was the lokaric way, losing the sun was the hardest. He continued.

"Still, while sunlit, the upper district is by no means inviting. There are very few entryways into the zone: a handful of closely regulated upper district teleporters and only two physical ports."

"Two ports?" a crewman asked. "How can any zone function with only two?"

"Few mystgoing captains have the stomach or nerve for trade with the Lokaryns. There are a few illegal ports, but again they aren't used all that much.

"After we pass the upper district wall, it will be a long while before we reach anything resembling civilization. The ship will be buoyed along this reach by vented myst and augmented antigrav. When we do get to the entryway into the main port there'll be a long bridge over a cavernous space. The far end of the bridge terminates in an entryway arch. From there the harbormaster will direct us. The rest, you really have to experience."

Gedrick took another long pull on his coffee and settled into the captain's chair. Seyschell had heard the whole narration, and took up a position at his side.

The passage into the Lokaryn Zone went exactly as Gedrick had described. But when they came to the arch, each crewmember stopped dead in his or her respective tracks and gazed upward with a certain awe.

"I love this part," Seyschell said quietly.

Everything about the archway oozed malevolence. If one strained to see the detail of its carvings, they could almost make out contorted heads frozen in the midst of agonized screaming.

The crew gaped silently, oblivious of everything else. It was at this moment that the beard of Second Lieutenant Rol Brend accidentally brushed the bare shoulder of Sail Mate Second Class Mezy Carinika. Carinka shrieked and spun without any consideration of coordination and landed sprawled at the feet of the equally startled lieutenant. The alarm was instantaneous and spread like myst fire. Fourteen men and women jumped, one man fainted, and one man ultimately went belowdecks to change his shorts.

Up on the bridge the captain couldn't help but look amused as most, but not all, of his bridge crew also gaped out the windows.

"And that's why seasoned Lokaryn Zone traders call that the Brown Bridge," noted Seyschell. "Gets the new guys every time."

"Clever," observed the first officer. "They try to psych you out before you even get through the front door so you'll trade less efficiently." Both Gedrick and Seyschell looked over at Neville. His skivvies remained unsoiled, and he looked like a man analyzing a puzzle.

Now past the archway, the ship headed toward her berthing. The first officer made short work of the close navigation and the clipper slowed as she eased into her slip.

Seyschell leaned over to Gedrick. "He's good. Can he..." She made a small gesture with her hand to indicate a ship moving across the myst.

Gedrick thought carefully. "I don't know" was the most complete answer he could offer.

The mooring lines were made fast as the ship settled to her temporary home. The crew breathed a short-lived sigh of relief. A few moments after she had made berthing, the entire docking facility began to stir. "Rumble" might have been a better word. Slowly the dock, and in fact the entire quay, began to settle lower and lower. The ship was not sinking. The entire dock area began to descend into the depths of the lower district.

The world above receded from view as gothic architecture seemed to crowd the immense well into which the ship slowly settled. From any angle the works were fierce, designed to emanate menace from every spire, bridge, and prominence. Every aspect looked as if it could skewer the unlucky passersby who strayed too close. Each was cast in deepening shades of darkness, illuminated only by the fears and psychoses of the observer.

Gedrick, while amused by the crew's reaction to the upper district entry, knew that he was taking a very serious chance with their futures. They were descending from their lives above into an unknown situation from which they might not ascend. His world had no certainties left; there was only the hope that he still had a few friends here.

"It may be a little late to be asking this," Seyschell said, "but how do we know that these guys aren't in on things?"

"We don't," Gedrick responded. "I'm betting on two things. One, Lokaryn clans rarely have common goals, and two, we have no place else to go."

Seyschell reached over to straighten his collar. "You'll see her, you know."

Gedrick took Seyschell's hands away from what she was doing. Holding them in his own, he looked at her with both kindness and sadness in his eyes. "No. I won't."

"Maybe so, but if the *Shicaine* is in Lokaryns', she'll see you."

Seyschell slowly removed her hands from his and resumed the task of straightening his collar.

"She has a very strong opinion about this: it reflects poorly on the finest ship on the mysts if her captain can't make himself presentable."

It seemed absurd to Gedrick to be primping while descending into a darkness populated by an overpowering number of beings who looked on humans as an entrée. Yet in this place and at this time, it felt right.

The first officer walked up beside the pair.

"Mutants for valets. What will they think of next?" he said.

"Humans as anchors?" Seyschell replied.

Chapman had to make an effort not to smile at her comeback. All evidence to the contrary, she did not feel like his rival.

"Yes, quite. Well, Captain, we're descending to a lower district dock facility of the Mal-Drevian Clan. One of the clan administrators is meeting you at the dock."

Seyschell finished her task and brushed some lint from Gedrick's lapel as she walked away. "Maybe they're having us for dinner," she said.

"Very well then," the first officer replied. "I shall dress according to protocol and as always, ladies first." It was Seyschell's turn to suppress a smirk. "OK, you two, enough. Any word on who's coming to meet us?" Gedrick asked. He realized he was feeling self-conscious at the prospect that *she* might be watching.

"Well, sir, that's the next thing that's a bit odd. Near as I can tell this…gentleman is a member of the clan lord's staff. He's not ambassadorial, nor involved with trade. He's a personal aide from what I can figure out. His name is…Solipher?"

"Sol?" Gedrick said.

"You know him?" Neville asked, surprised.

"Know him? He owes me one hundred caryns. He's terrible at Dranwyene, but can't admit it to himself."

"Perhaps you can get it from him and pay me the hundred and fifty you owe me," Seyschell said. The first officer shot them both a doubtful look, but said nothing.

With a loud thud, the whole platform abruptly stopped.

"Assemble some crew to man the side and render honors, Nev,"

Gedrick instructed his first officer.

The first officer had anticipated him. No sooner had he spoken the captain's order into the comm link than two dozen crew piled out onto the deck in dress uniforms.

Gedrick nodded toward his first officer in acknowledgment.

Long moments passed until a door finally opened. A smallish man walked out to the dock's edge and up the gangplank that extended from the ship. Stopping at the end, he looked over at Gedrick.

"Permission to come aboard, Captain?"

The Lokaryn waited at the end of the gangway for permission. "How extraordinary," the first officer remarked.

"Not really, once you get to know them," Gedrick replied. "Come aboard, Solipher. Come aboard and be welcome."

The Lokaryn came up the gangplank holding his hand out in welcome to the captain of the *Shicaine*. Chapman watched in amazement at the genuine camaraderie between the two. Solipher held Gedrick's hand in the handshake and then held his second over it in a gesture of warmth. The Lokaryn smiled at Gedrick. Contrary to what the first officer had heard about Lokaryns, it was not an icy smile.

"Welcome, Gedrick. You've made quite a stir with your visit. I'm surprised you'd risk it," the Lokaryn began.

"Well, you know us, we hate to make a stir," Gedrick answered diplomatically, not entirely understanding Solipher's comment.

"We'll have you outfitted in time to sail with the outgoing myst tomorrow morning."

"Thanks, but we'd actually like to stay for a while. We will, of course, pay dockage and all the fees."

The Lokaryn did not wait for Gedrick to finish his statement. "That won't be possible, I'm afraid. Your visit is well timed. We have a contract for you"

"Thanks, Solipher, but we really need to…"

The Lokaryn continued as if Gedrick hadn't spoken. "We need you to retrieve two Lokaryns for us."

"Well, thanks for thinking of us, but that won't be possible," Gedrick replied.

"More precisely, two Lokaryns and an android." Solipher put a slight emphasis on the last word with full knowledge that Gedrick and the *Shicaine* were known as liberators of sentient androids.

There was a silence that few of the crew understood.

"Solipher, you know that I...that...we no longer involve ourselves in that world. We need safe harbor and will pay well. Your clan lord will grant us haven."

"We have a contract for you that will make you rich beyond measure."

"Money is no good if I'm lying dead in the Badlands. Please contact your clan lord with our request."

Solipher's clan lord, Derring, had once been a part of the *Shicaine* crew. In spite of their history, Gedrick knew that she would be sympathetic to their cause.

"Gedrick, I need you to take this contract. On your return I guarantee you asylum."

"No. Tell your clan lord that the crew of the *Shicaine* requests asylum now. I can contact her myself, you know."

"No, you can't. I assure you of two things. The first is that you will hear my offer before you leave. The second is that you will take the contract."

There were times to argue, and times to listen. Gedrick sighed and nodded.

"The contract requires discretion, if not outright stealth. You'll have to cross to Phobes' Zone."

"Ravensford? Not a problem."

"Without stopping at any port between."

"On a straight run, assuming the winds are favorable, it takes weeks to get there. The *Shicaine* can't carry enough neutralizer to stay out on the myst that long. You should know that, Sol."

"We'll install dynamic neutralizers on your ship."

"Then problem becomes space and power. Even if the *Shicaine* had enough space for a dynamic neutralizer, which she doesn't, we'd run out of shipboard power in less than two days just trying to keep the ship afloat, let alone run the neutralizers."

"We've modified the neutralizer machinery; the technology has been worked on by our engineers. It won't add to your displacement by more than a metric ton."

"So then we run out of power running the thing."

"We will also provide energy cells based on a molecular-decomposition power source. The cells each generate ten megawatts per cubic meter and the array we've created for the *Shicaine* has forty units. It can be recharged with a thousand liters of ordinary myst if you ever manage to actually run down one of the arrays."

"You mean ten kilowatts," Gedrick corrected in disbelief.

"Megawatts, ten megawatts per cubic meter. The technology is yours to keep, but of course if you ever try to sell it or duplicate it for distribution, our agents will find you and return it and you to this zone."

An awkward pause ensued. Solipher was the first to break the silence.

"Well?"

"Well what? A neutralizer I don't need, and a power source I don't need unless I'm using the neutralizer that I don't need. And for these wondrous items I have to go stick my neck out when half the world seems to be trying to cut my head off. More than likely your technology will end up in the hands of whoever finally puts a broadside shot into us and takes the *Shicaine* as salvage. Now, did you have anything else to go with that terrific deal, like maybe body bags and a funeral barge?"

"Well, yes. One other thing."

"Solipher, honest to Thecla! Don't you get it? I'm not going and nothing you can say is going to change my mind."

"We'll fill the *Shicaine*'s holds to the brim with gems, precious metals, whatever you select."

"Excuse me?"

"You heard right. You bring the team in, or at least one key member, and we'll fill all of the holds of the *Shicaine* with as much as she can carry. You can keep the power cells and the neutralizer as well."

"Ah, damn," Gedrick said.

"It *is* a lot of money," Seyschell noted.

"No, Shell, not the money."

"What?" Seyschell asked.

"The Lokaryn they want retrieved. It's Derring. That's why Solipher is here instead of Derring."

Seyschell's eyes went wide open. "Then the android is Hemingway."

"Derring left the zone to retrieve him," the Lokaryn said.

"Someone's been targeting the *Shicaine* crew. It would make sense that they went after Derring and Hemingway."

"As I said," the Lokaryn interjected, "you will accept my deal." The Lokaryn stood with his hands clasped in front of him. He would never convey it, but he was desperate.

"How could you let her leave the zone, Solipher?"

"Well, Gedrick, she's a clan lord, it's not like we can ground her. I'm sorry, but if there were anyone else we thought could do the job, we wouldn't ask. We understand the risk this represents to you. However, we know that you are uniquely qualified to find the *lho-don*, and bring her back."

Chapman looked puzzled. "It means 'clan lord,' " Seyschell said.

"You know her, Gedrick," Solipher continued. "You know the railroad, and your reputation for extracting androids and people from difficult situations precedes you."

He leaned in as if to whisper, but Gedrick was not fool enough to expose his neck to a Lokaryn. Solipher understood and simply continued in a voice that only he and Gedrick could hear.

"We need her back, Gedrick. Without her voice in the council the clans are eyeing each other to take the power she's left behind. They'll destroy it all before they'll stop. I don't know how much longer we can control things."

The Lokaryn looked at Gedrick. He was asking the *Shicaine*'s captain to venture from haven out into a world where powerful and unknown enemies were trying to kill him.

The crew only imagined the riches that awaited each of them if the captain accepted. Each held a share of the ship's take as their salary for serving. Even the lowliest hand would be wealthy if the captain accepted. Seyschell watched her friend as he took in the situation. Meanwhile, Grizwald watched the dock, noting the number of Lokaryns that lurked in the shadows, while Chapman scanned the facility for any advantage, should the ship need to defend itself.

"Captain, time is short. Do we have a deal?"

Gedrick did not answer at first, and for all involved the world seemed to stop. He thought about the few options he had. They wouldn't let him stay. His last haven came with strings attached.

"Play the game," came the words of his old mentor, the captain of another myst-clipper, the *Impulse.* "Play the game on their terms and never let them see that they were playing your game all along."

Gedrick wanted to get the last known location of Derring and take off as fast as he could to get there, no matter the outcome. But he wasn't in this alone. He had brought his crew down into a Lokaryns' lair and was about to lead them into worse. They were loyal, but if they were to follow him, he'd better have something incredible to motivate them. Solipher seemed willing to provide that.

"Play the game on their terms," he whispered to himself as Seyschell looked over at him.

"Two cargo loads full of gems and seventy cubic meters of the energy cells," Gedrick said to Solipher.

"One and one-half loads and fifty cubic meters."

"One and one-half, seventy cubic meters, and twelve cases of two-hundred-year-old scotch."

Solipher winced a little at the last, knowing he'd have to part with it if he wanted to clinch the deal.

"Five cases per successful retrieval and another five if you do it before the equinox."

"Ever tasted two-hundred-year-old scotch, Griz?" Gedrick asked the immense bartender, who stood on the deck not too far from him.

"No, I avoid it. The only man I ever knew who tried it needed three years of electroshock therapy to break his craving after one glass."

Gedrick paused and looked at his crew. He couldn't expect life-or-death loyalty from his crew to rescue someone they never had met. But the promise of a spectacular payday was another matter.

"We accept."

A cheer went up from the crew. They were already figuring out how to spend their riches.

Gedrick recalled his mentor's advice on the subject of closing a deal: "And don't gloat when you walk away with their money and wives." He wasn't sure, however, if it applied to himself or Solipher.

No matter how draconian the results of using a technology, no matter how devastating it might be, no matter how graphically you describe the results, and tell them that there is no way to shield themselves from the results, that the device will harm or kill both user and target, there is always someone saying, "Great. Where's the On switch?"

—Unknown

CHAPTER 25

On the mysts
Thirty-five kilometers northwest of Thorpe's Zone

IT HAD BEEN A BEAUTIFUL funeral.

No expense had been spared in Lucy's service. Those who attended were told that her lover, killed in the same accident that had taken Lucy's life, had provided in his will for Lucy to be consigned to the myst in her home zone of Thorpe's Corporation in a manner befitting a CEO. Her family was solidly middle management; they could have never afforded such a funeral, but such was little solace.

The funeral barge departed Thorpe's Zone, slowly making its way out to the burial-ground markers. There was time for the mourners to mingle and recall their memories of the young woman who had died. For every fond memory of her life there was an equally vitriolic comment about the man they blamed for her death.

Hennix heard every word as he circulated among them. He attended disguised as an older gentleman who had known Lucy from one of the many establishments in which she had worked. His disguise was necessary to maintain the illusion that he had died in Thieves' Zone along with Lucy.

They reached the burial site after several hours and a thousand verbal cuts. The crowd fell silent as they stepped outside. Hennix stood there on the deck as the assembled bowed their heads for a final prayer. Her body was brought to the side of the ship on stretcher carried by four childhood friends, now grown. She wore a simple dress with a wreath of flowers in her hair. He had never seen Lucy wear such things, but her parents thought it appropriate. After a brief prayer, the burial shroud was zipped shut. He could not look as her body slid down the stretcher, but he could not shut his ears as easily. He heard the last of the sliding noise as she disappeared over the port side of the ship and into the myst. The ship quickly banked to starboard as it turned for home.

The assembled mourners returned to the safety of the cabin, but Hennix remained outdoors. Many harsh words had reached his ears, and he could not deny any of them. She was dead because of him. He had not caused her death, but he was responsible. He was not sure if he remained on deck to be with Lucy as long as he could, or to avoid the words that waited for him inside.

He stared into the myst. It looked so beautiful, with its traces of ionic activity, small tendrils of bluish white light, occasionally a red-orange, arcing out away from disturbances in the flow. So much of his life was spent in a synthetic world, with colors painted by imagination, that he often forgot that the real world had beauty too.

A voice shook him from his reverie.

"Sir, would you care to join the others before you're missed?"

Hennix suppressed a single laugh as he looked at the crewman. "I'll not be missed."

The crewman stepped back, not knowing what to say in response to the strange comment. The trip back to Thorpe's Zone would be long, and Hennix stayed on the deck, lost in thought. Much as he hated to, he needed to push Lucy's death to the back of his mind and look toward his task ahead.

He needed to find a ghost ship. It would be hard enough to do if he could ramp into the ether, but he couldn't risk doing so. The moment he entered the electronic world, he would be seen perfectly by those who hunted him. He had an additional problem: The ether worked on his willpower, calling him back. Like a junkie needing a fix, he wanted to jack in, he needed to jack in—but he couldn't. If he did, the elaborate ruse of his death would be wasted and his life forfeit.

More than an hour passed before the young crewman approached him again. To Hennix it had seemed like only a few minutes.

"Sir," the crewman began, somewhat hesitantly. "We have forecast reports that we will soon be leaving the area of sweet air, and have to secure the deck."

Hennix didn't turn from the railing. He remained leaning on his elbows propped up on the railing of the ship. The wind blew through his hair. He hadn't been out of a zone in nearly five years, and had forgotten what the mysts were like.

Without moving very much, a minute passed as the young steward stood not knowing what to do. Finally the man asked, "Sir, do you need some help in getting back to where you should be?"

Hennix flashed him a grim smile. "Perhaps I should have never left in the first place," he said.

"Well, you had to come out for the burial, and of course the sweet air is always nice if you enjoy that sort of thing," the crewman said, trying to be polite.

"Do you know where sweet air comes from, boy?" Hennix said, his tone reflecting his disguise as an older man. He was, in fact, far older than he ever imagined he would be, given his profession. Most net rogues died by twenty-five, a mark he had passed five years ago. By those standards, Hennix was ancient.

"No, sir" was the hesitant reply.

"You're sailing on it, don't you think you should know something about it? Myst is a complex mix of gases and liquids, and each of those parts can layer out according to its density. Like a thermocline in large bodies of water."

Word for word, he recited the lecture just as it had come from the chief engineer during the orientation lectures aboard the *Shicaine* nine years ago.

"When the gas part layers out above the liquid part, the lighter portions of the gas lie on top and the poisons settle, leaving air you can breathe without filt—"

Hennix stopped. The young man was supposed to clear the deck and now, having failed to accomplish this simple task, was being lectured about myst physics by a crazed old man. Hennix smiled and put his hand on the boy's shoulder.

"Don't worry about it, kid, I didn't understand it the first time I heard it either. I'll head inside in a minute. I won't get you in trouble with your superiors."

Once inside, Hennix stood away from the crowd. He'd heard enough on the trip out to last him several lifetimes. He was on his way back to a safe ground. No one knew he was alive. It was time for a drink. He waited for the bar to clear out a bit, then walked up to the android bartender.

"The longest tequila you've ever poured, and make it a double."

The android bent to take a bottle from under the bar. Hennix noted it was his favored brand, rare and expensive. When he had set up the funeral arrangements, he had given no instructions about the kinds of liquor to be provided at the bar. This was trouble.

The android placed the first drink on the bar.

"Hello, Hennix. We have some mutual acquaintances, most of whom want you dead." The android looked at him evenly.

Hennix thought for a brief moment about what the android had said then tilted his head back and drank the liquor. With his eyes closed, he gently placed the glass back on the bar, then held his breath for a moment, not even wanting to expel the vapors of the liquor. Finally, he let out a satisfied sigh. The android eyed him with annoyance.

"You have a drinking problem, you know that?" the android said.

"Well, let's see. A total stranger knows me by name after I've made every effort not to be recognized. The stranger hands me my favorite drink and then tells me that a bunch of people want me dead. This all happens at the funeral of my lover, who is dead because the people who want my head on a platter happen to be lousy assassins. And your primary concern is about my liver? You have a problem with perspective, friend."

The android's expression turned to one of puzzlement as Hennix held out his empty glass for a refill. "How did you know the drink wasn't poisoned?"

"Why would you say anything before I drank it if that's how you meant to kill me?"

"You net rogues are a pain in the ass, do you know that? I've been tracking you for weeks and you show up in the one place I was hoping you wouldn't. You haven't jacked into the ether for weeks, so no one can contact you that way. I've been to something like forty-five residences where you supposedly live and that stinking dive bar you love so much."

Hennix looked around the room. "Mind keeping your voice down? People are starting to take notice. You got a name?" He tapped the shot glass, indicating a refill. The android looked at him in disbelief and handed him the bottle.

"My name is Bowman," he said.

Hennix poured another drink and held it up in a fast toast. "To Bowman." The drink disappeared as fast as the first ones had. He started to pour another.

"I am going to kill you myself, if you don't stop that," the android said with exasperation.

Hennix shrugged. "Then no more toasts to you."

"Before you completely down the bottle, let me ask you: Have you bothered to look at the information you stole the last time you were in the ether?"

"No. Whatever it is, it's got a lethal program embedded in it. It killed Lucy." He stopped for a moment at the thought and poured another shot.

"Stop drinking and listen to me." The android leaned in. "You're not getting off this barge alive."

"So far, you're not making a good case for temperance," Hennix said, but did not pick up the shot glass.

"We think that the files you carry in your pea brain may hold information that could start, or prevent, a war in the zones. The people who are hunting you can't afford to have that information in the open."

"So they didn't buy the story? They think I'm still alive?"

"It was a good cover, but they aren't taking chances. They've sent a couple of teams to make sure you're actually dead. They incinerated the bar and everyone who happened to be in it at the time, and they intend to destroy this barge in the deep myst at marker thirty-nine. As long as the barge is destroyed they'll feel they've covered all the bases and probably figure that they got you. They'll continue to monitor the ether, of course, but they'll call off the dogs out here in the real world."

"So all I have to do to get them to stop is die out here with all of Lucy's family and closest friends?"

"Or we can both get the hell off in a life raft."

"There's a good plan. We hop off and I get to be responsible for not only Lucy's death, but that of everyone important to her."

"Listen to me. If this war begins, they're all going to die along with everyone else you and I care about. There are things going on that you have no concept of!"

"No. No one else dies because of me." Hennix ran a fingertip around the rim of the shot glass. "If you knew I might be here, and you know where they're going to destroy the ship, then you must know how. Bomb?"

"The vent system will cycle to intake when we're in deep myst. The lines should last about three minutes before they rupture, spreading myst throughout the engine room. The fuel lines will corrode and break; then one spark from a corroded electrical line and poof, the whole thing goes up and we go down."

"So we hack the program that controls vent cycling and take out the code." Hennix rubbed his hands together. "It will be easy."

"Not easy. It's pop-up code: it assembles itself from normal running code so it doesn't exist until the last line of normal code is run. Then it executes. If you destroyed the normal code, you'd still have a serious malfunction of the venting system. Same effect. If you can get to it, and if this ship survives, they'll know something is up and they'll really start coming for you. The bar and this barge are the work of a mop-up team.

Their prime team would make this look like a holiday in the Thieves' Zone Luxe Arc."

"So I can either abandon everyone to die on the ship, never jack into the ether again, and hope they stop looking for me while I let you guys dissect my head for this information that if I access might cause me to end up dead anyway, or stop the ship from sinking, in which case they'll send a squad of psychopaths after everyone and everything that might remotely be connected with me and I'll still have this crap in my head and still not be able to jack in."

He paused to take a breath.

"Plus, I might be responsible for starting or failing to stop a war. That about right?"

"That's pretty much it."

"My old captain used to say if you haven't found the third option, you just aren't trying hard enough. How about this? We hack the code, then cast off as many lifeboats as we can spare packed with whatever will blow up or burn hot. We ignite it at the myst marker on schedule, then take the ship to a safe haven."

Bowman looked at Hennix. "How long has it been since your last drink?"

"Trust me, it'll work."

"You're forgetting a few things. First, we're only three hours from the marker. Second, hacking the code isn't as easy as that, let alone doing it in three hours. Third, these people signed on for a funeral, not a hijacking. The captain just might not want to cooperate." The android finished by motioning toward the captain, who had come down to check on his passengers.

Hennix downed the shot in front of him and took on a look that the android would have sworn was an internal diagnostic scan if he hadn't known that the net rogue was mostly organic. Shaking his head briefly in the negative, Hennix reached for the bottle. He then took a long draw directly from the bottle. No small number of passengers turned his way. Murmurs from the crowd started to swell, and three portly old women who had been watching him with disapproving scowls on their faces finally broke from the crowd and made their way over to him. Hennix was at the three-quarters mark on the bottle when they got to him.

"Really!" the first one started in. "Drinking from the bottle! Lucy would not approve one bit...."

"The old biddies squad!" Hennix interrupted. "Lucy told me about your meddling and interfering in everything anyone ever did because you had no lives of your own!"

Shocked, the three ladies turned on their heels and scurried away underneath a cloud of "I nevers!"

"Did I really just say that?" Hennix asked Bowman after a moment's enjoyment watching their retreat.

"Yes, you did." The android felt the marker getting closer. "Now that we've had our fun, can we go?"

"Nope, if I'm insulting guests at a funeral, then I'm loose enough for what we have to do next."

He finished the bottle, wiped his mouth with the back of his hand, and set off in the direction of the captain.

"Holy mother of Thecla," the android murmured under his breath.

The last laugh favors the patient man.

—General Igor Chumley, founder, Chumley's Zone

CHAPTER 26

TARRO WOKE TO FRESH LINENS and the bright light of a well-lit room. His body ached as it never had before. The pillow that lay under his head was positively decadent. Next to his bed was a tray of freshly cooked eggs, sausage, and rolls. He knew at once that he was in far greater danger than when he hung from the pipes of the boiler room.

He tried to lift himself up on one elbow to survey the cabin, but the pain overtook him.

"Damn" was all that he managed to say before he fell back onto the bed. It was then that he noted the figure of First Officer Natrina Ma'Goran seated in a chair next to him.

"Good morning, Jayesh," she said with a small smile. "I trust that these accommodations are a little more to your liking?"

"Why?" Tarro asked.

"Captain's orders. I advocated for cooking you a little longer, but he simply wouldn't listen." A pout formed on her face. "Still, if you'd prefer the boiler room, it would be my pleasure to arrange it."

Tarro looked into her eyes and saw the spark of sadism ignite at the thought of returning him to the steamy hell.

"This will do," he said.

The smell of the fresh-cooked breakfast wafted over to him, and his stomach grumbled audibly.

"Hungry, Jayesh?" Ma'Goran asked. She leaned in close to his face and plucked a sausage from the plate. "You really must try one of these," she said, and slid it into her mouth almost seductively. She bit down hard on it and placed the remaining half to his lips. His training had taught him to reject such overtures but his instinct took over and he found himself accepting it.

"Mmmmm," she purred. "There's lots more, you know."

"What do you want from me?" Tarro asked.

"Just one piece of information. Why are you here?" Ma'Goran touched another sausage to his lips. He went to bite, but she pulled it just out of his reach. "Uh-uh-uh," she said. "You didn't answer my question. Why are you here?"

"You kidnapped me, if you recall," Tarro said.

The first officer looked at him without expression. "On the surface, that would appear be true, but let's just say that I'm a skeptic."

Tarro gave her the most incredulous look that his condition allowed him to muster. "Why would I purposefully allow myself to be taken aboard this ship? Its reputation is well known."

"Ah, that's the sticking point, isn't it?" Ma'Goran said. "You seem to be more intelligent than the typical recruit. Smart enough that you shouldn't be in this situation. You see, someone has been sending coded transmissions from this ship. Someone smart. Smart enough to evade identification."

Tarro attempted to look desperate. "You recruited almost fifteen others when you took me."

"True, but only three survive," she said. "Several even confessed to making the transmissions, but when we tested them, they couldn't even operate the equipment. So the question remains, which of the three is it?" She popped the sausage into her mouth. "These really are delicious." Tarro's stomach rumbled again.

"I need to know why you came aboard this ship and what your intentions are."

"I came aboard because I was forced to. My intentions are whatever you want them to be."

"I'm going to make you an offer. Tell me the content of the transmissions and whom you sent them to. If you do so, I will dispatch you quickly. One blaster shot to the back of your head. You'll feel nothing." She smiled at him, the picture of benevolence.

"And if I can't give you this information?"

"Then I will introduce you to someone who I guarantee will not be so quick. When she is done there will be little left of you. But what remains I will lash high on the mast. And then—" She paused for effect. "—we will go myst riding. It's an exhilarating experience when you enjoy the protection of the shielding. Unfortunately...you won't enjoy such amenities. Have you ever seen what myst burns to do a body?"

Tarro shook his head no.

"So do you have anything you want to say to me?" Ma'Goran asked.

"I have nothing to tell you."

"Pity. Especially if you are telling me the truth." She took the tray of food and placed it on Tarro's chest. "I suggest that you eat. You're going to need your strength."

Tarro watched the first officer leave the cabin, and when she was gone, he greedily shoveled the food into his mouth. In his short time aboard the *Blackthorne*, he had witnessed Natrina Ma'Goran's discipline practices. He knew he would need his strength. It wasn't until the door opened again and a shadowy figure entered the room that he realized just how much.

"Hello...lover" was all that Kell said.

If you like the person you are about to assassinate, then directly between the eyes is the proper etiquette.

—Thorpe's Corporation employee handbook

CHAPTER 27

Kwyne
Rohnin's Citadel

DAMIEN CAIRO STOOD AT HIS desk looking down into the polished surface as he collected his thoughts. Though he had just finished one of the most distressing meetings of his administration, he knew that worse was to come. He organized the events: First, word had reached his ears that a Lokaryn had been apprehended in one of the outer district arcs. By itself it would have been only an atrocity; however, the Lokaryn was caught in the act of feeding. It could not have been a more inflammatory situation. He thought about that for a long moment. It was the perfect flint. He could see the pieces on the chess board moving, but had difficulty discerning who was moving them. This was a diplomatic incident that would spark tensions that would take years, if not decades, from which to recover. Played poorly, it could very well ignite a war that Kwyne could ill afford. The meeting that had just concluded with his closest advisors did little to ease his mind as one bad scenario after another played out.

As was his habit, his chief of staff, Ko'Doran, remained behind.

The Nehreton was gathering. There would be the perfunctory discussion and then they would vote to execute the captured Lokaryn. He could not allow it, but neither could he prevent it.

Ko'Doran spoke first. "It is simply not done, Rohnin. We can't permit this."

"I know," Cairo responded quietly. "But how do we stop it? It's not like we don't execute people on a regular basis."

"Outcasting is not…" Ko'Doran started.

"Execution?" Cairo interrupted. "When we toss someone outside the protection of the zone walls, we all know what happens. We don't call it by that name, but the result is no different."

Ko'Doran remained silent. He understood his rohnin's frustration.

Cairo rubbed his temples.

"We should never have built that damn thing," he added after a moment.

"You had no choice. You were newly appointed; your power base had not yet been consolidated. To oppose building the execution chamber would have damaged you critically in the first year of your administration."

"So instead it will critically damage me now and we'll go to war with the Lokaryn Zone as well. This is much better," Cairo observed caustically.

"Sir, had you opposed the project, you would have been assassinated. The next rohnin would have built it anyway and we'd be in this same place. Well, I'd be in the same place. You'd be fertilizer in the Badlands."

Cairo was shaken out of his brooding by the irreverent comment and laughed out loud. "You son of a bitch."

"Yes, sir."

"Suggestions?"

"Option one, allow the execution. If you can avoid a war, then use the fact that we came to the brink of war as justification to destroy the complex."

"The public thinks it's a lighthouse. How can I justify destroying a lighthouse as a way to ensure the safety of our people?" Cairo asked.

Ko'Doran ignored the question.

"Two, oppose the execution. Force an override vote. If you win, the matter is settled."

"If I lose?"

"You would be forced to assassinate the more powerful members of the Nehreton, before they could assassinate you."

"So much for 'we don't execute people.' "

"They're not people, they're politicians. Players. A man in front of a firing squad can't shoot back," Ko'Doran observed.

"We should have found an argument to prevent this, Ko. It was only a matter of time before someone found a way to misuse it."

"Rohnin, I believe that our best option is to fight vigorously against the execution, allow it to go forward, and try to settle things diplomatically afterward."

"We can't do that," Cairo said simply.

"Why not?"

"It will not prevent a war."

"How could you possibly know that," Ko'Doran asked.

"I believe I know this Lokaryn," the rohnin said, "and if I'm right, the leadership of her zone will not let this go quietly."

"You know the Lokaryn? Is there something I should know?"

Cairo looked at his chief of staff. "Thank you, Primare" was all he said. The conversation was ended with that, and though Ko'Doran had much more to say, he knew it was time to withdraw. His friend and his rohnin had made up his mind.

"Thecla's blessing then, Rohnin Cairo," Ko'Doran said as he left the room.

Rohnin Cairo, former member of the Kuhbrik, two-term prelate of the Tenth Arc, professor of philosophy and defense arts at the national academy, and rohnin of Kwyne, knew that what he was about to do would end his reign and likely, his life.

He descended the stairs and entered the Assembly Hall. There he found the gathered milling about. They quickly took their places, and unlike so many other times, he allowed all the pomp and circumstance to be carried out. Now was a time to remind the Nehreton that he *was* rohnin.

After the preliminaries were completed, it was Prelate Var Kragen who walked to the center, slowly, in full command of the room. Every move of every prelate in the room conveyed gravity. The assembled prelates knew that this was a time of history; the eve of change.

"So, Prelate Kragen, you have found yourself a Lokaryn," Cairo began.

"No, Rohnin, we have found *the* Lokaryn. The Lokaryn who was responsible for the destruction of the tenement in the Third Arc a fortnight ago...."

"Our forces were responsible for the destruction of the tenement in hunting what may have been a Lokaryn in our zone. They used weapons that were far too powerful for such constricted places and they paid the price."

"They made the ultimate sacrifice and we must honor that. They pursued this Lokaryn, and now we have found that specific Lokaryn."

"My understanding is that the Lokaryn was staked in the encounter. Lokaryns aren't all that talkative when staked. So how have you determined that this is the specific Lokaryn who was involved in the assault in the Third Arc?"

"Even if this were not, Rohnin Cairo, it would not matter. This Lokaryn was caught in the process of feeding on a Kwynian citizen. Will you not protect your own citizens?"

"I am protecting my citizens, Prelate Kragen. Protecting them from a war we can ill afford; a war that will happen if we execute a citizen of a sovereign zone. *That* will take many more lives than one rogue Lokaryn in our zone."

"Even if that one Lokaryn happened to be feeding on the daughter of one of your prelates?"

There was an audible gasp in the room. Kragen had played this card perfectly. Cairo was stunned; he couldn't believe that his old friend would feed on an innocent, let alone a young girl. His mind raced, and that was the opening Kragen needed.

"Yes, Rohnin, this Lokaryn was consuming a young flower of Kwyne in her ascension to a life of service to Kwyne and her ideals. This monster plucked her from her home and led her on an ill path finally ending in that foul alley where she was rescued from his jaws."

" 'His'?" Cairo heard the word as a thunderclap. *His?*

Kragen too was taken off-guard by the rohnin's response to the word.

"Yes, Rohnin, 'his.' The Lokaryn is male." The prelate watched the rohnin's reactions. They did not make sense to him. Things made even less sense to Cairo. It wasn't his old friend Derring they had caught, it was a male Lokaryn. Where the hell had he come from? What the hell was he doing? Where was Derring? His mind raced, sifting through the new information. Then he considered the fact that it was a prelate's daughter. This provided a perfect reason to advocate for execution. Too perfect.

"Rohnin, the Nehreton brings to you a petition to execute a Lokaryn found in-zone feeding on Prelate Goli's daughter Chenara."

Before, when the vote was purely about a Lokaryn caught in-zone, Cairo stood some chance of bartering the vote to his favor. This, however, was entirely different. The daughter of one of their own. The vote would be wildly skewed in the passions of the moment. Cairo thought for a moment and then spoke.

"Prelate Kragen, does it strike you as odd the confluence of events? Lokaryns in Kwyne feeding on our citizens? Never before in the history of our zone has such a thing happened. And yet now we have two incidents in a short period of time."

"It has never been proven to happen, but just as the existence of Thecla's Paradise in the afterlife has never been proven we all still know that it's a fact."

"That one thing unproven is fact, does not make *all* things unproven fact. That the unprovable is truth in one sacred case is the essence of the Maker's special covenant with us and should not be used in such a manner. Prelate Kragen, we have never found a transgression by Lokaryns in our zone previously; now we have two in a short period of time. The first eludes capture through some fault of our own. The second is not only caught but caught in the act of feeding on a prelate's child? Doesn't that make you ask a few additional questions?"

"No, Rohnin, I focus directly on the source of a problem, not the extraneous."

"Who staked the Lokaryn?"

"What has that got to do with…"

"Who staked the Lokaryn? Shouldn't we be pinning a medal on the man or woman who was able enough to stake a moving Lokaryn?"

"Again, Rohnin Cairo, superfluous. This Lokaryn, for whatever else he may have done, was caught feeding on a citizen of Kwyne. Whoever she may be, the penalty is death."

"Prelate Kragen, if you persist in ignoring anything that doesn't fit your central theory, there will be war. You must understand this."

"Then let war come, Rohnin." Kragen turned and paced in front of the dais, his hands to the lapels of his robe lecturing more to the crowd than to the leader of Kwyne. "We are Kwyne, we will not shrink from our duty, we will not shirk our responsibility. We will carry the fight to the infidels' home and crush them."

"You do not understand the enemy you seek to provoke," Cairo said. "Kwyne does not understand this culture because we shut them out. We maintain our purity by shutting ourselves off from anything different from us, and as a result we are ignorant of the larger world around us. In that ignorance we paint ourselves as superior without measuring other cultures or ourselves against them. We seek to strike at what we do not completely see. Prelates, I served as an ambassador to Merchants' Zone and encountered Lokaryns there. In my studies, I have engaged their culture. They will not marshal their troops outside our walls and wait for us to engage them conveniently in battle."

"Thank you, Rohnin, for that insightful analysis. As I am a former colonel in the Kuhbrikian forces, you know I am exceedingly dense in military matters."

A silence came over the room. It was a bold, even brazen statement to make to the rohnin in front of the collected prelates. It was a challenge.

"Yes, *Colonel*," Cairo stated, going directly into his adversary's argument. "You were in the military, and a gifted tactician, as I recall. I also recall, however, that you never ascended to general-of-forces strata, owing to a deficiency of strategic thought."

With that, every person in the room knew that the two major leaders in their zone had gone to war with each other.

Though inwardly Kragen exploded at the rebuke, outwardly he remained calm. But he did not protest, and the rohnin continued.

"This execution will usher in an unwanted era for Kwyne. We will solicit a war with an enemy that we will not meet on the open plain. We will solicit this war under the pretense of self-preservation. The enemy will insinuate themselves in our midst, unseen and not comprehended until they strike. They could be anywhere, in any place, and we'll not know it."

"Then, Rohnin, our eyes shall be everywhere, our presence shall be everywhere, so that we *will* comprehend them, we will not be taken unaware."

"That is your answer? Will we cast our eyes everywhere? Into the homes of our citizens? All of our citizens? Will we make lists and have neighbors informing on neighbors, brother informing on brother, of any unusual behaviors? Will we catalogue the movements of people who like to be out at night, or buy live animals that could be used to sustain an enemy agent? Will we discard the freedoms of our citizens like an old warm coat that no long feels fashionable so that we may deceive ourselves that we have safety, when in fact we will be creating in our midst a greater danger? This is an enemy that you do not comprehend."

"Rohnin, you continue to use the word 'enemy.' Why do you not call them what they are? Lokaryns. They are the antithesis of everything that the Messiah's teaching has given us. They are not to be dealt with, but destroyed. Chapter 65:13 says 'Turn the wicked walking in your midst, else they shall not find rest in death and should be rent asunder.' An obvious reference to Lokaryns!"

"Var, I use the term 'enemy' instead of 'Lokaryn' deliberately: The enemy will not only be the Lokaryns. Haven't you figured that out? For starters, the generals in Chumley's Zone will join us."

"You see, my brethren, even the rohnin acknowledges that the military will come to the aid of a worthy cause!" Kragen pronounced.

"And that worthy cause is self-interest. They may have religious leanings, but they are more eager to deny Rossums Zone their greatest ally: the Lokaryns. They want Rossums weakened because it acts as a haven for thousands of their runaway artificials. With the Lokaryn Zone gone, they will expect our aid in subduing Rossums to reclaim their 'property.' So the military will ally with us, and the artificials of Rossums will ally with the Lokaryns. Now we have two formidable enemies, and one ally with doubtful motives. However, it doesn't end there. What about the phobes?"

"They will align with us!"

"That's right, they will. They abhor technology like you abhor the Lokaryns, so they pitch in with us against the androids. Our technology use is the lesser of the evils. So we have crystal casters and their Seb-Ichi special forces, but Thieves' Zone aligns with the Lokaryns and Rossums out of their antipathy for the military. Their militia consists of independents, a lot of technology, and a lot of wild cards. They are a diverse group drawn from all the zones. Now we're even having to fight against our own weapons and tactics. We have six of the nine major zones at war, with the two corporate zones remaining neutral to sell weapons to both sides and Merchants' Zone staying neutral to provide shipping to both sides. All because you feel the need to prove some point about Kwyne."

"Rohnin, this is all conjecture. We have the Lokaryn..."

"You have *a* Lokaryn. My intelligence indicates that this individual had nothing to do with the attack in the Third Arc."

The room again was stunned.

The revelation was a mistake.

"Rohnin, you have been withholding intelligence regarding this subject from the Nehreton?"

"I am rohnin. I have access to many sources that you do not. I do not report to you or to this body."

"Whether or not he was involved in the Third Arc, we can prove for a fact that this is the Lokaryn involved in the attack on Goli's daughter, and that is all we need prove to bring the matter to your attention for consent."

"I will not grant consent for this or any other execution. You will leave the stake in the body, and contact the lokaric diplomatic mission in the Ninth Arc to claim the body and get it out of the zone at the earliest possible opportunity." With that Rohnin Cairo stood. "This audience is ended."

Prelate Kragen, however, was not finished. "I invoke a Charter Call."

Though not surprised by the maneuver, Cairo had hoped to avoid it. He could see now that this crisis would propel itself not by reason, but inertia.

"Var, the road you seek to set us on will end poorly for all involved. Very well, by the laws of the Nehreton I will withdraw to my chamber and await the vote of this body. You will need seventy-five percent of the arcs to override my decision. Think carefully on what I have said, debate and allow for time to cool the passions of the morning."

And with that he left the chamber.

Ko'Doran joined him upstairs in the rohnin's office.

"Damien!" he started, forgetting all propriety. "What intelligence did you have about the Third Arc attack that you couldn't share with *me?*"

"I thought the Lokaryn in question would be a female."

"Why a female? What do you know that I need to know."

"It is complicated, Ko, and we haven't the time right now for explanations. Do you trust me?"

"Of course," Ko'Doran answered honestly.

"We must work quickly. First, did the girl survive the attack?"

"Chenara Goli? Yes she did. She's being treated for the trauma of the attack, but is expected to survive."

"Have we had any luck recovering the data feeds from the soldier's helmet cams in the Third Arc incident?"

"Yes, but the video that was transmitted was inconclusive."

Cairo thought for a moment.

"Isn't there a delay in sending the information?"

"Yes, there's a second or two delay while the data stream is encrypted; the cached video that hasn't been sent is stored in data chips in the helmet."

"*That's* the data we need. And we need it fast."

"There are a lot of data caches to sort through and they're all pretty damaged."

"Do the best you can. We also need to get the lokaric ambassador here."

Ko'Doran shook his head. "Not here. You just advocated for the Lokaryns downstairs. If anyone remotely connected with the Lokaryn Zone shows up in the rohnin's office, that will cement the vote, I guarantee it."

"You're right. Set the meeting up in the outer districts. Let's see if this Lokaryn of theirs was attached to the embassy."

"Even if he was attached to the embassy, he was still caught feeding on a prelate's daughter."

"True, but the girl didn't die, and if this Lokaryn was cleared to be in-zone, we've taken away two of their mainstays in arguing for execution. If the data in those helmets doesn't show him as the assailant in the Third Arc incident, then outcasting is the appropriate punishment. After that, the only thing they've got to push through with the execution is fanaticism."

They paused for a moment.

"Since when has a zealot ever needed more?" Ko'Doran said.

No one ever got more from a Lokaryn than they gave.

—Traditional wisdom

CHAPTER 28

THE VOICES SWIRLED INSIDE KELL'S head just as they had since she was a child. They started quietly at first, like a soft prayer in church, but quickly grew into a cacophonous uproar. They always got louder when it was time to feed, shouting and wailing until they had whipped her into a frenzy. Once the act of feeding was complete they sank back into the shadows of her mind, to pick over the bones of the psyche that she had just ingested. Sated, they returned to their quiet murmurs, but they never entirely went away. Had they done so, she would have missed them, for she loved each and every one of them, as a master does a pet. Though they had originally tormented her as a mortal, she came to understand them, and now that she was a Lokaryn, they conferred enormous strength. When it was time to feed, they sang to her, their voices both beautiful and wicked. And she was glad for it.

She stepped out of the shower, and picked up a soft snow-white towel. She took her time in preparing for the evening. Tonight would be special, an evening that she would remember forever. For tonight she would obtain the last piece of information that would allow her a vengeance sweeter than any she had ever known. She absently ran her tongue over the length of one fang as she thought about it. If all went well tonight, she would finally learn the whereabouts of Arles Timmerson, a man who had wronged her a lifetime ago. A man whose life was about to come to a horrific end as she fed on him night after night, until eternity dawned. Tonight she would seduce a man who would tell her where Arles Timmerson could be found. The voices sang a rejoiceful song.

It had taken her years to find the trail of the man she hunted, and years more to get this close. Now, at the brink, she allowed herself a moment of anticipation. She let the towel hang over a shoulder and cascade down her body. She closed her eyes and slid her arms around herself, imagining what it would finally be like. The two of them there, his fear intoxicating her. His hands strong around her arms, struggling against her, desperate to break free. She imagined the feeling as the tip of her fang slowly touched the heat of his exposed neck. The light pressure, on his skin. Resistance giving way as she pierced his flesh and entered him for the first time. Her fangs deep within his bloodstream and the exhalation as she began drawing in the life force that he possessed.

One of the voices brought her back to the present, scolding her. The voice of her mother. Did Kell want to go back into the closet? Was she done wasting her time thinking? If she stood there imagining the future, it would never happen. Kell shuddered as a cold, dark tension crept over her. She shook her head, returning to the present.

Tonight would be a different sort of intimacy. The man she hunted tonight was not Timmerson himself, but a man who would tell her where he could be found. She had studied this man well. He was an assistant to a subminister in Merchants' Zone, tasked with managing the comings and goings of the various merchant ships. Though he was little more than a low-level bureaucrat, no ship could legally enter Merchants' Zone without a permit from his office. He had access and he would soon give it to her. She knew the man's habits and his tastes. She knew that he had appetites that could not be filled just anywhere. Appetites that could be satisfied only in the outer districts, in dark places well away from decent people. She knew what he liked his women to wear, and from the arsenal that was her clothes closet she selected just the right weaponry. She knew that tonight he was going to be at a particular outer district establishment that catered to men who did not want to be recognized. His job required him to travel a lot, or so he told his wife, but he seldom traveled much farther than the outer districts of Merchants' Zone.

Kell slid on her undergarments and hosiery. These did not arouse her, but she knew they would arouse her target. In the back of her mind her voices shouted down the shrill denunciation of her mother. Through the din, she still heard the condemnation about such clothing, the cries of "whore," and the threats, always the threats. She grabbed the last of the evening's clothes quickly, threw them on the bed, and slammed the closet door shut with a shudder. Too many nights alone in a dark closet, her mother's punishment for things unholy. And unholiness took on many aspects: idleness, daydreaming, singing. But the voices protected her now, as they always had, from all that was left of her mother.

She took the dress and felt the satin as it fell about her frame. It accentuated her hips, and left the observer to wonder about what might be under the bodice. It suggested, but did not betray, that the answer would be pleasing. She selected the right height heels, as he liked his women tall, but not taller than he. There would be no makeup—she did not need it—and her hair would flow freely tonight. She looked at herself only briefly in the mirror, smiled a wicked smile, and left.

Kell arrived at the nightclub, which was more akin to an opium den in its appointments. All manner of excesses could be obtained here, and they were in plentiful supply for paying customers. She had made arrangements to be the featured singer, and the owner of the establishment had figured her for the spoiled mistress of a wealthy patron, a singer who couldn't cut it on her own talent so decided to buy the venue for a night. He didn't care. She had produced a sufficient amount of caryns, and his clientele generally did not come to his establishment for the entertainment. At least, not this type of entertainment. Listening to her first song, he found to his amazement that she had a voice that could only be described as otherworldly.

The evening established, Kell made her way around the room like a spider tending a web, weaving petty jealousies among the drunken men and women who vied for her attention. The place was dim with dark recesses and booths where patrons could sit unobserved. Blue light filtered down through swirls of smoke onto a baby grand piano, and Kell was working the room into a near climax when her target walked in. He moved with no particular grace and thought nothing of it when he was shown to a VIP booth, complete with privacy drapes. It was about time, at least in his mind, that he be given the respect due his position. A bottle was immediately brought to his table.

"Compliments of the lady," the waiter explained as he motioned toward Kell. The gesture was unnecessary. The man was already fixated on the woman who was the center of attention in the room. She finally looked over her shoulder, with head turned slightly downward, and brought her eyes up to meet his. When they connected, his pulse nearly doubled. At sixty, his lifelong excess of food and alcohol had left him more a man in his mind than in physical ability, but he suddenly found himself aroused. Very aroused. It had been years since that had happened.

She moved away from him with slowly swaying hips that brushed the satin of her dress from side to side like gentle breath on the skin just before an intimate kiss. Each time she moved near another patron, he felt a panic that he might lose this woman whom he had never had. The alcohol stirred his emotions—fear, rage, and more lust. He spent an hour trying to catch that gaze again, with many calls to the waiter to make sure that the bottle was from her. Finally, he gave the waiter one hundred caryns to have a request brought to the piano player.

The bait was taken.

Kell worked her way back to the piano, through several near fights, and picked up the piece of paper. She gave it back to the player with a very slight nod.

"This next song is a request from a new friend. Me and the boys will close the set with this one and I'll be back after I...freshen up a bit and get a drink—courtesy of my new friend."

The song was not the one that he had requested, but rather a slow and slinky ballad about a woman who wants to know what a real man can show her, and what her body might feel like in the hands of a master lover. She slowly lowered herself into the booth by the end of the song and on cue let the curtain drawstring loose.

The house DJ began playing dance music with a hard-driving beat.

This, too, was at her request. The sounds, though loud outside, were muffled by the heavy velvet drapes that now obscured the view of so many envious patrons.

"Silas Perno," Kell began, allowing her long blond hair to cascade over one shoulder.

At once the man was more than a little nervous.

"You know who I am?" he stammered.

"I know a great deal about you, Silas. That is why I chose you. Don't worry—I have no desire to worry Anna Mae with any of your doings here in the outer districts. You're really in Thorpe's Zone right now negotiating a trade agreement on behalf of the great trading houses of Merchants' Zone. Everybody knows that."

Silas Perno found himself frightened to death that this stranger knew so much, but he couldn't ignore his reactions to her. She was that first drink to a reformed alcoholic: irresistible, though the promise of lasting calamity rode with the fleeting pleasure.

"What do you want?" he asked, stalling for time.

Kell answered him by stepping onto the table and sitting directly in front of him, putting one leg to each side of his body. The music outside with its driving beat, the privacy of the booth, the liquor and the lust all converged upon him, brushing reason aside.

"You."

His fear forgotten or at least overtaken, he unfastened his pants and in a moment they were around his ankles. He struggled to get up to take her, but then, very suddenly, he found himself not on top of her but beneath her, as she straddled him.

"Now!" he growled though scotch-laden breath, and reached up to pull her down on top of him.

The voices concurred. She responded more quickly than his senses could perceive and answered by striking him in the center of his chest with the heel of her palm. The blow winded him instantly. Gasping for air, stunned by the strike, he watched as she started moving to the beat, smiling all the while.

"Tell me," she said, pausing to enjoy the moment. She was still gyrating, teasing him, as she started to dig her nails into the flesh of his chest. He could see the nails, he could see them long and sharp entering his skin, but he could not feel them. His eyes grew wide, his mouth opened, but no words came out.

"This is what you wanted—was it not?" she asked, baring her fangs for the first time. Horrified, the man struggled beneath her to no avail.

"I should have told you before we started that when we Lokaryns get 'aroused' it always ends in death for the mortal. We can't help it. Feeding is lust for us. You know how it is, lover. You always hurt the one you love."

He continued to struggle, which only aroused Kell all the more.

"But maybe," she purred, "just maybe I can stop if you tell me something that I want to know."

She was lying and he knew it. Perno looked up at her, knowing that his life was about to end. It was about to end in a den of perversion; his wife, his family would forever curse his name; his legacy would be shame for all time. Still, he had to try.

"Anything," he gasped. "Anything."

Begging was an excellent spice, Kell thought.

"Where…is Arles Timmerson."

She withdrew her nails, which were dripping with his blood, and allowed the droplets to fall onto her tongue. Delicious. The beat of the music seemed to intensify.

Suddenly, he became very aware of the pain from his torn flesh and he arched upward, spewing forth a string of impressive curses. She responded with a downward thrust, cocking one hand back, ready to claw into his chest once again.

"Timmerson!" she snarled at him.

"Saphinian run," he blurted out. "He always does the Saphinian at this time of year for some festival they have up there."

"Good." She smiled at him and bent down to kiss him. A malevolent thank-you. By reflex, as their lips met, he thrust his tongue into her mouth. She liked it. So she kept it.

He attempted to scream as she sat up, his tongue hanging from her mouth, and her own tongue drawing the blood in.

"Yummy," she said, licking the last of the crimson fluid from the dismembered part. She ran it across his own lips, then forced it back into his mouth. It would muffle the screams.

The lust had her now and there was no turning back. She had not lied about lokaric lust: Once started it ended in death. There was only one man she knew of who had escaped this inevitability—Arles Timmerson. Her mind lost in the fog of sensation, she became angrier and angrier as she rode the man below her. She thought of Timmerson and viciously plunged her hand deep into Perno's chest. This time she dislodged a large section of the musculature, and again she allowed the blood to flow onto her eager tongue. He could not disengage himself from her as she rode him, nor could he deflect her hands as they tore away chunk after chunk of his flesh.

Finally, she began to shudder, her voices singing in a chorus of delight. Perhaps she would finish and leave, he thought. As if reading his mind, she spasmed in delight, and he felt the bones in his hips give way. As his vision blurred from the pain, he saw that she was holding a beating heart in her hand.

His.

So quick was the move that had dislodged his heart, he had not felt the strike. Though his vision was fading, his still-perfect ears heard her climax as his heart, dripping his blood into her mouth, slowly stopped beating.

The last set of the night never came, and when the patrons of the club looked into the booth all they found was Silas Perno, with hollow chest and horrified expression, lying beside the singer's clothing.

Death comes to all. Use yours wisely.

—Preface to Chumley's Officer Training Manual

CHAPTER 29

Kwyne: Redemption Microzone

J'NATH WOKE TO PAIN.

It was a searing, penetrating pain, like being woken from a deep sleep by the flash of a white-hot poker drawn across the flesh of your back. He gasped and flew to his feet, ready to strike out and kill anything within reach, but there was nothing except the muted sound of conversation that drifted down on him from high above where he stood.

It was dark in this place. The walls were rounded and had a polished surface, yet he could feel what appeared to be seams in the finish. He tried to move through them, but each ended as a shallow groove. He circled the room, groping in the dark with his back toward the wall. Half-incorporeal, half-solid, he probed with his fingers, trying to find the pinhole to rescue himself.

Still the voices came.

Though he could not make out the details of this place, he could smell humans. And if he could smell that which was not present with him, it meant that somewhere there was a way out. He completed his turn around the room without any sign of the phantom breach.

All walls have holes, he thought, *all walls.*

He did not need his lokaric senses to tell that he was being watched. The conversation had subsided, but the feeling of being on display had not. He was still disoriented from the pain of his awakening, but images slowly filtered back to him. He remembered his last feeding, a street urchin. Though his clan lord would be displeased that he had killed an innocent, she would understand that he had not fed in days. She would take into account that even in a near-feral state, he had killed mercifully.

But he had been attacked while feeding. He couldn't recall if he had finished the girl or not. He remembered drawing her in, like the first breath of air after too long a time under water. Then came the blackness. The next thing he was aware of was pain, and then this place.

All walls have holes, there has to be an out, he thought.

Unless…

He stopped. While it was true that most walls had some imperfection that would allow passage of someone who could turn himself into a vapor, this wall did not. This place must be a prison for Lokaryns. There would be no cracks.

He would just have to make one.

He threw himself against the wall—to no effect.

"Open the door," he demanded. "This can still end well."

"Your attentions would be better served by turning them toward your soul," a voice replied calmly.

"Would you at least tell me what zone I'm in?" J'Nath said, changing tactics.

There was no answer.

A dim red light snapped on above him. It provided enough illumination for him to see that the walls and floor were mirrored. He stood in a circular chamber several stories high with a conical ceiling capped by a hatch, and in an instant he knew where he was.

The stories of this place were legend in the Lokaryn Zone. It was a place of execution, a place specifically built to kill his kind.

He understood the feeling he had seen in the eyes of those on which he had fed. That realization that they had reached the end of their days.

"Are you insane?" he yelled up to the disembodied voice. "You have no right to kill a member of another zone! If you do this it will mean war."

"We have every right: You were in Kwyne, without permission or diplomatic purpose, and found in the act of feeding on one of our citizens. You are being punished in accordance with well-known law. It is you who have committed an act of war."

J'Nath searched his memory. The last days were a blur. He had only just come to consciousness when he found the girl in the alleyway. He was starved to the point of being feral and was too far gone to even consider where he was. Before that he could remember only the feeding chambers with T'Gareth and the four-striper. Had the blood of so malevolent a creature overwhelmed him? He had no answers for the accusations he faced, but knew he needed to act.

"You *are* insane! You are willing to risk war over a street urchin? I had no idea where I was when I awoke. She was a street rat; someone your society threw away!"

"She was the daughter of a prelate."

J'Nath cursed his bad luck. Unbelievably bad luck…impossibly bad luck.

"The rohnin has sanctioned this?" J'Nath shouted in desperation.

"The rohnin has not the will for the word of Thecla. The faithful are carrying out the will of the Maker instead."

"You're invoking the book of Hass?" J'Nath said in disbelief. "That's a very slanted reading of the passage."

"How do you know a book of Kwynian law?"

"Because I was once Kwynian."

"Then you should understand that anyone assaulting a prelate's family does so under penalty of death."

It was then that J'Nath understood that this had not been about luck at all.

"Don't you see?" he implored. "They put her there for me to feed on. It ensured that you would have no choice *but* to do this and bring our zones to war."

Var Kragen, the owner of the disembodied voice, said, "We have a confession. You may proceed."

J'Nath could feel the vibration of the machinery before he heard the whine of the gears signaling his end. He looked around in a near panic. This couldn't be happening. Summoning all his strength, rage, and will, he threw himself into the wall. If he couldn't break the walls, then perhaps he could crack one just enough to mist his way out. He had only seconds before the upper hatchway would open, allowing lethal sunlight to pour into the chamber. He screamed a feral scream as he hit the wall. His mirrored image struck back with equal force, denying him any exit. They had, with malicious conviction, engineered a structure capable of withstanding such an onslaught.

The shock wave of the impact shook the viewing gallery where the assembled prelates had gathered to watch the unholy beast succumb.

Kragen lifted his hands and enjoined the room: "Let us pray for the soul of this misguided creature."

J'Nath continued to slam against the walls. They did not yield, so he surged for the hatchway, hoping to grab hold of something and prevent it from opening.

"Thecla, savior of humanity, hear our prayer for this creature," Kragen continued.

The Lokaryn reached the top but found only the same grooved, polished texture, with no leverage against which to hold the hatch. He felt it sliding ever so slightly under his hands.

"Angel of eternity, though he has wronged you we come to you in humble petition."

The outer hatch was open now; he could hear it clicking home in the recess that housed it. The inner began to vibrate in anticipation of its movement.

"We thank you for the gift of light, your most precious worldly blessing that gives life to all. We use it to purge your most profane foe."

The first minuscule ray of pure, intense midday sunlight punctured the room, striking J'Nath like a lightning bolt and throwing him to the floor in anguish.

"Have mercy on the sinners, those who would take your words and wonders and use them for their own ends."

Pulling himself up, J'Nath dragged his pain-racked body to the side of the chamber. Though little sunlight had entered yet, it was still more than enough to create searing agony within him. No matter how he moved his body he could not stop the pain. A thousand white-hot needles seared him, and razors cut him from within.

"We commit this sinner to eternity in accordance with your word."

J'Nath's mind was on fire now. With few moments left to him, he again launched himself at the hatchway, slower this time as his strength left him. He struggled upward into the pain. If he were to die in this wretched place, he would make sure no one else ever would. The structure of the chamber was vulnerable while the hatchway was opening. The leaves of the iris-shaped entryway did not have the same strength as when they were closed.

"Thecla be praised, rest in peace." And with that Kragen bowed his head in prayer, though many continued to watch the monitors for the spectacle that was unfolding.

He was almost to the top when the iris snapped fully open. There, J'Nath, engulfed in pure light, screamed out in a voice that few had ever heard.

His body hung there in the chamber, his arms flung out to the sides like an image of crucifixion. His life force poured out, as each neuron in his body exploded in a crescendo of pure energy that vented upward into the column.

It was seen for hundreds of miles around, and certainly by all Kwynian citizens. It was a warning to all who would violate the sovereignty of Kwyne.

As impressive as the spectacle was, the scream of agony was what brought the proceedings to a halt: So pure. So complete. So utterly human.

Finally, it was done. J'Nath was no more, and the chamber looked much as it had before. Information about the execution began to make its way from observers positioned in ships off the Redemption micro-zone. Kragen raised his head from prayer. He looked at the gathering. Their faces bore testimony to the horror of execution.

"Thecla's will be done. This ceremony is ended. We will be leaving with the evening tide for Kwyne. Go in peace. Our work here is done."

Senja Goli, prelate of the Ninth Arc and father of Chenara, knew differently.

CHAPTER 30

BY DARKNESS AND STORM DERRING and Hemingway traveled making their way across the rugged landscape. Chief among their problems was that the passage was getting easier.

Their journey had taken many days, and by all measures had been arduous. The storms, courtesy of the zone's government, had rendered the already treacherous terrain nearly impassable. Traveling by night only further complicated their efforts. A moonless night in Ravensford Zone rivaled the darkness of the lokaric lower district. As bad as these conditions were, had either of the travelers been human the trip might not have been possible at all.

Most dangerous, however, was that they were pushing toward the more populated inner district of Demminer Arc. This was where Stannis Klemm made his home. While mountains could be passed and rivers forded, even a single encounter with a local could spell disaster. One person gone missing could give the local security forces a fresh trail. Travel became easier as the terrain's severity lessened and the trappings of civilization increased, but the trip was accordingly more dangerous.

"We're at the crossover to the inner district," Derring observed as they moved through dense forest and approached a large fortresslike wall. Made of stone, it was impressive in size, some eighteen feet tall and massive at its base. At the top were arrayed crystals that generated an enormous energy field that separated inner and outer districts. On either side of the crystals were daunting spikes that arose upward from the top part of the stone structure on both sides at a forty-five-degree angle. The spikes acted as both lightning rods and conduits, protecting the field from the storm's disruption and funneling the immense energy into the shielding. Electricity pulsed along the course of the barrier, promising incineration to anyone foolhardy enough to attempt crossing save though the gates.

While the crossover gates themselves were capable of withstanding a great onslaught, they were not closed unless there was a state of alert or alarm, and the pair had gone to great lengths not to raise either one.

Derring looked up at the imposing site from their hidden vantage and took a deep breath.

"Open, and with what looks like only one guard."

"They're probably looking for us in the outer districts with ports friendly to lokaric trade. It would make a lot more sense for us to head *out* of the zone rather than into it. They can't be expecting us to try *this*," Hemingway responded. "It's the *dumbest* thing we could do—therefore perfect," he noted with a smirk.

"I see your *Shicaine* karma has returned," Derring replied, then looking at the electrified barrier added, "In what way is that not technology?"

"No moving parts."

Derring smiled a half-second smile. The bait was taken.

"Wish I could say the same for your jaw." A pause ensued.

Knowing that he'd been had, Hemingway smiled tightly and nodded his head.

"Waited for that didn't you?"

"Yep, I didn't overplay it, though, did I?" Derring asked with mock earnestness.

"No, no, it was good…really. Can we go get electrocuted or shot now?"

"Sure."

The two became serious again as they watched the guard's patrol pattern. After the third time they had it down.

"Do you see any sign of more guards?" Hemingway asked.

"No, but you never know what's inside the guardhouse. Could be more guards or even Seb-Ichi."

"Anything more than one or two Seb-Ichi and this is going to be…uncomfortable," Hemingway noted flatly.

Derring quickly swept behind the guard. With a small movement he was asleep in a chair and would not awaken for some hours. With that, the slow-moving jaws of a distant but lethal trap had been sprung.

Derring moved inside the perimeter wall, and then, finding nothing, signaled to Hemingway to advance. Once inside, they headed for a small cabin some hundred yards from the gate.

"Perhaps it's time to stick to the roads a little more," she remarked.

"I suppose so. We'll at least have a better chance of knowing where people will be. With our luck, if we cut across country we'd trip over the 'farmer's daughter' with a local boy anyway," Hemingway said.

Passing an outer split-rail fence, they were approaching the cabin door when Hemingway observed three quilts hung over a drying rack just outside. The patchwork trio was dripping wet from the storm, and the fabric badly tattered and damaged from the wind.

"Are we sure this is Phobes'? They're usually fanatical about waste," Hemingway said, motioning toward the quilts as he went inside the cabin.

Derring, however, stopped cold in her tracks.

He was right. Nothing was ever wasted in Phobes' Zone. They knew this storm was coming and here were quilts, items that had taken months to make, left out like a child's toy.

Derring slowly gathered the ends of the first quilt and spread them so that she could see the pattern in the flickering light of the oil lamps: Drunkard's Path. It was a quilt pattern used in the underground, but common enough for this area. The second quilt was badly damaged, but she could make out enough to see the centerpiece: Sunshine and Shadow. Not common for this arc, but a pattern that had been used on the railroad to indicate a lokaric conductor. Her heart beat quickened.

Hemingway leaned back out the door.

"Uh, Derring—would you like to shout loudly or maybe stomp

around so that you can bring as much attention to yourself as possible, or will standing in plain sight under that lamp do?"

Derring realized at once that Hemingway was right and quickly gathered the last quilt and scrambled inside. Hemingway went about the business of checking the cabin for supplies.

The cabin was a simple affair, with many bunks, bedding, a fire that the guard had been tending to keep warm, a long table with two benches, and a small larder with breads and water. To the far wall there was a tin for contributions.

Derring quickly flung the quilt out in front of the fireplace and there saw the pattern for which she had hoped: Storm at Sea. The center block signified their current position, and an eight-point star indicated their destination. Small quilted knots between the two marked off the distance to the next station and, possibly, home.

"Hemingway, they've found us! The quilts—they're using the old system to tell us that they know we're here and to bring us in!"

"You're sure?" Hemingway asked in disbelief.

Derring turned the quilt over. A patch on the back looked blank at first glance, but there was a very fine stitch in a color that matched the backing—the trace of the needlework was visible if held to relief in the light.

To D & H

Love M & P

"To Derring and Hemingway…" Derring began.

"From Mom and Pop, the Klemms' railroad names," Hemingway finished.

"Four markers northwest to the next station. We can make it to-night." Derring felt an excitement grow within her. She threw the hood of her cloak back over her head and started to head out the door when she felt Hemingway's hand on her arm restraining her.

"We can, but we won't. We've gotten this far by being smart. Let's not stop now."

Derring looked toward the door, then to the hand on her arm.

"You'll see them soon, Derring, one more night won't break up Mom and Pop's little operation," Hemingway said.

"I know, I know. Where should we shelter?"

"I think if the next station is to the northwest, then we head directly north. Tomorrow night we approach from the opposite side that they expect us. Gives us the advantage."

"Good, I agree. The terrain is getting more familiar. We should be able to find something without too much difficulty."

Hemingway drew the cloak over his head, and turned to Derring.

"With any luck, by tomorrow night we'll be warming ourselves by the fire at the Klemms'."

Try as he might, in his entire life Hemingway would never be more ironic than he was in that moment.

Derring tore off the patch with the inscription so as to leave no evidence, and the two flew out the back door, headed north.

The distance they needed to cover was short, and shelter readily presented itself in the form of a grotto cave, overgrown with mosses and, more important, undisturbed for a very long time. They immediately went to work setting up the dampening field.

"The rock will afford me extra protection and I can set up the field by myself with this much time. Why don't you go hunt, Derring?"

"No, I'll be fine."

"Yes you're right, it would be better to be good and hungry as we get into the more densely populated areas so that your control will be at its lowest just as the mission is at its most critical. Good thinking—that's why you're the brains of this operation, Clan Lord." Hemingway nodded a sarcastic affirmation and went about setting up the posts as Derring set aside a host of replies and instead headed for the exit, knowing he was right and swearing a vengeance upon him.

"Don't forget to close the moss behind you," Hemingway called after her.

It was an hour before Derring returned, but still before dawn. She came in without a word, spread her cloak on the floor, and sat down with her back against the wall.

"You didn't feed," Hemingway said flatly. "Didn't anyone meet that code of yours?"

"How do you know if I fed or not," Derring said with annoyance.

Hemingway waited a moment, then said, "Because you always pray for them after you feed."

Derring took a deep breath and assumed a position on her knees. Hemingway looked suspiciously at the Lokaryn.

"Hmmm," Hemingway mused. "What did you do? Kill a cow or something?"

"Wolf."

"A *wolf*? How long is a wolf going to last you?"

"It was a mean wolf."

Derring saw it coming but did nothing to dodge the backpack thrown at her; rather, she simply fell over on her side in mock mortality as it hit her, and the two were lost in laughter for a few beautiful seconds.

The day passed as they enjoyed rest and conversation. Dusk fell across the land and finally faded into night. As the evening storms started to gather, Derring and Hemingway collected their items to strike out to the next station. Taking a deep breath, they headed into the storm.

It is not known how the child Messiah of Kwyne survived her infancy or even if she had one. The earliest accounts of her existence begin with the miracles in the marketplace of Turin Tan.

—Tor' Manat
Kwynian Sacred Writings

CHAPTER 31

Kwyne

Rohnin's Citadel

THE EXPLOSION OF LIGHT STRETCHED so far into the sky that it seemed as if it might touch the very hand of Thecla herself. To many of her Kwynian children, it was a beacon that illuminated all of T'Amorach in the righteousness of their faith. Of equal importance, it was a warning to Kwyne's enemies: Unholy incursions would be dealt with swiftly and decisively. To all, it was a breathtaking sight figuratively and, for one ill-fated Lokaryn, literally.

From his vantage point high in the Rohnin's Citadel, Damien Cairo watched the spire rise into sky, eclipsing the waning sun. The surfaces of his office usually reflected, serenely, the sun that came though the zone shielding. At this moment, however, the light was in no way soothing. It glared off every surface in angry protest. But his eyes remained fixed on the rising plume and, as he drew his gaze upward, his face took on an aspect of mourning.

Slowly, and somewhat absently, he raised a mug of coffee to his lips and watched an uncertain future unfold. The coffee had long since gone cold but he did not notice. Nor did he seem to take notice as his primare, Donavus Ko'Doran, walked up beside him. Ko'Doran entered the room carrying two glasses of Tamgara, a Kwynian specialty well known for its ability to relax the body without clouding the mind. The rohnin immediately put down the mug and nodded in gratitude, as Ko'Doran handed him one of the glasses.

Cairo took a sip of his drink, and remarked, "One hundred and twenty-five? One hundred and fifty?"

"Longer. It predates the Cataclysm."

The two men fell quiet as they watched the column of light stretch to incredible heights. Though the pyre might have touched an almighty hand, it was the effect at its base that now took their notice. The energy release flowed over the dome of the execution chamber and into the myst below, igniting it instantly. Mystfires exploded with a ferocity that only those about to die had ever seen. The tempest unleashed now raged outward in all directions, spreading at unthinkable speeds. For the two men, the pain and gravity of the moment stretched out in equal measure as the act, now completed, begged the consequences to begin.

"So they actually went ahead with it," Ko'Doran observed.

"There was little doubt that they would," Cairo replied, and then, taking a sip of his drink, commented, "Tamgara is generally reserved for festive occasions. I assume we're not celebrating that." He motioned toward the execution zone.

"No, Rohnin, we are not. I do, however, have some encouraging news. The reports are preliminary, but I have received intelligence from Phobes' Zone. They are holding an injured soldier who claims to be a survivor from the Third Arc incident."

"A survivor? In Phobes'?" Cairo was incredulous. "How is this possible?"

"Our intelligence network has not been able to determine that yet, but the man is wearing one of our uniforms. And…" Ko'Doran paused, trying to wrap his own mind around the words he was about to deliver. "His ID positively identifies him as Sergeant Peli Domar, one of our unaccounted-for soldiers. There is no way that they would have that information otherwise."

Cairo stared at his primare, his chief of staff, and absorbed the implications of his words. After a moment of careful consideration,

Kuhbrikian logic kicked in: He knew that the "how" of the matter wasn't nearly as important as the fact that the soldier "was" in Phobes'.

"Why hasn't he been transported to me?"

"The man's injuries are severe enough that travel at this time would be risky. And, of course, the Phobes' government isn't simply going to return him before their Seb-Ichi can conduct a proper interrogation. Allies or not. Our Kuhbrik would do the same."

Cairo began to pace the marble, his mind racing. There it was: an answer just barely out of reach. Hemmed in by the requirements of diplomacy and politics. Frustrated, he slammed his fist against the polished desktop and spun around to face Ko'Doran.

"Dammit, Donavus! I need this man's information, and if I have to send in a Kuhbrikian strike force to obtain it, I will."

"Damien, I share your frustration, but we are on the verge of war with the Lokaryns. If we send a strike force into Phobes' today, I don't think they will look kindly on an alliance tomorrow."

"So here I sit while the Lokaryn clan lords meet to decide on war and the Nehreton runs amok."

Ko'Doran tried to find the words to defuse his friend's anger, but none were to be had. "You know that your position requires you to act in certain ways."

"Yes it does," Cairo said, and then in realization to himself, "Yes it does."

He looked squarely at his friend.

"Tell no one about this. Peli Domar is to be brought to the rohnin as soon as possible."

The words caught in Ko'Doran's ear. "I understand," he replied, barely able to conceal his alarm.

The rohnin continued: "I want Silas Jorvan and Millika Tallam in my office within one hour. You have authorization to use portals—direct portals into the citadel from their locations. After I meet with them, I will not be disturbed until after the delegation returns from the execution zone. Do you understand?"

"Yes, sir. But both Jorvan and Tallam are retired from the Kuhbrik and somewhat aged. I know that you served with them extensively, but of what utility…"

"Trust me, old friend, and prepare yourself for anything. One hour. Go." As primare, Ko'Doran was used to being privy to his rohnin's innermost thoughts. Now, for the first time, he was not certain what those thoughts were. Donovus Ko'Doran stood for a moment hoping there was more to do or say that might make the situation better. But finding nothing, he turned and exited with the strong feeling that he would never see his friend again.

The privateer myst-clipper *Shicaine* has been destroyed in the Sluice. There were no survivors.

—Chumley's, Thorpe's, Kwyne joint statement

CHAPTER 32

Lokaryn Zone
Outer Reef Lighthouse

FULLY LOADED, THE *SHICAINE* SLOWLY made its way out of the Lokaryn Zone and out toward deep myst. The rhythm of the ship had changed since it crept though the great arches of this zone: She had come in a refugee and emerged as an emancipator renewed. The ship was alive with activity now. The chief had all shifts of his crews working to install the new power generators. Chapman had four additional computers loaded aboard and installed in his quarters. He remained there when not on duty, feverishly working on no one knew what. His solitude was occasionally interrupted by meetings with the chief that were notable for their volume and breaking of items. The chief did not seem to win even one of the "conversations." Seyschell settled easily into the copilot's chair. The crew felt that she was not so much sailing the ship as flying it. And then there was the captain. Captain Gedrick walked with a different walk now. It was hard to put a name to it, but he seemed to burn. Not in a way that consumed, but rather in a manner that lit a fire in all around him. And he laughed now. Easily and well.

A wave of insincere protest rippled through the senior staff as the ship neared the end of the second day out. The captain had called a meeting—the first senior staff meeting since they left the Lokaryn Zone. While it did take them from the projects to which they had so ardently committed themselves, it meant that they were a crew, not a temporary assemblage. It meant the beginning of something great.

The morning came and all were early to the meeting except for Gedrick. As the ship's bell rang 7 a.m., he walked in on the fourth chime and assumed his position at the head of a long sturdy mahogany table. They were all there: Seyschell, the chief, Nev, and the rest of the bridge crew. Soon, he hoped, Derring and Hemingway would be among their number.

"Let's begin the briefing," Gedrick said. "Despite the increasingly imaginative speculation of the crew, at this moment our destination remains Ravensford Zone."

Neville Chapman looked doubtful as he said, "So it really is Phobes'? Captain, might I suggest that Solipher's request is not a realistic one? An artificial in Phobes' Zone would stand very little chance of eluding detection. Along with the limitations of a Lokaryn that could only travel by night, I don't see how they could survive."

Gedrick allowed himself a small smile.

"Nighttime is when they schedule storms, so it won't interfere with daytime and farming."

"I see. The lightning would blind the sensor grid temporarily, allowing both to travel for brief windows of time.

"Yes," Gedrick said simply.

"You have an exceptional knowledge of the workings of Ravensford," the first officer said with a new insight into his captain.

Gedrick said nothing in response, but continued on.

"The mission, however, has changed somewhat. Solipher informed me just prior to leaving that we will be looking for only two targets now: one android and one Lokaryn. The third target was executed early yesterday by the Kwynians."

Seyschell and the chief stiffened.

"According to the best intelligence available at this time, a Lokaryn named J'Nath was executed after being apprehended in Kwyne feeding on the daughter of a prelate."

There was a stunned silence around the table. Lokaryns could be killed, but caught? No one had ever heard of such a thing. Caught and executed passed belief.

"How do you 'catch' someone who can move faster than your eye can track and turn into a mist at will?" Griz asked.

"Planning," Neville answered flatly.

Seyschell spoke quietly. "The ramifications are…"

"Unthinkable," Gedrick finished for her. "Yes, I know. But it leaves two primary targets intact and in need of extraction."

"If they are still viable, then they would be best served by heading to the outer districts, where they could pick up transport from a carrier sympathetic to lokaric trade," Neville thought aloud.

"Which the zone's government seem to have anticipated. While we have gone dark on our communications, we continue to monitor communications traffic. At least the official traffic—we have no net rogue to ferret out the coded communications. Ravensford announced this morning that they've closed their ports to all outgoing traffic," said Gedrick.

"The food shipments from Ravensford farms feed most of T'Amorach. How long can that continue?" Seyschell asked.

"A very good question, but one that does not concern us. Solipher's offer notwithstanding, our mission is clear. We will rescue as many members of the old *Shicaine* crew as possible, starting with those we know to be at greatest risk. The purpose of this meeting then is to determine the most strategic way to accomplish it."

Seyschell was the first to speak.

"Gedrick…Captain, I hate to be the one to bring this up…" She took a deep breath. "While I agree with the rescue completely, before we go too far with this, what about…the deal?"

The whole room fell silent as Gedrick stood in the moment—a moment he had thought about every day for five long years. Seyschell shifted uncomfortably, but it was the chief who spoke next.

"No one wants to say it? Fine, then I will."

The chief stood and leaned out over the table.

"That 'deal' was a misbegotten piece of excrement that we should have told those miserable humps to shove back up their trousers." He slammed his fist on the table as if to emphasize the thought. "If they didn't have Kisner and Cade we would have never agreed to it in the first place, and a deal ain't a deal when someone puts a gun to your head and says sign. I don't care if it saved everyone, and I don't care if they come after us with every ship in the fleet. We should right here, right now renounce that bastard's handiwork, sail out of here, and get our crew back."

As he finished, he glared around the room, defying anyone to debate him on the point.

Seyschell looked from the chief to Gedrick and said, "Yeah, I agree with the chief." She nodded her head, folded her hands in front of her, and sat back with a happy smile on her face. The chief sat down, feeling better than he had in a long time.

Nev spoke next. "While I find Seyschell's endorsement of the chief's 'trouser' plan reassuring, it might help those of us who aren't as familiar with the *Shicaine*'s previous diplomatic dealings if we knew what the deal was."

Gedrick looked around the table and knew that the time had come.

"Fair enough. You may have to suffer for this, so it's only right that you know why we're probably going to be hunted by just about every zone government in T'Amorach." He took a deep breath and dove in.

"Eight years ago years ago the *Shicaine* became part of the movement to assist sentient machines in reaching sanctuary in Rossums Zone. I had only been traveling the mysts for a few years as captain of my own ship, but I was doing pretty well. Then I met our chief engineer here…"

The chief engineer cleared his throat a few times in a vain attempt to warn Gedrick off this particular part of the narrative.

"Sorry, Chief, but it *is* part of the story. As I was saying, we met when some of my crew took him out of a dumpster with a couple of bullet holes in him."

"I gave better than I got is all I'll say about that." The chief scowled around the room.

"Of course you did, Chief. So we fixed him up and in return he decided to pay his debt by going to work on the *Shicaine*'s engines and mechanical systems." He paused a moment. "We haven't been able to shake him since." Gedrick couldn't resist the light poke at his curmudgeonly engineer.

The individuals around the table were caught off guard by the comment, and in a moment good-spirited laughter filled the room. All those who had been subjected to the salty old man's crusty behaviors now savored the fact that the chief couldn't respond to his captain the way he might respond to anyone else making that same comment. A wave of laughter crested and subsided.

"At least I can focus on what I'm doing for more than ten seconds at a time," the chief retorted. "Left in your hands, the *Shicaine*'s engines wouldn't get you away from dock even if the tide was with you."

Another wave of laughter, including Gedrick's.

"Right you are, Chief. I couldn't argue that point." He held up his hands palms out, indicating surrender. The chief sat back and folded his arms, glaring at anyone who smiled at him. Despite the seriousness of the meeting topic, a camaraderie between past and present was being forged around the table.

"Where was I?" Gedrick said. "Yes, so we went on, having acquired another stray. No one thought much about it; after all, everyone who travels the mysts in the clipper trade is a stray of one sort or another. Now, usually no one looks for a stray for very long. This time, however, someone did. Months after the chief had been shot and long after anyone rationally would assume or care that he was dead, we were intercepted in the Cerissian Straits by a man looking for a wounded engineer. The man's name was Tarro. He was an officer from the chief's old ship who had been looking for him with unreasonable tenacity. As it turned out, he was an intelligence officer.

"The two had served together on a ship that aided the movement and Tarro wasn't going to give up the search for his shipmate until he found either the body or the man. I have come to find that particular trait of his can be either very helpful or very irksome. When it became obvious that the chief had no intention of leaving the *Shicaine*, Tarro, being Tarro, reasoned that the obvious solution was that the *Shicaine* should become part of the underground."

Neville was the next to speak. "And you accepted this logic."

"Tarro has a way of working on you. When his mind is set, you might as well realize that he's probably going to get his way."

"As I recall, you always profited from his persistence, Captain," Seyschell offered innocently.

"Who's telling the story?" Gedrick said with a mock withering look.

"A man with an impaired ability to get to the point, as I see it," came the dry reply of the chief.

"Small wonder they only shot you twice. Well, Tarro not only recruited the *Shicaine*, he signed on as the mission intelligence officer, as well. From there, Seyschell joined us, Cade, Hennix, and—"

"And Hemingway and Derring," Seyschell continued.

"Yes."

"And Kisner," the chief finished.

Gedrick looked at the table for a moment. "Yes. And Kisner. We sailed for three or four years, I lost track. After a while, I couldn't remember a time when we weren't working for the movement, when we weren't all together. Every mission was something new, and it opened worlds hidden to most people. I—we—learned about things that we never knew existed."

Neville immediately interjected. "Such as?"

"Such as the fact that sentient machines form families. Somehow certain groups form a bond. No one knows if it's in manufacture or during imprinting on a biological, but it happens. When one is returned to the whole, it's like a long-lost child returning home. That's a topic for another time."

The mood in the room turned from one of quiet amazement to sobriety, as all knew that the end-time was coming in the story.

"Finally, about five years ago, something went wrong. I still to this day don't know what. The mission was as routine as these things get—an easy pickup, an easy transport—but somehow they found us. Cade and Kisner were caught and the *Shicaine* was surrounded. For three days a standoff ensued. We had powerful friends in some of the zones, and Rossums even threatened war if we were destroyed. Finally it came down to a deal. Appropriate for a Merchants' Zone ship, right? We would be set free, but we would have to disband, and if we were ever caught together again, any of us, we would be executed without benefit of trial. No outcasting, no asylum in the Lokaryn Zone, just immediate execution by whatever means were handy. And not just the ones caught together—everyone would be hunted down and killed. So five years ago, the crew of the *Shicaine* was dropped one by one at their destinations never to see one another again. If they met in the street, they would keep walking. No contact, ever. I was allowed to keep the chief on. They didn't think of him as a participant, and I convinced them that I couldn't run the ship without him."

"So how do we know that this isn't what's happening now?" Griz asked. "The attempts at killing all of you? Perhaps two of your crew couldn't stay away from each other and now they're hunting you all down?"

"That though had occurred to me, but when they come for us it will be a massive mobilization. If they wanted Seyschell, they would have placed a Mastiff-class battle platform outside the lagoon, and leveled the rock wall and everything in twenty km of her village in a strike. She wouldn't have survived. There would have been forty ships chasing the *Shicaine*. And they wouldn't have used bounty hunters as their first line to hunt Seyschell in the Bitch."

"So if we reunite the crew—"

"Chumley's, Thorpe's, McAllister's, Kwyne, and Merchants' will all hunt us down. Lokaryns', Thieves', and Rossums will have to refuse us sanctuary. And anyone offering us aid will be executed as if they were members of the crew."

"Charming," Neville said, with typical understatement.

"Any thoughts?" Gedrick inquired.

Griz spoke next. "Captain, I know that I am here by your good graces."

"And I by your crack shot. Griz, I consider you a part of this crew at this point, though I have to say we've never had an official bartender before."

"We've had plenty of unofficial ones," the chief said offhandedly, as he continued to glare about the room. Gedrick rewarded the remark with a disapproving look.

"You asked for thoughts," the chief said in defense.

"Go on, Griz."

"Are there any contacts in Ravensford Zone that they might seek out?"

"There were a handful, but the ones that we knew stopped when we were captured. If they had been discovered, their lands would have been confiscated and they would have been outcast. I think that they would take Derring in; the question is whether Derring would seek them out."

Seyschell answered, "She'd try not to, but I don't see where she has a choice."

"I agree," the chief said simply.

"Well, then, we're off to see the Klemms."

"I hate to be the spoiler here," Neville said, "but with the official ports closed to traffic we'll need to find a way into the zone. And this being Ravensford, I don't see many options to sneak a ship of this tech level in undetected. We'll need someone with an impressive knowledge of backmyst channels and squirrelly ways into the zone.

Seyschell and the chief looked at each other knowingly, and said one name in unison: "Cade."

"I know where Cade can be found," Gedrick said. Cade had settled down, making him an easy one to keep a tab on. Most of the rest of the crew would be far harder to find.

"And he's on our way," Gedrick said with a smile. It was good to be back.

The greatest of battles, wars, or even empires have been won or lost in a single moment.

—Dhio Tyol, second marshal of Chumley's Zone

CHAPTER 33

Ravensford Zone
Winter Arc

DERRING AND HEMINGWAY TRAVELED QUICKLY now that they were in the inner districts.

They moved across the landscape like moonshadows fleeing the sun. Their senses were far superior to those of the farmers and workers they encountered; however, detouring off the roads to avoid these encounters proved time-consuming. While the storms still offered an electronic cloak for Hemingway, the sensor grid was growing stronger. The distance had seemed so short when they first saw it marked off at the outer-crossing cabin. Now it felt as if it were growing longer by the moment. Only a few hours' darkness remained as they came upon their destination.

The frustrations of the journey melted away as the two found themselves looking at another traveler's cabin. Cautiously, Derring circled and then approached the structure. A lamp hanging beside the front door beckoned welcome. The cabin was bordered by a large forest, which made for plentiful firewood and hunting. Though her heightened senses could not detect anything nearby, a foreboding took hold of her. She was in some small way comforted that Hemingway, with his abilities to perceive parts of the spectrum unavailable to her, had not raised an alarm. The only irregularity she sensed was the faint scent of blood. Human to be sure, distant and not exactly fresh, but recent. Breathing deeply, she could sense no ill intent. It was only a small amount, as if perhaps a traveler had injured her hand cutting trees or a hunter injured himself dressing a kill. Either was a very reasonable explanation, but something still tugged at the edges of her mind. She shook her head and refocused on the task at hand. Distraction could be fatal at this point.

Stealing toward the cabin, with a touch as light as a master thief's, she turned her gaze downward and was rewarded with a single quilt: Storm at Sea again. This time it indicated a northeasterly route, with a lighthouse instead of the eight-point star that they had found on the previous quilt. It stood for haven, which meant that they were close to home.

Derring was filled with a sense of relief and of loss. Once they were "rescued" they would again have to part ways. She cursed the damned deal that had been made so many years ago.

"Gedrick," she said aloud though quietly. The anger in her voice reflected in her expression, but her face softened a moment before Hemingway came up beside her.

"If you're still so angry with him, kill him the next time you see him." Hemingway prodded her.

"The thought had occurred to me. Then again, I've thought of un-plugging *your* power supply more than once."

Hemingway formulated a response but stiffened before he could get it out. A soft popping noise in the distance signaled their ruin.

Derring reacted instantly to the cue. Men were coming and she took the scent of bright metal. The pieces fell into place in her mind, but she did not have time to explain. Grabbing Hemingway's hand, she instinctively darted toward the blood that she had sensed earlier.

"Where the hell are you going Derring? If they're coming for us, let's stand and fight now while we can. Once the storm fades and the sun comes up we have no chance!"

"Trust me," she said cryptically.

The two scrambled through the underbrush of the forest pell-mell. The pursuers behind them were now joined by more in front of and to the sides of the lokaryn and android. Their arrival was punctuated by the soft popping sounds of portals opening, harkening the pair's imminent capture.

"We're ringed!"

"The last cabin was the setup for the trap and we fell for it."

Hemingway stopped suddenly and dropped his gear.

"Here as well as anywhere else, Der. It's a pretty place to die. For them I mean."

She grabbed Hemingway's arm again and yanked him forward.

"Derring! Where the hell are we going?"

His question was answered by a sight that truly surprised him. Impaled by a portal crystal, on a massive hemlock tree, was a quilt with the Fly Away pattern. There was no mistaking the meaning: Run.

The two looked at each other.

"It could be the coup de grace in a well-constructed trap. If we use this, it could drop us straight into the Badlands, or a cell or…"

She pulled the crystal from the bark of the tree, then ran the length of it under her nose and breathed deeply.

"Klemm put this here."

"You can tell it's Klemm's blood?"

"No, I've never had his blood, but I can still sense the blood of a righteous man and if the person who put this here had any malevolent intention, I would sense that. Can you think of any other righteous men running around in a dark forest staking quilts to trees with portal crystals and blessing them with their own blood?" she asked.

Hemingway thought about that for a moment. It seemed an eternity as the troops of Ravensford closed in. Only a few hundred yards now stood between them.

"Good point."

Reaching into her backpack, Derring pulled a flat strip of metal from of a piece of equipment, while Hemingway worked on cleaning the crystal of the blood, dirt, and bark.

"Make sure it's as clean as possible or it won't resonate properly," Derring said as she worked on flattening the metal.

"Really? You mean a crystal has to be clean in order to resonate?

Wow! Is there no end to the knowledge you've accumulated over the centuries?"

"No, I don't think so," she returned sarcastically as she took the crystal from him.

The troops in pursuit slowed down as they moved in on their quarry.

Derring placed the metal on the ground, then set the crystal on it, balanced on its point. She pushed her face near to it and hummed softly. Unlike the one in Kwyne, which had been tampered with, this crystal quickly began to glow.

Energy burst forth in every direction and illuminated the woods with shards of light so intense that the troops who caught direct sight of the spectacle were blinded.

The portal coalesced in an instant, and those not affected by the initial outpouring of light opened fire, severely damaging the tree bark all around them.

Hemingway, ever the skeptic, paused one moment at the threshold of the portal and turned to Derring before entering. "You know they could have killed Klemm and used his blood."

"True," Derring said, and punched Hemingway as hard as she could in the shoulder, knocking him into the portal.

The howl of pain was lost in the inkiness of the opening. Knowing he was right, she smiled a grim smile and stepped through herself.

They exited the other side some ten feet in the air over an empty field. Portals worked relative to one another, so placing the exit several feet above anything that might be passing by was a reasonable, if painful, strategy to avoid materializing inside a wandering cow.

Her reflexes allowed her to land without injury. She did not anticipate the blow that was about to come and could in no way deflect it as Hemingway punched her in the shoulder just as hard as she had hit him.

"Ow," she said, startled, and began rubbing her arm. Hemingway smirked and nodded his head with a slight tilt.

"I think we're close to Klemm's farm. The storm was over a while ago and the grid will be back up soon."

"Any other good news?"

"Yes, we lost a lot of night by coming west in that portal. Let's go."

They sprinted across the fields. Hemingway could feel the sensor grid like a faint and inconsistent breeze across his skin as one by one the crystal nodes came into harmonic resonance. Soon they would vibrate smoothly with one another and his electronic signature would be detected. Derring's situation was worse: the first tendrils of dark purple were stealing across the sky.

"There!" Hemingway shouted. "The silo, go!"

The tendrils of light progressed to blue, then red, while the gentle breeze of the grid became a persistent itch.

They covered the distance and began to climb up the side of a grain silo, which served as a safehouse. It was located on a fallow section of the Klemm farm. A four-foot-high bolt-hole below a false floor in its upper reaches provided a hiding place that no one had detected in all its years of use.

The sensor grid was monitored at the region's security center. There, a young woman stood with her eyes closed and her hands held palm down over a tabletop map of the area. The grid began to detect something...aberrant.

HEMINGWAY WAS FIRST INTO THE silo and began placing the field dampeners. Derring followed closely and leaped half the distance up the ladder, climbing quickly while turning to look out over the farm to see if there was anything of concern before they shut themselves away.

"Derring, come on!" Hemingway shouted.

The grid resonated more distinctly as the young woman's hands circled more specifically to an area. Suddenly the disruption was gone. Her hands came up off the table abruptly. Her supervisor, who had taken an interest in the sudden activity over the table, looked at her with a furrowed brow.

Miles away, Hemingway sat back as the dampening field flickered to life. On the ladder, Derring caught a most peculiar sight. Luginda

Woods had been looking at the silo, as if anticipating their arrival. On seeing the activity, she ran, seemingly frightened, across the narrow bridge that separated the Klemm farm and the Woods farm. Derring watched with a puzzled expression, a moment too long: the first ray of sunlight struck her exposed hand as she clung to the ladder's rung.

Excruciating pain shot through her as every muscle in her body spasmed—she couldn't even scream. Before she was remotely aware of the sensation of falling she was already halfway to the ground. She landed in the soft dirt with a loud thud, disoriented. The sun's light raced down the side of the silo after her.

Hearing the impact, Hemingway flew out of the doorway of the silo. The sensor grid, now fully established, lit up as Hemingway expended every ounce of energy he had to move as quickly as possible. He dropped down the full height of the silo, landing astride Derring, who was groggily try to grab one of the silo ladder's rungs. Wrapping her cloak about her as best he could, he began climbing back up the ladder. He too could see Woods running in the distance, but he focused on getting back into the shelter.

At the region's security center, the young woman quickly placed her hands back over the last position they had occupied. Closing her eyes again, she narrowed the circle.

Hemingway flung Derring into the silo and, after slamming the door behind them, dragged her across the floor to the trapdoor. Together they rolled into the opening.

The signal at the security center flickered one last time as he reached up to seal the trapdoor behind them. The supervisor knew there had not been an exact lock, but there was enough to report to command.

Derring lay on the floor unconscious, Hemingway cursed, and many miles away security operations began to mobilize.

The past is gaining on you minute by minute.

—McAllister's Zone saying

CHAPTER 34

THE COUPLE SAT AT THE dining room table sorting out bills and finances as they had on the last day of every month of the four years of their marriage. He, the older of the two by fifteen years, guided his young wife in financial matters. She, a quick study, had proven to have a knack for business and had made their fortunes grow considerably. Yet even in the post-Cataclysmic world the truism remained: Where there is society and government, there are forms to fill out.

And so it was that she typed away at the console, filling out a form to open a new set of accounts. A dull scene in an everyday life.

Name, the screen prompted.

Jillison Farmer, she typed in reply. Farmer was a family name from antiquity.

Marital status, it next queried.

Her husband looked over her shoulder. She felt his hand trace across her back and start to move toward her chest.

"I'd be happy to put 'Divorced' if you don't let me finish this form," she teased. His hand froze in mock terror, and then he lifted his palm up onto his fingers and scampered it back to its starting place like a frightened spider. Next he gently touched her cheek as he moved off to tuck their youngest child into bed.

Name of spouse, the form prompted. *Cadence Farmer*, she typed. Her husband had taken her name when they married, his name being one of the many things he had been forced to abandon to the past. He was lucky to have kept "Cade."

Address, number of children, ages of children, number of years married...

The form went on and on, and she answered questions until she was interrupted by a knock on the front door.

"I've got it," Cade shouted down the stairs.

Jillison heard the sound of the door opening and hushed talking followed by a silence.

"Who is it, Cade?" she called out, wondering why the door wasn't closed or the caller wasn't being ushered in. There was no response.

She got up from the table and went out to the front. She slid up under his arm as she often did when neighbors came to call. But the familiarity of the moment changed immediately when she laid eyes on the callers.

The male was of average height with blue eyes and brown hair that he had drawn back under a wide-brimmed hat. His cloak obscured the rest of his physique, making him appear somewhat nondescript. But it was the female that gave it away. She stood no more than five feet tall, with blond hair and green eyes. Had they called separately, Jillison might have missed it. But from Cade's description these two could only be Gedrick and Seyschell, the captain and copilot of the *Shicaine.*

Jillison knew of her husband's past when she married him. He had been honest with her, and she knew this day could come. The presence of Gedrick and Seyschell meant that Cade was in danger and, by extension, their family was in danger.

She knew what he had to do.

Cade turned to his young wife and kissed her.

"You know what to do and where to go. I *will* come back to you, to our life. I love you," he said.

He nodded to Gedrick and Seyschell. Then, taking nothing more than the clothes on his back and the bag that he always kept near the door for this moment, Cade walked into the past.

Jillison watched as her husband disappeared into the night. There in the doorway, she stared into the darkness for uncounted time until finally she returned to the form and slowly moved the computer cursor back several positions.

Marital status, it inquired.

Widowed, she entered.

Cook until the screaming stops, then season to taste.

—Translated from fragments found in a Badlands archaeological dig

CHAPTER 35

AND SO, UNCONSCIOUS, DERRING DREAMED.

The dreams of Lokaryns are the hardest things for a new convert to deal with. Many learn to live with them, some come to love them. Not so with Derring. For most, the loss of the sun, feeding from the living, and the unrelenting cold were only small inconveniences in exchange for the unspeakable power attained. The dreams, however, were another matter.

The first night after conversion, many new Lokaryns simply went insane from the images and had to be slaughtered. Many more ran into the daylight of their own accord. Since they had never fed, they did not experience the violent release of energy that older Lokaryns do when exposed to sunlight. The initiates simply ran as they slowly roasted, presumably to death. No one ever really knew. Who wanted to chase a mad Lokaryn into the sunlight?

The dreams were distilled from millennia of unspeakable acts, each generation of the shared unconsciousness building on the fetid psychic compost of the last, improving it and feasting upon it. The potency of the victim's emotions, thoughts, and feelings cured with time to an acrid blanket enveloping the sleeping mind.

Derring's mind.

She awoke violently, sitting bolt upright, drenched in the sweat of fever dreams. She immediately felt her sternum where light had struck her. It still burned, but was well on the way to being completely healed. Birds took flight from the rafters of the silo, frightened by the disturbance in the absolute quiet.

"Are you OK?" came Hemingway's voice in the dark. Derring spun rapidly, breathing heavily.

"What time is it?" she asked through the haze of her waking mind.

"Five."

Derring nodded, rubbing her face with the palms of her hands.

"Same dream, Der?"

Derring's aspect took on an expression that crossed many years and lifetimes. Hemingway had his answer without a word passing between them.

"Derry." The voice of a ghost called to her from a time before the cataclysm.

"Derry," it persisted.

"Hey Derry," her brother always began, knowing that she hated the nickname. Over three hundred years and his voice still rang in her ears as if he had just spoken the words.

Derring shut her eyes.

"What do the boy Lokaryns call a girl Lokaryn being chased by Kwynians while on her period?" Her brother would withhold the punch line until she responded. "Brae, don't you dare," she would say with mock annoyance in her voice.

"A Movable Feast!"

Then he'd laugh his head off at his own joke and her insincere protests to it. Inevitably she'd erupt into laughter as well.

"Brae, someday Mom and Dad are going to catch you with your little jokes and you won't feel so smart."

"Someday, but not today and not out here. We're camping in the great outdoors where nature rules, not parents."

"We're only a few hundred yards from the house, world explorer. Don't get too full of yourself."

"If I can't see the house, then we might as well be in another world."

In times past, Brae and Derring might have ventured relatively far from home, but not now. A war with a neighboring country threatened, and their home was close to the border. It was expected that, as always, the confrontation would be settled with diplomacy. Still, the whole family would be leaving this place tomorrow and heading away for safer regions until things simmered down.

"Speaking of feasts, how about some lunch?" Derring asked as she set up their tent.

She fought back the next memory, but it came through anyway.

Brae realized that he had left the bag with their food. "Nice job, dookhead," she shouted to him as he began the trek back to their house to retrieve it. Though there was no way she could have known that in a mere twenty minutes, the threatened war would begin with an attack on their complex. She regretted that these were the last words that she had spoken to her brother.

She could still hear the sound of that first explosion. Unsure of what had caused it, she broke into a dead run for the house. She wasn't even halfway there when she saw the smoke billowing into the sky. Fighting her instinct to run even faster, she remembered what her father had taught her. Use caution. Assess the situation. Be stealthy. And so, at a mind-numbingly slow pace, she carefully trod the remaining distance. What she found when she got there was horrifying: houses in flames and the moans of the dying. In a matter of moments, the entire settlement had been decimated. Her mind spun. Why would someone do this? It was not a military target, it was not… Then she spotted Brae.

He was lying on the ground about fifty feet from the burning ruin that had been their house, and the area around him was dyed a dark crimson. Forgetting her father's teachings and the possible danger she risked by ignoring them, she made her way to Brae as quickly as possible. He had been bayoneted and had lost a great deal of blood. He was not moving, and when she checked for a pulse she felt it fading.

It was at this moment that Derring realized that she was alone in the world. Her parents were consumed by the inferno that had taken the house, and her brother lay dead. Time would not heal these wounds. She could feel their deaths through the dreams. This was the form that her lokaric dreams took: each lick of the flame against the flesh of her parents and each inch of the blade as it pierced her beloved brother. Worst of all, the laughter and satisfaction of those committing the slaughter rang clearly in her ears.

It was in this moment when it all threatened to consume her that she felt a poke in her ribs and heard the voice of Hemingway reaching into the depths to pull from the abyss.

"How many Kwynians does it take to change a light bulb?"

"Oh Hemingway, please, don't..." she began, hoping to cut the punch line off at the pass. It was to no avail.

"Twenty. They form a prayer cell and pray all night for Thecla to send light. It works every time."

In spite of her self, Derring began to laugh through the tears that had formed in her eyes. She sniffed a few times and smiled at Hemingway.

"Do you believe that androids can reincarnate?"

"Yeah, I hope to be a vibrator with a fusion battery in my next life. Listen, I hate to be the here-and-now guy in this operation, but the sun's going down soon and we still don't have a next step. My guess would be that Klemm is at the farm waiting for us, but he could be waiting until dark to come out here in case there's any troub—"

Hemingway's sentence stopped short. Somebody was approaching the silo. Not one but two people, male and female. He strained to make out the voices as they approached.

"I don't know the male," Hemingway said in a low voice.

"I don't either, but the female's voice sounds somehow familiar. I can't quite place it." Derring was puzzled. It was as if the answer was staring her in the face, but she couldn't quite grasp it.

They're climbing up! Hemingway mouthed. Derring silently nodded, her pulse quickening, such as it was.

The two became immobile and were more silent than the noises made by the structure creaking in the evening wind.

"OK, we're alone. What did you want to talk to me about and why do we have to do it up here?" the female asked. Her voice was youthful but in no way immature.

"I wanted to be where we wouldn't get caught," the male stated with a certain bravado.

"Well, that shouldn't be hard, because we're not going to be doing anything to get caught *at*. You said you wanted to talk, Timan, nothing more."

"Lyrie," the male began, and abruptly stopped crossing over to the silo's access door. In that moment's pause, an expression of realization came across Derring's face.

Lyrie and Timan, grown up! Derring mouthed. She had not recognized Lyrie's voice, for the last time she had heard it was when the child was twelve years old, a year before the Shicaine crew broke up. Now, almost six years later, Derring marveled at how much she sounded like a woman. Hemingway smiled at that.

Mother hen, Hemingway teased, mouthing the words. Despite herself Derring felt a welling-up inside. She had held Lyrie and her younger brother on her lap many nights around the Klemm family table while they plotted and planned the many rescues and conduits for runaway artificials. The Klemm family could never know the profound effect it had had on her when they first accepted her enough to allow her to hold their children. On more than one occasion she had let herself imagine them as her own.

The boy started to talk again as he looked out of the door to see if they had been followed. "Ren wouldn't follow us up here, would he?"

"Of course he would, Timan, if I hadn't given him a distraction," Lyrie said, without much in the way of an explanation.

"What did you do?" Timan asked.

"Timan, we don't have a lot of time."

"Sure we do, our parents aren't going to miss us, they're all in the kitchen talking endlessly about whatever. The Woodses and are there too."

Lyrie knew what they would be talking about, but said nothing. The conversation she had overheard still confused her.

Derring and Hemingway looked up toward where the two were

talking. Every movement above them caused a small avalanche of dust to shower down. The most recent indicated that Timan was crossing to where Lyrie sat.

He stood next to the young woman, and through a small opening in the floor, the Lokaryn could see that the young man was looking down at her.

"Lyrie," he began quietly, "my love for you has grown so much, I scarcely think my heart can hold it."

It was at this moment that Hemingway's facial expression began to change from one of bemusement to what seemed at first like a mild case of nausea. It started with a furrowed brow, reminiscent of a person who, on sitting back from a meal, first takes stock of their well-being and finds that there is a distant, but definite discomfort.

Oh no, he mouthed to Derring, who despite their dire circumstances couldn't help but be amused at the android's reaction. Despite his wicked humor, which he unleashed often, Hemingway was not one to suffer fools gladly.

"I see your name in the stars and in the animals' eyes as I tend them," Timan continued.

The animals' eyes? the android mouthed in horror.

Hemingway's discomfort grew with each syllable. The furrowed brows were joined by darting eyes as if he were looking for the source of the abdominal discomfort that had passed from a hint of pain to a more present feeling. Derring watched him, enjoying the torture with a satisfied expression on her face.

"Our hearts were meant to beat together…"

The more the young man spoke, the farther down Hemingway's face the feeling traveled. His mouth now turned downward and his eyes widened as well. The sensation also traveled downward through what would have been his bowels, were he human. He began to shake his head. Still the young man droned on.

"I feel as if I must proclaim my love."

Unable to manually disconnect his hearing circuits, Hemingway reached into a tool pouch and held out a screwdriver to Derring. He gave her a pleading look, which she answered with a smile, a cocked eyebrow, and a small swing of her head indicating No. He shut his eyes and swung his head back and forth, more and more rapidly, trying to evade the sound waves.

"I wrote you a song…"

Hemingway's eyes snapped open.

"That really wasn't necessary," Lyrie offered in the vain hope that she would be spared his attempts at melody. While Timan was good man and an able farmer, she had heard his attempts at singing in the tradition of those who wandered the lands singing for meals. It was not pretty.

The young man began wistfully. And quite off key.

"The animals' eyes…"

"Oh for the love of…" Hemming could not contain the words, but immediately knew the drastic mistake he had made.

"Ren?" Timan shouted out. "Where are you? Get out here right…"

Lyrie interrupted him. "That wasn't Ren, get out of here quickly! Tell my father and the others! I'll secure the door."

Derring acted fast, with a gamble that relied on the memory of a young woman to whom she was most likely an imaginary friend of childhood.

" 'Tayshaw,' do not leave!" Derring said through the floor.

Lyrie froze. The disembodied voice called her by a name she had not heard since childhood. Since a dream in childhood. It had faded as the fancy of a child who imagines faraway things.

Timan was scrambling down the ladder, but Lyrie remained at the top, caught halfway between shutting the hatch and opening it to break hold of the dream.

"Derring?" she called out to the voice in disbelief.

"Yes, it's me."

"Why can't I see you? Where are you?"

"I cannot show myself to you yet."

"While the sun is out. I remember. But that wasn't your voice I heard just now, Derring. This isn't real, is it?"

"Yes, it is real."

Lyrie looked out over the horizon. The sun had just set, and she looked back inside the silo, allowing for her eyes to adjust. There, as if materializing in front of her, stood a young woman with raven-dark hair and blue eyes, her face framed in a cloak.

Lyrie ran to Derring and threw her arms around the Lokaryn.

"Derring, we have to catch the 'cowsinger' before he causes any problems," said Hemingway.

Lyrie's eyes went wide.

"You're the one they're looking for! You're an artificial!"

"Android. Introductions later. The boy?"

"I can take care of Timan," Lyrie said, moving quickly to the door.

"Timan! Come back. It was Ren after all. He..."

She never had the opportunity to finish the sentence. A flash of light came from the direction of the family house, and a moment later she heard an enormous explosion.

And word of the child Messiah's miracles began to sweep through Kwyne.

—Tor' Manat
Kwynian Sacred Writings

CHAPTER 36

Nehreton yacht
Myst marker 7

"WHAT THE HELL IS THAT?" the pilot said to the navigator, as she pointed out the glowing red cloud twenty degrees off the starboard bow. "Looks to be about five miles out."

"Never seen anything quite like it," the navigator responded. Though they both were experienced enough to know that the atmosphere and the myst often interacted in unusual ways, this was something new.

"It's actually kind of pretty," she remarked, noting it in the log.

"Yeah," he said. "I'll adjust course, I think this is close enough."

The pilot went back to checking the readings on the ship's instruments.

The ship continued silently through the myst, heading back toward Kwyne. The execution of the unholy had been carried out, and, in keeping with Thecla's teachings, the prelates were sequestered in the ship's chapel, deep in prayer. In the large reception room where the families and other witnesses traveled, the mood was decidedly more festive. Large trays of the finest traditional delicacies were offered, and the drinks flowed freely. The crowd broke into applause as a large slow-roasted boar was placed on the main table.

In the chapel, Var Kragen intoned, "May Thecla bless us for the work that we have done here today."

"And wash away our sins," the prelates responded.

Two miles off the starboard bow, the cloud accelerated toward the ship.

Out on the deck of the yacht, Andan Javik, guard first class, and his superior Sergeant Lojar Halre stood watch. "Did you get any of the boar?" Javik asked. "It's the best I've ever had."

"No doubt," the sergeant replied, knowing that this was Javik's first cruise aboard a Nehreton yacht. Excess was the rule. Halre had experienced many of these voyages and many servings of the first-class food.

Javik continued, "I would do more of these details for the food alone!"

The two men shared a laugh. Halre knew that this was one of the easiest details, with excellent food and double pay. These were not particularly dangerous duties and selection for the assignment was based more on etiquette and discretion than law enforcement ability. There was rarely trouble, with the exception of the occasional reveler who had had too much drink.

Up on the bridge, the pilot noted that although they were navigating away from the phenomenon, it seemed to be catching up with the ship.

"Adjust the course another ten degrees to port," she instructed the navigator, and made an additional note in her log. The pair remained unconcerned. The ship was well protected from atmospheric disturbances and the most it would amount to was a rough ride.

Kragen lifted a goblet from the chapel altar and said, "Let all who defile the sacred soil of Kwyne know the swiftness of her justice!"

"And may Thecla bless all who defend her!" the prelates intoned. They raised their glasses in response and drank deeply.

Uninterested in the boar, a small girl did battle with her brother over the outcome of a game: "I won that round!" the little girl protested. "Did not, did not!" her brother responded as he pocketed the ball. "Give it back," his sister yelled. "Not until you admit I'm the winner," he said.

The cloud was now one mile off the starboard bow.

"I heard that the Lokaryn was almost in a stupor when they found it," said the wife of one prelate.

"Well, I heard that it was feeding on that poor girl," said another. "Such a pity…so young."

The two women looked at each other with genuine sadness in their eyes.

"Can you imagine anything worse than having one of those…things…" The first woman could not finish the thought.

A half mile off the bow, the cloud started to dissipate.

"Well, whatever it is, it's starting to break up," the navigator noted. "It looks like a lot of fireflies now."

"Or eyes," the pilot replied. "If you ask me it's a little bit creepy and I don't like that we aren't shaking it."

"I wouldn't worry about it," the navigator said. "It's probably just supercharged myst. It's rare, but I know at least one person who's seen it. Supposedly it reverses polarity, which could mean that our ion skimmers are attracting it."

"I suppose," she said, unconvinced.

Down below, Sergeant Lojar Halre began his patrol of the ship's decks. Javik remained on post to rescue any drunks that threatened to fall overboard on this side of the ship.

"See you in a minute," he said.

He slowly walked from the port side to the bow, where he paused to light a cigarette. It would still be another hour before the ship docked in Kwyne and he could go have a drink of his own. Once he had done so, he'd regale the patrons with the story of the lokaric execution. Most of them would never have seen an actual Lokaryn, so the chances that he'd drink for free would dramatically improve. Throughout T'Amorach, a good story was always appreciated, and Kwyne was no exception.

The cloud was now two hundred yards off the starboard bow and closing in fast.

His cigarette finished, the sergeant continued his walk, rounding the bow and moving to the starboard side of the ship.

It was then that he saw it. It was moving fast and it looked angry. Worse yet, he knew there was nothing he could do to get out of the way.

Five seconds before the swarm reached the rail, he realized what it was. It was something that he had only read about, something that would likely have earned him a lifetime of free drinks. If only.

"Holy…" was the last word he uttered as he was hit by the full impact of the invaders.

For every political action there is an opposite and often unequal reaction.

—Tomanus Jungar, former rohnin of Kwyne

CHAPTER 37

HAD HE BEEN ALIVE TO tell the tale, the sergeant would have indeed drunk free for the rest of his life. He would have regaled the patrons with the ferocity of the attack, or the dread he had felt when he realized the nature of the glowing red swarm that had descended on the ship. But mostly he would have tried to relay the intensity of the pain. It was a pain that few if any had ever experienced—the pain of literally being torn apart as a Lokaryn changes from noncorporeal to corporeal form at the moment that it passes through your body.

It was a pain that the sergeant knew, if only for a moment.

The ship lurched on the myst as Lokaryn after Lokaryn assumed corporeal form and exploded through the walls of the reception room.

"What the hell was that?" the navigator screamed, as the pilot did her best to maintain control of the vessel.

"Let us pr—" concluded Var Kragen, as the ship was pitched, throwing the prelates around the chapel like rag dolls.

"Wow," the eight-year-old boy uttered in astonishment as his younger sister clung to his leg. He had always wanted to see a Lokaryn.

Within a matter of seconds, a cadre of thirty Lokaryns occupied the reception room.

In the ship's chapel, Var Kragen assisted his fellow prelates to their feet. He was not sure what had happened, but his best guess was that the navigation system had somehow failed and that they had hit a reef.

There were very few other logical explanations out on the mysts.

Andan Javik checked the other members of the security detail, most of who stood dumbfounded. Those who were moving were either fumbling with their weapons or ducking for cover against an enemy who was not armed. Without hesitation, he drew his weapon and fired at the closest of the Lokaryns, scoring a direct hit. The Lokaryn crumpled to the ground, and this brought the team to action. Immediately, they opened fire.

Kragen heard the discharging of weapons and knew that something serious was happening. He quickly made his way to the door, weapon in hand, only to find that it would not budge.

He immediately began searching for an alternate exit.

It was the Lokaryns' turn now. With a speed that was nothing short of astounding, they managed to avoid the security team's fire, and in less than a heartbeat were upon them. The air was soon filled with the sounds of screaming and snapping spines as they quickly dispatched the inexperienced team. Had they been Kuhbrikian soldiers it might have been a fairer fight.

Amid the broken bodies and waning moans of the dying, a Lokaryn stepped to the center of the room.

"Look at this," he exclaimed. "Our Kwynian friends are having a feast! Do you think they'd consider us rude if we helped ourselves?"

A female Lokaryn came forward.

"Why no, Gar' Dugan. I don't believe they would. They are, after all, well noted for their hospitality."

"Well, that is true," he replied. "Perhaps we should take a look at what's on the menu." The pair began to pace the room, inspecting the vast tables of food. In contrast to Gar' Dugan's mock joviality, the Kwynian families huddled together in fear. They had heard stories about lokaric feeding frenzies. After strolling around the room for a few minutes, the pair stopped in front of the pile of crippled soldiers who lay twitching on the floor.

"How kind. They even took our dietary needs into consideration," she said lustily, licking her lips for effect.

"By all means indulge yourself," the leader said as he waved the rest of the team in. They'd have to share, but everyone would get a taste.

Kragen found the intercom and slammed his hand on the button. "Security team, report at once."

"I'm sorry," a foreign voice replied. "They're indisposed at the moment. Who is this calling please?"

"What do you mean indisposed," Kragen demanded. "This is Prelate Kragen and you'd best…"

"I don't believe you are in any position to take that tone with me, Var Kragen," the voice replied. "We have your ship, and your security forces are in the process of being neutralized. Consider them casualties of war if you will."

"Kwyne is not at war," Kragen replied coolly.

"You do not consider executing our citizens an act of war?" Gar' Dugan said incredulously.

The picture clarified for Kragen. The situation was more serious than he had imagined, and it was of the utmost importance that he maintain a bearing of authority. He was, after all, the ranking governmental official on the ship.

"I consider the execution of the infidel to be a justified response to an incursion that violated the sovereignty of Kwyne and an attack on one of our citizens. If any act of war has been committed it most assuredly has not been by us."

A few moments passed, and Kragen spoke again: "Well?"

"Sorry, I was having a bite while you rambled on with that terrific little speech. It's true. Kwynians do taste like chicken."

The Lokaryn paused for effect and then became serious.

"What should be of greater concern to you, Prelate Kragen, is what happens next. Your security forces are forfeit, and should we meet any opposition as we neutralize them, so will be everyone on this ship. We are, however, willing to spare your children and families if you meet our demands."

"On what authority do you dare make demands," Kragen responded.

The Lokaryn replied, "On the authority that I have control of your ship. We have already determined that there will be casualties. We are now merely negotiating how many there shall be."

Kragen surveyed the room. His fellow prelates watched him intently, but none came forward to offer leadership. *Typical,* he thought. *Do nothing and later argue about what the right course of action should have been.*

"Speak your 'demands,'" he said aloud, "but understand that each life you take will bring consequences upon you and your zone."

"I think not," Gar' Dugan replied. "First, you will demolish the execution chamber.

"Second, your rohnin and each member of your Nehreton will submit a blood sample to us. Should you engage in any aggression against us, we will have your essence and we *will* track you.

"Finally, the Lokaryn that you executed was one hundred and eighty years old. You will turn over one hundred and eighty of your citizens to our feeding chambers."

"Outrageous!" Kragen responded.

The Lokaryn ignored him.

"It matters not which ones, but you have seven days to comply. To ensure your cooperation we will be taking your family members with us. They will not be harmed, but should you fail to meet this final stipulation, they will enter our feeding chambers instead."

Jarden Vander, prelate of the Twenty-third Arc, spoke up. "They're bluffing," he said. "They misted onto the ship, there is no way that they can mist off with mortals."

"True," Kragen responded. "But a zone that is responsible for producing the majority of T'Amorach's crystals is most certainly capable of setting up a portal, and one with a great deal more stability than can typically be purchased on the black market."

Before Vander could respond, the sound of agony rose in the room next door. It grew in intensity and each new sound was more sickening than the last. The Lokaryns had turned the volume up on the speakers as loud as it would go and the cacophony swelled. Men vomited as they fell to their knees. Kragen took a silent vow as he stood with his face burning, impotent to act. For most of the prelates it was the most horrific sound they had ever heard or could ever have conceived. Except for Var Kragen. He was Kuhbrik, he knew better. There were far worse.

And thus, locked in the chapel with no means to stop the carnage, Kragen did the only thing he could.

"Let us pray," he began.

The most sacred of all things to a Seb-Ichi is the joining of the warrior to a bondling. It will be their weapon in battle, assuming any form they can conceive of; it will be their eternal companion and protector. If separated, both will most certainly die.

—Seb-Ichi sacred texts

CHAPTER 38

Ravensford Zone
Ninth Arc, Outer District

THE VISIONS SWIRLED IN THE old man's head. A great conflagration issuing death and suffering on a grand scale. It was horrifying to see, and no matter where he turned, it filled his field of view. Worst of all, he felt it. All of it. Every nuance of suffering for every person the flames consumed. Had he not been trained in the Way of the Seb-Ichi monks, the visions would have overwhelmed and drowned him in their madness. So there in his mind's eye amid the flame and blood, the destruction and chaos, he sat in meditation, seeming oblivious of the plight of those around him.

Finally the trio came. The visions always ended with the same three faces. Three strangers who had always felt familiar. He could not identify them, nor could they respond when he asked their names. He was not sure if they had ended the destruction or caused it. This had frustrated him for years.

Over time, the occurrences had grown in frequency and intensity. While his mind fought to maintain its hold on reality, his body thrashed about, colliding with the stone walls of the monastery. It had left him with a constellation of scars. On the days that he was lucky, he was only black and blue. It often appeared as though he had been beaten.

While neither dreams nor nightmares, the visions first came as he slept. Eventually, however, they began to invade his waking hours. With little warning, they would erupt in his mind and when finished he would find himself at the bottom of a flight of stairs or at the foot of a ladder that he had climbed to tend the orchards. Sometimes he would be a quarter of a mile from where he had started. He began to carry his meditation mat with him and if he was quick enough, he could get on the ground before his body began to seize violently. Many times he could not.

The faces of the trio faded and he slowly became aware of his surroundings. He could hear water, which meant he was near the stream that ran along the south end of the monastery. The small waterfall that turned the mill was somewhat distant, so he was likely near the eastern fields. He could hear the one bad blade of the mill slap the water slightly different from the rest. Though he couldn't yet see, he judged that he was in the monastery garden. He heard a soft thud to his right, in the pasture where the horses were maintained.

Next came the sense of smell. The soft scents of the herbs from the kitchen garden and the aroma of the casks holding the ales that he brewed wafted through the air. The water too had its scent, as did the flowers along its bank.

The dull ache that had permeated his body rose up as well and the feeling was most pronounced at his wrist.

"Not broken so far as I can tell," came the voice of the monastery tender, a young man assigned to this least desirable of tasks: caretaker to a madman. He could discern the movement of his arm and wrist through no effort of his own. It was the young man, Vis-Shan, who examined his arm while he lay there.

"How bad?" the monk asked.

"The seizure? Not the worst I've seen you have, but still, impressive."

"They aren't seizures," the monk corrected.

His vision began to return as the perfect sky came into view.

"Yes, I know you say they are visions. By why would the Maker curse you so? Why this fate for a holy man?"

"Who am I to judge what the Maker has ordained for me. Perhaps my sins have earned me this, just as yours have earned you your role as my caretaker."

"Perhaps. But if our god treats you so, then perhaps you should consider the god of Thecla and we'll both be spared. You'll be made to leave and there will be nothing left to care for here and I can go as well."

"Ours is a life of sacrifice. The Hrazza are wise, who are we to say what form that sacrifice should take?"

The young man changed the subject.

"You are always hungry after these episodes. Come, I'll fix you food."

The monk took a moment and engaged in his breathing exercises. The experience had indeed left him famished and he rose slowly, his legs pliant as marshy reeds. He manifested his bondling as a cane to assist him.

The younger man helped to steady him and pointed him toward the kitchen. The monk could smell the mead from here.

Vis-Shan rummaged through the cupboard and found some pan bread. It was the least inedible of the food left. He placed the bread on a simple wooden plate and drew a mug of warm mead from a cedar barrel. Though it was tradition to store mead in oak, the monk liked the red flavorful richness that the cedar infused into the brew.

It struck the younger man as just one more touch of heresy, as he drew an extra measure for himself. He had to admit that the taste was pleasingly unique in a society that bred itself to traditional ways. Innovations were rare.

The monk watched as the young man set out the bread and mugs. The older man could read the younger with little effort. The younger man, for his part, knew what the monk was thinking.

"It's either this, goat's milk, or rainwater," the younger man said.

"You do not approve of this, yet you drink it and have apparently preceded me in doing so."

"I did not know that it required my approval," the younger man said as he drew in the rich flavor. "The locals seem to like it well enough to come up here and stock their cellars with it. At least the braver ones willing to do business with a madman."

"And that will fill our pantries in the next day or so."

"Yes. Heretical and profitable. You must be pleased."

The older man sighed. He had not realized until now just how intoxicated Vis-Shan was. "New traditions start. We use cedar instead of oak. There are new batches down there in walnut casks and olive casks. Who knows—the day may come when I fetch some trees from McAllister's."

"Small wonder they banished you."

"Small wonder you got to come along."

"If I hadn't, who would you tell your stories to?"

"I only wish that they were stories."

"You know, you Seb-Ichi are an irritating bunch. Here you sit in a desolate heap of stones on a pile of dung that no one cared enough to name, forgotten by everyone, and the only thing you care about are your precious visions. They're fits, just fits, there is nothing holy or sacred about them."

The monk sighed, noting that these outbursts and Vis-Shan's use of the mead had intensified.

"Vis-Shan, you are Seb-Ichi as well. Do not forget this."

"Seb-Ichi are charged with protecting Ravensford. I have spent eleven seasons bringing food to a madman."

"Thank you, Vis-Shan, the food is indeed fit for a madman, and it's nine seasons. You have been here for nine seasons. I'm curious what you will do if these 'fits' ever do turn out to be visions."

"Well, since you're the only one who has seen these 'visions' I guess you can claim anything that happens as part of it. A perfect little delusion."

"You've had too much mead, my friend."

"Or not enough. Why don't you show me? Why don't you show me your immaculate visions? Show me what's so worthwhile that the Hrazza grants you this grand palace in which to hallucinate?"

"Vis-Shan, I tolerate your behavior because I understand that you suffer here. Do not forget yourself. Do not ask for knowledge that you cannot comprehend and never forget that even if I am the least of the Seb-Ichi, I am still Seb-Ichi."

The younger man bowed, wobbled slightly, and stood up, laughing a mocking laugh.

"Or what? I'll be banished?"

He collapsed in a chair against a wall.

"Or I'll spend my days wishing things had never happened? It is you who do not comprehend. That *is* my life already! Every day I waken in the hope that today will be the day that either I understand why I am here or someone comes to tell me it was all a mistake."

The monk refilled his flagon.

"Every day I go to sleep without the knowledge of why, but in the hope that tomorrow will be the day. *Nine* seasons have come and gone. *Nine!* I understand now more than ever that no one is coming. I understand that on this pile of rock, on this dung heap of a mountain as the caretaker of the madman, I will die. I don't know why the Hrazza has selected me to be refuse, cast off for the use of an outcast, but they have. Here's to me!"

The younger man went to drink from his vessel, but it was empty. Again. He lurched to the cask and refilled his flagon, spilling significant quantities as he did. He left the spigot running while he drank the entire thing, then refilled it. He closed it with some effort and then made his way back, sloshing his mead as he did. Sitting down heavily, he slurred as he addressed the monk again.

"So, my grand master, share these visions. Share them with me. Seb-Ichi are the great teachers, the great defenders of the zone, surely you can educate me on this, the most central aspect of your life!"

"Vis-Shan, this is not what you want," the monk said, but the younger man only laughed.

"Know this, monk. You will wake up from your next 'vision' to find me dead. The next time you are unconscious I will find a way to kill myself. Better that than another day of this. The Hrazza are wise, who am I to question their judgment that I am refuse."

The monk knew that Vis-Shan's intentions were real, for he had had other visions. Among them had been one of Vis-Shan's body hanging from a rope in the orchard, another was of his body weighted with a large stone at the bottom of the stream. Never had there been one where the young man hadn't died. If he could affect these visions, then perhaps he could affect the others.

The younger man emptied his flagon again and fell over backward from his bench. He slowly came to his knees and then to his feet. He straightened his tunic and walked deliberately to the cask. With exaggerated movements he positioned the cup under the spigot, but it wasn't he who opened it.

"Drink," the monk said. "There will be less pain that way."

Vis-Shan gulped the brew, spilling much of it down his face. The fog that had taken his mind did not obscure the thought that soon he might die. He knew the monk would make it painless, but still he was vaguely scared.

"I'm ready," the younger man said as the monk reached out toward him.

His next sensation was of falling. Though immediate, it seemed to take a long time—forever, in fact. But when he landed, it was as if all was well. Perhaps he would not be condemned in the afterlife for his failure to serve as the Hrazza had dictated. He had scattered images after that, of the monk over him, ministering, and then of liquid silver heat. A slender bead of glowing metal rose above him and seemingly entered his vision.

Pain. Searing and consuming pain engulfed him and he spasmed as he felt the heat. His skin burned as the entire world was wreathed in flame, and in a moment all was silent.

Vis-Shan found himself on the floor of a monastery. There was music like a whisper on the wind, the air was cool and the breeze gentle. Here, there was a feeling of calm that he had never known. He looked up to see the sky framed by a courtyard of immaculate marble.

"Come on, we'll be late!" he heard from his left. Rolling over to his side, he watched two young men racing across the courtyard and in an instant he was with them. His mind's eye traveled behind them as if tethered by thought.

The two boys entered the temple, followed by a few others. One or two were left outside as the heavy doors swung shut. The two were met with a grave look from an imposing man that Vis-Shan had never seen before, but knew somehow to be the monk's mentor.

The men were adorned in ceremonial robes and brought before the altar to receive the greatest and defining gift of the Seb-Ichi, the bondling—or Traf'gala in the native tongue. It was the culmination of a lifetime—or lifetimes—of duty. The former were men and women who had made the decision to serve the order. The latter were those born of Seb-Ichi, those chosen to live the life. While the monk had to earn his right to carry the bondling within him, there were those whose lineage earned them the right from birth.

Vis-Shan sensed the monk's pride as he thought of his brother, a Seb-Ichi monk who had also earned the right for himself. Then there was the guilt. Guilt over the prejudices that he held toward Seb-Ichi and toward his brother's son, a trueborn initiate. Though the monk loved his nephew, he had suffered at the hands of those who felt birth afforded them a measure of nobility. Vis-Shan could hear the monk's silent vow that his nephew would never lord his position over others.

The scene rapidly shifted as the monk awoke in his room to pain. The bonding process took seven days and the initiate needed to be undisturbed during this time. On the second day, however, visions came of marauders slaughtering the whole of the monastery. Feeling every ounce of pain possible, he lurched from his bed days ahead of time. He stumbled across the room and out of his door, falling onto the floor in front of his ceremonial guards.

"You must go back!" they urged. No one had ever encountered a situation like this before. The guards were there to fend off relatives and well-wishers while the bonding took place, not to imprison the initiate.

"Take me to the Hrazza. 'They' are coming."

He crawled on the floor toward the chambers of the council, while the guards stood in stunned confusion. "Now!" the young man's voice commanded, so they dragged him in front of the first acolyte they could find.

Vis-Shan could see the vision as well as the monk could. There was a horde of Badlands raiders closing on the monastery quickly. Little time was left if any were to survive.

"They are coming," the monk croaked in a weak voice, as he lay on the floor in front of the acolyte.

"Who? Who is coming?"

"Badlands raiders. To the east."

Vis-Shan felt the world darken, and in that moment he cried out in the voice of the monk.

The monk awoke not knowing the time. He looked up at the same face that had been so disapproving when he was almost late to the bonding ceremony.

"You almost killed yourself, which is acceptable, but you almost killed the bondling as well, which is not. We tried to extract the bondling from you, which would have killed you of course, but it would not let go."

"The raid?" the monk asked in a weak voice.

"Deflected. It came from the east as you had seen, and we were able to meet it with sufficient force."

Vis-Shan knew the truth of it in his mind's eye. The force had been significant, but the advance warning had allowed the limited resources of the monastery to be focused and deflect the attack.

The monk had felt no achievement in the fact that his vision had saved the monastery, just relief before he blacked out. The scene shifted to the council chambers with the entire Hrazza assembled. There stood the monk with sentencing about to be passed.

"No initiate in the history of the order has risked the life of his bondling so flagrantly," the kol, the leader of the Hrazza, admonished. "No matter what the benefit to the monastery, your actions can not be condoned."

There was a general murmur of agreement from those assembled.

"Since you can not be separated from your bondling, it is the decision of this body that you shall be allowed to remain in the order.

However, in atonement for your indiscretion, you shall live the life of self-sufficiency and meditation." The kol looked at the monk sadly. "May you find peace in your days."

Then the visions began. Vis-Shan felt them, all of them, and vomited, writhed in pain, and blacked out. Before he did, he saw the three faces that the monk had described. The first was a military man, the second was a woman cursed, and third was obscured to him.

It felt as if he had fallen into an abyss when the darkness was broken by a sharp, piercing noise. A few seconds passed before the noise was repeated, and Vis-Shan opened a painful eye. He was hungover, but the truth of the visions remained with him. He closed his eyes again, only to be jarred by a more urgent knocking.

Disoriented and nauseated, he made his way to the front gate. He manifested his bondling as a cane to help steady himself.

"Yes," he replied, suppressing his retching long enough to talk.

"Open up, we need to talk with your master."

"Come back tonight," he countered, half hoping his reason would be accepted. "The mead will not be done until then." He slid down with his back to the door.

The knocking came again. "Open, damn you! We have a wounded man from the Kwynian militia!"

Vis-Shan heard that and stiffened. He slowly slid himself back up the door and opened it. There lay the man from the visions.

He closed the door again, mumbling, "Wait here."

He tuned to get the monk, but found him at his side as he did.

"Do you understand now?"

"No."

"Neither do I. Open the door."

It is not necessary to win the hearts and minds of the dead.

—Colonel Irlin Shammal, Chumley's Zone commander, Fourteenth Brigade
Motivational speech just prior to losing the Battle of Torin Lar

CHAPTER 39

Ravensford Zone
Demminer Arc, Inner District
The Klemm farm

SMOKE ROSE QUICKLY AS EXPLOSIONS continued one after the other.

Timan immediately turned around and began to run toward the sound, while Lyrie swung out of the door and onto the ladder. As she did, she felt an enormous force move over her head, followed by another.

Lyrie ran as quickly as she could through the crops of the field, making her way back to the house. She had covered only a few hundred yards when she heard Timan groan. Finding him quickly, she discovered that he was semiconscious but otherwise seemed unhurt. Unsure of what had happened, she turned him on his side and continued on her way to the house.

As she cleared the crop line and entered the kitchen garden, she could see clearly that the back of the house was in flames, the kitchen wall destroyed. Bodies of arc militia lay strewn about the yard, and Mrs. Woods knelt beside a smoldering body, wailing. Mr. Jospher looked into what had been the kitchen. He was crouched and backing away, preparing for an attack, while his wife was grabbing the children she could find and hurling them over short stacks of hay bales for some sort of protection. She had just thrown her middle child to safety when she was struck in the back with an energy bolt.

Lyrie looked frantically around for her parents and Ren. She heard sounds of fighting within the house and had started toward the opening when *it* erupted from inside the remains of the kitchen area. *It* was eight feet tall, and though it held itself aloft on two legs, it was in no way human. She stood gaping as the Thorpe's Corporation Assault Exoskeleton Mark 9 came to its full height outside of the house. Though stunned at the sight of the behemoth, she reacted quickly and dove behind a stone shed, as the flamethrower on its right arm came to bear on her. The monster closed on her position and with one swing of its mechanized arm reduced the structure to rubble. Assuming that his target was buried under the wreckage, the pilot moved on to his next target. Lyrie, however, had found other cover; as she dove over a mound of soil, she collided squarely with Ren.

"Ren!"

Ren was huddled into the dirt as much as possible. "What do we do?" he asked, spitting dirt.

"We protect our family. Gather your focus, and we'll start on the pilot of that metallic thing."

With a sudden crash an arc soldier erupted out of a second-story window, followed by another. Lyrie watched as her father scrambled out on the roof after them and swung down into the fray. He immediately set upon an arc soldier who was moving in on Mrs. Woods. Stannis Klemm's psionic force was fully engaged and he was expert in its use. It was the product of practicing every day of his life. The arc soldier quickly crumpled.

As Klemm turned around he found himself looking into the face of the man in the cockpit of the assault exoskeleton, who was smirking as he fingered the trigger. The flamethrower could not miss at this range. There was a blur and tremendous impact as Hemingway struck the mech broadside, buying Klemm enough time to evade. As the android scrambled up onto the cockpit, the pilot attempted to shake him off with violent movements that were to no avail. It wasn't until the last moment that he realized what the android had in mind.

After taking the feed from the flamethrower off the weapon and jamming it into a vent hole, Hemingway quickly covered the pilot with the flammable jelly. The man reacted as his training dictated and slammed the emergency escape. It was a poor choice. The ejection seat worked on rockets, and as they ignited, the entire cockpit burst into flame. The man flew upward on fire, screaming into the night as Hemingway dove clear. The illumination helped the defenders see their adversaries more clearly.

Another of the exoskeletons rounded the side of the house and bore down on Mr. Jospher. His son Ben, who was hiding behind bales of hay, saw what his father could not. He shouted in an attempt warn him, but could not be heard over the din of the battle. There was no time to manifest a thought message, and he reacted as the inexperienced do, without consideration of the consequences: He climbed over the bales and began to run, shouting and waving his hands. It caught his father's attention. It caught the attackers' as well. His father looked long enough for the image of his son being immolated to be etched in his mind forever.

Jospher turned to the exoskeleton and brought all his energy to bear. Lyrie and Ren sensed his target and added their focus to his own. As the pilot targeted his weapons on the seemingly defenseless man, his smirk turned to a puzzled look, then to one of horror as blood began to hemorrhage from his ears, nose, and eyes. He threw his head back, and his left eye popped out as the water in his brain tissue began to boil. Then, in a spasm driven by the fury of a father avenging a son, and in indescribable anguish, the attacker died.

As pitched as this battle had been, it paled in comparison with the one taking place on the front side of the house, where a single woman stood off a small army complete with exoskeletons. Klemm and the surviving members moved quickly to the front and saw Derring, or rather the aftermath of Derring, as she fought. As body after body crumpled they could trace her path. Klemm and Jospher moved to engage the troops that beset the Klemm farm, but were knocked back by the unseen force they knew to be Derring. Hemingway, defending his friend, blended into the blur of the battle. Running into the house for a better vantage point, Klemm and Jospher used their psionics training to incapacitate soldiers one by one until none remained standing.

A silence fell over the farm as the battle abruptly ended. An hour before it would have been the typical calm of a typical night. Now the silence was so shattered as to never bear mending.

Derring stood amid the fallen, Hemingway at her side. After the days that had just passed, anyone would have looked like the apocalypse incarnate. But now she was angry. For the second time someone had attacked someone she loved. This time it was a child, and as much her child as any she would have had if she were still mortal. She stood with Hemingway, staring into nothing, breathing heavily. Such a battle might have exhausted another, but her face betrayed the capacity for more carnage, and even invited it.

Lyrie came around the corner and stopped. She gasped at the ferociousness of the visage in front of her, frightened to her core at the raw destruction embodied in the Lokaryn and the android. She did not understand the cause of their anger and could not comprehend the outcome.

The silence of the moment was immense, until the solitary sobbing of one woman amid the dead rose up. Slowly they migrated to the side of a woman they thought they had known.

Mrs. Woods sat sobbing at her husband's side.

"Nera, wake up please. It wasn't supposed to be like this, Nera, beloved, Nera, wake up please."

Klemm was the first to speak.

"Wasn't supposed to be like what?"

"They only wanted to talk, they said. Only wanted the Lokaryn and the android. Nera, please!"

Klemm hauled the woman to her feet.

"What have you done, woman? What did you tell them?"

"You had no right, Stannis, you had no right to draw us back in. He wouldn't...so I did."

"Who did you tell? *Who!*"

Mrs. Woods only sobbed in his grasp.

Klemm released her, and she fell to the ground covering her husband's body.

He looked at the survivors. His children and wife were here; no matter what else, his world was whole. Jospher and his wife were here, and though their child Ben lay among the dead, Timan and Chirra survived. The Woodses' child Jarrel survived. Klemm's gaze finally came to rest upon Derring and Hemingway.

Tears welled up in his eyes. "I am sorry, Derring," he said. "I did not know…" He motioned to the sobbing Mrs. Woods.

Derring knew where the real blame lay. Even Hemingway had to look away as he dealt with the emotion of the moment.

"No, Stannis. I should have never come here…." Derring turned to leave.

Klemm grabbed her arm.

"No, we didn't come though this to walk away. Derring, this isn't your fault. We knew we were giving you haven when we put out the quilts, but now we need repayment of the debt."

Derring looked at the man she so immensely respected and hadn't seen in half a decade.

"They are coming," he said. "Soon. Now. Lyrie, Ren, Timan, and the rest—they'll kill them. You have to take them with you."

Derring looked at him, knowing the foolishness of his plea.

"Stannis, this was our only haven here, and it was a death trap. Your children will be better off here. Hemingway and I will make our way across country and draw them away from you."

Hemingway immediately agreed. "We can draw them with my electronic signature. I'll lead them as far away from here as I can."

"No," Klemm objected. "They will start looking right here and if we are here when they do, they'll kill everyone. They have to. No one can ever know what happened here. They used technology in an assault against their own citizens. They'll kill everyone here and then move on."

Derring knew that Klemm was right. Governments needed her dead, needed Hemingway dead, and a few farmers were a small price to pay.

"We have nowhere to go. This was our haven."

There was silence for long moment, which Ren broke: "The monk."

Klemm looked at his son as if he had been possessed by a spirit of a thousand years of wisdom.

"How do you know about the monk?"

Hemingway immediately asked, "A monk?"

Klemm nodded. "There is a Seb-Ichi monk who lives in the mountains of the Ninth Arc who is…"

"Mad," Jospher interjected.

"Different," Klemm countered.

"He has an…affinity for…technology. He might be sympathetic."

Derring looked at Klemm for a long moment.

"And he knows Gedrick," the farmer added.

The look of realization spread across Derring's face.

"Where?" she asked.

"No, not unless you take the children to safety."

"It's not safety!"

"It's better than what's here," Klemm countered. "That's my deal: Wait here for the reinforcements or head for the monk's with our children."

Derring looked at Hemingway.

"He's right, Der. Right now, anywhere is better than here," he offered.

"And you all stay behind to be slaughtered?" Derring looked at the surviving adults with a face that Klemm knew all too well. Derring wasn't about to budge.

Timan broke the silence that ensued. "Why not take a part of the…" He faltered for a moment, not knowing what to call the incarnation of everything his entire cultural upbringing had been taught to reject. He gestured once, then twice toward Hemingway, still at a loss for words. "It…the machine…and toss it in the creek behind the farm. It will act as a decoy."

"I am an artificial, I accept being called a robot or android, though neither is exact, but I will *not* be called a machine. Just like you, I need

all my parts. If you want a piece out of me you'll have to cut it out, boy."
Hemingway reached down, slid a combat knife out of one of the fallen
soldier's leg sheaths, and flipped it so that the hilt was facing toward the
assemblage of technophobes. "Who wants to do the carving?"

Derring quickly took the hilt of the knife and, spinning Hemingway
away from the group, leaned into his ear closely. "Stop it! These people
are not your enemies. They don't understand technology, let alone the
difference between an android and a robot. They meant no harm."

"I'm not taking the cowsinger anywhere, Derring. We can find this
monk of theirs."

Stannis came up behind the two as they whispered. "Hemingway,
I'm sorry for the boy's comment."

Timan bristled at being called a boy and from the apology on his
behalf to a…His mind couldn't bring itself to think the word.

"Timan's idea has some merit, however. The zone security forces
had several hits on the crystal grid from your equipment. If you can
spare a piece we can carry it down to the Yrithi River and tie it to
something that will float it downriver. It will be hours before they
discover the deception, and we can be well on our way to another arc
and then on to Thieves' or Merchants'."

"We only have the three field dampeners. If we leave one we might
as well leave all three. We can't define a field with fewer."

"Otherwise Hemingway would need to be deactivated the whole
time. OK. We'll come up with something. Head to…"

It was Hemingway who spoke next. "The arms and legs are out, as is
the torso, leaving the head. The only redundant piece is the eye. I don't
need stereoscopic vision to gauge range. Plus it will put out a good
signal."

"Your eye?"

He handed the knife to Derring. "Leave the optic track so I can
replace it." He turned to Mrs. Klemm. "Do you still have Grandpa's eye
patch?"

"He had a number of them, but I can guess which one you want,"
she said, and quickly went inside.

Stannis shook his head. "Are you ever going to grow up?"

"Artificials don't age."

Mrs. Klemm returned with the black eye patch that her father had used after losing an eye in a farming accident. In the past, Derring had commented that this particular one reminded her of the type used by a disreputable kind of sailor back when ships sailed water instead of myst.

Hemingway immediately loved it.

"Ready?" he asked Derring, who had been running a flame over the blade to approximate some level of sterility.

The android used his ability to shape his external skin to pull the eyelids away from the area about to be cut. Derring held his head with one hand and with a deft movement dislodged the eye from the socket and severed the stalk close to the eyeball. Hemingway recoiled, his hands flying up to his face and he stifled a scream. Leaning over with one hand over the eye and one propping himself up on his knee, he laughed so that he wouldn't scream.

"Takes a moment for the pain-suppression circuits to kick in," he said. "It's not my favorite period of time." Taking a deep breath, he reached up his hand, and Mrs. Klemm placed the eye patch and a clean dressing in it. She held his hand for an extra second.

"Thank you, Hemingway," she said quietly.

He squeezed her hand in return, and she let go of the patch. He quickly dressed the wound and placed the patch over it. Standing up, he faced the group. "What are you all staring at?"

"Just like a pirate, Hem," Derring offered.

"It's settled then. You take the children to the monk. He may be able to contact Captain Gedrick. We'll head toward the mountains and drop the eye into the Yrithi at the edge of the passes. They'll be able to follow the signal through the area, but the walls are too steep and the water too fast for them to get to it until after it comes out on the far side."

"Once that's done, we'll head to the outer district of the Thirty-fourth Arc and arrange transport to Thieves' Zone," Stannis finished.

"Where should we look for you?" Lyrie asked.

Mrs. Jospher offered an idea. "We could meet you at that establishment that you and Seyschell used to rave about all the time. It had an odd name—initials only. What was it you used to call it? The D-A-B? Is it a family-friendly place?"

A man who lives only for his legacy will never have truly lived at all.

—Ro' Torgan, twenty-eighth rohnin of Kwyne

CHAPTER 40

Kwyne
Rohnin's Citadel

THE FIRST PEAL OF THE old bell rang out across Kwyne in the Center Arc. The lateness of the hour caught some by surprise; for others the bell's ringing had been anticipated, as it marked the hour on the way to something else. Across the Center Arc the world remained unchanged. Distantly, at the port facility of the Fourteenth Arc they marked the time, knowing that the diplomatic mission would return no more than an hour hence.

When the first peal was completed, the second was anticipated and awaited. The old watchtower bell was anachronistic—people carried timepieces—but its ringing every hour on the hour was one of those small marks of stability. Unconsciously, people awaited the next tone.

Waiting in his chambers, Ko'Doran was momentarily distracted, then refocused on the words of caution from his rohnin: *Be prepared for anything…he should be brought before the rohnin.*

The third knell came in perfect meter after the second, while the rohnin's coffee sat in its mug going cold. Ko'Doran breathed deeply, while so many miles out in the mysts, souls surrendered to sate the darkness of the Lokaryns.

The fifth followed the fourth and the sixth followed that. As the seventh rang its hollow chime, Var Kragen concluded his report of the lokaric attack to the Center Arc watch commander. He was now waiting to be connected to the rohnin, and this time Damien Cairo would have no choice but to act. It was inevitable. Kwyne was going to war. And contrary to what the rohnin might believe, it was not a prospect that Kragen relished.

The hour would soon turn to eleven and the darkness of the Kwynian night would be fully embraced. On the street a simple man looked up with sad eyes toward the Rohnin's Perch.

The eighth rang true as the fuse slowly burned.

The ninth drew the moment closer.

On the tenth the world stood still. The simple man held his breath, Kragen felt in his soul that moment in battle when the tide shifts, and Ko'Doran, for reasons he did not comprehend, found himself contemplating the scripture that the rohnin had chosen for his seal, "God made love, God made hate, man decides which prevails."

At the eleventh strike of the bell, as the rohnin's coffee gave up its last moment of heat, as Damien Cairo breathed his last as the rohnin of Kwyne, as the world finally broke from teetering on the brink of war to free-falling into its dark abyss, in the Rohnin's Perch was born the spark of the new Cataclysm.

The flame ignited by the spark spread quickly, and the explosives released their energy willingly as both fiber and timber gave way to the enormous force. In fractions of a second, word and work became atom and energy as the conflagration spread.

Ko'Doran felt it before he heard it. It was like a symphony that began quietly and then rose quickly into a cacophonous crescendo. So intense were the reverberations that crystal shattered and pictures flew from the wall. The entire Citadel shook, and Ko'Doran wondered if the whole structure might come down on his head.

Without a moment of thought, he pushed the comm button that went directly to the Kuhbrikian security station, and to his surprise it worked. "This is Ko'Doran," he said. "Do you have the rohnin?"

"Negative," came the terse reply. "A team is on the way up now."

"What has happened?"

"A team is on the way up to you as well, Primare. Stay in your location. We'll brief you in the situation room."

The link went dead.

He knew that this was not good news. The rohnin's chief of staff was generally accorded a level of respect almost equal to that of the rohnin himself. The brusqueness of the dispatcher's tone was ominous.

Before he had time to contemplate the circumstances, the door to his quarters flew open and a Kuhbrikian security force fanned into the room, weapons raised.

Out on the mysts, Kragen awaited the rohnin's voice on the other end of the link. The Nehreton yacht was just five miles off the Kwynian coast now, and in spite of the moaning of the injured and the dying, the ship was relatively quiet. They didn't hear the explosion, but there was no missing the brilliant flash of light. It painted the night sky an eerie crimson and bathed the myst in a ghastly glow. The prelates gathered at an observation window, stunned by the sight and frightened by its implications.

"By Thecla's hand!" one prelate finally exclaimed.

Not likely, Var Kragen thought. He knew better. Only two things produced such a sight: a breach in the zone shielding, and highly concentrated explosives. For the first time in his life Kragen prayed that it was the latter. Should it prove to be otherwise, there would be little left to come home to.

Assessing that there was no imminent threat to the chief of staff, the security force escorted Ko'Doran to a bunker well below the Citadel.

"What has happened?" he again demanded.

"Sir, all that we know is that floors twelve through fifteen have been destroyed," the team leader replied.

Ko'Doran's face drew into a tight scowl. These were the floors that housed the rohnin's quarters, a place where he had been not a half an hour before.

"Where is the rohnin? Have you secured Rohnin Cairo?"

"No," came the simple reply.

Outside, smoke billowed up from the ruins that had comprised the pinnacle of the Kwynian capital, casting a grim pall over the area. It was late evening, but many restaurants and cafes were still open. The thunderous sound shook the foundations of these establishments, sending patrons pouring into the street in a state of disarray. Few were injured, but all were terrified.

"What just happened, Commander?" Kragen demanded.

"We are still assessing the situation, sir," the arc watch commander replied. "The Citadel has limited information at the moment."

This was not good news.

There were few security units in T'Amorach with more information than the Kuhbrikian unit stationed in the Citadel. This group was the elite of Kwyne's elite. The fact that they lacked information boded poorly.

"I will speak to the rohnin now," Kragen said, drawing on all of the command presence he could muster.

Ko'Doran sank into a high-back chair in the situation room, deep below the Citadel. Information was still sketchy, but one thing was now confirmed. The top of the Citadel had exploded and Rohnin Cairo could not be accounted for. Worse yet, the Citadel had just received word from the Center Arc watch commander that a yacht with members of the Nehreton aboard had been the target of a lokaric strike force. The situation was quickly unraveling, and Ko'Doran knew that he was going to have to rewind the spool before things spun completely out of control.

"Primare Ko'Doran, we have Prelate Kragen on the link," the Citadel communications officer announced.

"Put him through," Ko'Doran replied.

Ko'Doran's comm link barked to life.

"Primare Ko'Doran, with no disrespect, I was expecting to talk to the rohnin."

Ko'Doran nodded silently to himself. Up until three minutes ago, he had been expecting to do the same.

"So was I, Prelate Kragen. There has been an explosion in the Perch, and he has not been accounted for."

"His last known whereabouts?"

"In his residence, which appears to have been the epicenter of the blast. Prelate Kragen, I do not have the time to fully explore the volume of information that we don't have right now regarding the events unfolding. I have the preliminary intelligence on the assault on the yacht: The lokaric assault team has left you alive, so we will assume that they will allow you to continue on back to Kwyne."

"I see. And will you grant our ship landing rights?"

"For Thecla's sake, Var, would you for just one minute stop with the palace intrigue. Of course your ship is granted landing rights. In fact, make best speed back here. We need as much of the Nehreton intact as we can."

Far be it for the Lokaryns to have done us all a favor and kidnapped the politicians instead of the families, Ko'Doran thought.

"You know I will seek the rohnin's throne," Kragen said.

"Of course. Please know that I will oppose your election bid again."

Kragen's anger grew, fueled by the adrenaline of the attack, the frustration of standing by helplessly as the families of his colleagues and friends were spirited away, and the violation of an assault at the very heart of Kwyne. With supreme control he asked Ko'Doran the question that bubbled up through it all.

"Why would you oppose me, Ko'Doran? You have no favorite child this time. Cairo was selected in large part because Tomanus Jugar expressed his preference of successor. Cairo made no such selection. If the rohnin's throne has become open—and believe me or not, I pray it hasn't—then I would be a leading contender for rohnin."

"Because you are predictable, Prelate. Because I know right now you are in a fury under that calm exterior. Because anger makes for poor decisions. Predictability is a weakness in the face of our enemies and you, Var Kragen, are predictable. Your whole world view is contained in a single book, attainable by anyone and certainly read by our enemies. War is upon us. A leader may be a simple man in such a time with a single vision, but 'To have one's actions preordained…' "

" '…is to be defeated before the battle begins,' " Kragen finished for him. "I know the teachings. Now know this, Primare Ko'Doran: It is a time for actions, not diplomacy. You are a diplomat; you are a man of debate and dialogue. Men of decision have taken the field now."

"And a fine job they are doing. Your excursion to carry out an un-necessary execution has created a hostage situation and likely caused the death of the rohnin. Your men of action have unnecessarily brought us war."

Kragen knew that if he held the line for even a minute longer he would explode. He looked around the room and knew his loss of composure would gain him nothing.

"Ko'Doran," he said tersely, "you may do whatever you please. If you don't mind, I'd like to get the people on this ship safely home, then we can talk politics."

"I'll set up a portal to bring the ship in more quickly," the primare offered.

"No. I don't think so, Primare. We'll make our own way in."

"Then the best of luck to you, Prelate Kragen. Will you at least allow us to bring the family members in?"

"There are no family members left to bring in. They've been taken. We'll be at home port in an hour."

Ko'Doran sighed as he deactivated the link. Though it was offered in good faith, Kragen had declined the portal due to suspicion. Those who knew Ko'Doran even remotely would agree that he would not resort to a tactic such as killing his enemies. Kragen knew this as well, but would rather risk the myst in a crippled ship than trust the leadership of his own zone.

Kwyne was fracturing from within.

What is madness? What is vision?

Does it not depend through what lens we view it?

—Pater Done Sanwell
Ru Donache monastic order
At the heresy trial of Ga'tomas

CHAPTER 41

Ravensford Zone

Ninth Arc, Outer District

PELI DOMAR RAN THROUGH THE tall grass as if the wind itself propelled him forward. He felt the blades lightly thrash the skin of his legs as he chased his eldest boy though the field. The wetness of the soil between his toes and the coolness through the soles of his feet. He caught his son, then threw him into the air as if gravity itself held no sway over the love of a parent for his son.

He caught the boy again and spun him around, holding him high, until they were both drunk with dizziness. Then they collapsed laughing amid the greenery.

"Again," his son squealed with the inexhaustible energy of childhood. Though panting and red-faced, the child ran for the pure joy of running. He had no place to go, and would run at an amazing pace for as long as he could just for the purpose of his newfound ability to run. Such is childhood.

Such was the gift lost to Peli Domar. It was in this moment that he frowned and his son faded from view, his laughter echoing in the soldier's ears. He stood, looking around quickly, and surveyed his environment for threats. He spun a full 360 degrees and did so again crouching, his perfect legs carrying him as they always had without fail or question.

It was on his third time around that he saw the monk and flattened to the ground looking feverishly for a weapon, a stick or rock with which to defend himself.

The monk remained placidly in one place and, in a moment or two, Sergeant Peli Domar felt a fool for hiding from this man.

He stood. He looked to the ground and there were his legs as they had ever been. He looked up at the monk.

"Dream?"

"No, Sergeant Domar, this is not a dream. I am a Seb-Ichi monk. You were brought to me wounded and I am healing you. I have placed you in this state so that our first meeting might be a good one. It is, however, time to bring you back to the world of the living."

"You made these images?"

"Yes."

"How much of these images did you make? My legs…?"

"Both amputated, as you remember."

Domar sighed. "You could have left out the running and jumping."

"You can experience those things in the real world if you want."

"Yes I know, but synthetic limbs, they don't have the same sensation. That was so real that I can still feel the itch of a bug bite on them."

"So it can be for you. You need not rely on synthetic limbs. I can help you recover naturally what you have lost."

Domar smelled a trap. "In exchange for what?"

The monk's face took on a puzzled look.

"I had hoped that this would go better, but it is time for you to awaken, Sergeant Domar."

And with that, Sergeant Peli Domar felt a pain so extreme as to cause him sit bolt upright, screaming. The monk was the first thing to come into view. The sergeant saw the hand coming toward his head and with all the strength he could muster attempted to deflect it. Fueled by agony, he fully expected to break the monk's arm cleanly. What he would do after that he had not considered.

As the attack made contact, Domar found to his surprise not the splintering of bone, but an abrupt cessation of movement and a new pain emanating from his arm. He looked at the limb now wrapped in a quicksilver material that glowed with a faint blue light. The monk's hand gently made contact with Domar's forehead, and the pain abated as if a switch had been thrown.

Still breathless and sweating from the pain of awakening, Domar looked at the monk, who smiled at him serenely.

"How are you feeling?" he inquired. To Domar's surprise, the monk spoke the Kwynian tongue, but with an accent that confirmed he was not from Kwyne.

"Where is this place?" was all that Domar could say.

"You are somewhere safe," came the reply. "And for now it is best that this is all you know."

The monk examined the Kwynian soldier's wounds. Though the stumps of his legs were bruised and bluish, there was no sign of infection. He probed one of them with a crooked finger, and concluded that the pain block was working. At least the man would be in relative comfort.

"You are a very lucky man," the monk concluded. "The portal did an excellent job of cauterizing your wounds."

"I cannot feel anything."

"That is because I have caused your pain to be blocked.

"I wish to be returned to Kwyne."

"I'm sorry, that is not possible at the moment."

"Why?"

The monk paused as he carefully weighed his answer. Finally he responded: "Since your arrival there has been a great deal of upheaval in your zone. The situation requires that you be here for now."

The sergeant could sense that the monk was being honest, but he could not accept the answer. "You are a phobe, are you not?" Domar asked.

"We prefer 'Ravensfordian,' but yes, you are in what is commonly referred to as Phobes' Zone."

"Our zones are at peace and I have committed no aggression against you. If you're not going to send me home then I wish to speak to my ambassador," Domar said emphatically.

"No act of aggression other than trying to break my arm you mean?"

"Will you let me speak to my ambassador?"

"I can not allow that right now."

"Then I am your prisoner."

"Guest, prisoner, visitor. Use whatever term you like. Sergeant Domar, please understand that I could have caused your dream to be one of pure horrifying pain just moments before being sucked into the maw of the Grendel, or I could have simply had you believe you were debriefing your commanders about the incident."

Domar paused a moment to consider. This man was a Seb-Ichi monk, and without his legs Domar was at his mercy. Yet the monk did not threaten him and had done nothing other than tend to his wounds and take away his pain. "A fair point. What do you want?"

"At the moment the opportunity to help you regain your legs and some patience on your part while things get sorted out."

"You can regrow my legs?"

"Well, that's not the term for it, but in essence, yes."

"Will it take a long time?"

"Yes, but at the moment you have nothing but time."

"I see."

"Why don't you tell me what you remember of the events that brought you here?"

Domar thought for a while as Vis-Shan entered the room with a tray of fruits and a clear pitcher of ale—which he recently had sworn off.

"Hello, Sergeant Domar. I am Vis-Shan, the caretaker of this monastery."

Domar nodded slightly toward the caretaker and then looked at the monk. "I am sorry, I did not get your name," he said.

"I have no name, I lost it."

"You mean you don't remember it?"

"No, I mean it was taken from me. It is a long story."

"As you've noted, I have nothing but time."

"So I did. I imagine we will have time to exchange a great many stories."

"What do I call you, then?"

Vis-Shan spoke next. "I have a few suggestions."

The monk replied with a malicious smile: "Why don't you tell them to the donkeys while you clean out their stalls."

Vis-Shan smiled a terrifically insincere smile and took his leave.

Peli Domar asked again, "What do I call you?"

"Brother or Monk would be fine."

"As you wish."

"Now, let's get started on those legs."

Leaning in, he breathed deeply over each stump. No scent of the putrescence of pus. While this was a relief to the monk, it served to nauseate the sergeant enormously.

"Will you be sniffing anything else?" he asked with a look of revulsion. "I mean I'm grateful, but…"

The monk smiled in amusement at himself. "I'm sorry….What would you like to be called?"

"Peli will be fine. Sergeant Domar seems a little formal if you're going to be sniffing my body parts."

"Peli then. I'm sorry, Peli, I should have warned you. The healing arts are best served by using as many of your senses as you can."

"I see. We won't be using taste anywhere along the way, will we?"

"With Vis-Shan's cooking I would think not. Take a drink of the ale and lie back. Tell me the story of how you came to be here. It will take your mind off the process. It can be quite tedious."

Domar drew deeply of the first of what would be many tankards of this ale. He immediately went into a coughing spasm as fire exploded in his throat.

"I thought you said this was ale!"

"It is. Very strong ale, but ale."

The sensation of liquid fire quickly subsided and he was left with a gentle flavor that infused him with a sense of warmth. Like a lightning strike, it was violent and frightening at first, but then afterward the air held a remarkable scent unlike anything else.

He immediately took another drink and shuddered again. "Does it do that every time?"

"You eventually forget about the bite, but yes the flavor remains. Now, why don't you start your story."

Domar took a deep breath as the monk recharged his glass. "Well, it begins like most stories do, with a little thing. We got an alert about an intruder, but most of us figured it for a drill. We're Third Arc and the prelate in charge is ex-Kuhbrik and a true believer. He likes to conduct unannounced readiness exercises and we figured we were due."

The monk continued to work on the leg and Sergeant Domar did not notice as the bluish tinge of the stump began to pink up. The quicksilver metal of the bondling was fully engaged, helping to restore circulation.

"This is where things started to become unusual."

"Unusual how?"

"It would be hard to explain to you, I know phob…Ravensfordians don't like technology…."

"Try me, you might be surprised."

Domar poured some more of the ale, marveling at the sensation that continued to repeat itself. He laid his head back. "Sure, why not? We usually use close-support weapons."

"Pulse weapons and slug throwers," the monk added.

Domar's head snapped forward. "Are you sure you're a phobe?" he asked. It was then he noticed the bondling wrapped around his leg. He was becoming inebriated, but in a pleasant way. "I guess you are. So yes, pulse weapons and slug throwers. But this was different. Usually they mount us up and send us into a warehouse or some field with training mockups. This time we were going into a very heavily populated district, into apartment buildings and shops and areas where people would be."

"Was that all?"

"No, the worst of it was that authorization was given for Accelerators and grav-balanced dispersion weapons."

"You were bringing gravity-balanced weapons into a tight spot like an apartment? They mount those weapons on ships."

"I know. So rumors are running wild at this point. The weapons were total overkill, but a lot of the younger troops were more than happy to get their hands on the firepower.

"The platoon leaders were brought into the briefing and the arc security chief was doing the brief herself. That's when we knew it was real. They told us that there was a Lokaryn—*a Lokaryn*—feeding on the citizens of the Third Arc and an unknown number had been killed. It struck me as strange because I hadn't heard anything about anyone being hurt or even attacked."

"Bad information?"

"No. I think they wanted us to be angry when we went out there. They wanted us in a bloodlust."

"Sounds like they got it."

"Yes they did. My lieutenant and I returned to our squad and it was the sharpest formation I had seen in a long time. The word had gotten out that a Lokaryn was killing Third Arc citizens and we were going to pin its hide to a wall for the sunrise. We hit the area hard from all sides." Domar's face took on a distant expression. "The situation quickly got out of control on the ground, but the commanders pressed the assault. My squad entered a high-probability contact area with a tactical team waiting above in grav ships. They had a contact on what they thought was a beacon from a runaway android. What one had to do with the other I don't know, but this was our assignment. I was on the third or fourth floor, I don't even recall, and the order came down to hit the room hard. We hit it as hard as we could."

"As hard as you could? With Accelerator weapons?"

"I know. There was an open portal in the room and someone was going through it while carrying someone else. I swept the room and then there was an enormous sound and light."

"An explosion?"

"I think so. Explosions feel different than they look."

"Then what?"

"Stars and a beautiful night sky. I had never seen the stars look like that before. Usually they are a little distorted because of the zone shielding, but this looked more like the stars when you're out on the myst. I've done a few assignments on mystgoing ships, and stars are really clear out there. It was somewhat like that."

"Then what."

"Then *she* came into view."

"The Lokaryn."

"I think that's what she was. I've seen pictures and heard descriptions, but I've never met a Lokaryn before. She looked angry. She looked…hungry. I thought I was dead."

"She didn't kill you, though."

"No. She didn't. I cursed at her and told her to make it fast."

"What did she do?"

"She said…She said, 'Pray with me.' "

"What did she look like?"

"I was as close to her as you are to me right now and I can't tell you."

"Did she say anything else?"

"Nothing of consequence. She picked up what I assume was the runaway and was gone. Then there was gunfire."

"What did you do next?"

"I tried to buy her time."

"Why?"

"I'm not sure." Domar tried to form a coherent thought about why he would do such a thing, but none came. "I'm not sure," he repeated sleepily, the ale and fatigue starting to take effect.

"That is enough for now," the monk said as he finished tending to Domar's wounds. "Sleep well, Peli Domar."

The monk got up and walked to the door. He looked at the man he had seen in his visions one last time before closing the door, and whispered, "Maybe tonight I can as well."

To live in a zone is to live in a fishbowl. To live in a fishbowl is to pray that no one ever breaks the glass.

—Badlands cleric, identity unknown

CHAPTER 42

THE FUNERAL BARGE HEADED BACK to the Thorpe's Zone dock from which it had departed. As regulation and reason required, her speed was reduced to five knots. She approached the Gyronian Bend, a natural gateway into the zone, which was the first or last of civilization depending on which way you were traveling. It was here that a scavenger village subsisted on the vessels that so regularly wrecked along the reefs surrounding this entryway to Thorpe's. Villages such as this one on the fringes of a zone were a step below the outer districts but above the Badlands on the social register. The dilapidated buildings housed shops in which to barter, have a drink, or find whores who would cater to any appetite.

Atop one of these buildings, Hennix sat concealed with his back against some abandoned structure adorning the roof of what he supposed was a brothel. In his right hand he held the neck of a bottle of tequila, the bottom of which rested on his leg. In his left he held a compression automatic with a charge chambered and the safety off. From this vantage he could see the shipping traffic traversing the Gyronian passage.

He looked around at his surroundings—decrepit and filthy. "Like an alley cat," he observed out loud to no one at all. It was a perfect mirror of his mood. He was not, however, drunk, and the bottle remained as full as it had been when he took it. Raising it once more to his mouth, he stopped three-quarters of the way there and instead hit himself in the forehead before lowering the bottle to its original place on his thigh.

He sighed, understanding that he could not risk going into any of the buildings below, as there would likely be agents looking for whoever had engineered the destruction of the barge—agents awaiting the loud report of her demolition.

He thought about that for a long moment, and felt the desire well up within him to go down to the streets below and start hunting all those involved in Lucy's death. He wanted to kill them, one by one, until they were all gone.

The bottle of tequila took advantage of the distraction. His old friend and crutch was coming to him, to help ease the pain of losing Lucy, to help turn his mind from the problems of reality. The cork on the bottle seemed such a small barrier to him, so much so that he could smell the liquid on the other side if it. Since being unable to jack into the ether, he would need the assistance more than ever. He rationalized for a moment before snapping himself out of it. "No!" he demanded, and returned the bottle to its place.

"Patience," he breathed. The barge would be in view soon. He detested waiting for this, but he had no choice. He could not enter the electronic ether to verify the destruction of the barge. His pursuers would find his signal and begin the chase anew. Nor did he have the time to wait for news to filter through channels about the loss of one more insignificant ship entering Thorpe's Zone with a midlevel management family aboard. There was only one being he could trust right now: an android who was about to die.

Again his anger, and the bottle, began to rise. Though he could, barely, compel the bottle back to its resting place, his anger continued to build. He replayed the events that had dominated his thoughts for the last hours:

The funeral barge had been quickly secured. Though the ship's complement numbered some twelve in all, Bowman had taken the precaution of securing the ship's weapons locker before making contact with Hennix. It was of little consequence. While all mystgoing crew-members received basic weapons training during indoctrination, this was a funeral barge. The weapons in the locker were few, and it was doubtful that anyone would know how to use them effectively even if they could get to them. Once passengers and crew were safely locked up, Hennix and the android set a new course and went to work.

While Hennix knew that the risk of discovery increased with every passing minute, he was unwilling to let Lucy's family be sacrificed. It had required steering the vessel away from its most logical course, to minimize the distance when they placed the passengers and crew aboard the ship's lifeboats. The small crafts would then have to sail in open myst to get to Seyschell's village. It was a less than ideal plan, but if Lucy's family survived the passage, they would be safe in the village. The last instruction that Hennix gave the captain was the final proof to anyone aboard the boats that Lucy had fallen in with a truly evil man.

"Captain, the autopilots have been programmed with your course and a recorded message for the people who will give you haven. If you attempt to alter the programming, if you attempt to make any call for help, if you deviate in any way from the plan I've laid out for you, the computers will open the mystcocks and the lifeboats will be flooded, killing everyone. Do you believe what I'm telling you?"

A long tense moment ensued as the two men locked eyes. The captain, placing his duty to his passengers over his personal desire to flay the man before him, lowered his eyes and, face burning with indignation and humiliation, responded.

"Yes."

As Hennix turned, the captain grabbed him by the arm roughly. "Pray that we never meet again," he said, and then, just as roughly, threw the arm back at Hennix.

The boats away, Hennix and Bowman turned their attention to final preparations. Once finished, they stood outside the doorway to the only remaining way off the barge: the captain's gig, his personal craft for attending to the business of the ship.

"OK, what's next?" Hennix asked.

"You get in the gig," Bowman replied. "It's a fast boat and it should get you to the zone well ahead of this old scow. Kill any electronics that might send a signal and head north. There's a small village outside the port that this ship berths at; it's the best place to watch to make sure the ship goes up."

"And you will be…?" Hennix didn't like where this conversation was going.

"At the helm making sure things go as planned."

"I programmed the autopilot to take care of that. It will make small random course changes, slow down for no good reason, the works! It will look as if it's being piloted…"

"But it won't be able to compensate for unseen problems, will it?"

"Then I'm staying," Hennix said.

"I don't know if it's too many hours in the ether detached from your body, or the tequila, but you are not fully grasping the situation. The whole point of this exercise is for you *not* to die," the android said with exasperation. "Your skills are needed."

"And yours aren't?" Hennix replied.

"I knew the risks when I accepted this mission," the android said. "The only priority is to get you off this ship alive. Anything else is secondary. Besides, I have a backup plan. Before the explosion, I can signal for a portal from the railroad."

"That's a pretty slim thing to be pinning your hopes on. We don't know exactly when the boat is going up, and getting a signal out to create a moving portal is pretty unlikely."

"For humans maybe, but math is an android's primary language. I think we can pull off something like the calculus of a moving portal."

"Primary language, eh? Five minutes after I met you I assumed your primary language was bull—" Hennix never got to complete the sentence. With a blur of motion, Bowman shoved him through the door into the gig and slapped the door-closure mechanism. Hennix bounced off the far wall and, using the inertia from the bounce to carry himself back toward the door, hit it as hard as he could. Through the pain of the twin impacts he could see Bowman slamming his fist onto the emergency release, and with that the gig dropped violently away from the barge to the myst below. Hennix flattened to the floor for the abrupt deceleration that he knew would come when the ship hit the myst. The gig settled into a stable gentle motion.

Hennix fumed. For the second time in as many weeks, he would be causing the death of someone whose only mistake was to have the misfortune to be associated with him.

He realized something else in that moment, too.

Other than Hemingway, in all his years affiliated with Gedrick and the *Shicaine,* Bowman was the only artificial being with whom he had even remotely attempted to associate. The thought only served to compound his guilt.

So now here he was atop a roof, amid the garbage of a scavenger village. The gig was beached miles away, hidden beneath a pile of wreckage so that the scavengers wouldn't find it. A bottle of tequila in one hand, a gun in the other, and nothing but time to kill while he waited for the death of a friend he never made.

He saw the ship before he heard it. His pulse quickened. He did not want to watch, and knew he did not have to: no matter where he was looking at the time, the report of the explosion would reach his ears.

But, inevitably, he found himself watching anyway. The dusk had begun to fall as the ship came into view, distant, but its profile distinct against the blues of the coming evening. The saboteurs would do it here so that the spotters could confirm the event. Somewhere in the buildings below, they watched with smirks and a feeling of satisfaction. His breaths came now in shallow fits, the bottle and gun hung at his side, his pulse pounded, his head throbbed, and his mind cried out for the liquor.

"Get out," he whispered across the myst to the android.

The flash came first and was spectacular. The myst around the ship ignited into a secondary fireball. He had always thought the color of ignited myst was one of few things in the real world that could approach the beauty of the imaginary one. The thought now nauseated him.

The sound raced out across the fire, striking the village, shattering windows, and shaking the older structures. As the shock wave moved through Hennix's chest, he leaned over and vomited. In the few moments that it took him to stop retching, weathered and grizzled men were already piling out of the bars, running for the docks and their ships. These were not rescue vessels; these ships raced for the spoils of others' misfortune.

Hennix crouched down again, his attention focused on the second set of people to head down to the docks. These were few in number, better dressed, and they climbed aboard vessels in good repair. He recorded each one in as much detail as he could, and promised Lucy and Bowman that the day of reckoning would come.

He could not move for many hours now, lest some lingering agent ruin all that had been accomplished by Bowman's sacrifice. He sat back down and opened the bottle. It would be a long night.

The design project of the Garand-Trass myst-clipper can only be considered a complete failure. Of the four ships that have been tested, all suffer from uncontrollable patterns in "flight" mode. The chairman's suggestion that pilots without traditional flight experience might make more suitable candidates is without credibility.

—Letter to the board of directors of Garand Shipbuilding and Design

CHAPTER 43

Deep myst

THE FIRST OFFICER STOOD ON the command deck of the *Shicaine*: a ship of legend, a ship that no longer existed. His gut had told him that there was something special about her when he signed aboard, but he never imagined that it was her. He looked out over the mysts, ostensibly scanning for danger, but more to process the events that had recently transpired. Though it was late in the evening, the night crew worked to keep the sails in trim and the ship sailing at her best. They had entered a region of sweet air and he had ordered them to lower the shields for a while. This was when he loved life aboard the mysts the best.

The wind played across his face like a cool caress. He could breathe in the air that surrounded him without filters or fear, and he felt as if he were flying across a vast expanse, limitless and as gentle as the starry sky above him. In those moments, this world fell away and a new world was born.

The report of a sensor rocket, firing off the ship and racing out ahead of them to sample the air ahead, shook him from his reverie. He watched as the rocket arced out ahead of the ship in search of dangerous vapors that would necessitate the shields being restored. The flame of its thrust played out over the myst in a multitude of brilliant colors.

Chapman was not sure why the world was looking so beautiful to him in so many aspects, but he welcomed the respite from the tumultuous changes of the last several days.

The majority of the command crew had gone to bed, and he had the watch now by choice. It gave him the opportunity to think without being disturbed...much.

An ensign approached the Quarterdeck with a status report. While reading the details reflected on the screen, the first officer couldn't help but be distracted by the ensign's fidgeting from foot to foot.

"Ensign Brannagh, do you need to go to the head?"

The young woman stopped immediately and flushed a brilliant red. While First Officer Chapman was generally regarded as a perfectionist and a man you did not want to disappoint, he was also fair and had aided a number of the crew during difficult times. As such he was much like the favorite uncle to Gedrick's father figure among the crew.

"No, sir."

"Then why are you dancing on my Quarterdeck?"

"I'm sorry, sir, but aren't you excited? I mean—*Shicaine*. We're actually on the *Shicaine*. We've already been into and out of the Lokaryn Zone! Who knows what's next?"

Chapman looked at her enthusiasm and, in his thoughts, agreed. He was excited—but breaking into a tittering dance on the command deck might not be his best choice for maintaining the command structure. He handed the report back to the woman and, clasping his hands behind his back, said, "The report looks good, Ensign, and shows a steady improvement in your skills. You did, however, miscalculate the consumption report on the last leg of the journey. Please correct that before showing it to the captain."

Looking at the screen, Ensign Brannagh tapped it quickly and realized that she had in fact come up with the wrong number.

"I was off by three-tenths of one liter for the entire leg!" she protested, and stopped abruptly as the first officer raised an eyebrow. "Sorry, sir."

"The day you stop looking for ways to improve is the day you stop improving. Carry on, Ensign."

"One more thing, sir. Communications has been monitoring the situation in Kwyne—they sent up the transcript of the most recent traffic. Also, they're working on a systems issue with a repeating beacon they can't seem to filter out."

"Thank you, Ensign."

The young woman turned to leave the Quarterdeck knowing that she had failed in one important test just now—discipline. She vowed that tomorrow would be better and that she would not let her captain, or her mentor, down.

For his part the first officer thought more about a statement that Ensign Brannagh had made than about her outburst.

"Who knows what's next?"

He looked down at the report as the voice of Seyschell came from behind him. "It confirms the rohnin as missing, the ports are closed into and out of Kwyne, there's only one portal operating into and out of an outer district security arc, and the military has deployed their fleet— including the Mastiff-class battle platform—in a defensive perimeter around the zone. It remains to be seen how the other zones respond."

"It is surprising that someone a foot shorter than I am can read over my shoulder," Neville said. "Couldn't sleep?"

"No. I used to sleep like a baby out on the mysts—it was the one place I felt safe. Now I just don't want to miss anything. It's been a long time since I've been here and I don't know how long I'll get to stay. Oh, and they ran that report by me to look for errors before they gave it to you."

"Then you miscalculated the fuel consumption on that last leg of the trip," Neville observed dryly.

"Or perhaps I wanted to see if you would catch it," Seyschell shot back.

The first officer let that go past and leaned on the railing. Seyschell leaned onto the railing as well, quietly taking in the night. She had learned long ago to enjoy the night myst.

"What's next?" he said aloud.

"Hemingway and Derring," she answered.

"No, not that. I'm not sure what is gained by the assassination. No one has assumed the throne by assassination in generations."

"More like millennia. The right of assassination rarely ends well for the assassin; few have served more than a few years, and it's always a time of instability until the assassin himself is killed."

"You seem to know a lot about Kwynian politics."

"I knew a guy once from Kwyne. He served with us for a while."

"Was he a politician?"

"No. Not much use for politicians on a myst-clipper."

"Fair point."

"He was just a guy," Seyschell said. "Kind of a bookworm, ex-military. Good with weapons and explosives. Anyway, if it isn't the right of assassination, then it's someone outside the zone. The most obvious candidate is the Lokaryns."

"True, but it doesn't make any sense. If the Lokaryns attack Kwyne they know that Kwyne will respond."

"And Chumley's will honor the mutual protection pact and that will drag Thieves' Zone in on the side of the Lokaryns," Seyschell continued. "Ravensford will honor the Kwynian pact as well."

"And that will drag in Rossums on the other side. The next thing you know, six zones are at war, with the other three building and supplying weapons. Merchants' will make huge profits. Thorpe's will sell a decade's worth of weapons in a few months." The first officer took a deep breath.

"Meanwhile, Thecla only knows what the bioengineers in McAllister's have been breeding to unleash on the world. Bioweapons have no off switch." Seyschell had seen her fair share of McAllister's abominations.

"So who benefits?" Chapman said. "The weapons manufacturers and merchants make some profits, but if the Lokaryns are destroyed, there goes the crystal supply for the zone shields."

"And if Ravensford is destroyed, there goes the food for the zones," Seyschell finished.

"Too much risk for even a great return on profits."

The discussion was interrupted by the navigator on the bridge calling out on the communicator: "Sir, that twix that the communication shack has been hearing is now coming through on the bridge systems."

"Got a 'myst phantom,' First Officer? Tsk. Tsk. Sign of a sloppy ship." Seyschell had quickly learned that any imperfections in the running of the ship were enormously irritating to the first officer. This would be a great source of amusement for Seyschell.

Chapman breathed in again, expanding his lungs fully to embrace the night air. He held the feeling as long as he could, and when he exhaled, he felt his body relax a bit. "I note that it started when you and Cade came aboard," he said. "Perhaps if I tossed you overboard it would stop."

"You're welcome to try, sailor." Seyschell shot him a playful look as he turned to tend to the problem. She then turned back to the railing and watched the starlight over the myst.

Inside, the first officer walked over to the bridge communications station and looked at the readouts. The communications officer was working to isolate and eliminate the signal.

"I think I have it eliminated, sir!" Knowing, as Seyschell did, that imperfections irritated the first officer, the young man did not find this as great a source of enjoyment.

HEXA—DALON—FAHTA—HEXA, the readout reported.

"It would appear not," the first officer observed.

"Sorry, sir. Every time I isolate the signal and feed it to the filter, it screens the signal once or maybe twice; then it comes through again."

"Does it change frequency?"

"No, sir. Same frequency, exact timing, no variation. It's automated. There is no answer when I try to respond to it."

HEXA—DALON—FAHTA—HEXA.

The first officer leaned over and tapped the panel with his finger.

"I tried that, sir. This phantom doesn't scare easily."

Neville was mildly embarrassed. The finger tap was a habit from previous ships he had served on. Those ships had been plagued by myst phantoms: inexplicable irregularities in the functioning of the ship's electronic and mechanical workings. The superstitious alleged that these were the callings of wandering souls long lost to the mysts. Ever the pragmatist, First Officer Neville Chapman would often lecture younger shipmates that in truth they usually resulted from corroded circuitry interacting with high levels of static electricity, and that finger tapping might scare away phantoms—if they actually existed—but would have no effect whatsoever on modern electronics.

HEXA—DALON—FAHTA—HEXA.

Chapman instinctively tapped the panel with his finger again while he thought. The communications officer said nothing.

HEXA—DALON—FAHTA—HEXA.

Chapman stared at the console and wondered if this was one of the chief's jokes. The man seemed to live for tormenting the first officer and it required no great leap of the imagination to picture him down by his engines tapping out the pattern, knowing full well that it would drive Nev crazy. He looked through the window to see if Seyschell was enjoying his torment, but she continued to look out over the mysts.

HEXA—DALON—FAHTA—HEXA.

He pushed buttons and turned dials, yet the pattern continued. He attempted to attenuate the frequency compensating for the lower myst density in the region. Finally, in frustration he tried the old trick and tapped the panel once again.

"Call her in here," he instructed the communications officer, who was happy to leave the station and the frustrated first officer in order to get Seyschell.

HEXA—DALON—FAHTA—HEXA.

"Damn!" Neville exclaimed. "Thought I had it. Do you or the chief have anything to do with this?" he asked as he turned to look at Seyschell, whose face had gone ashen.

"What...are you...working on?" she stammered.

Chapman looked at her with puzzlement. "What's wrong?"

"Get Gedrick," she said.

"Why?" Chapman replied. "If this isn't one of the chief's jokes, then it's just a communication beacon gone bad that we can't filter out."

"Get. The. Captain," she said again, emphatically.

"I'm not going to wake him for a bunch of gibberish," the first officer responded.

"It's not gibberish," Seyschell replied. "Your myst phantom is a ghost."

In the game of cat and mouse,
every so often the mouse feasts.

—Badlands proverb

CHAPTER 44

TARRO'S MIND WAS FILLED WITH horrific visions as he fell into the void. Kell drew him in softly at first, their blood intermingling in some kind of macabre dance. He could sense the malevolence with which she savored this moment. He knew that he was dying, but he wouldn't give her the satisfaction of crying out as he fell.

Just like so many before you, he could hear her think.

The darkness framed everything as he hurtled downward toward a dark bitterly cold place. As he did, images flew by him as if he were in a house of horrors, yet each was palpably real. He stopped abruptly, yanked like a puppet on its stings, coming face-to-face with a person he had never known.

"I had a life. I had a husband who loved me," the woman sobbed. Tarro knew in an instant that this was one of Kell's countless victims. He did not know what to say, and before he could offer any words, he was pulled away, violently crashing into a new image.

This one screamed in fury, lunging out of the darkness. He was halted as if held by manacles on his hands, though most of his arms were lost into the blackness from which he came. No coherent words came from the man's mouth, only the frothing of a mind made feral. Tarro had no doubt that had the man not been restrained he would have attempted to kill Tarro in an instant.

Tarro shuddered as he was again yanked into a new setting. He forced himself to focus on his surroundings.

"The banquet has just begun, lover," came Kell's voice from every direction.

He spun wildly, falling and hitting invisible walls and floors. With enormous strength of will he managed to slow himself. But he quickly realized that she was toying with him, making him feel as if he could gain some margin of control.

He felt himself come to a stop, and in an instant, from every side, he was inundated with the faces and bodies of Kell's victims. Thousands of them, tens of thousands, and the faces and bodies were not always connected.

In that moment he went from being utterly alone in an endless darkness to being swept into an ocean of pain. Face after face burst into his view, screaming, crying, pleading, and then in a moment was gone.

Soul after soul buffeted him and he could feel Kell watching. He drew on his training now to think amid enormous distraction. It was not unlike the battlefields he had known. In that moment he transcended this place. The battle no longer contained him. He stepped outside of it and could think.

Why so many faces? he thought.

He looked into the tormented mass of humanity, an endless train coming at him. Then he saw the one he knew. Someone from the *Shicaine*, someone Kell had killed from the old crew.

He understood. She was throwing her victims at him pell-mell, hoping that there'd be one he would recognize. And when he did, he'd react. It was human nature.

Time was short now, and he did the only thing he could think of. He ran.

He could hear her laughing.

"Where do you think you are going? There is no way out. Surrender your secrets to me and I shall make your stay here relatively pain-less...Jayesh."

His act of flight was utterly amusing to Kell, who enjoyed bringing strong men to their knees.

"So much for your bravery. In truth, Jayesh, I though you would last longer than this. Perhaps Captain Loh'l was wrong about you after all."

He ran blindly through the scenes of torment, not knowing or understanding where he was going. He was just trying to avoid that person in this place who would identify him. The whole of the crowd that he had fled now pursued him like ravenous wolves looking to devour him.

He did not know how long he had run. Perhaps a minute, perhaps a day, perhaps longer, but the longer he could conceal his identify, the longer he could protect the *Shicaine.*

He knew that the only reason he was allowed to run was that it amused the Lokaryn, and that once she became bored with it his eternity would be this place of torment. He turned and dodged and ran crazily, until he suddenly came upon a place that even Kell herself had forgotten existed.

He ran full force into a door. It was closet door and it splintered from the impact. In that moment the wolf pack that pursued him stopped and gasped. There before him stood a young woman. She had the appearance of a girl about to fully bloom into womanhood, physically developed but awkward.

She looked Tarro directly in his mind's eye and in a shaky voice uttered two words: "Help me."

Before he could respond, the cacophony of voices swelled up and the throng was on them. They grabbed at the girl, tearing at her, pulling her back into the mass. In a second she was gone, her voice drowned out.

He knew that the only way to her was to plunge himself into the very heart of that madness. He hovered for a moment. Was it a trap, or had he witnessed the last remnant of the psyche's humanity, crying out for help, turning to him for salvation?

In the end, instinct was stronger than reason.

He followed her and found himself in a world like none he had ever experienced. Unspeakable terror, devastating loneliness, souls stolen and absorbed, beasts who tore at him, trying to devour his very essence. As he pushed and shoved and punched his way through the mass, he noted that they not only tore at him, but equally at one another, as each aspect vied for dominance.

Tarro fought viciously and he had an advantage. *He* had a goal, to find the girl. The others fought mindlessly. Finally, he saw her. She was on the ground, cowed and trying to make herself as small as possible. Tarro smashed the last obstacle between them, an old woman who stood screaming and beating the child. With a merciless blow he send the image flying, then stretched out his hand and pulled the frightened girl into him.

"You're safe," he reassured her, stroking her hair.

"My name is Kell," she said in the smallest voice he had ever heard.

"Kell." It was a name that he recognized.

The ground began to shake around them and the voices screamed in a mixture of revelry and fear. "Hold on," he said to her, as the reverberations intensified, trying to launch him from her world. The child held fast, but he could tell that he was becoming less real in this place. She fell through him down into the mob.

With a loud groan and pain he awoke in the room, still alive. He was unable to speak, but could see the Lokaryn staring at him, visibly shaken.

"Kell," he said weakly.

"Sorry, lover," she replied. "You're just not my type."

Artificial or biological, are we not all composed of atoms?

—Rossums Independence Proclamation

CHAPTER 45

Ravensford Zone

IT WAS SELDOM THAT DERRING had heard the android pray, yet this particular prayer was as heartfelt as any she had ever heard. Though Hemingway said it only in a bare whisper and the winds of the rainstorm swirled around them, the virtue of her lokaric hearing allowed her to pick out the words:

"Please, Thecla, for the love of all things holy, either shut this kid up or kill me now. Lightning strike or blow me off the mountain, I don't care which."

Ren had been asking Hemingway questions steadily now for about two hours as the group climbed into the mountains and away from the Klemm farm. They worked up the side of the mountain, knowing that every mile increased their chances of survival—if just fractionally. Ren's incessant questions did little to slow them; if anything, Hemingway seemed propelled forward at a faster rate. High above the plains they could still see the farmlands receding in the distance.

"How fast can you run?" Ren asked.

"I don't know, kid, how the hell fast can you run?" Hemingway asked as he mentally repeated the prayer for an uncounted time.

"Can I see your insides?" Ren went on.

"You show me yours and I'll show you mine." Hemingway only half meant it. While Ren was irritating him to no end with questions, the android was impressed at the fact that the young man didn't utter a single word of protest at being dragged up the side of a mountain in a cold rain. His lip was already fattened from one fall. His arms and legs were torn and bruised, but his focus was entirely on his new biomechanical companion.

Lyrie also pressed on in silent determination, helping the others as needed. Her mind was elsewhere as well, though she did not share her thoughts as readily as her brother.

Chirra and Jarrel worked to gain purchase on the slippery rocks, encouraging each other to continue. Timan sullenly kept up. While he was not happy about the situation, he chose to accompany Derring and Hemingway that he might stay close to Lyrie.

Derring was the last one of the group who might need a rest break, but the first to suggest it.

"We'll rest here for a short while. Hemingway, would you scout ahead for routes?" Derring knew the android would jump at the chance for a moment's respite among the unexplored jagged and hazardous rocks. He disappeared from view in an instant.

The night still stretched out before them for some hours, but Derring knew they would soon need to seek shelter from the coming daylight. It was then that the situation might become uncontrollable. Should one of their charges decide to bolt from whatever shelter they found, there was little that either Hemingway or Derring could do to stop it. She worried how the children would adapt to nocturnal living, even for a short while.

The group was tired and eagerly accepted the rest. Timan was the first to speak:

"Ren, you embarrass yourself and dishonor your father by talking to that thing."

Ren had unfortunately inherited his father's fuse. While slow to start and slow burning, the explosion would come once it was lit. "His name is Hemingway and he helped to save us. Why wait until he's gone to say anything? Why don't you say something when he gets back?"

"I won't belittle myself by talking to that thing."

Lyrie stretched aching arms and legs, trying to ignore her brother and Timan.

"Are you OK, Tayshaw?" came the voice of Derring.

Lyrie smiled for a moment.

"Yes, I am fine," she replied.

"Why the smile?" Derring asked.

"I thought you were a dream, Derring. An imaginary friend from childhood. Yet here you are and I don't know how to deal with all of this."

"Would you like to know what you did the first time I ever picked you up?" Derring asked.

"I don't know. Would I?"

"I picked you up and caught you on my right shoulder. Just at the point you were closest to my ear—you sneezed."

Lyrie caught a laugh. Part of her was mortified at having done such a thing, and another part saw the joyful expression on Derring's face as she related the tale and felt happy as well. "That's disgusting."

"It was then I knew you and I were going to be friends."

"Why?" Lyrie asked.

"Wait until a child of yours does it to you; then you'll understand. I am pretty sure, however, that you got snot on my eardrum."

"Yuck!"

"Couldn't hear out of that ear for an hour." The two laughed out loud. A moment later they saw the flash of an explosion.

The security forces had arrived en masse at the Klemm farm and, taking no chances, they poured as much firepower into the area as they could, starting with an explosive strong enough to flatten twenty farms.

Several seconds later the group on the mountain heard the report of the explosion. The six stood and watched as the fires rose into the night, not noticing when Hemingway joined them silently.

"Those bastards and their technology did this!" Timan cursed.

Ren ignored him and took Lyrie's hand. "Mom and Dad are as far away as we are." The rain dripped down his face as Lyrie leaned her head toward her younger brother. The tears that ran down her face were lost in the rivulets of water, as the bickering of childhood gave way to the bonds of family.

"This storm is heading down into the valley. It should be there soon, if not already. The fire will die out soon," Chirra said, ever the optimist.

"Can't you all see it? Technology brought us to this." Timan turned to Derring and Hemingway and sneered. "Why don't you leave us? We can find our own way."

"Timan," Hemingway said, "no one is impressed with this. We have a long hard road ahead and you're already getting on my nerves. And for the record, farm boy—you couldn't find your way to your own…"

The report of thunder drowned out the end of Hemingway's statement for most of the group, but Timan himself heard it, as did Derring, whose eyebrows rose slightly at Hemingway's crude image.

Timan's face reddened and, trembling in anger, he moved toward the android. To make matters worse, Hemingway broke into an uncontrollable smirk. The two squared off, with Hemingway grinning like an idiot and Timan caught somewhere between the rage of a man and the tears of a child. Derring rolled her eyes.

While Hemingway had a clear advantage over the young man, he was not foolish enough to dismiss Timan altogether.

"You going to do something, farm boy, or do you just want to sit here and lock eyes all night?"

A tense moment passed and no one knew what would happen next.

"Eye," Ren said. "Unless you're hiding something under that eye patch, Hemingway. You can only lock 'eye.'"

There was silence that gave way to stifled snickers from the group. Hemingway's inane smile grew larger and he burst out laughing. He looked over at Ren and said, "You're all right, kid."

As he turned back to Timan with words of armistice on his mind, it took him only a fraction of a second to realize he was about to be attacked. He dodged and Timan's punch missed narrowly. The inertia of the attack carried through and the young man ended up sitting unceremoniously in the mud.

Hemingway reached toward him to pull him up.

"Not bad, kid, but why don't you save it for…"

His anger at a full boil, Timan acted on instinct as his psionic abilities burst forth. They struck Hemingway square in the chest, manifesting as what some might describe as a telekinetic bolt. Hemingway arched backward violently and was blown backward down the mountainside.

"Timan!" Lyrie screamed.

Timan looked to where Hemingway had fallen beyond view. He at once felt a rush of power and the nauseating feeling that he had made a terrible mistake.

He looked over at Derring, who sat without emotion. She could have killed him in the seconds he watched Hemingway fall. Mistake number one. Lyrie looked at him with contempt for the act, not support for his stand against technology. Mistake number two. As he looked at the assembled group he noted that they all said nothing, but watched with faces that seemed to be expecting something. Chirra seemed almost to be looking...behind...

Mistake number three.

Timan spun and found his throat in Hemingway's grasp.

"Knocking an artificial, who's built to function in the most extreme conditions the myst has to offer, down a hill? Wow! Now, that's killer instinct. I almost, nearly, bruised a circuit."

He then pulled the young man close to him so that they were almost nose-to-nose.

"I'm a patient man..." Hemingway started, only to be interrupted by Timan's choking voice.

"You—are—not—a—man," Timan said as he worked at the artificial's hand, gathering himself for another attack.

"No joke, cowsinger. You get one of those. Next time either finish the job or I'll drop you off a real cliff and not even think twice about it."

Hemingway released his grip, throwing the younger man back. Timan gasped for air and rubbed his neck. After a second of collecting himself he started toward Hemingway again only to be stopped by Jarrel's hand in his chest.

"This doesn't get you anything, Timan," Jarrel said. "The more time we waste here, the worse off we'll all be. You have to get Lyrie and your sister away from here, whatever that takes."

Timan stood, feeling rage but hearing his friend's counsel. He turned from Hemingway and walked a short distance away with his friend.

Without another word, the group continued on. They had walked for a while when Derring pointed to a small cave in the mountainside.

"We'll overnight here."

Hemingway looked it over and, waving a hand, motioned Timan to walk in front of him. "After you," he said, wanting to keep the young man in his sight at all times.

"As it should be," Timan replied.

The child Messiah was brought before the council at the great hall of Turin Tan, where the heads of the vanquished were embedded in glass and lined the archways into the hall. As she passed, the heads of those long dead began to wail and scream for mercy. This she granted with a touch of the arch, leaving only empty glass blocks and a frightened council.

—Tor' Manat
Kwynian Sacred Writings

CHAPTER 46

THE MAN SLOWLY MADE HIS way through the tunnels beneath the ancient capital of Kwyne. A soft violet light emanated from the crystal in his lantern, playing across the stone of the crypts as he passed. It took enormous discipline to suppress his desire for speed, knowing that a single mistake could leave him hopelessly lost in the centuries of passages or, worse still, at the bottom of an open forma.

As he moved deeper into the catacombs, his shoulders brushed the walls with each step. The earliest tombs of the leaders of Kwyne were simple niches carved into the rock walls of underground tunnels. Within these small recesses were placed stone coffins bearing the remains of the rohnins and other luminaries. The widest tunnels that could be excavated at the time would not permit the passage of the increasingly elaborate coffins large enough to be worthy of a rohnin, and the stonesmyths of the time had assembled the sepulchers around the bodies, using an ingenious system that locked the structure into place once completed. As Kwyne grew in stature and engineering ability, so did the diameter of the tunnels they dug, but here in the older section the way was narrow.

Although the tunnels were cold and forbidding, the smell of decay had long ago abated, leaving only history behind. He tried not to dwell on the fact that this was a sacred place and his presence was a sacrilege. Given that he had just blown the Rohnin's Perch into the pages of history, he wasn't as worried about this trespass at the moment as he might otherwise be, but he felt a deep need to apologize to the dead who surrounded him, and he wasn't sure for which of the offenses he had committed.

Above each crypt he passed was carved the name of the occupant, a later addition made once Kwyne was established. Prior to Kywne's rise to power, the tombs were unmarked to prevent disinterment by political rivals. The names were added by the Fossore, the order of clergy that tended the catacombs. Like the rohnins, they were an unbroken line that could trace their lineage to the beginnings of Kwyne. They had added the inscriptions when Kwyne had grown sufficiently in power to defend itself. They carried out the orders to construct each tomb and, when necessary, defended the place as if it were the final resting place of Thecla's heart itself. The men and women of the Fossore lived here, meditated here; they married and had children, who were raised into the order from birth. When one passed without a successor, a new member was chosen in a process that rivaled that of choosing a rohnin. The Fossore never came above ground, and over the years their bodies adapted to their subterranean life. When the opportunity arose through McAllister's Zone to modify their bodies and genetics to better serve the cause, they embraced it fully. They were fanatical about their duty. Thus the catacombs had none of the air of neglect that one would expect of tombs so ancient, but were an immaculate homage to the Maker's chosen one.

The man kept to the wall farthest from where the Fossore cloister would be. He was too distant to be heard and he was counting on the Fossore to be in prayer, but the caretakers were an unknown in this plan and he was taking no chances.

He halted, set his lantern down, breathed deeply, and sighed: He had come upon the tomb of the first rohnin.

"Kuna Latte." He whispered the name, despite knowing he was at the far periphery of the catacombs and much too distant for anyone to hear him. He felt humbled by the sense of history. The men entombed within represented an unbroken chain, a chain that was anchored to the very beginnings of Kwyne. He looked at the simple gravesite, the name etched into the stone, and Kuna Latte's epitaph spoke volumes about the man:

For the Maker and for Kwyne

"I hope you understand," he quietly said to the corpse, his hand reaching out to touch the stone of Kuna Latte's final resting place.

With Rohnin Cairo out of the way, it was likely that Var Kragen would become the next rohnin. He felt a swell of disapproval from the gathered leaders of Kwyne.

"I'm sorry," he said simply. "Cairo needed to die that Kwyne might live."

Even the brief moments he had spent here were too long. He would need to move more quickly now. He picked up the lantern and checked the map that he carried with him.

Turn left at the tomb of the next rohnin, he thought, and set off again.

After making his way through several more centuries of tombs, he arrived at the first golden age of Kwyne. The floor abruptly transitioned to a smoothed if not polished stone. The passageway opened wide enough for a procession, and a new entryway presented itself. The older area thus became a side gallery to the new. The man was relieved as the feeling of claustrophobia lifted somewhat.

The two areas were separated by an iron gate. Its lock was largely decorative, and thus easily picked. The man thanked the diligence of the Fossore that there was no dust to disturb, so that his movement through the area would remain undetected. He proceeded with as much stealth as time allowed.

It's a time of crisis, he thought. *The Fossore will be in prayer for a while longer. Then they'll be out in force preparing the tomb of Rohnin Cairo.* He paused a moment as a tight smile came across his face. *There will be nothing to bury.*

With a deep breath he pressed on.

He came to a rotunda, the ceiling vaulted some fifty feet above him. It was a hundred feet across, with a perfectly clear crystal statue of Rohnin Tonla commanding the center of the room, stretching some thirty feet toward the ceiling. Tonla's generals from the Abborran Conflict had their crypts arrayed around him in a circle marked with somewhat less massive, but still imposing, statues. Each was dressed in the battle gear of the day. Though this burial area was usually reserved for the rohnins, it was permissible that the leader have those important to him buried here. These men and women were credited with the salvation of Kwyne, and were afforded a final home in this sacred place.

The floor and walls were a perfectly polished obsidian, and the sconces on the wall held bioluminescent broth shining endlessly in a multitude of colors. The play of light across and through the crystal was mesmerizing. The organisms in the liquid fed off the energy of those passing by—thus the Fossore themselves were the fuel that lit the chambers from this point on. It enhanced their bond to this place immeasurably.

Moving on in time and geography, he passed through the galleries and knew he was approaching the rohnins who ruled during the ascension of the Prophet. It was rumored that Thecla's Heart, the Prophet's remains, was here in these catacombs, although others speculated that it was in catacombs under the ruined city of Turin Tan. He did not have time for speculation.

He found his pace quickening even more than his heartbeat as he worked his way down another corridor toward what he supposed to be the center of the complex. It was here that the Shrine of the Relic of the Messiah existed. He knew that it did not actually contain the Heart of Thecla, a burning beating heart, wreathed in pure white flame. Still, to be so close to his messiah was beyond words. Thecla was a young girl when she performed her teachings and was killed by a government fearful of her influence. She had been slain by an archer's arrow and by the accounts of the believers of the time, the archer burst into flame, burning in a writhing agony for three days. After her assassination the heart remained, burning in its pure fire, untouchable to all except the purest of souls. Millennia passed and its whereabouts were ultimately lost in the river of time.

A sense of majesty and peace infused him as he approached this place. First there was a marble floor, dark and polished, with veins of red running through it. Bioluminescent organisms ran through the small fissures in the marble, making it pulse with reddish energy. Then there was the main vault containing the crypt. It was massive, but not ostentatious. The walls were adorned with murals, some a hundred feet high and truly magnificent. The paints were created from pigments using the same organisms that lit the room and the murals offered a warm radiance. Rather than being a dark place of graves, this place was a luminous celebration of the leaders and prophets of Kwyne.

The man knew he did not have time to stay, though he could have easily spent a lifetime in just this room. He could not help but pause for a moment at the Mural of Thecla before the council. It depicted the back of a small girl, standing before the imposing dais of the council of Kwyne. Beyond the council were the citizens of Kwyne who had come to see the condemnation. Though dwarfed in size before the assembled, she seemed all the more powerful in the conviction of the word.

"They did not deserve it and yet you sacrificed yourself for Kwyne," he said softly.

The mural grew somewhat brighter at the whisper.

Fool, he thought, *why not belch loudly and make it easier for the Fossore to find you.* He moved quickly out of the area and into a side gallery that should lead to what he hoped was his final destination.

IN THE PLACE THE MAN was bound for, two other men, one old, one young, stood waiting.

"Beheading!" exclaimed the younger of those two men.

"No, not beheading," replied the older.

"You're right, too quick. One cut and the show is over. Even though there would be three of us." The younger man paused for a moment. "Hanging!"

"No, not hanging. And you can stop this anytime you like." The older man pulled his cloak around him. He did not like being in this place.

"True, hanging wouldn't be severe enough, though if they didn't fracture the neck in the initial drop there would be a brief period of struggle." Again the younger man paused. "Burning! It's slow and a real crowd pleaser."

The older man looked over toward the younger with an exasperated look on his face. "Wood."

After the Cataclysm, wood was scarce, and using such a precious commodity for such a task was unthinkable.

"Drawing and quartering...now, there's a possibility! It's slow, especially if preceded by extensive branding and removal of the hands, feet, and eyes. It could be a real crowd pleaser so long as they left the tongue in place for screaming."

"Captain?"

"Yes, Sergeant?"

"With all due respect, shut up."

When the man came upon them his thoughts were still back on the beauty of murals in Thecla's crypt, but he had heard at least part of their conversation. They hadn't changed much; eternally irritating one another and inseparable. The man emerged like a shadow from the side gallery, startling both.

"I have just killed Damien Cairo. We will speak no more of him."

The older man shook his head grimly.

"Yes...Major."

The major looked at the older man.

"That will do." He paused for a moment. "You disapprove."

"I serve."

"And you, Captain?"

"I serve, but wouldn't mind getting out of here."

The older man nodded. "He's right, nothing more to be gained by being here. Unless Thecla herself is returning."

The captain started to pull up his backpack. "If that little tart shows up, I'd like to give her a piece of my mind."

The two other men looked at him. The wiry captain was quite intelligent, but he had an unfortunate tendency towards heresy.

"Why are you looking at me? I didn't just blow up the rohnin."

The sergeant spoke next. "Where to now, sir?"

It was not the major who spoke next, but a fourth man. "Thieves' Zone, I would imagine." The voice came from the darkness.

They all spun with weapons drawn toward the voice as Primare Ko'Doran stepped out of the same gallery that the major had left just a minute before.

"The Fossore?" the major asked quickly.

"Still in prayer."

"Why are we going to Thieves' Zone?" the captain asked.

"For a meeting with Var Kragen," the major answered.

"A meeting?" asked the captain, incredulously. "With *Kragen*?"

"Yes. If Kragen doesn't play his part in this properly, the survival of Kwyne will be unlikely."

"Kragen is complicit then?" the sergeant asked.

"Yes, but he doesn't know it," the major said. "We must ensure that he moves in the directions we need him to."

"I agree," Ko'Doran said. "I will ensure that Kragen is at the lokaric ambassador's residence."

"We're going to the lokaric ambassador's residence?" The captain ran his hand over a balding hairline in disbelief. "I hope you know what you're doing, sir."

The trio pulled on their gear, and the major turned to Ko'Doran. "I'm sorry."

"Don't be. I thought about it and you were right. Damien Cairo had to die. It had to be done. It is my hope…Major…that you will complete your task and Kwyne will be born anew."

The major placed a crystal on the floor and spun it. He then took out a harmonic generator and pointed it at the gem. A low hum emanated from the device, causing the crystal to glow. A portal opened quickly and the first two stepped through, leaving Ko'Doran and the major alone for a moment.

"Good luck."

"How did you know?"

"Cairo had to die and you needed to meet with Kragen afterward to ensure that your plan would continue unimpeded. It was the only way and the only place to do it."

Ko'Doran said nothing more. The portal continued to ripple with dark energy as the captain stuck his head back though. It hung there disembodied for a moment.

"Do you mind? I'm not facing Lokaryns alone," he said.

"Go," Ko'Doran told the major.

The major pulled a small remote from his pocket. He pushed the button and watched the screen on the device for the return signal. Once satisfied that the remote had activated, he nodded an acknowledgment toward Ko'Doran and disappeared into the inky portal.

Some distance away, in a recess that even the Fossore had not found in the many years since he had placed it there, and would not find for years to come, a transmitter started to send a simple message into the ether.

HEXA—DALON—FAHTA—HEXA.

First, mix reptile DNA with avian DNA. Next, add a smidge of electric eel for the spark and three large phosphorus glands, then brew the mix in an ungodly amount of growth hormone for three months. There you have it—a winged flamethrower capable of carrying two grown men into battle.

—McAllister's Ltd. announcement of the first completely de novo genetic hybrid

CHAPTER 47

Ravensford Zone

TIME PASSED AS THE GROUP settled into the dank cave. Stannis Klemm's obsession with preparedness for an unknown catastrophe was here represented in the backpacks he had readied for his children. Prepared and quickly retrieved from a root cellar, the packs still smelled slightly of that musty environment. They had been updated often and all the supplies were kept fresh. He and his wife each had one, Lyrie and Ren also each had one. There were additional packs, which were divided between the two groups.

Lyrie took a glow crystal from her pack and set it far back in the cavern. Should anyone see the light from the entrance, they would assume it was only the bioluminescent plants that grew so well in the conditions found in such a cave.

Ren had fallen asleep, as had Chirra. Jarrel and Timan sat apart from the group talking quietly, while Hemingway listened, feigning sleep.

Lyrie sat near Derring and made an inventory of her knapsack as the Lokaryn watched.

"You are remarkably like your father. You know that, Lyrie?"

"I've been told that before, and it's not always meant as a compliment," Lyrie responded, without looking up. She continued for a moment before stopping. "Can I ask you a question, Derring?" she asked quietly.

"Anything, Tayshaw," the Lokaryn replied.

"How is it that I can remember you and I can't remember Hemingway and the railroad?"

"It was kept from you, Lyrie. When we came into the zone, your parents told you we were friends visiting. We had to keep Hemingway away from you and Ren. It would have been hard to explain why he was asleep all the time or standing inside a dampening field."

"I remember Gedrick and his brother Kisner."

"They weren't blood brothers, Tayshaw, but their friendship was stronger than the bonds of most brothers I have known."

"I remember Gedrick most because he always had crystals that did the most amazing things." She smiled awkwardly at Derring. "I used to think he was your husband."

There was a small pause as Derring collected her thoughts.

"Did you?" Derring said, noting just a hint of covetousness in Lyrie's tone.

"There was a woman, she was small but she used to give us all rides. Everyone at once. Strange. It doesn't seem possible now, but that's how I remember it. I remember being jealous because Timan liked her."

"A woman's prerogative," Derring observed.

"What was her name?" Lyrie asked.

"Seyschell, and she did carry the whole gang of you around. Seyschell is not an in-zoner. She is a mutant, and blessed with strength and agility."

"There was an older man too. He used to scare us. I think he did it deliberately."

"That was James Montgomery, the chief, and yes, he did it deliberately. Though I think you used to like it," Derring said.

"There were others—the tall man with the funny laugh."

"Tarro."

"The quiet one."

"Cade."

"There was the man who always smelled of drink—whiskey, I think it's called."

"Tequila. That was Hennix."

"So much is coming back to me now. Tell me how my father got involved with all this."

"Simple, really. The captain…"

"Gedrick!"

"Yes. Captain Gedrick was originally from a Ravensfordian family. They were fairly prominent in their arc and very well connected. Though Gedrick's father disowned him when he was not much older than Ren is now, there were still some who would talk to him. They aided him despite his interest in technology. Later, when he joined the railroad, he knew who he could trust on the subject, and one of those people put him in contact with your father."

"The monk. The monk put him in contact with my father. It seems strange to think that a Seb-Ichi monk is sympathetic to artificials."

"Well, you'll be meeting him soon. After that you can tell me how strange it seems."

"He must be a little odd. If they assigned him any further away from the center of things he'd be out in Merchants' Zone."

"Fair point, Tayshaw. Now may I ask *you* a question?"

"Yes," Lyrie said tentatively.

"You know I am a Lokaryn."

"Yes."

"Yet you don't seem very bothered by it."

"You're Derring first. To me, you'll always be Derring first."

Derring did not respond to that. She couldn't. She turned to look out of the cave and sat with tears quietly streaming down her face. Lyrie shifted to lie down to rest and found a comfortable place for her head on Derring's lap.

There the Lokaryn stayed, motionless lest she disturb the moment. She stroked the young woman's hair with a touch lighter than air and sang a song with a voice less than a whisper.

Hemingway could barely make out the words as she sang in the lokaric tongue. He knew it to be an ancient human song about a mother and her child.

After some hours, when all had fallen asleep, Hemingway rose and walked silently to Derring. He looked at her as she sang another song from an age gone by.

When she had finished the song, silence filled the space between them. Derring didn't look up, she didn't acknowledge him in any way except to say, "Please, Hemingway, don't ruin this for me. No jokes, don't…" Her whisper faded to nothingness.

She looked up at him, finally, and his face betrayed neither cockiness nor mirth, only his friendship and love for her. She nodded ever so slightly, and her friend sat down beside her.

Hemingway said nothing, but lifted his arm and placed it around her shoulders.

Derring started to sing again in a voice as soft as the wind itself. She laid her head on Hemingway's shoulder, her face a mix of bliss and sorrow—

The hours waned to a single one and the group started to wake. Ren made his way to Lyrie with the light touch of a bull.

"Lyrie, wake up," he said as he shook her. Hemingway removed his arm from Derring's shoulders as he heard the others stir. He sat with his back to the wall, his arms folded and eye closed.

The sun had started its final descent in the sky as the group gathered together to discuss the next leg of the journey.

"Take the river," Ren said. "Once we're over the range, the river system will run pretty much in the direction we need to go. All the water on this side of the range runs down into the inland sea, but the out slope runs toward the outer district."

"How bad would the waterways be at this time of the year?" Derring asked.

"It's the growth part of the season, so the rains are pretty heavy. The storms you've been using to travel by have been every night for the last month, so the creeks and rivers will be pretty swollen."

"White water?" Derring asked.

"Yes, definitely," Lyrie replied.

"Well, that rules that idea out, then," Hemingway concluded.

"Why? We can handle white water, we've all been down a stretch of white water before," Timan stated with a touch of indignation.

"In the dark? Mile after mile of it, with no idea of what's ahead or underneath you? Waterfalls, rocks? Using whatever we can steal or cobble together to do it? Are you willing to stake your life and the lives of your friends here on that? Next idea," Hemingway said with a decided irritation in his voice.

"What's the matter?" Timan asked. "Are you worried you'll rust?" He shook his head in disgust. "You really are an arrogant—whatever the hell you are—aren't you?"

"Enough!" Derring said, with a frightening tone in her voice. "I will not sit here while you two go at it again! We've wasted enough time with this nonsense."

"Derring," Lyrie said quietly, "Timan has a point. With the psionic field that the five of us can generate, we can reach out fairly far downriver to probe the hazards. By linking minds, we can react much faster than you'd think."

Ren nodded. "It would get us there faster than any other route, and the chances of being found, especially when the river gets larger down into the delta, are pretty low. We'd be moving faster than they think we can."

Derring looked doubtful. "What do you think, Hemingway?"

"I'd normally say caution, but the attack at the farm has probably put the entire zone on alert, and the decoy won't last very long. We still have at least another night's travel before we're over the range and far enough down the other side to pick up water we can travel on. Night's coming, and we don't need to make a decision right now. Let's pack out our gear and get ready to travel."

Night fell gently as the storms gathered. The crystal grid was more spread out at this altitude, making it far less sensitive. This made it easier to travel without waiting for the storms to fully develop. The rain became a cold wet affair and ultimately turned into snow as they continued to climb.

"Hide!" came the voice of Chirra, who, while linked to the minds of the others, had probed out ahead of the group. She was the most sensitive of them and usually took point. "Fliers!" she said. Her eyes went wide on the word.

"Bury yourself in the snow," Derring commanded.

The group scrambled for cover, as animals with enormous wing-spans flew over head in expanding circles. The cold of the air accentuated the steam coming from their mouths. Their bodies were as dark as night; their eyes like blood.

"The engineers in McAllister's have been working overtime," Hemingway noted quietly to Derring as he covered himself with snow.

"Those things used to be mythology until somebody figured out what great weapons they'd make and engineered one."

"Wyvern? Really? I thought they just made them bigger. That one has to have a fifty-foot wingspan."

"It has four limbs, but wyvern have two and a tail. That thing used to be called a wyrm. This does not bode well. Those things are cold-blooded, meaning his rider must really be pushing the thing hard to get it to come up this far. They're looking for us."

"Well, that makes one decision a little easier anyway. Once we get over the range we start looking for watercraft."

"Agreed."

Unable to detect them through their icy camouflage, the winged colossuses glided off toward lower latitudes. The group quickly dug themselves out of the snow and resumed the journey. They crested the range toward the middle of the night and made good time down the outslope. Finally, they stopped in a cave that promised some warmth. Lyrie reached into her pack and took out a small reddish crystal that produced both light and heat. The group huddled around it. All except for Hemingway and Derring.

"There's about an hour left before sunrise," Derring said. "I'll go scout ahead and see if I can find the waterway and something suitable to sail on it."

And with that she was gone. Hemingway set up the dampening field and the rest set about rationing the supplies for the evening.

Minutes before sunrise, Derring reappeared in the cave. She had an expression that conveyed a disappointed effort, but said nothing. The day again passed in relative calm. Timan and Hemingway remained wary of one another, though no further engagements were had. Night again approached as the septet gathered their belongings and readied themselves.

"We'll head down the western side of the slope," Derring said. "There's a long run with good cover. The wyrms I know of don't have good night vision, though I can't speak for the riders. I wouldn't put it past the McAllister's breeders to have figured out how to give those things heat sensing."

She turned to Hemingway. "The longer we're in the open, the greater the chance something will go wrong. You keep them moving, I'll find transportation."

The last rays of light had left the sky and with them Derring was gone into the night.

"Let's go," Hemingway said, throwing his pack and Derring's over his shoulder.

"Hold on," said Chirra. "There are people coming this way."

"Intention?"

"It doesn't work that way. We can sense them, but not their thoughts." The expression on her face soured.

"Must be mercenaries. Nice habits your zone has," Hemingway said. "How far away?"

"Within a half mile. They've stopped. There's something wrong. Oh…"

"Break the link!" Lyrie commanded.

"What's happening?" Hemingway could see the expression on the young girl's face turning to one of terror.

"They're being killed," Chirra said with a horrified expression. Her eyes were wide open and staring into nothingness.

"Derring," Hemingway said simply.

Timan went to his sister and, touching his forehead to hers, brought her mind back to the cave. Lyrie and Ren joined in as Jarrel cast a new psionic field around the cave to make sure that no one else was coming. He was careful to avoid the minds of the men dying.

It was over quickly, and Derring soon returned to the cave.

"We have to move, now. Mrs. Jospher was found at the site and made to talk. She told them the plan in exchange for a guarantee that her children would be safe. The mercenaries, instead, have instructions to kill everyone. The council is spreading the story that Rossums Zone sent a team into the arc that destroyed the farm—hence all the technology at the site. The story has everyone from the farm as being killed. The arcs think that they're hunting for Rossums assassins."

"How could you know that?" Timan demanded.

Derring said nothing but gave Timan a look that said everything.

"He begged for his life, didn't he?"

"The dying often do," Derring said flatly. "We have to move on. There are teams scouring the ranges, but they haven't had time to get a lot of them into the area yet. This will only get worse, and it's only a matter of time before we run into Seb-Ichi."

"There's a small trading town along the east side of the ridge," Lyrie said. "The pass road goes through it. Miners go there to barter. I'd bet we're not too far from there."

"It would also make an excellent staging area to search this part of the range," Hemingway observed. "This isn't going to get better. I say we have little choice. Those men were miners who were more than happy to kill for a few dollars. I'm sure the bounty will continue to go up to attract Thieves' Zone's assassins and mercenaries."

"OK," Derring said, "the trading post it is. Let's go."

The group traveled in silence, making good time toward the trading settlement. By daybreak, they were out of the snowcap and had set up camp in an abandoned mine. The day passed largely in silence, and at nightfall Derring scouted the settlement. She found limited but adequate crafts to bring them downriver, and then observed the comings and goings in the settlement's drinking establishments. As dawn approached, she made her way back to the group, who were growing weary of being in the confined space.

"How did it go?" Hemingway asked, as Derring appeared in the cave without much warning.

"Rumors are running rampant down there," Derring said, putting down her pack. "The bounty is large enough that pretty much everyone is abandoning mining for the time being and fanning out into the woods. Fortunately, no one has missed those men we ran into last night. Yet. Even though hunting parties will be out for days at a time, they will eventually be missed."

"So they know we're here?" Hemingway asked.

"No, this is going on all over the outer districts, according to what I've heard. Apparently we've been sighted in every arc on this side of the inland sea and some on the other side as well," Derring said.

"Did anyone bother to ask why Rossums would just all of a sudden send a team in to kill a bunch of farmers?" Lyrie asked.

"No, nobody's asking that particular question. Mix a little fear and prejudice, then throw in some money. People were more than happy to respond without too much question." Derring noted that not much had changed on that subject since before the Cataclysm.

"What if someone finds us here?" Ren asked. A knowing silence was all that came in response. "Oh" was all Ren said, after a moment.

"Why are you surprised, Ren?" came the voice of Timan. "That's what she does to mortals."

The day passed largely in silence as the stress of the journey began to rend the fabric of the group. Hemingway sat in his dampening field; Jarrel and Lyrie tended the psychic wounds of Chirra. Ren kept mostly to himself, while Derring appeared to be meditating. But it was Timan who was most affected. He sat apart from the group, his anger building to a slow boil. His father had been killed by technology and his mother forced into the position of being an informant. The woman he would marry and his own sister now worked to protect that thing that caused it all. How much his life had changed in a handful of days. And all because of that damn artificial. He swore to himself an oath that he would make it right.

The word of this miracle and others began to spread. The crowds that gathered to her grew to armylike sizes. The council deliberated.

—Tor' Manat
Kwynian Sacred Writings

CHAPTER 48

Kwyne
Center District

AFTER DISEMBARKING, KRAGEN WALKED SILENTLY to a portal station a few yards away from the ship, which had been set up to allow the delegates quick access to the capital. Without much thought, he entered the blackness. It was much like walking though a door, and once on the other side he found himself in the Center District of Kwyne. Though the hour was late, there was a restlessness to the area, and security forces were present in large numbers on every street.

The news spread as fast as a Badlands organics storm, and a crowd had quickly gathered in the vicinity of the Citadel. There, Kuhbrikian forces formed a ring around the ruined structure, unsure of what they were protecting, but knowing that their presence implied a stabilized situation. Some mourners intoned prayers, while others left mementos to honor the memory of what was believed to be their recently deceased rohnin. Restaurants stayed open in order to accommodate the swelling number of people.

Debris and dust were strewn all around the Citadel, and a number of small fires had broken out. Most were quickly brought under control, but not before unleashing a blanket of smoke into the air.

Var Kragen quickly surveyed the scene, as medics rushed toward the portal to tend to the prelates and the other wounded.

"Are you hurt, Prelate Kragen?" one asked him.

"Negative, but there are plenty on board who are."

"They'll have our full attention, sir."

"Carry on."

Kragen headed down the dock with N'orin and Balazar on his heels.

"Var," N'orin implored, "hear me out." The squat man had a reputation as a conniver and he was not going to let this opportunity pass.

"Our rohnin is not an hour deceased, N'orin, if in fact, he is deceased at all."

Ever the opportunist, N'orin replied, "You saw the explosion, with your own eyes. He could not have survived."

Kragen turned on his heel and stared at the man he knew to be his equal in title only. "Are you so hungry for power that you cannot wait even until his corpse is found?"

Balazar sensing the danger, interrupted.

"Of course Prelate N'orin meant no disrespect to Rohnin Cairo." Balazar's diplomacy skills were well regarded and he was someone whom Kragen did consider an equal.

"I do not," N'orin agreed. "But, Kwyne is in crisis."

"The law prescribes a period of mourning," Kragen responded.

"The law also recognizes the right of assassination. In this circumstance there is no period of mourning," Balazar observed.

N'orin seized the moment. "That's right! We can ill afford a period of mourning while our enemies mass at our gates. You have witnessed with your own eyes what the unholy have done to our families." He paused, then added, "What they have likely done to our rohnin."

"So you would have me claim the mantle of a murderer?" Kragen asked.

"We would have you claim the mantle of righteousness, of savior of Kwyne," N'orin responded.

"Damien Cairo may have been misguided in his interpretation of the word of Thecla," Kragen said, "but he did serve Kwyne honorably. To claim succession by right of assassination will forever cast him as unfit."

"Yes it will," Balazar said. "And you are correct, he did serve Kwyne with honor."

He paused, choosing his next words carefully.

"But ask yourself this, Var. Which is more important? Preserving one man's honor, or that which he served honorably?"

"I will need to pray on this," Kragen said.

"As is right and proper," Balazar replied. N'orin nodded emphatically, the wattle under his neck shaking furiously.

"In the meantime, I must meet with Primare Ko'Doran. There is much information that I do not have."

Taking their cue from Kragen, the prelates headed in the direction of the carriages that were parked nearby. From there they would travel the two miles to the old Nehreton Assembly Hall and begin to lay the groundwork for what they hoped would be the ascension of Var Kragen to rohnin.

The prelate of the Third Arc was also heading in this direction but, as was often his way, he chose to walk. This would allow him time to mentally prepare for his meeting with Ko'Doran and also to take measure of the situation in the streets.

The walk was for the most part uneventful, because the majority of the populace was gathered at the Citadel in ever growing numbers. He passed a handful of people heading in that direction and noted one common thread: fear.

In the post-Cataclysmic time, Kwyne had never had an attack on her soil, and the people were clearly distressed. The air was heavy, and even with the zone's superior environmental system, faint traces of smoke lingered like ghosts.

"Prelate Kragen," a voice called from behind.

He turned to find a young mother running toward him, breathless and desperately clutching her baby in her arms. He recognized her but at first could not place her. Then he realized that her husband was in the security force of his arc. He had been slotted to be on one of the teams that had been lost in the explosion while attempting to capture the Lokaryn. In a life-altering twist of fate he had been sick. By the grace of

Thecla there was one less widow and orphan that day.

"Prelate Kragen," she said again, her chest heaving as she caught up to him. "Are the rumors true? Is the rohnin dead? Are we at war?"

"Breathe, child," Kragen replied.

"If they have killed the rohnin, then no one is safe," she said, mostly to herself, trying to reason it out. Her eyes grew watery and she began to sob. Kragen put his arm on her shoulder.

"Kwyne is safe. Your baby is safe."

She looked up at him, wanting to believe but not entirely convinced.

"The best thing you can do," he said, "is to take your baby home, be faithful in your devotions to Thecla, and raise your child well."

The young mother looked the prelate in the eye. Drawing her baby closer to her, she pulled away from him. "We pray every day and every night. It may save our souls, but it won't save our lives. Can't you see that? Don't you have any idea what to do?" And with that she was gone.

"Thecla be with you," was all he could say in response. They were words that he had said all of his life, and suddenly they felt empty. They echoed in his head as he continued down the street. The night seemed to grow even darker as he contemplated his role in Kwyne's future. He would need Thecla more than ever, and hoped that his steadfast devotion over the course of his life had earned him some small measure of her blessing.

As he got closer to the Citadel the air seemed to thicken, as the soot and fear cast a grim winter visage upon the landscape. He knew this feeling from Badlands campaigns that he had fought and it rarely forecast good tidings. He pressed on through the heaviness and the gathering throng until he was in reach of the epicenter. What he found he would later refer to as the most frightening and the most hopeful moment of his life.

Before him some ten thousand citizens had gathered in Tonla Square, the area that surrounded the Rohnin's Citadel. Medics and clergy tended to those who had been wounded by the debris, while others prayed. Most simply watched silently as the scene unfolded. The once red bricks were strewn on the ground covered in a greyish-brown dust from the mixing of earth and mortar. It only served to intensify the somberness of the mood.

Kragen paused for a moment and took in the scene. He was proud of his people for turning out in force. The spirit of Thecla was indeed alive and well. They would need it for the days that lay ahead. What struck him more, however, was the realization that the emotion he had seen in the young mother just moments before was amplified immeasurably by the masses that stood before him. *A dark day for Kwyne,* he thought.

He prayed a prayer of apology to Thecla but more so to Damian Cairo, wherever he might be. It was unfortunate and it was unfair, but Kwyne could not survive thirty days of mourning.

Without a word he moved through the crowd and hoped that he would be forgiven.

Better living though avarice.

—Merchants' Zone motto

CHAPTER 49

THE CAPTAIN OF THE *River Rat* was a man who fancied himself a king. He was, after all, the captain of a ship and answered to no man. His ship was barely more than a barge—and a sunken one at that, on more than one occasion. With some repair work and a liberal amount of bailing, she was raised from the mud of the upper river to sail again. It was true, however, that he answered to no man, as no man, or woman, would employ him. So this king was left to patch the *Rat* and to haul supplies to make a living. He lived close enough to starvation to provide the spotty motivation to deliver his goods on time, or at least close to on time.

The *River Rat* was an awkward affair as boats go. Shallow-draft, as all riverboats must be, she was some thirty-five feet long. She was built as a barge with no decking or superstructure. On acquiring the vessel, her current captain "found" sufficient wood to nail decking over the open floor. At the stern of the boat he cobbled together a small wheelhouse. There were wood-covered portals on the front of the structure that raised and lowered on frayed rope. There was no glass in the portals, though, as he could not "find" any while he was building the structure. The whole thing was shorter on one side than the other, giving the boat a seeming list to starboard when viewed from behind. The captain would steer while sitting in a recliner scavenged from some unknown brothel. The recline ability of the chair had been broken for some time, so an insulated crate that doubled as a wine locker served as the footrest. Discarded bottles rolled back and forth in gentle response to the rocking of river waves.

The engine crystals and propulsion conduits sat beneath the wheel-house superstructure and could be accessed through a hatch at the feet of the captain as he sat in the chair. It was a simple arrangement. Crystals could be used to generate heat; water flowed into the conduit, was heated to steam, and was ejected out the back of the boat, providing propulsion. The heat from the engine kept the man warm on cold nights if he left the hatch open.

Forward on the ship was another makeshift structure for transport-ing cargo. Perhaps fifteen feet in length, it was crammed with all manner of junk, both in boxes and stuffed in various nooks and crannies. When not in use as an auxiliary cargo hold, it doubled as a living area for the captain. Forward of this structure was another equally unsound cabin that served as the primary cargo hold. It was approximately the same size as the first, though a stovepipe stuck though the roof of this area. It spoke volumes about the captain's cooking ability that he could not sleep in the same place that he cooked. The decking between the two structures was raised about two feet above the gunwales, making for about four feet of clearance between the two structures. Material could be stored above or below this decking as needed. It too was filled with junk and bottles.

It was late at the docks of the Satara Trading Post. Rain had started a half an hour before and quickly intensified to an uncomfortable level. The lightning was particularly unwelcome this close to the water. The dockmaster, an older balding man of thin frame and small paunch, looked disapprovingly at his pocket watch, noting that he had only one ship that was scheduled to dock tonight that still hadn't made port. It was with a combination of annoyance and relief that he watched the *River Rat* strike the pylons that were intended to guide her to her berth. A competent river pilot might nudge the pylons one time out of ten, but the only word for the *River Rat*'s performance was "ricochet." The dockmaster sighed and rolled his eyes.

"He never fails to hit the pylons," noted a younger man training to be a dockmaster.

" 'Assault' is more the word. He also never fails to be late," the older man noted sourly.

The dockmaster was unwilling to move from inside the shack that served as his office and shelter from the current storm, until the chaos that always accompanied this particular ship's docking was finished. It was a hard-driving rain that would soak him to the bone. Unlike most Ravensfordians, he hated the growing season.

The captain threw a rope to the nearest person on the dock without alerting the person that he was doing so. It struck a worker who was wearing a black and worn rain-slicker to fend off the elements. The man's rain hat was pulled low, ostensibly to keep the wind and water from his face.

"Can you tie a bowline, man?" the captain shouted, the slurring of his speech not inconsiderable.

"Aye, Captain, a myst-clipper couldn't slip my knots," the man replied through the driving rain.

"Not a name to be using in these parts!" the captain said jovially, as he threw the second line. The man caught the line in the air, quickly tied the *River Rat* to the dock, and watched as a parade of men and women, all nasty looking characters, began to disembark. "Good lad, tie 'em tight! Find me later in the pub and I'll buy you a stout."

"The captain is a damned drunk, almost killed us all more times than I can count," one woman snarled as she walked by the man in the rain slicker.

The dockmaster came out from his shelter with a clipboard in his hand and a harsh look on his face. The younger man accompanied him.

"Captain," the dockmaster addressed him flatly. He looked briefly at the man in the slicker but did not recognize him. He returned his attention back to the source of his irritation immediately.

"Ahhh, dockmaster!" the captain said expansively. "Will you allow me to buy you a drink?"

"No. What is your cargo?"

"No cargo tonight! Only passengers."

"Purpose of their visit?"

"You'd have to ask them."

"They're all gone, so I'm asking you."

"I don't pry."

"Well then, ready your ship to cast off. We've no more space for your vessel since you missed the docking curfew."

"Curfew?" the captain protested. "I've never heard of such a thing."

"Well, with all the commotion in the zone these past few days, the dockmasters and harbormasters have been granted authority to secure their docks however they see fit, and I see fit to impose a curfew."

"Starting when?"

"Oh I don't know, what do you think?" The dockmaster looked over at the trainee, who had a wicked smile on his face. The man in the slicker smiled at that as well, but said nothing.

"About thirty minutes ago," said the trainee. "Shame really, you just missed it."

The dockmaster gave the younger man an approving look and said, "About thirty minutes ago. Shame really, you just missed it."

"All right, all right, I'm not swearing to anything, but I think they may be here to find that 'thing' everyone is talking about."

"Mercenaries? You're transporting mercenaries now? This is just what we need. The miners are all off in the hills and now this. They'll as likely kill the miners as the fugitives."

"It pays a lot better than bringing up dry goods."

The irony of the statement was lost on the dockmaster. "Listen to me, Captain. I'm going to make you a deal, and the best you've had in a long while. First, you don't *ever* bring another mercenary into this post or I won't allow you to dock ever again. Second, if you can manage to get here before the damn rain starts during the growing season, I'll cut your docking fees in half."

"On behalf of the crew of the *River Rat*…"

"You don't have a crew."

"I accept," the captain said, knowing full well that next time he would simply discharge the mercenaries a short distance down the river before he got to the dock. He shot his hand up in the air to cement the deal. The dockmaster took his hand and found himself struggling for balance as the captain pulled himself up onto the dock.

"Thanks," he slurred. "I'm off to buy supplies to make the *River Rat* even better than she was!"

"The chandlers are all closed at this hour."

"Then I will find someplace interesting to await their opening," the captain said, with great conviction and a pocket full of cash. He immediately oriented himself toward an establishment of ill repute.

"I might suggest you remain with your 'ship,' Captain; there are many new faces in town and we make no guarantees on the safety of the ships docked during the storm season."

The captain of the *River Rat* made no indication that he had heard the wise counsel of the dockmaster. The man in the rain slicker shrugged.

"He can't say you didn't try to warn him."

"But he will try. The man is a…I'm sorry, I don't know your name?"

"My friends call me Hem, got in last month. Perhaps you'll allow *me* to buy you a drink sometime."

"We'll see, 'Hem.' " The dockmaster did not trust easily. "Now, if you'll excuse me, I'm getting out of this rain. I would suggest you do the same."

Of course my name doesn't inspire fear, that's why I chose it! My enemies never saw me coming.

—General Igor Chumley, founder, Chumley's Zone

CHAPTER 50

Kwyne
Rohnin's Citadel

ON A SUBTERRANEAN LEVEL OF the Rohnin's Citadel, Primare Ko'Doran sat in a briefing room and awaited the arrival of Var Kragen. Although the Perch, the topmost structure, had been blown off the building, the rest, including the Nehreton Assembly Hall, was remarkably unscathed. Ko'Doran thought deeply about that as he waited. How curious the assassin had acted with such precision. In the old meeting chamber, some half a mile away, the prelates began to gather. He contemplated this and suppressed the dark wish that the explosion had taken this area of the building as well.

Outside in the ashen winter, a throng continued to gather, and Ko'Doran had instructed that as many clergy as possible be dispersed to help keep the calm. Thousands of grieving people had the potential to be unpredictable, and he was taking no chances.

A Kuhbrikian staff sergeant entered the room. "Primare, Prelate Kragen has arrived."

Ko'Doran nodded. "Is there any update on the search for Rohnin Cairo?" he asked, hoping that he might somehow be spared the impending conversation.

"I'm sorry, Primare, no."

"Escort him in then," the primare replied.

Var Kragen entered the room, followed by a steward carrying libations for the two men.

Ko'Doran rose and extended his hand to the prelate. "Welcome, Var. I regret that we meet under these circumstances."

"As do I," Kragen replied.

Ko'Doran motioned for the prelate to sit.

"Before we begin," Kragen said, "I wonder if we might pray together." Though such prayers were often done as a formality, Ko'Doran took comfort in the suggestion and nodded. They bowed their heads and intoned together:

"May we gathered here in Thecla's name,

arrive with peace in our hearts,

and speak truth from our mouths.

May the almighty guide us in our thoughts

and bless us in our deeds.

May we serve Kwyne with fealty

And her people with devotion.

We ask this in our savior's name."

Ko'Doran picked up his glass and contemplated the contents. "I'll be briefing the Nehreton shortly," he said. "The rohnin remains missing and we believe that he is dead."

Kragen nodded. He had thought as much.

Ko'Doran said, "This has not been made public."

"But is well suspected nevertheless," Kragen noted, referencing the scene in Tonla Square.

"We will not release speculation," Ko'Doran said.

"There will be no need to," Kragen replied.

Ko'Doran looked at him curiously. "Do you have information, Var?"

"Yes. Do you mind if I light my pipe?" He would need to appear at ease now if he was to convince Ko'Doran of what he was about to say.

"Given the circumstances, I see no harm."

Kragen reached into his pocket and removed the pouch. When he was done with his ritual and the pipe was gently sending smoke to the sky, the primare looked at him expectantly.

"Rohnin Cairo is dead, and you will not find his body."

"What?" Ko'Doran said sharply.

"Do you wish me to repeat it?" Kragen asked.

"I wish you to explain it," Ko'Doran replied.

"I am claiming the rohnin's throne by right of assassination."

The words hung in the air for several moments as each man carefully considered his next step.

"I don't believe you," Ko'Doran said.

"It's only necessary that the Nehreton does," the prelate responded, "and I will convince them."

"And I suppose you expect me to believe that you also convinced a swarm of Lokaryns to attack a Nehreton vessel?"

"Of course not, but it was inevitable that an attack would come."

"And you offered them a golden opportunity with your stunt at the execution chamber, didn't you?" Ko'Doran was angry now.

"Rohnin Cairo's response to recent lokaric incursions was impotent."

"And yours was reckless."

Kragen took another puff on his pipe. "My response was decisive. It sent a message, and in response the Lokaryns have clearly revealed their intentions. Better to have our enemy operating in the light." The impossible nature of his metaphor was lost on him in the moment.

"You think that the Nehreton will believe your case?"

"They will see the facts."

"Which are?"

"That Kwyne is under attack from an unholy and deadly enemy, that our people are frightened, and that we can not remain rudderless for thirty days."

"The period of mourning," Primare Ko'Doran said.

"The period of mourning," Kragen replied.

Ko'Doran watched as Kragen drew on his pipe again and found his respect for the prelate growing. Kragen did not kill the rohnin, of this he was certain. And he was right that the period of mourning could present a problem. "Bring him before the rohnin," Cairo had said.

"When will you make your claim?" Ko'Doran asked.

"Immediately."

"I see."

"It is unlikely to change the outcome, but it is your right as Primare to oppose me."

Ko'Doran marveled at his own next words, "I will not. And once you have made your claim, you will have my resignation."

"I would prefer not," Kragen replied.

"You understand that I will continue to investigate the events of today?"

"I'm counting on it," Kragen said.

The two men rose and nodded to each other, as was the custom at the close of a meeting.

"One more thing, Var," Ko'Doran said.

The prelate turned to face him again.

"I trust you remember the lesson of Gen' Roba and Shub' Wegroeg."

Ko'Doran knew that no clarification was necessary. Both men well knew the story of Shub' Wegroeg the Usurper, who, after claiming the rohnincy by right of assassination, was soon assassinated himself by his primare, Gen' Roba. To all but historians, the name of the rohnin was forgotten, but the primare was remembered as a hero.

"I'll see you in chambers" was all that Var Kragen said.

"Yes you will, Var," Ko'Doran replied, although he added, "I have one task yet to attend to before we meet in full session; I may be somewhat delayed."

"I of course trust that the primare knows his duties and will carry them out in accordance with the best interest of Kwyne."

Said the one-legged whore from Thieves'…

—Beginning of a limerick from Thieves' Zone

CHAPTER 51

HEMINGWAY PULLED OFF HIS HAT and motioned toward the alleyway that was seemingly deserted.

Lyrie, Ren, and the others poured forth from it immediately.

"Onto the boat," Hemingway said.

"That?" Lyrie said in disbelief.

"Yes, that. No one will miss it and no one will care when this guy begins raising all sorts of complaints about his boat being stolen. They'll probably think it broke loose from the mooring and sank downstream. Now get on!"

"It probably *will* sink downstream," Ren noted as he stepped down into the boat.

"Where is Derring?" Lyrie asked. "We can't leave without her."

"With mercenaries in town, she's likely still feeding," Hemingway said.

"She just fed!" Timan protested. "How often does she need to eat?"

"Look, kid, she's feeding," the artificial said while he examined the controls on the makeshift bridge. "If you have a problem with that why don't you go take it up with her?"

"If she needs to feed this frequently what's to stop her from feeding on one of us?" Timan asked.

"On you specifically? Not me. She can go a long time without feeding, but she's feeding now because she has the opportunity. She may have fed only a couple of nights ago, but that's a couple of more days she'll be able to go. Now get on the boat."

Timan stepped onto the boat and the group quickly surveyed the craft.

"He left the propulsion crystals hot," Ren called out.

"Perhaps he's up to something that needs a quick getaway?" Lyrie asked.

"I get the feeling that he has a habit of needing to make quick getaways. Probably stirs up trouble wherever he goes," Hemingway noted.

"There's no wheel, he uses a tiller and it's patched in about three different places," Chirra called out.

Looking down into the rear compartment that served as one of the ship's holds, Hemingway was greeted with a patchwork masterpiece of boards running in every direction along with rags and tar stuffed into the gaps. "Perfect."

"Permission to come aboard?" came the voice of Derring.

Hemingway popped his head back up from the hold. "Proceed at your own risk," he lamented.

She looked over the boat and cast a dubious eye at her friend.

"I figure the better the boat, the bigger the stink they'll make when it's gone. The dockmaster hates the captain of this thing and when he shows up complaining that his boat is gone, the dockmaster isn't going to make much of a fuss about it."

"Makes sense," Derring said.

"Ren, cast off the bowline. Chirra, get the stern. Timan, would you push us away from the dock?" Hemingway issued instructions as Derring looked on with an amused expression on her face.

"Ready for the captain's seat?" she asked.

"On the *Shicaine*?" he shot back. "Absolutely. Or maybe I can find one of the other Garand-Trass clippers out there and make a living for myself. There's still some fifteen left." As he spoke, he guided the ship around the pylons and out of the shallow cove that served as this area's harbor.

"Do we have any idea what the river ahead is like?" Derring asked, looking for a navigational chart.

"Wet," Hemingway deadpanned. "Hey, while I'm thinking of it, can you all swim?" The five Ravensfordians and the Lokaryn looked at Hemingway in disbelief.

"Just asking," he said as he steered out into the current.

An hour later, the sound of heavy footfalls disrupted the quiet of the night as a man sprinted down the dock with several other men in pursuit. An angry shout went up from the pursuers as the man jumped from the dock into what they presumed to be a waiting boat. But instead of a loud thud on the deck of a vessel, his pursuers heard a splash, followed by a string of inventive curses as the captain of the *River Rat* found himself waist-deep in river water and mud.

Satisfied with his predicament, the men who had chased him from the last establishment he'd been making trouble in returned to their drinks laughing, pleased with the new story they had to tell. Unable to find his ship and assuming that she had come loose and would run aground somewhere downriver, the captain of the *River Rat* crawled onto the shore and stumbled along the riverbank after her. He made it almost to the border of the settlement before sitting down to rest and falling asleep.

Out on the river, the group quickly began to doubt the wisdom of sailing beyond waist-deep water in their newly acquired ship.

"How are we doing?" asked Derring, after about an hour of travel.

"As long as everyone keeps bailing and the water stays smooth we stand a chance," Hemingway observed.

"According to Lyrie, this river has long stretches of white water."

"Well then," Hemingway said, but didn't finish the sentence.

"Do you want me to take over the tiller for a while?" Derring asked.

"No."

"What do we do when dawn comes?"

"The obvious thing would be to find shelter, but what if we pushed our luck a little?"

"What did you have in mind?"

"It wouldn't be a huge stretch for someone to connect the dots: a missing boat in an area that's a reasonable travel distance from the Klemm farm. So they figure out that we're on the river, which gives them a very narrow area to search. Since Mrs. Jospher has talked, we have to assume that they know about you. They'll assume that we have to stop during the day, but if we don't..."

Hemingway let the idea hang in the air.

"And if we get stopped? Then what? I can't jump out to defend anything and the crystal grid is likely to be strong along the river. You step out of that dampening field and we'll have the entire Seb-Ichi legion swimming after us."

"Each has its risk, but my vote goes for the unexpected."

"And mine for caution," Derring replied.

"I hate ties. Want to flip for it?"

Lyrie said, "One could assume that since it is our lives you're playing with, we might have an opinion worth more than the toss of a coin."

Derring's eyebrow shot up. She was surprised at how stern the young woman sounded. "Yes, of course, Lyrie, you're right," she conceded. "It may still take me a little time to get used to the idea of you as an adult. I am sorry."

"I'll get the others," Lyrie said quietly, and left the two.

She returned quickly and the whole group gathered around the wheelhouse and listened as Derring and Hemingway each presented their plan. Ren sat steering the boat, feeling as if he were holding court.

"So there you have it," Hemingway said. "Push on through the day and hope no one stops us, or try to hide both ourselves and the ship before dawn and hope no one comes looking."

Chirra spoke next. "What if we take a middle road, look for a suitable hiding spot, and failing that push on through the daylight hours. While I agree that with the town full of mercenaries someone will become suspicious, I don't think they'll put it together that quickly."

Lyrie finished the thought: "It's likely they'll all be out in the field searching by the time the captain sleeps it off."

"One thing more," Hemingway said.

The group looked at the artificial, who in turn looked at Timan.

"I want your word, Timan, that you won't give us up."

"I got the message, 'artificial,' that these men will kill us regardless of our innocence. You need not worry about me."

"Then give me your word."

"It would mean as much to me as promising the chair over there that I wouldn't turn us in," Timan scoffed.

"Then give me your word," said Lyrie, looking at the man she was to marry with the beginning embers of contempt. They locked eyes as he looked over at her. She took his gaze, which started as a glare but softened to disapproval. He could see no way around this, though if she were his wife it would be different.

Hemingway immediately stood behind Lyrie with his arms crossed and his chest puffed out, and grinned a moronic grin as he motioned toward her with his head.

"We're wasting time. I give *you* my word, Lyrie, that I will not 'give up' anyone in this group, living or otherwise, while we are on the water."

"Very well. Let's get to work with inventory and repairs. Ren, take the tiller for a while," Hemingway said, as the group dispersed about the boat continuing to repair the craft as best they could.

"Aye, aye," Ren said.

" 'Aye, aye'? Where the hell did you pick that up?"

"We have water and sailboats here, Hemingway. Plus these crystal-driven boats are not considered technology. We do know a thing or two about ships."

"Well, aren't you a man of the world."

"Can I ask you something?" the young man said to the artificial.

Hemingway took a deep breath, bracing himself for the next on-slaught of questions. "Sure, kid. Why not?" As he finished the sentence, he saw a small bottle over Ren's shoulder and reached over him to get it. "Here you go, Captain, a little nip to keep the night air away."

Anything to slow the questioning.

Ren looked at him with widening eyes. He had never drunk liquor before, though he was always curious about it. "I don't think I'm supposed to."

"Supposed to what? You mean while you're sailing in a stolen boat with an artificial and a Lokaryn, two real favorites of folks around here, and trying to escape slaughter by your government, you're going to follow some rule for children? Ren, wake up! It's graduation day, kid. From here on out you're an adult. Every day that you survive now is its own reward. Every day you live is a day you've earned for yourself, so live it."

"So drinking that swill is supposed to be some sort of reward?"

Hemingway was fast becoming irritated at the pragmatic nature of Ravensfordians. "No, this is a new experience. You may like it you may hate it, but at least experience it." Hemingway held out the bottle.

Ren took it warily. Giving the bottle a doubtful look, he uncorked the top, and after a quick sniff he drew the liquid into his mouth and swallowed.

Hemingway awaited the explosion with much anticipation. Ren contemplated the sensation for a moment; then, without so much as a hiccup, he smiled.

"Not bad," he said pleasantly, though his throat burned intensely. He would not give the artificial the satisfaction of seeing him cough and gag.

"Well, I'm glad you liked it," Hemingway said insincerely. He nodded and gave a little smile as he did.

"Not much of a reward for living through the last few days."

"Trust me, kid, there are far greater things than that out there, but you have to be willing to try them."

"I see. And what if it goes wrong? What if while you're out there trying new things you make a mistake?"

"For starters, kid, artificials never make mistakes, we call them logic flaws." Hemingway smirked as he said it. Despite himself he found that he liked and even respected the young son of Stannis Klemm. For the first time he gave Ren a completely honest answer. "It all comes down to who you want to be in this life. You can live a long life staying at home, never venturing past your front gate, or you can chance it to go outside the gate—maybe living a shorter life, but everyone I know who's done it hasn't really regretted it."

"You have no regrets?" Ren asked.

Hemingway fell silent and Ren continued to work the tiller. Finally, the young man said, "I know I'm not all that worldly and all, Hemingway, and I may not know what regret looks like, but that sure sounds a lot like the things I've regretted."

The comment had the effect of snapping Hemingway from his silence. "It's not, kid."

Ren awaited additional explanation.

"Sometimes you can't control what others do. You belong to something bigger and you trust others not to break the faith."

"Gedrick?" Ren asked.

Hemingway stopped at the doorway to the front passageway with his hand on the doorframe and looked over his shoulder.

"You're a smart kid. Don't let it get you in trouble." And with that he was gone.

The council quietly set the plan in motion and summoned the child Messiah to again appear before them. She traveled with an old woman and a young boy that no one knew anything about. All three approached the courtyard entryway to the great hall as the assassin drew his bowstring taut.

—Tor' Manat
Kwynian Sacred Writings

CHAPTER 52

Kwyne
Center Arc
Old Nehreton meeting hall

THE MOOD IN THE NEHRETON was a mix of somber gravity and claustrophobic discomfort. The prelates had gathered in what was called the Old Hall, the former meeting place of the Nehreton. It was an aging building that had long been relegated to an existence as a historical footnote on the grounds of the rohnin's formidable home, the Citadel. During Kwyne's growth, the burgeoning populace was represented by an equally burgeoning Nehreton, who outgrew the chambers of the Old Hall some generations after the Cataclysm. The new Nehreton hall, a much larger structure designed to accommodate many more generations of growth, became a part of the central structure of the Citadel and was topped only by the Rohnin's Perch. With the destruction of the rohnin's chambers atop the Citadel, the structures below could not be assured of physical safety, and thus the entire Nehreton crammed into this far too small, but safer space.

It was hot in the hall, as body heat and close confines conspired to make the prelate's ceremonial robes feel like personal crematoriums. The few fans, which might have moved even a small amount of air through the mass of bodies crammed into the dusty wooden hall, were off. All noncritical expenditures of power were suspended to conserve energy that might be needed later for the zone shields.

The first prelates who had entered the room had made the error of lighting cigars from the candles that burned to provide supplemental light, and the smoke mingled with the sweat and tension in an acrid stench. The few thin windows, a dozen feet above the crowd, were pried open, or simply broken out to allow for some air to circulate.

At the head of the room stood Ko'Doran. He saw the discomfort of the prelates and, had the circumstances been different, he would have enjoyed it. Despite the environment, and the situation that faced them, the leadership of Kwyne continued to whisper their small secrets and deal their small deals from inside their personal hells. Rumors followed the trains of smoke around the room. Rumors that the rohnin was alive, others that he was indeed dead. Some said he had been killed by the Lokaryns, some said that it was Rossums, others still that it was suicide. The chambers were more subdued than usual, but it was not somber enough in the room for Ko'Doran's liking. The prelates had not been briefed, so perhaps it was only natural for them to conduct business as usual. Still, it irritated him. For all they knew the rohnin was dead and he wanted the room funeral quiet. Such was in his power.

He nodded to the sergeant at arms, who called the assembly to order and as protocol dictated, a prayer was said. The formalities completed, Ko'Doran ascended the first level of the dais to address the prelates. Behind him, on the next level up, sat the throne of Kuna Latte. Moved from the Citadel just after the attack, the chair was a massive stone structure and had proven an enormous task to move so quickly. But the primare deemed it important that the symbol of Kwyne's guiding principles be prominently displayed before the Nehreton and the Kuhbrik was more than eager to provide the manpower to accomplish the task.

"Good evening," he began with the chair so conspicuously empty behind him. It was raised high enough that even in this crowded place all could see it. "Tonight is a grim night for Kwyne."

He noted that several heads nodded as he continued.

"We have suffered two attacks this evening. I know that some of your families fell victim to one of those and my prayers are with you and them. Be assured that we will do everything in our power to bring them home safely. We know from survivors that the vessel was attacked by Lokaryns, however, we do not know if they were in fact working as agents of their government, or as a rogue element."

He paused to allow them to absorb that information. Finally, he continued.

"Rohnin Damien Cairo is believed to be dead in this evening's explosion at the Citadel."

There are moments when the world stops and every moment after is different, be it good or bad. Kwyne was a society carved from conflict that had endured over the millennia through war and hardship. They knew what it meant to have been decapitated before the battle had begun in earnest. That fact now sat in the room like a hungry predator.

Across the room, N'orin looked at Kragen, attempting to gauge his reaction, but the older prelate's face remained impassive. Suddenly their grand plan seemed like an extremely narrow sliver of wood bridging the chasm between the world that was crumbling around them all and a renewed Kwyne. Images of the lokaric feeding chambers filled his view for a moment, and then he was pulled back to the Old Hall and the primare's words.

"Though we will have due time to honor our rohnin's work and memory, let us have a moment of silence so that we may offer our own prayers for his soul."

The prelates bowed their heads, and N'orin used the opportunity to whisper to Balazar. "Do you think he will do it?" he asked with a hint of panic. Balazar discreetly nodded yes, and gave his counterpart a look of disapproval.

When the moment had ended, Ko'Doran took a deep breath and said, "I will take your questions."

"What exactly are you planning to do to save our families?" a young prelate from the Sixteenth Arc inquired. He was a recently elected prelate whose wife and two small children had been taken.

"I am conferring with the Kuhbrik to determine an appropriate extraction plan." Ko'Doran felt it was an insipid question, but an expected one. They would need to focus on the survival of Kwyne if their families were going to have anything to come home to.

"When will the official period of mourning begin?" came an indistinct voice from the throng.

"At sunrise tomorrow. In accordance with our laws, we will begin the selection process for Rohnin Cairo's successor thirty days from then."

Ko'Doran looked around the chamber. No other prelates sought to be recognized. Between the heat of the room and the events of the day, exhaustion was claiming them.

Yes, he thought bitterly, the children of the Nehreton had had a very full day indeed. He knew what would come next. He had his part to play and would do so.

"As there appears to be no other business…"

As if responding to a cue in some macabre play, Kragen rose slowly.

"I wish to address the assembly," he announced.

Murmurs began to fill the chamber.

Somewhere in the crowd one prelate turned to another and whispered, "Another speech from the Kragen the Pious? Just what we need. Perhaps he will pray for cooling winds and do us all some good." The other prelate simply returned a grim smile and nodded.

Var Kragen ascended the steps to the dais as prelate of the Third Arc for the last time.

He came shoulder-to-shoulder with the primare. Ko'Doran stood facing the crowd as Kragen stood facing the throne. For his whole life, Var Kragen had wanted this moment. Now that he was here, his guts churned with resentment of the circumstances that brought him to it. The crowd began to murmur. Why was the prelate not turning around? They thought he was having words with the primare, but neither man seemed to talk.

But Ko'Doran did talk. Though his lips barely moved, his words moved the man of faith to the most pious and pure act of his life. He quoted from the book of Sacrifice: "Each to his own destiny. Thecla's will be done." Kragen thought about that for a moment, and in an equally imperceptible way said only a name.

"Gen' Roba."

Var Kragen waited only one more moment. His lifetime would end here. There would be no time after this, there was no hope for his future. He would become, in this next step, all he would ever be, and his hopes for his own future would be replaced by the utter servitude of his hope for Kwyne.

It took all the military discipline in his being to force his right foot to move forward. As he did, he could hear the rising of voices behind him. The heat and foul air forgotten, the prelates started to shout at the sight of the sacrilege. The upper dais was for the rohnin only.

Turning to the crowd, who felt shock, anger, and a host of other emotions, all as volatile as myst heating to a boil, he raised a short curved sword over his head. It gleamed in the firelight of the candles and crystal light that illuminated the chamber.

"*Isbakunm caralu mort!*" he shouted, quoting the scripture. "I claim the throne of Kuna Latte by the right of assassination."

Logic failure.

—Ren Klemm
Captain of the River Rat (Acting)

CHAPTER 53

HEMINGWAY JOINED THE REST OF the "crew" in the forward compartment, where they had found and laid out some of the river charts. The paper was stained and smelled of both urine and alcohol. It took the better part of an hour to find the maps amid the clutter, and almost as long to determine the correct one.

Derring spoke as she looked at the chart. "There are a number of channels and tributaries to the river. It gets quite large as we go along, which means when we get to the lower river there should be a fair amount of traffic to hide in." The ship lurched to the right slightly, and everyone grabbed on to something to stop from losing balance.

"Sorry. Obstacle in the water," came the voice of Ren from the back of the boat.

Lyrie spoke next. "It's going to get much worse from here. There's a division in the river coming up in a few miles. The right is a channel they cut to smooth the passage to the lower river. The drop is gradual and snakes down the mountainside. The left is the more direct route, but the drop is more severe and the water is extremely rough."

"This old bucket probably wouldn't take it," Timan noted.

Hemingway pointed to a large red X over the left route. "I think the previous owner felt as much, but she's a sturdy old thing. She'd have to be, the way the captain drove her into those pylons."

"Unfortunately the charts only show as far as the crossover into the extreme outer district. There is a military post that spans the river to prevent anyone from using the waterway as an entry point."

"Or in our case as an exit point," Chirra noted.

"It's a fair bet that the security will be significantly increased," Derring observed.

The ship lurched to the left this time.

"Ren! Do you mind?" Lyrie shouted back to her brother.

"Sorry! Obstacle in the river," Ren responded.

"So we're decided, then? At least on the route to the lower river? We chance the right channel or we could all wind up swimming."

"Agreed."

"Ren?" Hemingway called up to the young helmsman.

"Aye?"

Hemingway rolled his eyes but made no comment.

"Steer for the right fork on the river. The left has too much white water."

"Aye, aye, artificial!" Ren shouted back. Hemingway missed the cue.

"Once we get onto the lower river we should begin to look for safe harbors."

After looking over the maps for a while, Lyrie pointed to a seemingly large settlement. "I've heard of this one. Port Corilys is at the base of the mountains. It's a large post that a lot of the supplies for the farm come in to. Dad goes every so often, but he's never taken us."

"It's the outer district, and I'm sure not much of a family spot." Hemingway replied.

The boat again lurched to the left.

"Ren!" Lyrie shouted.

"Sorry. Osb-stical in the river."

Hemingway's eyebrows shot up as the boat began to rock and bounce more severely. He sprinted back to the wheelhouse. There he found a smiling Ren leaning on the tiller with a bottle in his hand.

Derring was there as well with a confused look on her face.

The others caught up quickly.

"What's going on?" Lyrie asked.

"He's drunk!" Chirra said in disbelief.

"Oh, crap," Hemingway said.

"What did you do?" Derring asked Hemingway.

"I gave the kid a drink. I didn't tell him to keep drinking."

"But you left him the bottle."

"I didn't think he'd keep drinking!"

"He's a kid who's never had a drink before, which by the way impairs judgment, and then you leave him the bottle. Your brain does how many teraflops per second and you didn't think he'd drink more?"

"We have bigger problems than that right now," Lyrie said, pointing over the ship's starboard side.

The right access to the channels drifted away as they all stood watching. The *River Rat* picked up speed now, as the current from the left fork of the river took hold and began to accelerate it down the mountainside.

"Ren, I said take the right fork," Hemingway shouted over the increasingly noisy river water.

Ren smiled pleasantly and replied, "Logic failure."

Onboard or overboard.

—Myst-clipper saying

CHAPTER 54

IT WAS GOOD NOT TO have drowned.

Ren's logic failure had placed the *River Rat* on the rapids, and despite many near calls, Hemingway had been correct: Though the ship wore a rickety overcoat in its nailed-on boards and cabins, it had a sturdy backbone. The psionic abilities of the Ravensfordians had saved them all on more than one occasion, while Hemingway's skills at the helm made the passage survivable, if harrowing. Lost in the adrenaline of the experience, no one knew how long it had taken, but they now traveled on the smoother waters of the foothills.

"How's the captain?" Hemingway asked.

"It's doubtful that he'll ever drink again, but he should survive. The bottom section of rapids tossed him around that cabin quite a bit. He's been hanging his head over the starboard bow now for about half an hour. Every time I think he can't bring up anything else, he starts again. It's fairly impressive to see."

"Well, he needs the practice if he's going to travel with the *Shicaine*."

There was a pause as Derring looked at Hemingway.

"What makes you think we can reach the *Shicaine*?"

"We won't. They'll reach us."

"You think they know about us?"

"It would make sense. The last I heard of Captain Gedrick he was still out on the mysts. He was traveling the northern routes, and he gave the ship an alias. So far as I know he's out of the pirate business, but he's out there."

"It wasn't piracy. How long ago was this?"

"Well, it wasn't purity either. About three or four years."

"*Years?* He could be dead, for all you know."

"Maybe, but I don't think so. I think the situation in Kwyne probably created a bit of a stir, and now with the phobes buttoning up the zone, I think people in the myst-clipper business are lining up to make some serious money running the blockades."

"It doesn't take long for information to get around, that's true."

The sound of terrific retching came from the bow of the boat.

"I think that boy is going to vomit up his own anus," Hemingway said.

Derring ignored the comment. "So you think Gedrick will equate the disturbances in Kwyne and Ravensford with us?"

"I think that if you and I have been targeted already and our only link is the *Shicaine*, it's a fair bet that he's probably already been the target of a disturbance of his own."

"Why? Why go after the crew after all this time?"

"The deal was that if anyone made contact, we'd all be hunted down."

"But why do it in a way that reunited us? They could have killed you and let me think you were still alive to draw me out."

"Maybe we're live bait for bigger fish. Maybe the only way to get to Gedrick and Kisner and the rest was to have us. Maybe someone wants the *Shicaine* crew intact for some reason. Who knows, but I think if Gedrick catches wind of the upset in Phobes' Zone here and someone is on his own tail, he'll put it together and head to Klemm's farm."

"And find what?"

"A reason to come to the monk's."

Derring thought about that for a while. "And then?"

"We get on the fastest ship on the myst and get the hell out of the way of whatever is going on."

"Somehow I don't think it will be that easy."

Chirra burst into the cabin, extremely excited.

"Ship!" she blurted out.

"Calm yourself, it was to be expected," Derring said.

"It's coming right at us. It has guns."

"We could use that fast ship right about now. Timan, take the tiller," Hemingway said, as he moved forward.

"Keep a straight course," Derring shouted. She grabbed a bottle of the captain's "whiskey" as she did.

Lyrie and Hemingway exchanged a look, Lyrie's questioning and Hemingway's confused.

"The rest of you remain in the aft cabin."

"What the hell good is that going to do? Go overboard."

"Trust me. It's too close to dawn and if we get split up, we're really in trouble," Derring said.

"Really in trouble she says," Timan muttered to himself. "I'm traveling with an artificial and an undead in a stolen boat but I wouldn't want to get in trouble." He shook his head and focused on looking nonchalant as the security cruiser came along side.

"This is the Ninth Arc Security Force," the man lied. "Heave to and prepare to be boarded."

"On what authority do you intend to board my ship," Timan tried to bluff.

"We have more guns than you do. Heave to!" The officer of the deck on the security ship was a tough-looking character with far more scars then brain cells.

"I'm waiting. On what authority?"

"We have instructions to inspect any suspicious-looking vessel on the river."

"Well, as you can see we're not that."

"Heave to or be fired upon. We have authority from the arc government." In this he told the truth; however, he lied as he continued, "Suit yourself, we've already sunk one ship tonight."

Timan idled the steam vents as the security ship came along side.

The sound of boat hooks slamming onto the *River Rat*'s deck made a jarring sound.

A small boarding party of three jumped down onto the roof of the rear cabin as others stood guard with crystal pulse rifles on the deck of the larger ship. The leader of the boarding party hopped down to confront Timan.

"Well, do you have a name?"

"Yes I do, do you?" Timan's defiant streak rose to full bloom.

"You might not be so smart if I blew this ship out from underneath you."

"I am Captain Jos…lin."

"Well Captain Jos…*lin*, what are you doing out on the river so late?"

"For us it's early. We started out a few hours ago."

"You are light in the water."

"We have yet to pick up our cargo."

"And that is?"

"Mercenaries. For the search upriver."

Hemingway and Derring could both make out the conversation and looked at each other with growing alarm. Hemingway whispered to Derring, "Great, Timan, and we'll be picking them up where? You don't know any destinations down here except the one we're going to."

"And where will you be picking them up?" the leader of the boarding party asked.

"We're not sure."

Hemingway rolled his eyes. "Perfect. An even dumber answer than I anticipated. He should go back to singing about cows."

"You're not sure? You aren't a very bright cargomaster, now, are you?"

"These are mercenaries, they have enemies. They wouldn't tell us where they were, only that we should travel downriver in this area by the western bank and they'd signal when they saw us."

"And how will they know you?"

"Look at the damn silhouette of the ship, man! You think I'd build it like this without a purpose? It's pretty unique."

Hemingway looked surprised. "OK, that wasn't bad."

Derring shot him a look. "Shut up."

"What's in the cabins?"

"Crew, mostly sleeping. I'm resting them, we have a long day ahead of us."

The leader of the boarding party turned and poked his head in the door of the first cabin to find three "crew" lying in makeshift sleeping areas. He nodded to one of the boarding party to check the forward cabin. Timan could barely contain himself, he was so nervous, and it showed.

"Is there a problem, Captain Jos-*lin*?" The man always used the same halting pronunciation that Timan had originally used to avoid saying Jospher. He did not know if their names were out yet. He began to sweat while Derring sat in the forward cabin looking sadly at Ren and uncorked the bottle she carried with her.

"No, I just don't think you want to look in there."

"I will look anywhere I damn well please, Captain Jos-*lin*, and when I am done looking, then we will decide the fee for not blowing your ship out of the water."

Though he would never admit it to anyone else, a part of Timan was looking forward to Derring destroying these men.

The second man jumped down between the two structures and moved toward the forward cabin. With an enormous racket a wild figure lunged from the doorway and was on the man at once. The man screamed as Ren vomited profusely on him. The smell of the liquor that Derring had waved under his nose set off a new round of retching and vomiting. The man threw Ren to the ground and watched as the young man pulled himself to the railing and continued to vomit. The men aboard the pursuit ship and the men of the boarding party broke into laughter as the man covered in vomit heaved himself over the opposite railing and began to retch.

"Sorry about that, he can't hold his liquor," Timan said truthfully.

"Check out that cabin!" the head of the boarding party bellowed.

The first man continued to vomit and the third man just shook his head.

"Not a chance. Floor's probably covered in the stuff."

"Come on, we have better things to do than shake down this old scow. They have nothing but rotgut whiskey, and there's a ship heading downriver that looks like it might actually have something of worth. We're going to miss it if we keep on with this. Let's go!"

The leader of the boarding party sneered at Timan, who stared straight ahead.

"Don't let me catch you on this part of the river again. Mercenaries or no. Do you understand?"

"Yes," Timan answered. Staring straight ahead.

The *River Rat* sailed on as the boarding ship departed. Once they were out of range, Derring and Hemingway moved quickly from the front to the rear cabin and joined the others. Ren continued to vomit where he was.

"That was too close," Lyrie said. "We should put in somewhere."

"No. If the locals can act like that, it means that the river security is occupied elsewhere. Probably working their way upriver, the long and safe route. Ren's mistake…"

"Loooogic flaw," Ren tried to shout while retching.

"…may have steered us around the worst of it. I say we keep on as we are."

"And when we hit the outpost?"

"What's the difference if we cross it now or later? We still have the same problems. With some luck maybe we can find a chart of the lower river so we can time our crossing for night."

"We push on, agreed?"

"Agreed," they all said in turn.

"Agr…" Ren did not finish his statement.

Meet Alexi Tovash!

—Boran Culver, proprietor, Custom Personalities

CHAPTER 55

Thieves' Zone
Outside the perimeter wall

IT WOULD BE SO SIMPLE a thing to end his life right now.

Hennix sat on the rooftop toward the end of one of the longest nights of his life. The dawn would certainly not make it any better. In fact, the only thing that he could see stretched out before him was an endless number of endless nights and endless days until someone found him and put a bullet in his head. Why wait? Why not now? A small gathering of rats, in total agreement with him, watched him closely in the hope that he might soon become food.

He had nearly finished the contents of the first bottle. He downed the rest as he looked out over the mysts towards where the funeral barge had exploded. The last of the local scavengers were making their way back to shore, where the trading and bargaining would begin. He cracked open a second bottle and wondered if any of their bounty included parts of Bowman, or if the 'droid had somehow managed to escape. Either way, there was nothing that he could do about it.

As the human scavengers departed, carrion birds were venturing over to investigate what was left. The site was strewn with remains: Hennix had ensured that the plentiful galley stores were positioned for maximum dispersion, so that food would litter the surface and attract the birds. In order for the plan to work, it had to appear that everyone on board had died.

The first birds found a banquet laid and set upon it energetically.

This caught the attention of others, and it wasn't long before a feasting and squabbling flock covered the area.

Satisfied by the display, Hennix prepared to set the last piece of the plan into action. He drew a set of well-used tools from his ragged satchel and laid them out in front of himself with care. Then he drew out a small metal box, no larger than a thick deck of cards. He placed his left thumb on a scanner embedded seamlessly into the lid. It activated immediately, and a small beam of light evaluated the thumbprint. This was followed by his right index finger on the same pad and his left ring finger on a second pad on the left side of the box.

"Can't be too careful with Mr. Tovash," he said. "My life depends on this man."

A small sound emanated from the box, which he knew to be a fuse burning through the inner sealant, and with a very faint popping noise the object was again still. Looking at his small audience of rats, Hennix held the box out as if toasting to their health.

"Meet Alexi Tovash!" he said, and opened the box, placing it directly in front of him. A small luminescent cube floated in supercooled mist. "Don't look so puzzled, my friends," he told the rats. "It's really quite simple. Hennix is a hunted man. Even with all of this, they still may be on the watch for me. I can't risk porting into the ether to find the *Shicaine*, as the bad guys would read my signal before I had a chance to do any sort of search." He picked up the bottle of tequila for more anesthesia. "Furthermore, since net rogues aren't welcome in some 'civilized' areas, there are sensors all over the place that will eventually pick up my ether port. In sum, comrades"—he lifted the bottle to toast them—"I can't travel, I can't port, and I can't sit on this roof for the rest of my life, so Hennix is a little bit screwed." He drank deeply from the bottle. "Even if I could travel, some small behavior on my part could give me away, and I wouldn't even know I was doing it."

He picked up the box. "But Alexi here is a whole other person. Quirks and habits all his own. The poor guy is going to have a *very* bad day. Starting now."

He began to remove the processor from his head. It was excruciatingly painful, and several times he had to stop and drink from the tequila bottle. Finally, he removed the last of the two-inch screws and, suppressing the urge to scream, pried it out.

He gasped as it popped free.

"Start the clock, if you would," he said to the nearest rodent. "In thirty-five minutes, I stop breathing. The ether port is rigged into our nervous system to control breathing, heart rate, metabolism, and everything else so we can stay in the ether longer. The brain adapts to this and eventually the chip takes over. Consequently," he went on as he prepared the Tovash implant for insertion into the port, "without this wired into my brain, everything shuts down in…thirty-four minutes. Roughly."

Hennix had that much time to make his modifications and to get the device reimplanted into his head.

As he examined the unit to make sure that he hadn't damaged it, he dug around in his satchel and pulled out a small square device, which he plugged into the main port. The device made a whirring noise and began the process of uploading the personality overlay. As it did, the light from the white glowing cube dimmed until extinguished. Hennix had designed the program himself and, once installed, it would completely suppress his identity. Anyone he met would believe him to be Alexi Tovash. Of equal importance, he would believe it. This would allow him to be able to jack into the ether safely and sift for information. He had segmented a small part of his processor to scan for certain patterns. If found, these would trigger the personality overlay to abort. If not found, he would live the rest of his life as Alexi Tovash. Either he would find what he needed to avenge Lucy's death, or he would be spared the pain of ever knowing she existed. It wasn't ideal, but it was the only option he had.

Satisfied that the unit was undamaged, he slid it back into the port, reinserted the screws, and tightened them down. He put away all his tools and the small black box.

The next part would be the hardest.

Pressing the reset button.

Once it was pressed, the processor would reboot and he would lose consciousness. During the time he was out, the program would activate a small army of nanites to restructure his facial bones, lengthen his vocal cords, and make a number of other changes, including severing his hair stalks and impeding further growth. Once finished, they would shut down at the direction of the program. When he revived, he would for all practical purposes be a different person.

He looked to the sky and hoped that Lucy would somehow be watching out for him from wherever she was.

"If this fails, *bon appétit*, boys!" he said, raising the bottle to them again, and taking one last drink. Still holding the bottle, he lay down with his head pillowed on his duffel. His expression somber now, he said a silent good-bye, as much to himself as to anyone else, and pressed the button.

"I THINK HE'S DEAD," SAID the boy with the stick.

"He sure smells like it," said the boy with him. "What the heck happened to his hair?"

The pair stared at the figure on the ground. His shirt was torn, and there were clumps of blond hair all over the duffel under his bald head. His right hand was wrapped around the neck of a tequila bottle.

"Poke him again," the second boy said.

The boy with the stick leaned over and gave the man another sharp poke in the ribs. This time the man flinched, and the boy jerked the stick back.

"He's waking up. Take his bottle," the second boy urged.

"I'm not gonna take it, you take it," replied the boy with the stick.

Before either boy found the nerve to swipe the tequila, the man opened one eye.

The boys ran.

ALEXI TOVASH AWOKE ON A roof disoriented, reeking, and with absolutely no idea as to how he had gotten there.

He propped himself up on one elbow and promptly vomited. His stomach was a churning mass, his head was in a vise, and his whole body ached.

The bottle he was clutching might have something to do with that. He opened his hand and let the bottle roll away. A flicker of movement and a scrabbling sound drew his bleary attention to a couple of rats scurrying along the base of the rooftop's wall.

More than a couple, he saw as he sat up. But they were keeping their distance.

"I don't blame you," he told them, having caught wind of himself. His face itched and was sticky with drool and vomit. He swiped a hand across his mouth, and it came away covered in hair. Blond, human hair. He looked around and saw the same hair all over the duffel bag where his head had been. He ran the hand over his scalp and found it completely smooth. Not shaven smooth, but hairless smooth.

"What the hell?" He got up slowly, much to the protest of his head, which now pounded in response to the effort.

He looked out over the edge of the building and then back to where he had been. He sat down next to the duffel and began pulling out the contents. First he found a full bottle of tequila. It matched the one he had been holding and an empty one standing off to the side.

"Why the hell would I pack three bottles of tequila?" Shaking his head, he dug deeper. Two boxes were next. A small one that was completely seamless and a larger one resembling a toolkit. He could not find a way to open either.

Digging further down he found fresh clothes, weapons, a few other equipment kits, and a large wad of cash. He quickly looked around to see if anyone was watching, then laid one of the energy pistols across his lap.

All the way at the bottom of the bag was a lined pouch. He pulled it out and opened it to find a handwritten letter.

Mr. Tovash,

Your application has been selected and you have been chosen above the other applicants for this mission.

Your memory has been erased by our agents in keeping with standard procedures. Should you be successful, your memory will be restored to you as is customary.

Please proceed to the Drunken Angry Bitch, in Orlehachs' Arc of the Thieves' outer district. There you will meet your contact. We advise extreme caution, and use of deadly force is authorized.

Good luck.

At the bottom, in a different handwriting scrawled diagonally across the page, was a brief note.

Good luck, Alexi. Be careful on this one, it's not like the other missions. H

"So what the hell am I?" The weapons he pulled from the bag seemed to be from Thorpe's. Perhaps, then, he was a Thorpe's "adjuster"—their name for an assassin.

"I think they overdid it on the memory wipe." He thought a bit more about his situation. Why the hell would an adjuster wake up on a rooftop hungover?

"OK, from the top: I am Alexi Tovash. This much I know for certain."

If you wake up not locked and primed,
you start the day two steps behind.

—Children's rhyme from Chumley's Zone

CHAPTER 56

Deep myst
Aboard the *Shicaine*

GEDRICK'S VISION BETRAYED HIM. BOTH his natural and cybernetic sight were failing in the swirling images that surrounded him. Flickers and flashes of passionate moments so real as to break the heart, but never realized

"Captain, you seem distracted," came the voice of the one woman he had ever loved. Her voice was gentle, playful even. Though he could not see her, he could feel her presence moving through him like a spirit.

"No, not distracted. This isn't real." It was the great paradox of lost love—always there, but never there. His eyes took hers in. They were a surreal blue, an unreachable depth that drew the breath from him.

"Does that matter?" she said. "Here, we can be together. Here, you are safe." Her eyes were all that he could see now, but he could feel her body near his: the movement of her breasts against his chest as she breathed and the strength in her hands as she held his.

He closed his eyes and leaned toward her. In his mind's eye he could see the moment in its clarity and perfection. He would gladly give his life to remain in this moment forever. As her lips parted to receive his, the words fell from her mouth:

"Bridge to Captain Gedrick."

The world shattered like exploding crystal. Light scattered as the pieces fell back to reality and he along with them.

"Bridge to Captain Gedrick," the intercom squawked again.

Gedrick opened his eyes. He glared at the ceiling above his bunk for a moment and then looked at his timepiece. It was 3:17 in the morning. He had been asleep for perhaps two hours. He pressed the flashing button on his comm link and began to rub his eyes.

"Gedrick here," he said, betraying none of the anger or resentment he felt at being awoken.

"Captain, we need you up here," the first officer replied. "We've been pulling in a pretty strange repeater for about forty five minutes." Not sounding completely convinced, he added, "It's probably just a ghost."

"Mr. Chapman. Is Seyschell up there?"

"Yes, sir."

"Mr. Chapman, you never gave much credence to myst phantoms. I would suggest that you look at my former copilot and watch for that small smirk starting to form at the edge of her mouth," Gedrick replied.

"Well, Captain, I'm looking right at her and she very much looks like the Lokaric Council is here for her soul."

"You've been had and I'm going back to bed."

The comm link suddenly barked as if in rebuttal, "Dammit, Gedrick, would you get your ass up here! It's no joke." It was Seyschell this time, and she sounded genuinely alarmed.

"I'm on my way," he responded, and quickly began to get dressed.

Up on the bridge, the color began to come back into Seyschell's face. "Care to explain that to me again?" Chapman asked.

"Your myst phantom is a ghost," she repeated.

"What the hell are you talking about?" the first officer asked, using a rare expletive.

"Let Gedrick explain," she said, suddenly unsure of exactly how much information he had shared with his current second in command. Recent events indicated that obviously it was not much.

It took Gedrick less than two minutes to get dressed and arrive on the command bridge. A crewman handed him his customary cup of coffee, which he gratefully accepted. "It's extra strong," the man said. "I have a feeling that you're going to need it." Gedrick nodded and then looked at the two expectantly.

Chapman began, "We've been receiving this repeating—" and was interrupted by Seyschell: "It's a railroad extraction code, Gedrick. You won't believe who it's from."

"Kisner?" Gedrick asked hopefully.

"Would you forget about Kisner? It's not a member of the crew."

Gedrick looked at Seyschell, not understanding why she wasn't coming right out and saying the identity of the sender. Chapman had pulled a piece of the initial message off the printer and handed it to Gedrick. As was often his style, if he had a reaction, his expression did not belie it. He looked at the paper and then at Seyschell and then back to the paper.

HEXA—DALON—FAHTA—HEXA

Hexa—the code for extraction.

Dalon—a prearranged pickup location.

Fahta—the code for the person who needed to be picked up.

Hexa, repeated at the end—danger was imminent.

He read the words again, his mind scanning for the underlying meaning. Two answers presented themselves: Either reports about the sender's death were erroneous, or it was a trap. Had he been a betting man, he wouldn't have put his credits on either choice.

After what seemed a small eternity to both present and former first officers, he asked simply, "You're sure of this?"

Seyschell nodded. "It's been coming in every thirty seconds on a repeating loop, for the past half hour."

Gedrick nodded. "Have the crew set course for Kwyne, Nev. I'll provide the exact coordinates as we get closer."

Chapman unable to stand the suspense any longer, blurted out, "What does the message mean?"

"It's an extraction code, Neville."

"An extraction from where?"

Gedrick considered his next words carefully, "Thieves'," he finally said.

An uncomfortable silence ensued.

"And who might need an emergency extraction from Thieves' in the middle of the night?"

Gedrick exhaled deeply. "Soon enough."

A signal broke the silence of the bridge alerting everyone to an incoming message on the display:

HEXA—DALON—FAHTA—HEXA...

The child Messiah stopped, kissed the old woman's cheek, then stepped away from her companions. She turned, looked up to the archer, and held her hands out wide. The arrow slipped the bow and flew straight toward her heart.

—Tor' Manat
Kwynian Sacred Writings

CHAPTER 57

Kwyne
Center Arc
The Catacombs of the Fossore

IN THE DARKNESS OF THE catacombs came a skittering noise. Slowly moving about the crypts with the loving care a spider bestows on an entrapped morsel, one of the Fossore traced the cobbled stones with an inhuman appendage. His face was human enough in its expressions, if not in its construction. On that face he wore a concerned expression. He had left the prayer service earlier than most to resume his duties. It was with no small degree of nausea that he considered the fact that in a very few days the Kwynians would be coming below to entomb their now-dead rohnin, Damien Cairo.

He liked dead rohnins better than the living ones. Less trouble, and most of all they could be trusted far more than their living counterparts; they were a part of history when they entered this realm. Yes, far less trouble.

He moved along, hoping to outrun the wave of unpleasantness that had greeted him a moment ago. He sighed and accepted the coming intrusion as inevitable. Those from above would be here for only a few hours. The representatives, those still human enough to interact with the

Kwynians without revolting the visitors, would do the greeting. The Kwynians would conduct their ceremony and be gone. A few, the historians of the group, would want to tour, but never more than briefly. He picked up his pace as if to leave the unpleasant thought far behind. As he did, a small rodent scurried across his path. He quickly and neatly speared the animal and, consuming its head, stored the rest in a small membrane on his back for later consumption.

He licked what remained of his lips and moved on. When he came to the Mural of Thecla before the council, he was again greeted by another wave of nausea. He stopped cold, his weight shifting across multiple legs that tapped on the floor as each raised and lowered. He breathed in the air here. The nausea grew more intense. He raised his head and, looking about the room, spotted a section of the mural that glowed more brightly than the rest. He vaulted over the sarcophagus of a revered general and stopped himself from hitting the wall at a full run with two powerful forelegs. He breathed deeply and was consumed with the pain in his stomach and his head.

He reared back and came to a fearsome height as he did. He let out a scream that would alert the entire community. It wasn't a shrill panic shriek, but rather a low ominous tone that pulsated through the rock and passages. As it spread, it was felt in the chest of every nearby Fossore who added to it.

Soon the entire catacomb rumbled with the alert.

"Intruders!"

Like hornets pouring from a nest under attack, the Fossore poured from every crevice of the catacombs and from the levels below, the places they had dug for themselves, their civilization below their sacred task.

Countless numbers swarmed up into the catacombs, filling every space until there were few places left to hide. They followed the trail that grew stronger and stronger and were ultimately joined by many others. Finally they found the one place, the last place that the profane could be. The first moved slowly forward; he had uncovered the incursion and would be given first kill. His appetite was difficult to sate, and he would consume this intruder with relish.

The stone door held no historical value and was expendable for the element of surprise. He took a deep breath and, running full force from a short distance away, hit it with all his might, exploding the door into dozens of deadly projectiles. He burst into the room, expecting to see dying or stunned prey. He brought himself up to his full height, forelegs with bared barbs ready to impale the interlopers, but as he spun to look at every corner, he found nothing.

Many miles away, the major and his traveling companions completed the first leg of their escape.

Belief in the preordained is the mark of a weak mind or a weak will or both.

—Akiro Tonla, third rohnin of Kwyne

CHAPTER 58

THE CASK OF RED ALE loosed itself from Vis-Shan's grip and began to roll away toward the bank. The young man fell to his knees trying to grab it, but missed by a lot. Picking up momentum, it went airborne when it reached the bottom, finally landing in the stream with a great splash. Someone down the river would make a lucky find later.

The monk watched the whole scene from the kitchen with mild amusement. It was not the first time this had happened, and the younger man's frustrated reaction was typically so comical that it more than made up for the lost ale.

The older man took a sip of green tea and waited for it.

Usually, his young aide was fairly animated, wildly flailing his arms and cursing. But not this time. Instead, he remained still, a living monument to defeat. The lack of reaction bothered the monk more than the outbursts. In the days since he had shared his visions with the younger man, Vis-Shan had been quieter, more contemplative. He no longer made threats of suicide, and the monk wondered if in his head he had moved from threats to planning. And yet in some other way, Vis-Shan seemed more at peace.

The monk got up from his seat at the hand carved kitchen table and went outside.

"Come now, Vis-Shan," he called out merrily, "it's no big deal.

There are plenty more where that one came from." Vis-Shan remained still and quiet. The monk tried again, "You've just made some poor farmer's day, my son!" On these words Vis-Shan fell facedown on the dirt path that ran from the brewery to the house. Had he been prone to levity, the monk might have thought it a joke for his benefit. But this thought was soon banished when the young man began to convulse on the ground.

"Vis-Shan!" the monk called, breaking into a run. His aide had finally made good on the threats of suicide. The elder man gathered his focus in preparation to stave off the poison that he was now convinced Vis-Shan had taken. Upon reaching the young man's side, he placed his hand on Vis-Shan's forehead to discern what he had taken. Vis-Shan's thoughts held the truth: There was no poison. Instead, the monk found himself pulled inside a vision.

The monk recognized what was happening immediately. Though the images were different from his own, all of the elements were there: confusion, chaos, and a foreboding sense of doom. But this seemed less dreamlike. It was as if Vis-Shan had a clearer vision of what was to come and, for reasons that the monk could not explain, he found the clarity less than comforting. But like his own visions, he was powerless to do anything but let the drama run its course.

The scene unfolded with an explosion high above the outer district crossover point, at the left channel of the lower Sengoran River. Beyond this area was the entry to the extreme outer district, and the monk knew that he must be seeing the bridge of the military outpost that spanned the river. The sun was shining, and even though the water was high because of the growing season, the river was usually placid.

But not at this particular moment.

Instead, it roiled and rolled as a battery of artillery was loosed upon it from high above. He thought it a pointless waste of ammunition until he noticed one small detail. In the midst of the churning waters was what could only be described by the loosest of definitions as a boat. It was clear from the trajectory of the bombardment that this was the intended target, though to the monk's amazement the small craft was somehow managing to evade the maelstrom.

"Twenty-eight degrees to starboard should do it," he heard a gun-nery major yell. The battlement unleashed another volley and the boat lurched to port as the pilot desperately tried to evade the incoming fire. It missed the ship by the smallest of fractions but managed to create a large wave that crashed into the starboard bow and washed over a young woman who was desperately trying to hold on. Her efforts for naught, she slid across the deck and over the port-side railing.

"Should we put a sharpshooter on her, Major?" a young corporal asked.

"Negative, stay on the boat. The river will take her."

"Aye, sir," the corporal replied.

"Tell the tower gunners to charge their cannons," the major ordered.

The corporal broke into a run, and soon a low hum began to reso-nate from the towers at each end of the bridge.

"Span defense, focus!" the major shouted. "You're not fighting with blunderbusses."

The lower Sengoran defense team was a defense team in name only. In truth they were a highly trained fighting force, second in skill only to the Seb-Ichi themselves. They guarded an important access point in and out of Ravensford and if not feared, they were at least respected by most ship captains. "What is the problem?" the major yelled. "You should be able to blow them out of the water with a full drunk on after the spring harvest festival!" His face was red with anger. How was it that they were evading his overwhelming force?

The monk, being strongly connected to the vision, realized the an-swer before the major did. There could only be one explanation: Seb-Ichi. He said a silent prayer that this fact would remain hidden from the defense team. As if in repudiation of his wish, the air was shattered by the repeat of a high powered sniper rifle. The monk watched in horror as the boat began to pitch violently on the water and knew that whatever Seb-Ichi protection it had been afforded was now lost. As if to accentu-ate the point, the cannons high up in the towers let loose their deadly cargo with devastating effect.

It was over in a second and the monk wept bitterly as he felt seven souls snap their tethers and begin the long journey to Shi-Hol. The last thing he witnessed before the world went dark was the body of Vis-Shan lying still and broken on the left bank of the Sengoran River.

The initial merging of corporate culture with assassin philosophy, while motivating, created a very chaotic and frankly counterproductive business model. This was remedied by the introduction of "backers," the person or persons contracted to avenge an assassination. This created stability and unheard-of profitability. Our institute was of course instrumental in bringing about this change.

—Robert Inski
Better Corporate Profits Through Directed Assassination
The Inski Institute

CHAPTER 59

Deep myst
Aboard the *Shicaine*

HEXA—DALON—FAHTA—HEXA.

The message repeated.

Neville Chapman stood looking at a roomful of strangers, most especially his captain, with whom he'd served these four years. A moment before, he'd thought he knew Captain Gedrick at least on some level.

"Set course, helmsman," the first officer instructed. "The captain has the conn." Then, without asking permission, without a word of explanation, he turned and walked off the bridge.

It took only a moment's shared look between Gedrick and Seyschell for the captain to follow his first officer into the companionway.

"Neville," Gedrick called, following him down the passageway. "Neville!" he repeated more emphatically. Then: "Mr. Chapman!"

That had the effect of catching the first officer's attention, and he stopped abruptly and stood as his captain caught up. "Sir," he said stiffly.

"You knew there was a past to this ship when you signed aboard."

"The past is not my concern at the moment. The lack of a future is."

"Meaning?"

"Do you think me ignorant, Captain? The rohnin of Kwyne is dead. Assassinated. Suddenly we receive a mysterious message from Kwyne: an emergency pickup. Since when do we consort with assassins?"

Gedrick took a deep breath. "All is not as it seems."

"They're going to kill this entire crew, everyone who has shown you any sort of loyalty. Have you considered that? You asked for the trust of the crew and they gave it to you without question. The magnitude of the forces that could be arrayed to try and assassinate a zone leader will crush these people. They are common sailors who tossed away their lives because they trusted you."

"They had the opportunity to leave."

"They thought they were protecting you. They didn't know they were getting into *this*. Who else is coming for us now?" Chapman turned and started to walk away.

"Are you leaving the ship?" Gedrick found himself demanding of his first officer.

As the words left his mouth he found himself transported into the past. A time some fifteen years before, when he was a young officer then serving aboard the *Impulse.*

"Are you leaving the ship?" came the inebriated voice of Gedrick's captain: Arles Timmerson. He was slurring his speech and leaned heavily to one side. His right hand held a bottle of whiskey; his left rested on the pommel of his saber.

"You know I have been intending to leave for some time now. My ship is ready in the dockyard."

Timmerson interrupted. "And that old scow won't last ten minutes on the myst."

"I think it will."

"I won't come to your rescue when you screw up, Gedrick. You're turning your back on this ship and crew."

"Captain, you know it's time for me to move on. You said it yourself, I'll have a ship of my own someday."

"You can have the *Impulse* when I die. The routes, the contracts, the works."

"I don't want to think about you dying, though if you keep drinking like you have these past few weeks, it's going to be soon."

Timmerson continued to draw deeply from the bottle as Gedrick continued.

"Captain, I'm grateful for—for everything. You've been like a father to me, but…"

"Get out. If you're going, get out," Timmerson spat as everything within him screamed for the young man he considered a son to stay.

"I don't want it to be like this. We can help each other on the myst. All those contracts you've had to pass on because you didn't have a captain you trusted to take the second shipment."

"I said get out."

"Drink has the better of you. All too often these days."

"Get out or I will throw you overboard," Timmerson snapped.

"If and when you finally decide to sober up you old bastard, send word and we can talk like men. Until then, crawl inside your bottle and drown in your self-pity." Gedrick turned viciously away from the older man and grabbed his last duffel, throwing it over his shoulder. He stormed out into the companionway, angry and bitter that it would end this way. He had contained most of his anger, which was no small feat for the young brash officer.

The older man was not so able, however.

The whiskey bottle came hurtling out of the room and smashed against the far bulkhead. Gedrick dropped his bag and spun as he heard sharp metal sliding out of it scabbard. As he did he found Arles Timmerson in a fury with his sword drawn and moving quickly toward him.

"Let's see your Seb-Ichi training save you now, phobe!" Timmerson spat.

Instinct now took over, as the time for words between the two crumbled to dust. Gedrick manifested his sword as his bondling reacted to the threat. It initially projected from his hand as a blunt spear, striking Timmerson squarely in the forehead in an attempt to subdue the man. Gedrick pulled the blow to avoid killing him. It was a mistake. He hadn't used enough force to subdue the enraged man, who was now within striking distance.

Gedrick pulled the bondling back into a saber configuration just in time to deflect a slashing attack to the chest. Timmerson laid on the attacks. He was beyond thought and rationality now, uncoupled from reason, as anger and alcohol melded into rage. He wielded the sword without any consideration of the consequences.

Gedrick was making his own mistakes. He parried each blow, waiting for a chance to disable but not kill the man who was attacking him. This forced a retreat through the passageways of the ship. His anger, though immense, did not match the feral onslaught of his captain. While he did not want to kill the man, he did want it to hurt. Enough that he would never forget it. If Timmerson were maimed then so be it.

They fought viciously out onto the deck as the crew watched the first officer and the captain battle. Gedrick found himself less and less able to contain the attacks he was throwing at the captain. While Timmerson was a dangerous man, he was also thirty years the senior of his first officer and was beginning to fatigue. His attacks were getting more wild; his sword was becoming less accurate. It was at this moment that Gedrick knew he could kill the man. And he wanted to. His anger grew with each moment of the fight, till he was not conscious of his actions from moment to moment. If he loosed the bondling, Timmerson would die. With a sweeping motion, he knocked Timmerson to the ground and pulled the bondling into a razor-sharp blade poised above the man's chest. He screamed and plunged the sword downward while the captain lay flat on his back with the wind knocked out of him. The tip of the sword broke the older man's skin and drew blood. Though he had not inflicted a deep wound, Gedrick could sense it through the bondling, and it was enough for him to regain himself. Stunned at what he had just done to a man he called friend, he yanked the sword out of Timmerson's flesh.

Gedrick turned away, emotionally exhausted and breathing heavily from the strain of the fight. Timmerson, however, regained himself and was on his feet with an unnatural agility.

"I'm not done with you yet," he growled as he brandished his sword and swung again.

Gedrick's bondling instinctually manifested again and deflected the blow.

"The fight is over, old man. I'm leaving." He withdrew the bondling again and inhibited any further action. It was to be his last mistake of the day, as an even more enraged Timmerson struck his final blow.

The last memory Gedrick had of the *Impulse* and Timmerson was his former captain's sword being driven into his eye as he lost consciousness.

On the *Shicaine*, Gedrick's reverie had allowed Chapman to continue on down the companionway to his cabin. Gedrick sighed deeply, collecting himself before proceeding to the first officer's quarters.

After knocking on the door, he entered slowly and found his first officer sorting through books on his shelf. An empty duffel sat thrown on the bed, though nothing was in it.

"Are you leaving the ship?" Gedrick asked quietly.

"I'm not sure," the first officer answered honestly. After pausing a moment, he continued.

"How many years have I been aboard this ship? Whatever her name was, I've served to the best of my ability. To not have your trust now shows my failure as your second-in-command."

"I trust you, Neville. I have trusted you with my life and more importantly with my ship and her crew. This is the only way I know to protect you from my mistakes. Once you know the full truth, any possibility of protecting you and the others from it is lost. I don't believe the person we're picking up is an assassin. I can't tell you why I believe what I believe until we get there and I see who has sent the message. I trust you Neville, but telling you more, leaves you no way out."

"It seems to have worked out the same in any case."

"Perhaps, but I wish it hadn't. The question now remains, do you still trust me?"

"Captain, can I ask you a question?"

"Of course."

"What happened in the passageway just now?"

Gedrick sat down heavily in the chair next to the first officer's desk. It was a chair that had been occupied by many seamen and young officers receiving counsel or reprimand from the first officer over the years.

Gedrick related the tale that he had just relived. Chapman eventually joined him at the desk, sitting in his customary chair.

"So you are Seb-Ichi?"

"Not quite. I was selected at birth because my father had served and had earned the right to have his children bonded, but I did not complete the training. I took an interest in technology in my early teens and by the time I was fifteen coming on sixteen, my father had disowned me for it. It was pretty scandalous. One of the bonded interested in technology? It would be like a Lokaryn as rohnin."

"Have you talked with your family since?"

"Some of them, it's been a while, but not my father."

"You said he struck you in the eye. He must have missed. I don't see any scar or difference between the eyes."

"No, he took the eye and the sword split the skull on the side. Had it gone straight in, I would have been killed on the spot."

"It looks flawless."

"I ran across an old member of the *Impulse* crew years ago, who told me the rest of the story. Timmerson was apparently so shocked at what he did he just stood there stunned as I slid off his sword and onto the deck. The old man fell to his knees and picked me up and just sat there crying, cradling what he thought to be my dying body. He had contacts and resources no one knew about and one of those was a small clinic in Thieves' Zone where some escapee scientists from Thorpe's and McAllister's had set up shop."

"Androidics and Biological Sciences."

"Their respective zones would pay a lot of money to get those guys back; however, they used Timmerson to run supplies for them and in turn they owed him a lot of favors."

"And he called one in getting you fixed."

"Yes he did. A few of them in fact. I was told by the staff that the old man staggered in carrying my body, dropped an enormous amount of money on the chief officer's desk, and staggered out again in tears."

"The result?"

"They gave me an option of a regrown natural eye and skull plate, or a cybernetic one. I chose a cybernetic core within a natural eye and a layered computer within bone to replace the section of skull that had been destroyed."

"Hybrids? Wow—that must have cost a fortune and then some."

"It did, and I didn't use all the money Timmerson had left for the procedure. I had enough left over to make extensive repairs to my ship, and purchase my first cargo rather than carrying for others."

"I always wondered how you were so good at determining fraudulent goods."

"It's a lot easier if you can see them on a microscopic level."

The two men sat in silence for a moment.

"So it really was a scow?" Chapman asked.

Gedrick smiled at that.

"Calling it a scow would have been a compliment."

"Did you ever see the old man again?"

"No, never. I tried to contact him a few times over the years, even tried to find out what ports he was going to be in, but I never had any luck. After the incident he discharged his entire crew and apparently rigged the ship for solo operations. He only carries small cargo for clients who require discretion. He uses an androidic crew to handle the ships ops."

"I won't stop you if you want to leave, Nev. I need you and the crew needs you. But if you get off now, you might still not be associated with the ship. We can make sail for Merchants' Zone instead of Thieves' to drop you off."

"But then again I might."

"Yes. Then again you might."

"First Officer?" came the voice of the helmsman over the comm link.

"Chapman here."

"Preparations are complete for departure. What are your orders?"

As the first officer opened his mouth to talk, he wasn't sure what words would come out, but he began speaking anyway.

"Make sail for Thieves'."

Dream it. Build it. Pray it doesn't kill you.

—McAllister's Zone saying

CHAPTER 60

THE SLAUGHTER FADED INTO A faint and unpleasant memory that was quickly relegated to the background of Vis-Shan's mind as he began to regain consciousness. His body felt stiff and he was unable to move anything. He heard the splashing of water in the distance, which meant he was near the stream that ran along the south end of the monastery. He also heard the soft mumbling of what sounded like a prayer.

T' doran me' grazi slovint.

He could not yet distinguish all of the words.

Tradana megora s'orduvi.

He felt a hand press against his forehead.

Vis-Shan, gur servanti enroda Shi-Hol.

It was the last word that fully registered: Shi-Hol. Someone was administering the Seb-Ichi Prayer of the Dying to him. How strange, he thought. He didn't feel sick; in fact, he felt no pain at all. Was death really as easy as this? It had only been his fear of it that had prevented him from carrying out his threat of suicide. *If only I had known*, he thought, and his world went black.

The monk lifted Vis-Shan's limp body and carried the young man to his bedchamber. Like most Seb-Ichi, Vis-Shan kept few personal effects in the room. Effects were a distraction and this was a place of contemplation. The elder man placed his charge gently on the meditation mat and wiped his brow. Though hardy for his age, carrying one hundred and fifty pounds of dead weight caused him to break a sweat. All he could do now was wait. Vis-Shan was unconscious and for how long he would remain so was uncertain. He had administered the Prayer of the Dying to him more as a precaution than anything else. The vision had shown him that Vis-Shan was much stronger than he had given him credit for being. Still, he owed his young aide this blessing just in case.

With Vis-Shan ministered to, the monk went to the kitchen and prepared a cup of green tea. He had managed to shake off most of the vision that he had shared with his young aide, but knew that soon enough he would have to revisit it.

"Is Vis-Shan all right?" a voice asked from behind him. It was Peli Domar, his other charge.

"He will be, Peli. Please, sit."

The Kwynian maneuvered with remarkable agility for a man whose legs were just beginning the regeneration process in the crystalline encasements that the monk had fashioned. In the short time that he had been here, the Kwynian soldier had shown amazing adaptability and resilience. He was a man used to pulling his weight, and though still in the early stages of his recovery, he had insisted on helping around the keep. The monk would have preferred him to rest, but realized that keeping him busy could be a positive part of the healing process. Perhaps he would teach him the basics of brewing ale.

"Would you like some tea?" the monk asked.

"Yes, please," Domar said.

A steaming cup was placed in front of him.

"What happened to Vis-Shan?" Domar asked.

The monk considered this for a moment, thinking about how much to reveal. He had asked the soldier to trust him, and perhaps it was appropriate to return the favor.

"Vis-Shan has had a vision, and I believe that your Lokaryn was in it." He let the words hang in the air. He did not tell the man that hers was one of the faces he had seen in his own visions.

"I see," said Peli Domar, considering it. "Are visions common among the Seb-Ichi?"

"No. In fact they are exceedingly rare. Vis-Shan has never had one before."

"What does it mean?" Domar asked with true concern in his voice.

"I honestly don't know," the monk replied.

The two continued talking while Vis-Shan lay recovering in his bedchamber. His mind felt as if it were tightly wrapped in a thick cocoon, but snippets of their conversation wafted through. Unlike his mentor, he knew what the vision meant. And, more important, he knew what action and sacrifice it would require of him. For the first time in his life, he realized that the dreary days of tending to the monk had been about something larger and of greater importance. With this insight, he slipped back into unconsciousness.

Hours passed.

The monk and Peli Domar ate a simple dinner of pan bread and four root stew that Domar had insisted on preparing. To the monk's surprise, it was rich in taste and in texture.

"You surprise me, Peli Domar," he said. "I would not have expected a Kwynian to prepare such a fine dish from the land."

Domar smiled. "Early Kwynian society was not dissimilar to your own. Many years before the Cataclysm, a large number of my people were farmers."

"It is delicious," the monk said, as he savored another spoonful. "Still, I'm surprised that a soldier would take the time to learn the family recipes."

"Survival skills are essential in my profession," said Domar, adding another ladle full to the older man's bowl. An impish grin crossed his face. "Of course, if you were ever to dine in my home you would soon realize that it is an essential skill there as well." The monk look puzzled. "My wife," Domar explained, "is a beautiful woman and a wonderful mother." He paused, considering his next words as if she might somehow overhear them. "She has a great many talents and skills, none of which translate to the kitchen. My poor children survive because I can cook!"

The monk burst into laughter and raised his glass. "To your wife," he said.

Peli Domar raised the ladle. "To my wife!" he replied.

Domar's face suddenly lost its mirth.

"What's wrong?" the monk asked.

"My family expects me to be gone for extended periods," Domar said. "But soon enough they will be notified that I have not returned."

"Don't worry, Peli. I promise you that they will know you are alive and well."

The smile crept back onto Domar's face. "Then my children shall not despair of ever eating well again."

The monk laughed, recharging their glasses this time with mead.

Vis-Shan heard the laughter but was unable to respond. He had spent the better part of the evening lapsing in and out of consciousness. When he was finally able to maintain wakefulness, it was several minutes before he realized that he was in his bedchamber and that the laughter was coming from the kitchen. With a great deal of effort he raised his upper torso from the comfort of the down mattress that had been placed over his meditation mat. Everything ached. *If this is what the old man experienced every time he had a vision, perhaps I have not been as sympathetic as I should have been,* he thought.

Uncounted minutes passed as he worked to center himself.

He inhaled deeply and held it, imagining the oxygen flooding his every cell. He did this several more times until, at last, his body felt cleansed. The name for the technique was Param Gra Nor. It was a Seb-Ichi meditative practice that had been developed to refresh the body when a period of rest was not possible. Vis-Shan tentatively placed one foot on the floor. When he felt the grain of the wood against his skin he decided that his legs were working and put the other foot down. Standing proved to be more of a challenge, as his legs were wobbly. He fell back on the mattress twice before he was finally able to support himself. With gingerly steps, he walked into the kitchen where the monk and Peli Domar were drinking.

"Vis-Shan!" the monk exclaimed. "I am pleased to see that Shi-Hol has not claimed you!" he said merrily.

"I'm not sure that I am." Vis-Shan smiled weakly.

Peli Domar got up and helped the young Seb-Ichi to the table. The monk was inclined to scold the soldier for pushing himself too hard, but decided that allowing him to assert his independence also had therapeutic value.

"Perhaps you would care for some stew?" Domar asked. "Thank you," Vis-Shan replied.

Domar placed a warm bowl in front of Vis-Shan, who tasted it tentatively. "Trust me, Vis-Shan," the monk said. "It is quite good. I had two bowls myself."

Vis-Shan began to dig into the stew.

"How do you feel?" the monk asked.

"I feel ashamed," the young man replied.

Domar looked at the two men quizzically.

"I did not understand the power of the visions," Vis-Shan continued to his mentor, "and I am sorry for the many times that I was less than understanding."

The monk appraised the younger man. "There is no mark against you, Vis-Shan, nor is there any way that you could have understood."

"You have the visions as well?" Domar asked the monk. "I thought they were exceedingly rare."

"They are. I have had these visions most of my life, but up until today Vis-Shan had never had one. I recently allowed Vis-Shan to share in one of my visions and I fear it has opened the floodgates."

"To what?"

"I'm not sure," the monk replied. He turned to Vis-Shan. "I know that this life is not what you would have chosen for yourself, Vis-Shan, and despite that fact you have served me well. I regret that I have passed my affliction on to you. For that I am truly sorry, and I will do everything I can for you to prevent it from ever happening again."

It was Vis-Shan who spoke next. "I do not view what I have experienced as an affliction," he said almost joyfully. "I have been blessed with a vision of the future. A future, which I may play some role in shaping."

This statement alarmed the monk. "You mustn't, Vis-Shan," he cautioned. "This future can only bring about your death."

"Why?" Vis-Shan asked.

"You did not see it?" the monk said with surprise.

"Yes, I did. But what if what we saw was just one possible outcome? What if the vision was a gift?"

The monk considered this for a moment.

"How so?" he said.

Vis-Shan finally asked. "What if the vision was an opportunity to explore the scenario? To try different strategies? It revealed to me what I most likely would do in the situation. I have now seen my mistakes, with no harm to myself, and am free to try again."

"What are you saying?" the monk asked.

"I believe it's important to aid that ship," Vis-Shan replied, simply.

"How?" the monk asked. "You have no idea when the ship will be passing near the outpost."

"But I do," Vis-Shan countered. "The hara crops were flowering, meaning that harvest time was near, and it was exceedingly dark out."

"New moon," Domar offered.

"Exactly."

The combination of the two facts meant the night was very near and little time was left to prepare, or even to consider what was to be done.

A million objections ran through the monk's mind, but he decided not to voice them. Instead, he said, "Eat, Vis-Shan. You need your strength."

The three men sat in relative silence as Vis-Shan finished his stew. Finally, he got up and announced, "I think I shall lie down." The monk helped him back to his chamber and Peli Domar cleared the table.

A few minutes later, the monk emerged and sat back down. The glasses were refreshed with mead. Domar knew how to facilitate the coming conversation.

"You had a vision that foretold my coming, didn't you."

"Yes," the monk said simply.

"And you've had visions of the Lokaryn that I encountered."

"Yes."

"Do you believe that Lokaryn to be on Vis-Shan's ship?"

"Yes."

"Vis-Shan seemed to feel that the people on that ship warranted help, even though they were transgressing against the outpost."

"Yes. The visions impart some feeling of intent. I assumed he sensed no malice in the occupants of the ship. I know it may be hard for you to believe, considering your history with this particular Lokaryn."

Peli Domar thought back to the moments after the portal blast. "Pray with me," the voice of the Lokaryn echoed in his ears.

"I am finding that many long-held beliefs may not be serving me well anymore."

Silence again fell between the two.

"I don't have the gift of these visions, but I can tell you this," Domar said. "I think Vis-Shan is correct that the vision is a tactical asset. I also believe if we allow him to go off on his own…he will die."

We have been unable to find Chairman Garand to serve him with termination proceedings. We also note that inspection of the dry docks at the Thorpe's Ninth Arc Proving Grounds are empty of mystworthy ships. Including the four ships damaged in the trials. I would strongly recommend to the board that your retirement accounts are put in order.

—Letter to the board of directors of Garand Shipbuilding

CHAPTER 61

Deep myst off the Sarengagh Reefs
Aboard the *Shicaine*

"GRENDEL OFF THE PORT BOW, closing fast. Prepare to abandon ship," came the unnaturally calm voice of Seyschell as she entered the bridge.

The first officer stood with his hands folded behind his back looking out over the decks. Unmoved by the information, he said: "That is indeed bad news. Master at Arms, we need to lighten the load in an attempt to make an escape. Please start with any small blondes that you happen to see."

The master at arms looked at Seyschell, who smiled at him sweetly, and tugged at a short blond thread of hair to accentuate the idea. Considering the option of actually trying to move Seyschell, even in jest, he thought the better of it.

"I'll go see if I can find any, sir," he said, and immediately left the bridge.

"Brave lad," Chapman called after him. "Bring back some coffee."

Seyschell sat in a chair beside the first officer, and both looked out at the horizon. "Have we made the Hyrinoth Lighthouses yet?"

"We're about an hour beyond them."

"Really? We're making excellent time."

"We'll need to if we're to keep this schedule. A straight reach across the mysts to Ravensford was difficult enough, but the detour to Kwyne makes it nearly impossible. Even with the new power cells, the sheer distance involved…"

"On the upside, only we know exactly where we're going."

"So far as we know."

"We've blacked out communications and cut systems from the ether so the net rogues will have a hard time picking up our trace. The Lokaryns think we're heading straight to Phobes', and our pickup doesn't know that we're leaving for Phobes' afterward. Anyone who gets close enough to pick up a transponder signal will read us as a freighter from Chumley's, and no one is going to interfere with any ship from Chumley's."

"That's all well and good, but there's always one more wildcard than the ones you counted on. Always. Don't forget that while people are looking for us, we're trying to find others. Those others are being actively being pursued by half the major zones. We're eventually going to bump into someone we don't want to see."

Silence fell between the two until the helmsman voiced a progress report.

"Sarengagh Reefs in fifteen minutes, sir."

"Navigator, tide?"

"We're nearing high tide, about forty-five minutes away in this area."

"Damn," the first officer said quietly.

"Damn? That's perfect for heading over the reef," Seyschell said.

"Yes it is, isn't it?" observed Chapman.

"I'm not following you."

"Right now, I'm assuming that everyone who wants us dead knows exactly where we are, what we're doing, and what we had for breakfast this morning."

"And if we go over the reef?" Seyschell asked.

"We'll have enough tide and time to get over the reef, but if some-one is waiting for us, there's not enough of either to get back. We'll have our back to a wall with few options."

"I see your point."

"Captain," the first officer said into the comm link.

"Go ahead," came the response.

"Sarengagh in fourteen minutes. High tide is forty-five minutes away."

"Very well, make for the reef. I'll be up in five minutes."

"Aye, aye, sir. Sarengagh Reef." The first officer then switched the comm link.

"Sailing master, rig for shallow draft. We're going over the reef."

"Aye, aye, Mr. Chapman, shallow draft. We'd appreciate any extra lift the chief can spare."

"Understood. Chapman out."

"You aren't going to share your concerns with the captain?" Seyschell asked.

"If I've had the thought, he's had the thought."

"Wrong, First Officer. He's a smart man, but he isn't omniscient. In fact he's downright reckless at times. He gets so focused on his goal and is so used to bailing himself out of trouble that sometimes he doesn't think things through enough to avoid the trouble in the first place."

"We'll see in about four minutes from now." The first officer then switched over the comm channel to the engine room. "Chief?"

"Aye, Mr. Chapman?"

As the first officer opened his mouth to speak, he heard the voice of the captain in the background.

"How's the experiment coming, Chief?"

"I'll tell you after I clear the link with the bridge, Captain."

"Go ahead, bridge."

"The sailing master would appreciate as much antigrav as you can spare to help with the reef passage."

"Tell him to trim his sails properly and he won't have to ask for an ounce."

"Very good, Chief, I'll let him know he can expect an extra twenty percent; after all, you have the new power cells."

"Unproven cells, Mr. Ch—"

"Bridge out."

"Some things never change," Seyschell noted.

Down in the engine room, Captain Gedrick repeated his question to a similarly warm response from the chief. He still managed to make it to the bridge in his five-minute window.

"Captain on the bridge," the master at arms called from the hallway. Gedrick looked at him quizzically, not understanding why he was standing just outside the bridge.

"Good morning, everyone."

"Good morning, Captain. Sunrise in a few minutes, the reef in about ten."

"Some things do change," Seyschell whispered to the first officer.

"Meaning?"

"Gedrick was never much of a morning person. Before sunrise? Now that's something. You must be a good influence on him."

"Not my doing. He was on this schedule when I got here." Chapman thought about the conversation he had just had with Seyschell. "Captain Gedrick? We have enough draft and time to get over the reefs and I appreciate the time savings; however, if anyone is looking for us on the other side, we could have a problem."

"We couldn't get back over the reef."

"Correct, sir. We'd be very much trapped."

"Well, I don't know about that, but it would get interesting in a hurry. While I agree with your assessment Mr. Chapman, we'll head over the reef. Let's be prepared for trouble on the other side."

In the distance the myst fountained high in the air against the jagged reef. Though it was beautiful, one spark could set a mystfire to burn for hours, taking the *Shicaine* with it.

"So what experiment were you talking about, Captain?"

"It's still a little nebulous and I'm working out the technical problems with the chief. When I have a better idea of its feasibility I'll share it. Otherwise you'll think me a lunatic."

"You're relying on the chief to disprove you're a lunatic?" Seyschell said. She then looked at the first officer. "Beat you to it."

"I wasn't going to say a word. Thankfully, I can rely on you to say enough for both of us."

"Leave it to Mr. Chapman to get two digs in with one sentence. Isn't that correct, gentlemen?" Gedrick asked the bridge crew.

"Aye, Captain," came the unanimous response.

"Aye, Captain," came the master at arms's response a fraction of a second later from outside the door.

The forward watch called out "I see the reef. The channel is at the two-o'clock position about three minutes away."

"Let's go to work," Gedrick said with a wicked smile. "Mr. Chapman."

"Sir?"

"What do you know about Garand-Trass myst-clippers?" Gedrick began to prepare the pilot's crib.

"Let's see now: Morgan Garand was a shipbuilder in Thorpe's and Conrad Trass was a designer. Trass was the progenitor of the foils we use on all ships today to achieve lift. He was the first to achieve 'neutral buoyancy,' allowing clippers to stay out on the myst much longer. Before this, the power constraints to lift a ship over the myst made interzone travel extremely limited. But after Trass's design became fully realized, the world opened up. Most designers would have retired at that point, but he kept going and it's commonly believed that he went mad. His designs became increasingly bizarre, until finally he came up with a design that he swore would revolutionize travel in the zones. It was spurned by every reputable shipbuilder in T'Amorach. Garand, however, thought the design was viable for reasons passing understanding and, after a lifetime of respectability building reliable mystgoing ships, he put it all into Trass's designs."

"Very good. A good history of the two. Now, what was the result?"

"Disaster: four wrecked ships, and fifteen or so ships in dry dock, somewhere. In traditional sailing mode they were reported to handle well enough; however, they could be operated in a powered-flight mode. Trying to 'fly' a ship that was meant for sailing was an aerodynamic nightmare. In test runs they proved to be uncontrollable. The ships were mothballed as too expensive to maintain as normal sailing ships and too dangerous to use in powered flight. I went to find them when I was a midshipman at the Academy. I was doing a structural evaluation of the project as my thesis. I figured they would be available at one of the design institutes in Kwyne or in Thorpe's; however, no one at the Shipbuilders' Institute or any of the other major institutes could tell me where I could find them."

"So what do you surmise?"

"That they're being held somewhere inaccessible to the common folk like myself."

"Or?"

"That they're out on the mysts plying a trade and that is the reason why the chief is so damned protective of certain areas of his engine room."

"Very good, Mr. Chapman. How long have you known?"

"More like suspected. There are subtle differences in the hull that were giveaways to Trass's design. It was difficult, however, as you modified the hull somewhat, but that's why I joined the crew in the first place."

Gedrick stared at the first officer.

"All this time you thought you were putting one over on him and he's been putting one over on you. I love it," Seyschell laughed.

"Shut up and sit down in your damned seat," Gedrick said, almost laughing himself.

"Reef in two minutes thirty seconds, sir."

The helmsman and navigator worked together to line the *Shicaine* up for the deepest channels through the reef. Gedrick smiled and shook his head at the first officer; then sat in the pilot's crib as Seyschell settled into the copilot's position. Chapman coordinated operations among the sailing master, the navigator, and the engine room.

Gedrick and Seyschell sat side by side in the seats, separated by an electronics console. Placing headsets on, they adjusted the mics to a comfortable position. Quickly, they slid down into the berths and the electronic readout flickered to life as a yoke drew up from the floor.

"Reef in two minutes."

"Sailing master," Seyschell called into her comm link.

"Aye, bridge."

"Pin her ears, Mr. Isen."

Responding to a command usually reserved for securing the ship before a storm, the crew scrambled into the rigging to haul in the sheets. They made fast work of it, assisted by the ship's androidics. Then they descended the rigging like so many spiders fleeing the web.

The yardarms then spun to align with the masts and the mast lay back against the decking. The ship floated for a moment, slowing as they lost the wind.

"Helm," Gedrick called.

"Aye, sir," the helmsman replied

"Release the ship to my station."

"Aye, sir."

Gedrick looked over at his first officer, who wore an amazed expression on his face. To know about the ship was one thing, to see it in action was another. The *Shicaine* had been hiding one last secret, at least from the crew if not from Mr. Chapman. With a nod from the captain, First Officer Chapman knew what to do. It made perfect sense. His study of the Garand-Trass Project, and his patience, was about to pay off.

"Chief, prepare for all power to the captain's command," Chapman announced to the comm link.

"The captain had better have strapped himself in tight for what I'm about to give him." If the first officer did not know better, he would have sworn the chief was smiling on the other end of the comm.

"Navigation, prepare for real-time threat notification," Chapman said.

"Aye, aye, all threats will be passed through to the captain's nav screen along with course recommendations," navigation replied.

"Sailingmaster?" Chapman called over the bridge railing.

"The deck is secure, Mr. Chapman."

"Very well. Sensors to maximum, shielding to maximum. Captain, the ship is ready."

"This is the captain speaking. Please secure for storm running." It was a command given when the ship was expected to encounter rough myst. The crew belowdecks scrambled to finish securing all items that might be thrown about.

"Mr. Chapman?"

"Aye, Captain."

"You might want to sit down."

"Yes, sir."

A few seconds after the first officer had secured himself to his seat, the captain and Seyschell started what seemed to be a small war as their hands flew over one another on the shared overhead console. More than once one slapped the other's hand in an effort to keep the controls set the way they preferred. After the short duel, all fell silent.

Gedrick sat back a little in his chair, waiting for the call. It did not take long, as the forward lookout shouted:

"Reef!"

"Chief."

"Aye, Captain. All banks at your disposal."

A moment later Gedrick whispered "Now," in a voice only Seyschell could hear, as he brought the engines to quarter power. The ship lunged forward and lifted from the myst in a dramatic motion. His left hand became a blur over the pilot's pad as he slowly moved the thrust forward with his right. The ship was now engaged at quarter speed, and he thought he must be imagining things when he noted that the power levels remained virtually untouched.

"Chief, am I reading this correctly?" Gedrick asked into the comm link.

"Yes, Captain, we're using less than five percent of available power."

The *Shicaine* skimmed over the reefs as the crew gathered at her sides to watch this seemingly impossible feat unfold before their very eyes. While the first officer's concerns about tide and timing were correct for a myst-clipper, they did not apply to a Garand-Trass clipper powered by lokaric-engineered fuel cells.

"Mr. Chapman."

"Yes, Captain."

"What is your estimate for arrival at the Falon pickup point?"

"Assuming we maintain this speed, I would estimate the day before yesterday, Captain."

"We'll bring the ship back to sail power once we're on the other side of the reef and we know that no one is following."

"In that case, I would estimate five days' sail time to Thieves. From there, another two weeks to Ravensford."

"Three weeks is a long time to wait for rescue."

"Yes it is."

"If we were to power the journey, how long would it take?"

"Assuming no problems and continuous operation, we could at least halve the time. Can the power cells actually sustain that sort of expenditure?"

"We don't know yet. The chief is still learning his way around them."

After two hours' hard traveling, Gedrick had taken the first shift and Seyschell the second. The ship had cleared the reef and was well beyond it when the captain ordered normal sailing operations to resume.

"That's the problem with 'flying' a ship designed to sail; it's incredibly fatiguing. We only have two pilots capable of powered sailing," Gedrick said.

"Three, sir. I can handle the ship under power," Chapman said flatly.

"Nev, you're an excellent pilot and helmsman, but this isn't something you pick up as you go."

"I see, and a Ravensfordian and a Badlander just happened to be born with the innate knowledge of how to work a Garand-Trass clipper." The first officer prosecuted his case calmly. He stood on the brink of realizing a dream and would not be deterred.

Gedrick opened his mouth to speak, but nothing came out. Seyschell spoke next.

"He's right, you know. Give the guy a shot. If it works out you've just increased our powered time by fifty percent."

"And if we crash, we'll all be swimming in myst." Gedrick sighed. "I'll think about it" was as much as he would commit to. The first officer suppressed a smile and made a note to reread his own thesis as soon as he returned to his cabin.

The arrow found its mark, but the child Messiah did not fall. Instead pure white fire exploded out from her. The assassin burned for days after all other fires had died. His agony stretched out the whole time. Where the child Messiah once stood there now remained a beating heart wreathed in pure white flame. The young boy that she had traveled with was pure of heart and could carry the heart. All others who tried were consumed by it.

—Tor' Manat
Kwynian Sacred Writings

CHAPTER 62

THERE WAS A FRENZY OF activity inside the residence of the lokaric ambassador to Thieves' Zone.

Acting Clan Lord Solipher had arrived unannounced and requested that Ambassador G'oran prepare for a most unexpected visitor: the new rohnin of Kwyne. G'oran did not completely trust Solipher; they were from different clans, and those clans had not always agreed on matters of zone governance. But different clans or not, Solipher was a council member and that carried weight. A lot of weight. And so G'oran made the appropriate preparations.

Solipher had not told the ambassador that there would be additional visitors. He was not entirely sure who could be trusted and it was best to keep information on a need-to-know basis. They would portal into his chambers and only reveal themselves if necessary.

"Clan Lord Solipher," a voice came over the comm system. "Will you join us for feeding?"

"I will," he replied.

Feeding at a consulate was very different from feeding in-zone. Because most host zones tended to frown upon the concept of feeding chambers, it was necessary to portal blood in. Once removed from the body, it tended to lose essence fairly quickly, so deliveries occurred several times a day.

Solipher descended the grand staircase to the main floor of the residence and entered the feeding chamber. Because it was most often used for functions with dignitaries from the other zones, it had been furnished like a traditional dining room. A large wooden table occupied the center of the room with a chandelier high above it. The chandelier was a wonder of Ravensford engineering, comprised of seven strands of crystals not dissimilar to seven strands of pearls. Each was suspended from a center ring and resonated on its own unique frequency, which caused it to emit a single band of the light spectrum. The energy from the top crystal flowed into that of the next until, finally, a waterfall of liquid light emerged from the last. The seven spectral cascades streamed into a rotating collecting pool, which mixed them. The result was a low-intensity light both breathtaking to behold and not harmful to its hosts.

The center of the table was adorned with a large fountain that circulated the evening's meal. It was designed to preserve freshness by maintaining the proper level of warmth and oxygenation. G'oran handed Solipher a snifter. "Thank you, Ambassador," Solipher said as he took a sip. "Excellent!" he exclaimed with true surprise.

"We acquired it this morning," said G'oran. "A three-stripe, I believe."

"I had no idea that life at the consulates was quite so good."

"We get by," G'oran replied with a smile. She paused for a moment. "So tell me, Solipher, do you really think that you can avert a war?"

"Yes, I believe I can."

"I agree," G'oran admitted. "The question, however, is should we?"

Had G'oran not been legendary for playing the Grendel's advocate, Solipher might have been taken aback.

"Why, G'oran, you almost sound like a Traditionalist."

"Oh not at all," she demurred. "Our culture is much stronger with the clans working together."

"Go on," Solipher urged, taking the bait.

"You have to admit that no matter what our structure of govern-ance, Kwyne will never be an ally."

"Clan Lord Derring would disagree."

"True, but Clan Lord Derring has not been heard from for months. Can you even be sure that she survives? Perhaps, Solipher, you are 'acting' clan lord in name only."

"I am not ready to address that claim."

"Understood. You honor her well." She paused. "Before you choose a course of action, I would like to share with you a piece of information that has come to my attention."

"Go ahead."

"I cannot vouch for the veracity, of course, but we both know that more often than not Thieves' Zone rumors contain a grain of truth."

Solipher waited, letting G'oran have her moment of drama.

"There are some whisperings that the Kwynians have made progress in finding Turin Tan."

"Really," he said without much enthusiasm.

"Really," she replied.

"We have heard such whisperings before," he said.

"True," she responded, "but I find it somewhat odd that this rumor comes to me days in advance of the assassination of a neutral rohnin, a rohnin who is then replaced by a hostile one. Is it not possible that these are related events?"

Solipher let the information sink in. "I am skeptical, but I appreciate that you have mentioned this to me. You have my gratitude."

"Thank you, Solipher. Your gratitude is well known."

Solipher nodded.

"If you'll excuse me, I think I'll finish my meal in my chambers. You've given me a lot to consider."

"As you wish. Good evening, Clan Lord."

"Good evening, Ambassador," he replied with a raised eyebrow.

Solipher ascended the grand staircase and headed back to his chambers. He removed a small iron key from his jacket pocket and unlocked the large wooden outer door that opened up into the main suite area. It was almost time. The suite was lavishly furnished, as was customary to both ambassadorial residences and the lokaric culture, with plush couches and dark hand carved tables. On each end table there was a standing version of the cascading crystal light source, similar to the chandelier in the dining area.

He sat down and gently swirled the contents of his snifter. He watched the crimson liquid slowly drip down the sides of the glass, tiny tributaries soon to be reunited with the darker sea below. This was his favorite part about dining out-of-zone, and he savored it the way a wine connoisseur did the rarest of vintage. It was a very different experience from feeding in the chambers and he loved every aspect of it; the texture, the bouquet, the way the droplets fell from the glass onto his tongue. Deliciously intoxicating, he thought.

A small wall clock began to chime, and Solipher made note that his guests would soon arrive. As if reading his thoughts, the air began to shimmer in front of the silver service on the far wall. The emerging portal grew and took shape until it reached the size in which a man could step through it. Finally it stabilized. Although he had seen many wondrous things in his long existence, Solipher was still mesmerized by portals. He understood how and why they worked, but when he saw one, he felt like a child who had just witnessed the magician's beautiful assistant enter the box and disappear. Astounding!

Three men entered the chamber and, the trick complete, the portal closed behind them.

"It's good to see you, Major," Solipher said in greeting.

"And you as well, Solipher," the major replied. The two shook hands, and after mortal drinks were offered and accepted they got down to their business.

"As you can see, I have taken care of things on my end," the major began. "I trust the appropriate arrangements have been made on yours?"

"Yes," the clan lord said. "Kragen has accepted my invitation. Ko'Doran saw to that. He did so with a great deal of reluctance, but he will be here on the morrow."

The major nodded, understanding. "Kragen's mood is of little import to me, so long as he is here. Once he is dealt with, we can begin the next phase."

"*Y'ord utluck bezina seprimus*—may good fortune follow us," Solipher said, as their glasses clinked.

Rights? You can have all the rights you want in the afterlife when you enter Shi-Hol.

—Response of a Badlands tribunal prior to the execution of thirty insurrectionists

CHAPTER 63

Deep myst

Aboard the *Blackthorne*

THE COMMANDER OF THE *Blackthorne* walked the deck and watched as his crew scurried around him like ants. For all intent and purpose, they were ants to him. He worked them hard, and when they failed, or if they simply displeased him, he crushed them. It had the effect of making the rest work all the harder. After five years, he had it down to a science, and he had profited handsomely from it.

But it wasn't about profit for Loh'l.

His ruminations were interrupted by a slender pair of arms that wrapped themselves around his waist.

"So deep in thought?" a smoky voice asked.

The voice belonged to a woman who stood almost his height, with raven-black hair and piercing green eyes. He could feel the strength in her arms as she pulled him close to her well-muscled body.

"Are you here as my first officer, Commander Ma'Goran, or my lover, Natrina?" Loh'l asked.

"I'm armed," she replied.

"That doesn't answer the question," Loh'l observed. He took a deep breath and then said, "If any other member of my crew put their arms around me, I would have them thrown into the myst."

"If any other member of the crew put their arms around you, I would throw them into the myst myself," she replied, smiling at him broadly. He returned it, knowing full well that she was speaking the complete truth. Natrina Ma'Goran was an able first officer and a dangerous woman. It was on the second point that she had come to his bed. She recognized his potential and each took to their role: he the commander and she the teacher.

She was a lover whose deviance had at first shocked him, but she was hypnotic, and he found himself very much enjoying the freedom that she brought. Soon his appetites surpassed hers, but she would not be outdone. Nor would he, and over the ensuing years their competitiveness on the subject became feared on the *Blackthorne*. On more than one occasion the disciplining of a crewmember had served as an appetizer to the entrée of their lovemaking.

She released her grip and moved beside him. He knew what she wanted. To say no to this woman would have its consequences, but he remained captain and exerted that control when needed.

"Have you worked out the next phase of things?" she inquired.

"Yes. Cut to the chase, Commander," he replied.

"You are going to use her, then?"

"Yes. As I have said I would all along."

Ma'Goran looked at him darkly. "It is bad enough that you must accept assistance from T'Gareth. Send me instead."

"No."

"I believe that I have shown myself to be an able 'negotiator,'" she countered.

"Yes, you have," he replied.

"She is unstable!"

"Yes, she is."

"And this does not trouble you?"

"It troubles me greatly, but where Arles Timmerson is concerned, she is single-minded. She also has the advantage of being able to mist onto his ship. As talented as you are, Natrina, I do not believe that this is one of your skills."

"I can portal, then."

"Assuming we knew the exact location of the *Impulse*, that might be true."

"We have his course plot," the first officer responded.

"We have the course plot that he filed. I have served with him and I assure you that to him, it is merely a guideline. You are too valuable to this ship to risk portaling you into the myst."

"You and I both know that I could survive it," she said.

"Your genetic recode suggests that you could survive it, but your zone's scientists have been known to be wrong about such things."

Ma'Goran knew the captain was right. Though the scientists of McAllister's had provided many significant genetic modifications to their zone dwellers, they had produced an equal number of failures. The ability to breathe myst was one that had mixed success. Though the gene had been successfully spliced into her DNA and activated, she had not gone through the testing period. A real-world test would let her know, but should it fail she would die.

"I concede the point," she said, hating to do so, "But when her usefulness is over, I hope that you will allow me the honor of disposing of her."

Loh'l considered this for a moment, and a smile slowly crept across his face. Natrina versus Kell. It was an image that he found arousing.

"Very well," he said. "But first, we attend to the Timmerson matter. Have a crewman notify Kell that we are ready."

"I'll do it," Ma'Goran said.

"Very well," Loh'l replied, a little surprised that his first officer wanted to take care of so menial a chore personally.

Ma'Goran walked along the aft deck until she arrived at the companionway to the crew quarters. The area was gunmetal grey and impeccably clean, another hallmark of life aboard the *Blackthorne*. As she made her way down the long corridor, she encountered Jayesh, who was dragging the corpses of two deceased crewmates in a makeshift sling.

"Where are you taking those?" she asked.

"To the engine room, ma'am," he replied, attempting to sound nervous. It was the reaction he hoped she was seeking.

"And their belongings?"

"Turned in to the purser, ma'am."

"Very well, Jayesh. You may return to your duties. Rotting corpses tend to get juicy, so make sure that this deck is pristine when I return."

Ma'Goran watched as he resumed dragging the corpses down the narrow passageway. Loh'l had briefed her on the man's encounter with Kell, and she remained skeptical of the outcome. Men simply did not react in the way Jayesh had.

Once Jayesh was out of sight, the first officer knocked on the door of the guest quarters.

There was no reply.

Kell watched as the door opened and the first officer of the *Blackthorne* entered her quarters without permission. She knew that the woman did not like her and she was happy to return the sentiment. The voices liked the first officer very much and pushed Kell to kill her. It was advice that she would suppress. The voices had been extremely stirred up since her encounter with Jayesh and since then had urged her to kill anyone with whom she had come into contact.

"Natrina." She acknowledged the first officer, but did not use her proper title. "I don't believe I invited you to enter."

"You didn't. The captain has asked me to inform you that we are ready to pursue *Impulse*," the first officer replied formally.

"Timmerson!" the voices began to chant.

"You have his location?" Kell asked.

"No, not his precise location, but we have his course plot."

"The only thing reliable about Timmerson is that he is unreliable. The filed plan will only get me so close."

"Then one can only hope that you are up to the task, Kell." The first officer of the *Blackthorne* stood well inside the cabin showing no concern about making a fast getaway. Kell looked up slowly from what she was doing. Her heart had begun to beat faster, and she could sense that Ma'Goran's had as well. She looked over at the raven-haired woman, who carried a hint of menace in her eyes.

"Meaning?" Kell asked in a measured voice.

"From what I've observed your abilities are...lacking," the first officer said. Kell could sense that she was flushing ever so slightly, but she did not sense fear.

"Really? Enlighten me," Kell said, with equal menace in her voice. She found her desire to kill swelling. The voices swirled in her head now like circling vultures. She turned to face the first officer and breathed deeply. The sensations from Ma'Goran were confusing to her. Her heart was beating faster and faster, she flushed more deeply now, and her breathing was becoming erratic. Kell sensed something growing, but it wasn't fear. She found herself starting to struggle for control.

"Drink her in, we want her," the voices pleaded.

"The captain told me that you were unable to break, Jayesh," Ma'Goran continued, taking a step toward the Lokaryn. Then, leaning in: "I had never heard of a Lokaryn failing in such a task. That leaves me to wonder if you are incompetent, complicit, or just so crazy that you can't complete a simple task given to you."

"Take her," the voices throbbed.

"So simple a task? Then why don't you take him to your bed and see how well you do—or won't your master let you off the leash long enough to experience it?" Kell mocked though a small sneer. She found herself awash in sensations. The heartbeat of Ma'Goran pounded in her brain.

The voices in Kell's head screamed for Ma'Goran. The two women stood less than an arm's length apart now. Kell could feel the vibration of Ma'Goran's jugular on her teeth. Ma'Goran searched for the trigger that would bring the Lokaryn to her blade. She convinced herself that she could bait Kell and kill her. Once the Lokaryn was dead, Loh'l would have to use her to go after Timmerson instead. She had not anticipated the power of the sensations. They stoked a desire dangerous and sublime.

"In fact, the way he described it, it sounded as though Jayesh broke you."

"Perhaps you'd like to understand more intimately what Jayesh experienced."

Ma'Goran looked at Kell, tilted her head to one side, and swept the hair away from her neck with a small movement while her hand worked the hilt of a blade. Kell could sense everything, exhilaration, arousal, confusion, all coming from Ma'Goran.

The two women stood face-to-face for a long moment, neither giving an inch. Ma'Goran swam in the intoxication of the evil that radiated from the Lokaryn's crescendoing rapture. Kell's voices had worked themselves into a screaming frenzy, but it was so much more than simple blood fury that rose within her. Rising up from the cacophony of lust for blood came a singular voice steady in its rhythm and request. "Timmerson," it chanted over and over.

Soon the rest of the voices joined in calling for Timmerson. Kell slowly retreated from the haze of the passion to kill. If she destroyed this woman, Loh'l would not help her find Timmerson.

"Everything in its time," Kell said to herself, turning away.

"Tell your master that I am ready. Now leave my cabin," she said.

Ma'Goran gained control of herself and said nothing. She left the cabin and, once in the companionway, leaned against a bulkhead, breathing deeply as she did. She was unsure of what she had just done or why she had done it. She only knew that she'd enjoyed it more than any sensation she had ever known.

Outsmarting a man is all well and good, but getting him to outsmart himself—now, that's impressive.

—General Igor Chumley, founder, Chumley's Zone

CHAPTER 64

Kwyne

VAR KRAGEN LOOKED OUT THE window of the carriage that carried him down the street. Rain had fallen not too long ago in this region of the arc, and the report of the horses' hooves on the stone was punctuated by the occasional splash of a puddle that lingered as a reminder of the cleansing shower. For the first time in his life, the sound bothered him.

He had always found it remarkable that even the dirtiest street or building always seemed renewed after a rain. Even if only briefly. How often had the blood of a righteous battle been washed away while he was in the Kuhbrik? It had not gone unnoticed by the reluctantly conscripted demigod that not a single drop touched him now. Ten minutes ago, he had been ushered into the carriage in an alcove below the old Nehreton meeting hall for an emergency meeting with the Lokaryn Zone ambassador. For security reasons, he could not even open the window.

Var Kragen was suddenly isolated from the world in so many ways now. Seconds after he had utter the words 'I claim the throne of Kuna Latte by the right of assassination,' it was as if a steel cage had sprung up around him. His security and continued existence now were essential to staving off the chaos that threatened to consume them. Yet he had a dangerous task ahead of him. The message from the Lokaryns' embassy had been simple: "Meet before midday...else war."

It was a meeting he could not refuse. He'd taken the precaution of anointing a successor in case the diplomatic mission should fail. The brevity of his reign would call the legitimacy of his successor into question, but at least there would be some guidance for those left behind.

He rode along silently, accompanied by N'orin and Balazar, who argued furiously over the coming meeting. Kragen might as well have been alone; he neither participated nor listened. Instead, he looked out the window as the two continued sparring. So much had changed in the past few days. Even in the past few hours. Before all of this started, he was simply a prelate. One of many in the history of Kwyne. Now Var Kragen was no longer "just" a prelate. In all the millennia of Kwyne's existence, he would be one of the very few who had assassinated a god. At least, history would record it that way.

In his entire adult life, he had allowed himself only one flight of fancy: ascending to the rohnin's throne. He imagined stepping upon that sacred ground, called to the duty of ultimate leadership in a time of Kwynian crisis. He thought perhaps to be called upon as the savior after a lapse of leadership. He would have liked to have been Jungar's chosen one, but that honor fell to the recently deceased Damien Cairo. Now he would even have taken an election, a close election, over the reality that stood before him. History would paint him as an assassin, a murderer. He couldn't remember any rohnin who had ascended the throne by right of assassination serving Kwyne with distinction.

Kragen sighed, comforted somewhat in the knowledge that he was, in truth, not a murderer. Thecla was just. He might yet be granted a long and peaceful reign. After all, his first act had been one of sacrifice for the good of Kwyne. His first act had also been to lie to everyone.

The two prelates continued to bicker as he remained lost in his thoughts. The ambassador's residence itself was in Thieves' Zone, in an outer district set aside for diplomatic functions between governments that didn't talk to one another. Here, Chumley's Zone held its diplomatic mission to Thieves' Zone and vice versa. Thorpe's and McAllister's, the two corporate zones, held embassies with each other here despite their ongoing war. And of course the lokaric consulate for Kwyne was here, though the Lokaryns were perfectly happy to set up a very lavish embassy for the Kwynians at their own expense in the Lokaryns' upper district.

Traveling from the Center Arc of Kwyne to the Diplomatic Arc of the Thieves' Zone by horse-drawn carriage would be an impossibility if not for the portal transportation system that linked the zones. Though convenient, the portal system was far too energy-intensive for common use. It was reserved for high-level diplomatic functions and, of course, the extremely wealthy. The portal station was completely cleared of all personnel. A special team from the Kuhbrik operated the controls that now opened a conduit to Thieves' Zone, and they would remain here.

The members of this unit knew that it was the eve of war and that Var Kragen was going "somewhere" that might avert the conflict. Like all true warriors, they abhorred war, but if called upon they would unleash a horror on their enemy that there could be no comprehending. All trained for it. All dreaded it.

The two mares that pulled the carriage stopped for an instant when confronted with the portal. Unnatural and utterly black, it was not a thing that any living creature went into lightly. With a prod of the driver's whip, the horses pushed on and the carriage followed.

Once on the other side, the driver reined the horses to a stop and the party got out. They were in enemy territory now, so far as they were concerned. If Kragen were to die, Kwyne would be thrown into chaos. With their enemies ready to loose war they stood at a perilous moment in time.

They quickly filed into an armored antigravity vehicle, one of eight identical vehicles that quickly sped off. Two vehicles apiece on each of four routes. Inside, the prelates continued their debate until finally Kragen took a pouch of tobacco and a pipe from his left pocket, and said simply:

"Thank you. That will do. I will have silence for a moment to collect my thoughts."

"Var," N'orin began, "what makes you think you have the right to silence us? We know the truth."

"The truth, as it stands right now, is that I killed Rohnin Cairo. By the right of assassination I am the new leader of Kwyne and I will not be made a puppet by anyone. When we decided to do this, it meant all the way. There is no way to undo this; therefore, it is reality. You had best learn to accept it."

The prelates looked at each other in apprehension as Var Kragen smoked his pipe. The pungent aroma of the tobacco had N'orin reaching for a window, but a security officer intervened, knowing that a smoke plume from one of the eight vehicles would give away their position. They all sat and suffered while the rohnin considered the coming challenge. Finally, he exhaled and extinguished the contents of his pipe. After carefully cleaning the bowl and stem, he replaced it in its velvet pouch. Then he tied the drawstring—a single throw of a knot, right over left—and placed it with the bowl facing forward in his left-hand pocket.

When they arrived at the lokaric embassy, the aides very quickly wanted to get out, but the rohnin was not yet ready to go.

"Join me now," he said solemnly, with head bowed. "Everlasting Maker, we come before you now in an hour of need. Ever have we been faithful to your word and we thank you for your prophet who brought your word to us. We go now into the lair of the most unholy of places. We pray that you guide us and protect us in this time..."

Kragen trailed off, not knowing what else to say. The silence was broken by the abrupt opening of the door by a servant of the embassy. A cloud of tobacco smoke greeted him and he wrinkled his nose at the smell of it. For their part, the occupants of the vehicle breathed deeply of the fresh air, hoping that they would never have to experience Kragen's tobacco in a closed vehicle again.

"The ambassador awaits your audience," the servant said, with a small bow.

They were ushered into an ornate room. The paintings on the walls were old and had an otherworldly aura about them. Artifacts that had survived the Cataclysm often had this quality. So did their subjects: The people in the paintings didn't seem concerned with their own mortality. They looked as if they thought they would live forever. Though the Kwynians could not have known it, there was no Lokaryn in any of the portraits.

Some short time later the servant returned.

"Please come with me," he said.

The security detail moved forward to secure the room before their rohnin entered. They fanned in rapidly, only to find a man seated at a desk looking entirely amused as they scanned the room for threats. The rohnin came in and motioned to the team.

"That will do," he said, dismissing them.

"Permission to post a guard in the room."

"Permission denied," the rohnin said. "Our host didn't bring me all this way to attack me. Besides, if he were to, you couldn't defend me. Not here. We are all in Thecla's hands now. Go outside and pray for us."

The detail commander turned to leave the room and Kragen caught his arm. "But from one old soldier to another, keep an ear open," he said.

The Lokaryn stood and beckoned to them to come forward. They did so, unaccustomed to being directed in such a fashion.

"Prelate Balazar," the Lokaryn said. Balazar made a slight, courteous bow of the head. "Prelate N'orin," he said next. N'orin continued to look around nervously. "And—" He paused a moment and looked Kragen over. "—the Eminent Var Kragen."

"*Rohnin* Kragen," the newly installed leader of Kwyne corrected.

"Indeed? Welcome."

The Lokaryn did not wait for a response; instead, he closed the book that lay upon his desk with what appeared to be regret. He tapped it a few times in thought and then looked up.

"A state of war technically exists between our zones. Our armies are mobilizing and we have contacted other zones that we feel will be sympathetic to our cause to ask them to join us. We understand that the Rohnin's Perch was destroyed in an explosion late last evening and that you cannot account for the rohnin himself. You have been sent to us as the interim government."

"I am here as the government of Kwyne," Kragen again corrected.

"Your reign may be a short one. In twenty-four hours a force representing all the clans of our zone will start to infiltrate Kwyne. They have been given instructions to target any living being within your zone."

"You mean kill," Prelate N'orin said matter-of-factly, interrupting the Lokaryn.

"Yes, kill. Further, a force of net rogues who have been given asylum will launch an all-out assault on your computer grids. We anticipate that you will be able to resist for little more than eighteen hours, assuming you've been diligent about your security and are not just posturing about it in the Nehreton. We will consider the following. If you surrender five percent of your population to us for our feeding pens, and destroy the execution chamber, we will hold our invasion."

N'orin and Balazar sat stunned as they listened to the offer. Rohnin Kragen acted.

"Ambassador. You treat us as if we are paupers. Kwyne is not some child that must beg for its existence. If we were so easily subdued, you would have long ago marched our entire population into that pit of yours. Kwyne has existed for millennia, you know that. Through the Cataclysm, and through wars. More wars than your kind has ever fought. We have no wish for conflict, but if you want a war, then bring it. If you want to kill us here and now, then do so. We are three against how many? But Kwyne, the millions of faithful, the Kuhbrik, the commoner, with faith in the Maker and the Prophet, will not yield to you willingly. Each dranz of blood you take will cost you threefold of your army. Kwyne will never bow…"

The Lokaryn held up his hand with a slight smile on his face. "Kragen, you really are a pompous ass."

"That's Rohnin Kragen," N'orin said, emboldened by Kragen's stand.

"I think not. You killed your rohnin?" the Lokaryn asked.

Though it galled Kragen to say the word out loud, *this* was the purpose for creating the lie.

"Yes."

"Really? Quite a thing to have assassinated the leader of your precious Kwyne. A person you revere as a god."

"Do you have a point, Ambassador?"

"No point, I simply don't believe you."

"My ascension does not require your belief…"

"Only the complicity of fools," the Lokaryn finished for him.

Kragen looked at the ambassador and knew at once that he was missing some fact.

"It dawns on the man that he does not know something that he really should. Tactics and not strategy, such is Var Kragen." The Lokaryn looked at him with disdain.

Kragen's mind raced but without result.

"Var," came a familiar voice. "What are you doing?"

Was it a trick? Could the Lokaryn seed the voice of the dead rohnin in his head?

Damien Cairo walked out from behind one of the walls of books holding an ancient tome in his hands. His finger held the spot where he had stopped reading.

"What have you done, Var? *You* blew up the Perch? *You* attempted to assassinate me?"

Kragen stood face-to-face with a specter.

"Rohnin?" Kragen gasped with the voice of a strong man who beheld the fulfillment of wishes unspoken: The rohnin was alive; he did not have to assume the assassin's mantle.

"No," Cairo said, shaking his head with a smile. "The rohnin is dead. You killed him, everyone knows that now that you've made your grand announcement."

"Rohnin, you must return."

"My assassin wants me to return? I'm afraid not; I'm dead and therefore released from all obligation."

"Rohnin, if I may. Please, a moment alone."

The ambassador shared a look with Cairo and motioned to a doorway. Kragen followed Cairo to the door, his confusion mounting. The relationship between his resurrected god and this undead emissary seemed almost…friendly. The ambassador looked at his desk and, tapping the book twice more, said, "Are you sure about this, Damien?"

"I am," the rohnin replied simply.

Cairo opened the door and ushered Kragen into the private study. The last thing he saw before closing it was N'orin and Balazar gaping at the ambassador.

"Sit!" the Lokaryn snapped at them and, in unison, the two prelates did so, like trained animals.

Cairo allowed himself a smile as the door closed. Turning to Kragen, he said. "You must have a thousand questions, Var, but I'll start with a few of my own. First, you are not the assassin, correct?"

Kragen was relieved to have the question put to him. His duty was to answer his rohnin truthfully. Sometimes duty can be a blessing.

"I am not."

"Honesty is a good start to this conversation. I thought you more strong-minded than to believe fools such as N'orin and Balazar. They convinced you that claiming the right of ascension through assassination would speed the transfer of leadership during this crisis, correct?"

Kragen felt like a cadet being reprimanded for a failing grade on an exercise. "The speed of events caught everyone off guard…"

"The speed of events did *not* catch everyone off guard, Var."

A moment or two passed as Kragen searched for the meaning of the statement. And then: "That's how you knew to be out of the Perch. After the vote, an assassination attempt wasn't an absolute. The situation might have been defused."

"Var, listen to me closely. An assassination attempt *was* inevitable. It was logical. Someone is pulling strings to create a crisis, perhaps even a war. The Lokaryn you executed was not the one that was in Kwyne earlier. The audio cache from the helmet cams has at least three instances where the assaulting forces refer to the target as a she."

"The Lokaryn was female?" Kragen began to feel nauseated. "Then who was the Lokaryn we found?"

"He was a younger Lokaryn named J'Nath. Think about it. A Lokaryn, found in Kwyne, in the same arc shortly after the attack. That's bad enough. But found feeding on a prelate's daughter?"

"That would incense anyone," Kragen said.

"That would incense everyone," Cairo replied.

"Rohnin, I will walk the Prophet's Path as atonement, should you deem it appropriate, but you must resume the throne."

"No, Var, I'm a martyr and you did it. You are now the rohnin of Kwyne."

Kragen's mind raced, searching for the successful argument to convince the rohnin to return. The realization was slow, but bitter.

"You knew," Kragen said, looking into Cairo's eyes. "You knew I'd step forward and claim the throne by right of assassination."

"I knew somebody would. You were, of course, the most likely to do so. You have a part to play in this now, Var, and I need you to play it well. Kwyne needs you to play it well."

"So I am to be painted as an assassin for history so that you can slip your responsibilities?"

"Your choices were your own. I need Kwyne to turn away from war at a time when her soul is set on it. We will use politics to our advantage. Do not trust N'orin. He will seek the throne before this is done. Balazar is the one. He is your Ko'Doran. You and Balazar must have a falling-out. It must seem as if civil war is about to break out."

"How will that help us?"

"You'll be buying me time to defuse the situation. The Kuhbrik and the upper-echelon forces of each arc will have sunlight crystals in a fortnight. That will help to balance things."

"How do you know the Lokaryns can be trusted?

They could use our inaction to attack."

"I know it's difficult to imagine, but Apostatic Lokaryns have no interest in war. If it helps you to know this, the raw material for the crystals came from the Lokaryns."

"They will not work. If the Lokaryns provided them—they will fail when called upon and our men will be slaughtered."

"I am not a fool, Var. The raw material came from sources I trust. They were smythed under the eye of the tarran's smyth himself—they will work. They will be flawless."

"You say you are averting a war, yet you are prepared for one."

"I am."

"If we are prepared, then why not strike first? Don't you think we can prevail?" Kragen asked.

"No, I think we would, but at what cost?"

"The war won't stay confined to the Lokaryns and Kwyne," the new rohnin said, picking up the thought.

"No. Just as I predicted, Rossums and Thieves' have pledged assistance to the Lokaryns. Before I left, I contacted the commander in Chumley's and the tarran of Ravensford. They will join us. Merchants' will remain neutral as expected. McAllister's and Thorpe's will as well, supplying weapons to both sides."

"You arranged for Chumley's and Phobes' to ally with us."

"Yes."

"But you didn't want this, you have always argued against force."

"I always argued against using force without just cause. If we are attacked, we must be prepared to answer."

"Where will you go?"

Cairo said nothing and instead reached out to shake Kragen's hand.

Kragen took it and with his other hand held out Cairo's copy of the holy book, charred from the blast, but still intact. "The Maker's blessing on your journey and may Thecla guide you."

Cairo reached out and took the book. It was like a piece of him had been restored.

"Thank you, Rohnin Kragen," Cairo said. "May Thecla guide you."

"You are welcome, Rohnin Cairo," Kragen said with respect. "May she guide us all."

Without another word, Damien Cairo left. Var Kragen found himself standing in a room filled with a thousand tomes of ancient and modern knowledge, a man in search of answers. The irony of his situation was not lost on him. His answers could only be found though experience. Var Kragen was now the right hand of God, with countless faithful at his side. He had never felt more alone.

Morgan Garand and Conrad Trass were never seen again. The ships they built have never been accounted for. From time to time stories of exceptional feats of mystmanship surface, giving rise to the idea that the ships are out there. If so, their recovery becomes paramount to the Garand Corporation and Thorpe's Zone in general.

—Thorpe's board communication

CHAPTER 65

Deep myst

Aboard the *Shicaine*

"ALL SENIOR CREW LAY TO the bridge," came the shrieking demons of the comm link.

In Seyschell's religion there was a special place reserved for the damned. It was a place where things that were seemingly pleasurable erupted into torment. The touch of a lover became sharpened knives. The kiss of the sun became a blistering burn. Sweet nectar became acid, and it was on this last point that Seyschell, having attended the card game in the engine room, compared the chief's moonshine to the afterlife. She dressed and slowly made her way to the bridge.

Her head swam, her body objected, and her stomach could just as well be removed and she would be the better for it. She had won at Dranwyene against the chief the night before just as she had sworn to do, but the chief had the last laugh. She awoke in her bunk naked, and the room was a wreck. She must have had nightmares—the bed headboard had been crushed where she grasped it in the night. She would replace it with a sturdier alloy later.

As she entered, the first officer looked over at her and smiled a cryptic smile. She furrowed a brow and retraced the evening: Had she done anything she would regret?

Dumb question, she thought. *I never regret anything.* It was, of course, a lie.

Yet her mind retraced the night.

Engine room.

Bridge crew.

Cards.

More cards and the chief getting irritated.

The chief's moonshine.

More cards, more liquor.

The trail went cold after that. Like a curtain drawn over her memory.

How drunk could she have been? She had a pocketful of the chief's caryns.

When she opened her mouth to talk, a rasping noise escaped. "Good morning," she croaked.

She cleared her throat and attempted to straighten herself in the vain hope that a dignified entry would compensate for her loss of voice.

The bridge crew had other ideas and simultaneously replied in an overly loud manner.

"Good morning!"

The sound struck her like a wave of flaming myst.

She stopped cold and smiled weakly. Her hand shot out for a console on which to steady herself.

"Can I be of assistance?" the first officer asked innocently.

Seyschell's eye went wide. Those words, "Can I be of assistance," raised the curtain on at least one foggy element of the night.

She froze. She recalled the chief's look as she rose from the table, unsteady. The first officer and Cade attempted to help her to her feet. She was as drunk as a first-time sailor.

"Lost your capacity for decent ale while you were away, I see," the chief laughed.

If she made a reply, it was surely too slurred for any to comprehend.

"Can I be of some assistance?" The first officer had grabbed her hand to steady her. She pulled away slurring something to the effect of not needing anything. The next thing that she recalled was being carried to her bunk by the first officer. Her arms were around his neck and she could recall enjoying his scent as she nestled in closer. And closer.

Again the curtain fell. What happened between that moment and the morning retreated into the darkness of the night.

"Captain on the bridge," came the voice of the master at arms.

"Carry on," Gedrick said quietly. He, perhaps alone, Seyschell thought, had a modicum of sympathy for his chemically wounded former first officer.

He came up behind Seyschell and gave her a hearty slap on the back and a little shake of the shoulders. Then again maybe not, she thought.

"Well, since our former first officer does not appear to be up to the task of powered sailing this morning, it looks, Mr. Chapman, as if your opportunity has arrived."

Gedrick looked over at Seyschell with the distinct impression that this was a problem that was deliberately manufactured to allow the current first officer a shot at the copilot's seat. Seyschell looked back at him with the knowledge that she hadn't intended to succeed this well.

"Are you ready, Mr. Chapman?"

"Aye, sir. I trust the betting is closed, Master at Arms?"

The master at arms looked back at the first officer with a face as innocent as a newborn's and asked, "What betting would that be, sir?" He knew full well that the crew had been betting on how long the first officer would be able to control the ship before the captain would have to rescue him.

"Put me down for a hundred caryns, on thirty minutes," Chapman said.

"If there were betting on the subject, sir, which I am sure there is not, I wouldn't be able to take your bet since you can influence the outcome."

"Mr. Chapman, if you are finished managing your investments, could we set to this? We're wasting good sailing conditions."

"Aye, sir."

The entire crew took a deep, deep breath as if they could hold it long enough to swim out of the myst.

Neville Chapman didn't look like a man about to have a heart attack, but he did feel like one. He lowered himself into the pilot's crib like a man getting into a tub that's entirely too hot. He took a deep breath and buckled in.

"Most of the controls are exactly the same," Gedrick said as he slid into the copilot's position next to the first officer. "You just don't have any margin for error in anything you do. The pitch, yaw, and direction of the ship are controlled by the orientation of your hand over that sensor pad. If your hand twitches left to right, the ship will follow the signal. Easy enough."

The sergeant at arms stood nearby. Chapman looked over at him.

"Seriously, how's the betting going?" he asked in a conspiratorial voice.

"Not bad. Two to one the captain takes the ship over from you in the first minute."

"Nice to know the crew has faith in me."

"Not a matter of faith, it's a matter of physics. For what it's worth, the captain put a fair lot down."

"I thought you couldn't take bets from someone who could influence the outcome."

"Well, he's the captain after all isn't he? Besides, he bet on you to hold the ship for the entire run."

The adjustments were made in the pilot's crib and the deck was quickly prepared for powered sailing.

"Are you ready, Nev?"

"Yes I am," Chapman said.

"You have command of the *Shicaine*."

"On my mark. Three—two—one—mark."

The power flowed to the propulsion systems and he at once felt connected to the ship in a way he never had before. The ship surged forward. He had seen falcons and hawks in Ravensford Zone glide with the barest hint of a wingtip touching the water. The *Shicaine* now moved that way under his command.

Suddenly, the feeling was gone and he felt nauseated and exhausted as if he had gone drink for drink with Seyschell the night before. He had only piloted for what felt like a minute. So short a time. What had he done wrong? As his vision cleared and he came back to the moment, he found a grinning Gedrick collecting a large sum of caryns from the sergeant at arms.

"Go lie down. You're going to feel like you were drinking myst for a few hours. It will pass," the captain said.

"Why so short? Did I make a mistake?"

Various members of the bridge crew began to laugh. A few shook their heads in amazement as they went back to their duties.

"Mr. Chapman, you were at the helm for about ninety minutes."

"Sir?"

"It happens. You lose track of time. It must be similar to what net rogues' experience in the ether. You have to be careful, you can exhaust yourself to the point of collapse and never feel it coming. Now go lie down."

It wasn't until this point that Chapman realized that Seyschell was sitting at the nav table with her feet propped up. Her mouth was wide open and from it emanated a rather raucous snoring.

"Permission to leave the bridge?" he asked.

"Permission granted."

Chapman felt as if he lacked the strength to walk back to his stateroom a few dozen yards away. After climbing out of the pilot's crib, he willed himself to walk, albeit slowly, from the bridge. Once off the bridge and in the companionway, he leaned on the wall for support. A number of bridge crew watched after him with wicked smiles.

He had always heard the phrase "Asleep before the head hit the pillow." For the first time in his life he experienced it. And he dreamed of flying a myst-clipper ship throughout the most well-earned sleep of his life.

Villages burned and bodies turned to dust, but humanity endured. Such as it was.

—Starpoint Shanachie, Badlands

CHAPTER 66

SIXTEEN YEARS OLD.

Confused.

Condemned.

Chenara huddled against the cold. There was no light, no heat, not a single comfort in her cell. Though she couldn't remember the last time she ate, she did not feel hunger in the usual sense. Instead she ached. Her chest burned. Each time the guard approached on his scheduled walkthrough, she felt herself falling into a haze. She could feel his body heat and she could hear his heart beating. It made the wound at her neck burn all the more intensely.

As he left, she would suddenly snap out of the fugue state and weep uncontrollably. She did not know what was happening to her, only that something was terribly wrong.

The bite began to burn intensely, more intensely than ever before, as she felt a new sensation building within her. It was a profound, feral hunger, and she knew all too well who was approaching her prison.

She had adopted a position with her back toward the door. It was less painful when the viewport to the cell was open and shadowy light filtered into the room. She could feel the burn on her back, but it was infinitely better than when the light hit her eyes.

The viewport opened. The man who stood there said nothing.

The girl did not turn around to look. She knew it was Senja Goli, prelate, chief politician, and theological leader of her home arc. Her father. She spoke after only a few seconds of silence. "Father, I am in trouble. I am ill and these people won't let me out of here. They won't tell me what I've done; they hate me and won't tell me why. Please, Father, help me."

"You are beyond anyone's help now, girl. Your mother and I tried, but you had to have your way. You stopped being my daughter when you ran away. Now your sin has brought you to this. You should have done as we said, read the scriptures and followed them. You chose to stay out of the light of Thecla's teaching. Now you will pay the price of the wicked. I have only come to see for myself what you have become."

"Father, please. I am ill. I want to go home. I didn't do anything."

"You disobeyed me, you disobeyed your mother. You defied us and ran away from the home that we gave you."

"You only gave us whatever was good for your career. Every time you got a new position we had to parade around like the perfect family. I only wanted to have a few friends of my own. Not the ones who had parents that you needed to advance your career." It seemed absurd to her to be having the old arguments in this place.

"It fed you for sixteen years, you and your mother. She doesn't complain."

"She doesn't complain because your bodyguards comfort her," the young woman spat. Senja Goli took in a deep breath. Though he knew it to be true, he would not take the bait.

"Your mother and I will pray for your soul." With that the portal abruptly shut, leaving the girl once again alone and scared.

It was hours, no more than a day to be sure, before the portal opened and shut quickly. Then the door opened. The hallway windows had been covered over so as to not allow any sunlight in. How she longed to feel at least a single ray on her face. She did not yet understand.

The guards were heavily armored, and they held weapons of every description. They stood back from her as if she were diseased or somehow dangerous. Snipers lined the overhead walks, and stun nets roofed the walkway, ready to fall free if there was any disturbance. Every time a door open or closed, the sound of an airtight seal accompanied it.

She wondered why all this was necessary—airtight doors and enough weaponry to carry out a small insurrection. She was a teenage runaway, not a heretic. A guard motioned her to exit her cell completely. She did so. Though not the sunlight she craved, spotlights as bright as the noon sun snapped on, illuminating her from every side. The guards looked on uneasily. Quite different from the terror they had concocted in their minds, this looked like a scared little girl. Wrapped in a dirty blanket for warmth and standard-issue prison clothing, equally dirty and torn.

The guard motioned to her to walk down the hallway. There was only one other door in her sight. Perhaps her father was being dramatic and all this was a show. This was her lesson so that she would fall into line. After being on the streets, the assault in the alleyway, and now prison, she would gladly toe the line for the warmth of her bed and her mother's cooking. Even school didn't seem so bad.

She walked down the hallway, looking at the guards with a slight fascination. She had never seen such a sight. For her father to go to all this trouble for her…maybe he did care after all. She resolved to give him a chance when she got home.

Now at the door, she did what must have been very odd in the eyes of the guards. She thanked them and stepped through.

The door shut behind her and the airlock cycled. She felt the small room begin to rise like an elevator, and after a short but slow ride, the room stopped. The roof opened like a camera iris, and the floor continued up until she came even with another floor. As it did, the white light of the elevator was slowly shut out, ending in a halo under her feet, and then it was gone. This new room was bathed in red light. Though it was dim, she found her vision was good enough to make out some detail.

The walls were mirrored. It could mean only one thing. She had heard this place described many times at the dinner table. It was a symbol of Kwynian wrath against the unholy. Against all sins. She touched the wall with a trembling hand and looked at her image reflecting off into infinity. She fell against the wall and cried. She sobbed, and her hair fell across her face.

"Daddy, please help me," she called out. She could never have anticipated what happened next. Her father did indeed answer her. From high above, a panel of the mirrored walls slid back, revealing an observation gallery. She could see faces peering over at her, many of whom she recognized. Several had cocktails in their hands.

"My fellow Kwynians," the prelate began, "several days ago we caught and executed a lokaric spy. That agent was caught in the act of assaulting a Kwynian citizen, a child of Kwyne. My child."

"Daddy, please, I want to go home, I want to see Mommy!" she shouted, but her father continued, not remotely acknowledging his child's continuing pleas.

"These are times that require us to be strong. They require strong leadership and they require sacrifice. This creature was once a child of Kwyne, but now is the embodiment of all that is unholy, of all that Thecla despises. Today we will respond in accordance with the scriptures; the scriptures that will keep us strong against evil and which save us in this world and the next."

"Daddy! Please! Someone please help me. I want to go home!"

"Scripture *demands* that we cleanse this child. This purification will cleanse us all of…"

The prelate's voice stopped and the room quieted.

"Of what, Senja Goli? Bad parenting skills?" Thus came the voice of Var Kragen, rohnin of Kwyne. Kragen's presence had transformed the festive occasion to one of sobriety and duty.

"I had received word of what you intend to do here, but had to see it for myself to believe it. Is this what we've come to? Executing children who defy their parents? The line will indeed be long."

"She is a Lokaryn, Rohnin. She was bitten. She is sin that walks among us. The scriptures demand…"

"Demand? The scriptures demand? Show me where the word 'demand' occurs even once in any of the holy books and you may continue this abomination without another word from me."

Down below, Chenara stopped weeping and listened in amazement. Her father had always used the term "zealot" in a very derogatory way when describing Kragen. She had seen him preach and knew him to be extreme, yet here he was the one voice that stood between her and death.

"How can you all stand here with *drinks* in your hands as if this were some sort of party? I see some of you with escorts who are not your spouses. A remarkable number of attractive cousins are in town, I see. And here you all are, milling about waiting to watch the execution of a child. Is that what scripture demands? Is this Kwyne?"

"She has become a Lokaryn, she must be purged, Rohnin Kragen. I am sacrificing my child for the purity of Kwyne," Prelate Goli pontificated, summoning all the false indignation he could.

"The scriptures demand no such thing. They direct us to help her, to search for a cure for her, to counsel her and pray for her."

"I tell you, she is a Lokaryn!"

"We don't know that. She has not transformed, she has committed no crime against Kwyne or scripture that warrants death. If the transformation is not complete, you will be incinerating your daughter. The light won't kill her like a Lokaryn. Instead, the heat in the chamber once the upper hatch is opened will be more than enough to burn her to death."

"No!" the girl screamed from below. "Please don't burn me, please don't burn me. I don't want to die."

Kragen leaned over and looked at the girl below. "You would do well to pray right now. Your actions have brought you here. Pray for forgiveness from Thecla and you might yet find deliverance."

Kragen turned to a guard. "Get her out of there and to a healer. Now!" The guard left immediately, glad to be out of the room.

Var Kragen stormed out of the room with a new understanding. Cairo was right. There could be no leadership while tending the Nehreton.

The terms "salvageable target" and "siribium-tipped hollow-bore diamond ordinance" are not compatible.

—Thorpe's Corporation ordnance manual

CHAPTER 67

Zone shelf myst
Thieves' Zone

THE AX SPLIT THE FIRST officer's head cleanly in two from the crown to the stem of the neck. At least, that's how it felt when the knock came on his door. It was followed by two successive blows, each more piercing than the last. When he finally managed to pry open an eye it was in response to the aroma of strong, almost burnt coffee. He found a very concerned-looking captain standing by his bedside holding a cup in one hand and an urn of black consciousness in the other.

"How long?" the first officer croaked.

"About twelve hours. Drink this, all of this, and report to the briefing room in fifteen minutes."

With that Gedrick was gone. Chapman slowly rose from the bed. With great effort, he slid one leg onto the deck and began shifting his weight until he was finally seated in more or less an upright position. He had been hungover before, but this was worse in every way. Gedrick had left the coffee out of reach on his desk. Heaving himself up, he planted his feet firmly on the floor and pushed off the bed. He arced over and caught himself on the desk with his left hand while the right scooped up the pot and sloshed some contents into the cup. He more dropped than put down the pot, before taking the cup in hand. He quickly brought it to his lips and sucked it down.

Slowly his senses came back. The first to return, regrettably, was the sensation of temperature, and he realized that he had scalded his tongue. No matter; his headache was abating in response to the coffee. He poured a second cup with slightly more acumen and it disappeared as fast as the first. His tongue was becoming leathered, but the headache continued to wane. He became aware of his hearing and the sounds of the ship. Someone was outside his door.

"Who's there?" he said through the gravel that now inhabited his throat.

Midshipman Neylione peered in the door with the look of someone who had just stumbled upon a deathbed scene.

"The captain gave orders that you were not to be allowed to go back to sleep," the midshipman said nervously. Chapman said nothing but noted a pail of water at the young woman's feet.

"What is that for?" he asked, knowing full well its intended purpose.

"Watering your plants."

"I don't have any plants."

"My mistake."

"Captain's orders?"

"Captain Gedrick gave the instruction not to let you miss the briefing, and told me to be inventive. It's all I could come up with on short order."

"I see. Not very inventive, but probably effective." With that Chapman closed the door, walked to his bathing area, and splashed some water on his face. After a third cup of coffee, most of his mental abilities had returned. He changed into a new uniform and headed for the door. He paused for a moment with his hand on the knob, then pulled the door open very abruptly. He caught Neylione listening intently for signs that he had returned to sleep. She snapped upright, stepping back to give way to her superior officer, and stepped directly into the pail of water. She stood there at attention, with one foot in the pail, immobile.

The first officer looked her up and down and, adjusting his collar, said, "You might want to clean this up before someone slips on it."

"Aye, aye, sir," she said, without losing her composure.

He still carried with him a cup of coffee and doubted it would survive the trip to the briefing room. He detoured through the galley, where he found Seyschell with the same plan in mind.

"The coffee really helps," she said, looking fairly unfazed.

"You took the helm for a while this morning?" Chapman, asked amazed.

"About two hours ago, for about an hour," she replied.

"I can't even imagine doing that after the way you looked this morning."

"I do love my mutant genes."

"Let's go, we'll be late."

They arrived in the briefing room a few minutes early, and as Chapman entered the room he received a round of applause and a number of handshakes for his performance at the yoke earlier in the day.

"Attention on deck," came a voice from the crowd as the captain walked in.

"Please be seated," Gedrick said. "As you all are apparently aware, we have a third pilot for the *Shicaine* for powered operations." He nodded toward Chapman and continued. "This allows us to go onto a schedule of three to four hours of powered ops followed by eight hours of sailing until further notice. Mr. Chapman, you will select an individual to carry out your duties as first officer until such time as we no longer require powered ops at such an intense level or Kisner rejoins the crew to take your place."

"McCormick is ready," Chapman said.

"Commander McCormick, you are acting first officer until Mr. Chapman or I say that you aren't," the captain announced.

"Yes, sir," McCormick answered.

"Select a replacement for your duties. In the meantime, we'll be going on a twelve-hour cycle of powered ops and sailing until further notice. The chief thinks that he can give us more power with the new cells. Mr. Chapman, you're limited to sixty minutes, however; I need you fresh for you next shift."

"Aye, sir."

"Get a good meal and brief, McCormick. We should be to rendezvous point Fahta in three days if we can continue at this rate of travel."

"Can we assume an immediate departure for Phobes'?"

"You can. Powered ops in twenty minutes. Dismissed."

Chapman still felt the ill effects from his first experience piloting the ship. He took a deep breath, imagining the cumulative effects. A rather painful slap on the back was accompanied by the sound of Seyschell's voice.

"Be careful what you wish for, young man," she said, laughing as she left.

Chapman returned to the galley, where the cook had assembled a large plate of food. The thought crossed his mind that a man about to be outcast into the Badlands was often given a good meal before being thrown over the wall.

He sat down to the table and was quickly joined by Gur McCormick, a Thorpe's escapee who had joined the crew some four years ago.

"Thank you," she said.

"Wait until you've done the job for a week before you thank me," he said, watching the clock closely.

"Any advice?" she asked.

"How long have you been under my tutelage?"

"As an officer, two years."

"All my advice to you has been given save this."

"Yes, sir?"

He continued chewing a morsel as McCormick watched him, waiting patiently for him to reveal the secret of success in her new post.

With his mouth half full he said, "Don't screw up."

He got up and walked out, hoping he had left enough time to get to the head before he was to be in the pilot's crib.

"Five minutes to powered operations. Deck crew secure for storm running," he heard over the shipwide system.

To Chapman, the next three days became a blur of strapping into the pilot's crib and exceptionally strong coffee. The chief had a concoction that he swore would ease the postpiloting symptoms. After his first sip he was reasonably sure it was made from old socks the chief had been fermenting in the engine room, mixed with liberal amounts of myst and the Grendel's urine.

While it was effective at preventing the symptoms, after one dose he understood why Seyschell and Gedrick preferred to deal with the situation using only brutally strong coffee. In any case, he found the combination of the shorter piloting time and general acclimation to do more than the chief's brew. He managed to keep close tabs on Commander McCormick and was well pleased with her progress.

Before he knew it, the three days had passed and they approached the rendezvous point. The ship reverted to sail power as Gedrick worked to make the *Shicaine* just another merchant ship on the trade routes: nothing unusual about her at all. Yet the *Shicaine* did not sail directly to her destination; rather she tacked extensively and even reversed course to flush out any would-be pursuers.

The ship was alive with nervous energy. They came along side the physical portion of the zone wall that protected Thieves' Zone. Here the wall was solid and not projected shielding. The walls were made of thick rock and stood some ninety feet high. From behind this sat the machinery of the force projectors.

Inside the command bridge, Cade worked frantically at the nav table trying to find the back channel that would allow them to navigate inside without attracting much attention.

"I have some bad news, Captain. I think they may have closed the channel."

"Options?"

"There are others, but it would mean overland travel away from the ship to get to the rendezvous," Cade said. "If we can enter here we can sail straight up to it."

"If the channel is gone, what choice do we have?" Gedrick asked.

Chapman was the next to speak. "Commander McCormick."

"Sir."

"What is your assessment of the situation?"

"Me, sir?" she asked, a little alarmed.

"You are the first officer of this ship, yes you."

"Overland creates a situation where the command crew will be separated from the ship, and so far every time the captain leaves the ship he has been attacked."

"Technically, I wasn't attacked in Seyschell's village," Gedrick corrected.

"Since the back channel is no longer an option, I would say we go in through the customs gate."

The entire bridge crew stood silent. The customs gate was an outer district warlords' shakedown for the new or unwary traveler. Anyone foolish enough to enter though a local gate rather than a zone gate was subjected to steep fees for passage that could be had elsewhere for a fraction of the cost.

"Brilliant," Gedrick proclaimed.

"Brilliant? You must be joking, they charge us thousands of caryns just to breathe the air," Seyschell said.

"Money we have, access we don't," Gedrick said. "They'd never expect us to come in like fools."

"Plus the locals aren't going to care much about the comings and goings of an inexperienced captain," Chapman said.

Seyschell thought for a moment, then nodded her head. "They make their money and have a good laugh while we slide through unexpected and undetected. It could work."

Chapman allowed a smile in the direction of his pupil and gave her a small nod of approval. McCormick did not react outwardly but inwardly felt as if she had vanquished the Grendel with a single blow.

They all stood looking at her and while distracted, she suddenly realized they were waiting for her to give the command.

"Oh, sorry. Helm, make course for the Nineteenth Arc customs gate."

"Mr. Chapman."

"Aye, Captain."

"Feeling deceptive today?" Gedrick asked with a wicked smile. He knew that a younger man would be more believable as a new captain.

"Not at all, Captain," Chapman deadpanned.

"Very well, *Captain* Chapman. See if you can negotiate us through the gate for a believable, but not painful amount of money," Gedrick said.

"Aye, sir."

"Cade?" Gedrick continued.

"Sir?"

"Please plot an inefficient course to the gate. Something that a first-timer might do."

"Yes, sir." Cade turned to the task.

"Helm, nice tight adherence to the coordinates that Cade gives you."

"First Officer McCormick," Gedrick said.

"Sir," she answered.

"Please have a number of the crew turn out in formal uniforms."

"Already done, sir."

"Bring us in then."

The *Shicaine* pulled up alongside the Nineteenth Arc customs dock and tied up loosely to the pier. The crew lined up on deck in formal uniforms while a weasel-faced man looked over the ship and headed up the gangway. He walked past the sailor at the head of the boarding ramp without so much as a glance.

"Permission to come aboard granted," the man said under his breath. He suddenly wished he had held that breath as he caught the trailing odor from the man.

"Greetings, Captain," the man said, sizing Chapman up.

"Greetings." Chapman fidgeted a little, trying to look uncomfortable. The smell from the man helped enormously.

"What brings you to the Nineteenth Arc?"

"Business."

"Well, that's a surprise on a merchant clipper. What kind of business?"

"Private business."

"Again, a surprise. But we don't much like surprises, so why don't you tell me what you're doing here."

"Excuse me, but as you're a customs-house agent, wouldn't you like to know what our cargo is?"

"What is your cargo?"

"We are carrying nothing."

"Just came to visit then?" the man said, with growing impatience.

"We were commissioned by an agent in Merchants' Zone to come here and try to obtain certain materials."

"What materials?"

"Excuse me, but if I am carrying nothing then why does a customs inspector want to know what I may be carrying in the future?"

"Let's just say if you want to find 'certain' things that may be difficult to obtain and even more difficult to transport…"

"I would do well to have a friend?"

"So the conventional wisdom goes."

"And would you know where I might find such a friend?"

"I might, for smallish fee."

"Up-front fees can cause bad feelings. I prefer percentages. You connect me with the right supplier and I'll give you a percentage of the take when I return. If the take is good, you know I'll be back and I'll want to make you happy. If it's bad I won't be back and I won't be out a fee and looking to recoup it from you."

The weasel-faced man looked him over. Money in hand was infinitely better, but in his position he could afford to take a risk.

"Forty percent gross."

"Two percent net."

"Ten percent net and an additional two percent over a hundred thousand caryns."

"We have an understanding then. What is the certain item?"

"Detonator cores and siribium-tipped hollow-bore diamond shards. Seven hundred."

"Ow," the man said, impressed. His mind had calculated numbers that set his greed center into spasms. "Have a little spat with someone did we?"

"Me? No. I'm at peace with all of T'Amorach, but my employer has certain interests to protect and those little beauties will tend to fend off..."

"Anything."

"Anything. So, *friend*. Do you know where an honest merchant might find these certain items."

"Seven hundred would take a while."

"We can wait a single night; then we have other business to attend to. It might be some time before we can return."

"Seven hundred is a tall order in one night," he muttered, wiping sweat from his lip. His mind raced through legal and illegal venues to obtain such an order. His mouth moved, listing them, and his breath seemed to become more fetid as he neared hyperventilation.

Chapman interrupted. "It seems as if this may be a problem for you. Let us pay you a fair amount for your time and we'll inquire in some of the outer district establishments that have been recommended."

A small degree of panic seeped into the edges of the man's demeanor. The money to be had was considerable. He couldn't let the opportunity pass without at least trying.

"Tie up at Pier 490, due northeast, the dockmaster will be expecting you."

"We'll make our way over there discreetly. But we will arrive there sometime tonight."

"What is your ship's name?"

"*Opportunity*."

"Excellent name. Very good. I'll get to it then." The weasel-faced man scurried off the ship, across the dock, and into his shack.

The *Shicaine* slipped her tie-up and made her way into the outer district of Thieves' Nineteenth Arc. Chapman made his way inside the command bridge to find Gedrick, Cade, and Seyschell all standing in utter silence.

"No good?"

"No, actually, you're a natural at it. It didn't cost a cent. Yet. But why siribium-tipped diamond shards?"

"Well, I figure if we're going to be getting into tangles out there, the gunnery master is going to want some hitting power, and the hollowed shards can be packed with explosive. The siribium and diamond can penetrate most anything and the explosive will take care of business once inside."

"Seven hundred rounds?"

"Handy to have."

"You turned a ruse into a requisition?"

"Yes, sir, I did."

"Yes you did. Mr. Chapman, is there no end to your talents?"

"One would hope not."

"Though I suspect modesty may be one still in development," Seyschell observed.

"As is discretion," he shot back.

"Knock it off, you two. Make for the rendezvous. We'll swing by Pier 490 and check on your requisition in a few hours."

"Aye, aye," came the response of the helmsman.

"Make trim for harbor operations," McCormick instructed.

"Mr. Chapman, Seyschell, you'll be coming ashore with me."

"Captain," McCormick interrupted, "permission to send a security detail with you."

"No I think these two will do. Too many people will draw attention. But if it will make you feel better I'll smyth a quick crystal for escape from the rendezvous point to the pier."

"Sir?" McCormick asked

"Yes, Commander?" Gedrick replied.

"You can smyth crystals?" she asked with some confusion. Merchants did not smyth crystals; phobes did that.

"Carry on, Commander," Gedrick instructed.

"Aye, sir," she said.

"ETA to rendezvous point?" Gedrick asked.

"Forty minutes, sir," Cade responded.

"Briefing room in twenty minutes. Check out your preferred weapons loadout from Gunny and secure any additional equipment you need from ship's stores," Gedrick instructed.

"Aye, sir," Seyschell and Chapman replied in unison.

Twenty minutes later the trio assembled in the main briefing room.

"This should be simple enough. The site is abandoned. Cairo should be alone. We know each other so identification should be easy enough. Once we've made contact we'll come back to the ship and check on Mr. Chapman's requisition. Once clear of the harbor, four hours of sleep and then press on to Phobes'. Questions?"

"No, sir."

"No, sir."

"Very good. If anything happens, the priority is to get the rohnin aboard the *Shicaine* and get to Hemingway and Derring. Whoever comes back, the priority is to assemble the remaining crew. Starting with Kisner."

Chapman noted that Seyschell bristled a bit, but said nothing.

"Captain, docking in five minutes," came over the comm.

"Very good," he responded. Then, to his team, "Ready?"

"Captain, did you have a chance to 'smyth' the crystal you wanted to bring?"

"I took care of that the day we received the signal. I have two spares. Ready?"

After a weapons check, the trio departed the ship and moved at a good clip toward an area that looked to be shunned by even the homeless.

They reached their destination without incident: a warehouse that was seemingly the work of a patient demolition team. One wall had already started to buckle, and light streamed in from any number of areas where the structure had failed. There was the scent of machinery in the air, though none was visible. The wind blew dirt and rustled papers around the cavernous insides of the place, though no other sound could be heard.

They looked at one another.

"Now what?" Seyschell asked.

"Waiting would be wisest," Chapman said.

"How about a look around? I'd rather have a lay of the land than fight blind—if it comes to that," Seyschell offered.

"Fair point," Chapman conceded. "But with some discretion, if you don't mind."

"Agreed, then," Gedrick said. "Seyschell, you take the right, I'll take the middle, and Neville, you go up the left. If we need to get out of here in a hurry we go out the nearest exits and meet up back at the *Shicaine*."

"Just like the old days," Seyschell said, and with that she was up like a runner in the starting blocks—only to have Gedrick's hand pulling her back down.

"Dial it down a notch or so, Shell, we don't need to go headlong into problems we can avoid. Got it?"

Visibly deflated, she nodded. "You're right. Low and easy, boss."

The three split up, moving out onto the warehouse with weapons drawn. Gedrick used the cybernetic capabilities of his eye to analyze the structural elements of the old warehouse. It was made of granite, much like an old castle, so that the caustic myst wouldn't dissolve it away should the outer district wall ever be breached. High above the floor, olden windows with thick metal baffles allowed some small element of light through. The floor was a mass of refuse from old slabs of building granite and wrecked machinery piled high.

Seyschell moved quietly, her heightened senses listening for any nuance of movement against the floor. A small sound caused her to snap around as silently as a whisper, bringing her pulse rifle to bear on a small rodent, which eyed her with curiosity.

Across the floor, Chapman crept slowly and silently, trying to imagine the best places from which an assassin could fire. In his mind he tried to plot Gedrick and Seyschell's likely locations based on their probable moving speeds.

Seyschell is more reckless, he thought. *She'll be a few yards ahead of Gedrick, but she'll stay to the wall. Gedrick will walk the middle, trusting the bondling to protect him.* Looking down, he saw a footprint on a piece of paper that drifted by. It was caught by a cross-breeze and shifted in a new direction. As it did, he saw a second print, different from the first. The rohnin was to come alone, but there was more than one person in the warehouse with them now. The cross-breeze came from across the warehouse, and looking in that direction he realized the light pattern had shifted. Someone was moving behind Seyschell's position.

They might as well have been separated by the Central Chasm for the distance Chapman would have to cross to get to Seyschell.

She smelled the electronics before she sensed anything else. The hair on the back of her neck bristled and she brought her gun to bear even before she spun around to find a pistol muzzle squarely in her face. Her finger brought pressure to bear on the trigger, yet she did not squeeze it home. Her mind raced; this man could have shot already. She barely had time to think when she sensed Chapman moving from behind her target. He jammed his pistol behind the man's ear as she became aware of another man. She swung her rifle around, centering on his chest, but the second man already had his weapon thrust up under Chapman's chin.

The whole thing took less than two seconds, but there they all stood, each with a gun targeting a vital organ, caught in the moment, not sure what would happen next.

"It would seem that our teams have captured each other, Rohnin Cairo," Gedrick said.

"Indeed they have, Captain Gedrick. Would you like to wait and see how it turns out or should we suggest that they all lower their weapons before somebody sneezes and they blow each other into Thecla's arms?" Cairo replied.

The four lowered their weapons, all looking a little sheepish as they shook hands and introduced themselves.

"An auspicious start," Gedrick said, with small irony.

"Any introduction to new people that you live to walk away from is a good one," Cairo offered. "Now let's get out of here before we make any more introductions."

The soldier ends when he runs out of bullets. It is then that the warrior takes over.

—General Igor Chumley, founder, Chumley's Zone

CHAPTER 68

Ravensford Zone
Outer district monastery

VIS-SHAN AWOKE EARLY, HOPING THAT by doing so he would avoid his mentor. The rays of first light had not yet penetrated the gloomy shroud of darkness, and he kept his lamps extinguished to improve his chances of escaping detection. Quietly, he packed a small bag of supplies along with four days' rations for the journey that lay ahead. It was a several-day trek to the outpost, and he would have more than enough food should today not be the correct departure day. On the off chance that he was wrong, it would not be by much, and his years of isolated living with the monk had taught him how to live off the land anyway.

He shouldered his bag and, taking a light step toward the door, grimaced as a floorboard creaked in response. Though a sound typically heard in the house, it had never sounded so loud. He paused a moment and listened, as if the sound might provoke a call and response. It hadn't. He slowly turned the tarnished doorknob and gingerly opened the door. The hinges responded with a high-pitched squeak. It was his own fault; the old man had asked him to oil them and he had not done so. He had only himself to blame for their complaining. He waited another moment and listened carefully.

Silence. He only needed to get through the kitchen now. With the subtlest of twists, he turned the knob and eased the door open. The back exit was within his line of sight just a mere five feet away.

"I thought that you might sleep in all day," the voice of the monk boomed, shattering the early-morning serenity. Vis-Shan jumped a foot in the air, dropping his ration bag in the process and scattering the contents all over the old wooden floor. So intently had he been focused on the back door that he had not noticed the old man and the Kwynian soldier sitting at the kitchen table drinking tea. The pair broke into laughter as a piece of fruit rolled under the table.

"I damn near soiled myself," Vis-Shan exclaimed.

The monk raised an eyebrow. "A colorful descriptor, Vis-Shan. Please, sit a moment and let us discuss this."

The younger man complied. "I had hoped not to disturb your rest," he said by way of explanation.

"What you hoped was not to see me before you left," the monk said.

Vis-Shan smiled sheepishly, knowing that he had been caught. "It was not my intention to deceive you, but I know that you do not approve of what I intend to do."

Peli Domar watched intently as a small silence ensued. It was the monk who broke it first. "Vis-Shan, I have meditated all night on this hoping to find an answer." The younger man looked at him expectantly. "I regret that I cannot offer you one. I simply don't know if what you saw is the future or just a possible outcome."

"Neither do I," the aide replied, "but I believe that I must save that ship. Believe me when I tell you, I have no desire for a suicide mission."

"A sound decision," Peli Domar said. "Perhaps I can teach you how to avoid one."

The Ravensfordians looked at the Kwynian, who continued to surprise them.

"Do you have a map?" Domar asked.

"Yes," the monk replied. "It's old, but not much changes in this region." Vis-Shan nodded in agreement. The monk left the room and returned a few minutes later with a yellowed parchment, which he unrolled and placed on the table.

Domar looked at it with puzzlement. "I don't understand the markings," he said.

"That's because it's in the Seb-Ichi tongue," Vis-Shan replied. "We're here," he said, pointing to an unremarkable-looking area of the map, "and this is where the attack will take place."

There was a legend under the region that Vis-Shan had noted, which Domar attempted to pronounce. "*Sor gord sulgara*'—what does that mean?"

"It roughly translates to 'gateway to the void,'" the monk replied. "When the map was made, Ravensford was a bit more xenophobic."

Vis-Shan nodded. Not all that much had changed. Ravensfordians still zealously guarded their way of life.

Domar continued to study the document. "What's over here?" he asked, motioning to an area close to the river marked simply as "Sharv."

"Sharv was a crystal-mining town, but the mines have long been dry." The Kwynian soldier thought for a moment. "Is it true that crystal shards emit energy signatures?" he asked.

"Yes," Vis-Shan replied. "Why?"

"If the area naturally emits large amounts of crystalline energy, it might be difficult for anyone to detect our presence." Vis-Shan looked at his mentor, waiting for him to confirm the information.

"He's right," the monk said. "Unrefined crystals take a very long time to dissipate their energy. Sharv was one of the largest operations in the zone, so it will be littered with fragments and shards."

"Enough energy to throw off a sensor grid?" Domar asked.

"I should think so," the monk replied.

The soldier nodded. "Then this is where we go in."

Now they both looked at him quizzically. "'We'?" Vis-Shan asked, the puzzlement evident on his face.

"You intend to go with me?"

"There's little that I can contribute learning how to brew ale," the soldier replied, "but I am well experienced in this type of work." As if the issue was settled then, he returned to scrutinizing the map. Vis-Shan looked at the monk and shrugged as if to say, *What do I do now?* The old man simply shook his head and without further response left the table.

Vis-Shan sat there silently and contemplated the apparent change in his plan while Peli Domar calculated the amount of time needed to get from their current location to the abandoned mining town. The young monk had planned on making the trip alone, but recognized his lack of experience. The soldier could be helpful. Still, timing was critical, and while the Kwynian was making tremendous progress with his prosthetics, he could not afford to miss the ship.

Domar broke the silence. "If I'm reading this legend correctly, Sharv should be about a day and a half's trek. That's going to be cutting it close."

"Likely longer, if you come," Vis-Shan added, instantly regretting that he had called attention to the man's prosthetic.

The Kwynian sighed. "I keep forgetting about that."

Domar replied, "These work so well around here that I forget they aren't actually mine. Terrain will be an entirely different matter."

The young Seb-Ichi looked down. "I'm sorry," he said, feeling shame that he had commented on the soldier's condition.

"Don't be, it's something that we need to consider."

A few more moments of silence passed before the monk returned, holding a small pouch in his gnarled hand. "I think that this may aid you," he said, handing it to Vis-Shan, who emptied the contents on the table.

"Portal crystals?" Domar asked as he examined the shimmering rocks.

"Very good," the older man said, impressed with the soldier's knowledge.

Vis-Shan picked up one of the gems and studied it intently. "This bears the mark of the tarran's crystalsmyth!" he said with genuine surprise. "How?"

"I will explain later, if you return," the monk answered. "Consider it an incentive. The crystals will allow you to get in and out more efficiently." He looked at Peli Domar. "And I assure you that they will be a good deal more stable than the one that brought you to us."

"I hope so," the Kwynian replied with a tight smile.

There are places even demons dare not go.

—The scripture of Bow

CHAPTER 69

CHENARA WATCHED FROM ABOVE AS three figures hurried about a body that lay deathly still on a hospital bed. Her mother was there as well, sobbing. The scene was hazy, as though she was viewing it through a myst cloud, and although they were talking, only bits and pieces of their words filtered through to her.

"Hello?" she called, hoping to get their attention, but they continued in their ministrations as though they had not heard her at all. Frustrated, she called out a second time, and again she got the same result.

"Can you save her?" Chenara's mother asked, her frenzied panic almost at a full boil.

"We're doing all that we can for her," the senior healer replied, "but her temperature is at a very dangerous level. If we can't bring it down..." The woman did not finish the thought.

The first assistant healer did. He was a man of moderate religious leanings. "If your daughter has been bitten and we can keep her temperature down, we may be able to save her." He did not add that it was likely that Chenara would be left in a vegetative state. "However, if the transformation has begun, only Thecla will be able to save her."

Chenara's father entered the room, fresh from the recent proceedings of the Nehreton. "If the transformation has begun," he said, "she is not worthy of Thecla's mercy."

At these words, his wife began to sob uncontrollably. The senior healer bristled at the prelate's callousness and, ignoring his station, pulled him aside sternly.

Chenara watched with a detached fascination. She had never seen someone treat her father in such a manner. In another time she would have relished it, but now it didn't seem to particularly matter.

"Prelate," the senior healer said, "your words are not helping your daughter."

"My daughter is dead," the prelate hissed.

"Your daughter is not dead," she replied, "and may yet recover."

"Tell me, healer," he said, emphasizing the last word for effect, "how many have you seen recover from the unholy bite?"

"None," she admitted, "but we theorize that part of the process of conversion involves the victim dying from extremely high fever. We have a new treatment based on that."

"An *experimental* treatment based on a *theory*," he said, shaking his head, emphasizing the words as he said them. "Would it be fair to say that the chances of my daughter recovering are speculative?"

"Yes," she said reluctantly. "But, it's your daughter"

"But nothing," he said with finality. "That is not my daughter."

Chenara was floating as if lying on her back during a gentle morning tide, increasingly oblivious of the goings-on below. She discovered that with very little effort she could spin and dive and do somersaults. It was the freest feeling she had ever experienced, and she did not want it to end.

The senior healer walked away from the prelate with a curse forming under her breath. She did not suffer fools gladly and she suffered zealots even less. In her estimation, the prelate scored high on both scales. Better that she ignore his blustering and tend to her patient instead. Arguing with him was not going to help Chenara.

Something shimmered in the air, distracting Chenara from her ethereal gymnastics: a thin gold thread gently wafting in the currents created by the air purifiers. "Beautiful," she gasped, immediately wanting to possess it. She did a spectacular dive hoping to catch it, but missed by just a fraction.

"Prepare the sites," the senior healer said to her two assistants. This was going to be tricky. The drug was experimental and had an extremely short half-life. It needed to reach the brain within a fraction of a second, and the only way to get it there that fast was to send it directly through the arteries that fed the brain. They gently positioned the girl and began the difficult process of establishing the lines. Long minutes drew out.

Chenara attempted another dive, her hands outstretched, grasping for the shimmering cord.

"Right carotid artery established, I'm in the internal carotid," the first healer said as the blood pulsed within the clear tubing of the injection machine.

"Left is as well. Same position," the second healer responded a moment later. The pulsations showed an incredibly fast heartbeat.

"Her heart is beating over two hundred times a minute," the first healer noted.

"Yes, it has been since we first examined her. She is tolerating it, though who can say for how much longer," the senior healer replied.

The shimmering cord dangled in the air, tantalizing the young girl. There was nothing in her life that she had ever wanted to possess as much. Nothing that had seemed this important.

"Turn her and we'll get the last artery started," said the senior healer.

"Left the best for last?" the first asked.

"The hardest, anyway. This one has to be right up inside the brain or the medication will dissipate too quickly. If you nick anything along the way, she'll bleed into her brain and most likely die," the senior said.

"I'm sure that will upset the prelate to no end," the first said in a whisper.

"Her blood pressure is dropping!" the second healer reported, watching the monitors.

As if to answer her wish, Chenara discovered that the gold thread formed a beautiful necklace around her. How had she not noticed this before? She would have the beautiful strand.

All of it.

"Pulse has quickened," the first noted. "Should I administer it now?

We don't have the third line."

"Push the medication. Increase the flow rate," the senior healer said.

The second responded, "The arteries will blow. Give me a minute to start the third line. We only get one shot. Miss it and her fate will be just as bad."

"Push it, I said, she'll be dead before you can get the needle out of the sheath!" the senior healer said. The anger in her voice was palpable.

Chenara began to wrap the cord around her hand. It was warm and throbbed as if possessing a heart of its own, each beat infusing more life into her.

"Her pulse is becoming unstable!" the first healer said.

The senior healer stormed over to the injection controller, dialed up the flow rate, and slammed the button.

The young girl's body jerked up on the bed as if pulled by some unseen force. Her back arched and she convulsed, dislocating her shoulder in the process.

"We're losing her," the first healer said.

The senior healer dialed up the rate and stood back. There was no more to do except wait, as the last of the dose flowed in.

The cord began to pull back, and Chenara suddenly felt as though she were on the end of a fishing line. She yanked again, but there was no slack. She let a little out of her hand, but it immediately retracted into the haze and continued to tug at her.

"Pulse is coming down," the second healer said. "One-sixty, one-twenty…"

The cord shimmered more brightly now, and Chenara was beginning to lose the tug-of-war.

"Blood pressure is coming back to normal levels," the first healer reported.

"Pulse is stabilizing," the second healer added.

For Chenara, it was like being sucked into a vortex as the cord pulled her through the haze at a dizzying speed. The last thing she would remember before her world went dark were the faces of the medical team that stood over her.

"We've got her," the second healer said.

"Yes, but *what* have we got?" the first asked.

Kill whomever you want, however you want. If you win, you can write the history as you please. If you lose they'll paint you as a monster anyway.

—Unattributed

CHAPTER 70

Ravensford Zone
Nineteenth Arc
Lower Sengoran River

TRAVELING BY NIGHT ON THE lower Sengoran River was generally not recommended. The rapids were tricky and the lack of settlements meant that there was little ambient light along the shore by which to guide a ship. The darkness made navigating around the protruding boulders all the more difficult, and more than one ship had been lost in its craggy currents. Fortunately for the crew of the *River Rat*, the night watch was made up of an android and a Lokaryn, two species with the best night vision in all of T'Amorach.

The trip downriver had been uneventful, a fact that greatly concerned Hemingway. It was a point that he had been perseverating on for the better part of an hour, much to the annoyance of Derring.

"For Thecla's sake," she finally exclaimed, "will you please give it a rest. We've been over this a thousand times already."

"Actually twenty-eight," he replied, ever the smart-ass.

She continued. "Hem, this route makes perfect sense. We're heading through the outer district and we're doing so by boat. It's the hardest type of transportation to come by, so it's the one they're least likely to suspect."

"Until we come to a very big garrison at the end," he added. "I'm not sure how we're going to deal with that."

A DAY'S TRIP UPRIVER, THE garrison commander was reading a message that had just come over the communications lattice. Its crystalline structure made it a more complicated device than the comm-link technology that was used in the other zones, but it was just as effective. The lattice was versatile in that it could transmit both written and verbal communications, and it was accessible from almost anywhere within the zone. As a result, it did not take long for the word to reach the commander that the ship of a disreputable captain had been stolen. The man had drunkenly told his story to anyone who would listen, and with the heightened state of alert, the right people had been listening.

The commander assembled the senior leadership team in his ready room and shared the information that he had just received.

"It sounds as though the story is suspect at best," his second said.

"I agree," said the third. "Likely no more than the ramblings of a drunk who hit the docking pylons one too many times and damaged his hull."

The remainder of the team nodded in general agreement. The first spoke again. "What are our orders, Commander?"

"We're to take the ship out."

The command team seemed satisfied. There was not a lot of action this far out, and unloading some armament would be good for troop morale.

THE CHILL OF THE NIGHT air woke Lyrie as she realized that Timan had once again stolen most of the blankets. The last three times he had done this, she responded with escalating force, culminating, finally, with a sharp poke to the ribs and a forceful reclaiming of her share. Recognizing the futility of the situation, however, this time she simply drew her knees up and tried to keep warm with her cloak.

Timan continued to sleep soundly, as evidenced by a loud snoring that all but rattled the walls of the small cabin they shared. She stared at his back with disbelief that a human could produce such a noise. As her mind wandered, her thoughts would not allow sleep to reclaim her. So many days during her awakening sexuality she had dreamed of being alone with him, of being with him and afterward sleeping next to him, feeling his body pressed close to hers. Somehow her dreams had never quite looked, or sounded, like this.

Recent events had caused her to look at her intended in a new light, and at the moment it was not one that reflected favorably upon him. She had told herself it was stress that had brought out this side of him. She felt the weight of his disapproval that she did not spurn Hemingway or admonish Ren for actually befriending the artificial. It churned her up inside, but even more, his closed-mindedness made her angry. He should have been able to feel the pressure of her stare burning through his back. Rather he snored on placidly, enjoying the entirety of the blankets.

Lyrie wondered if her father had ever anticipated this situation while preparing his daughter for adulthood. Though she could never be sure, she decided that more than likely he had. At the moment it wasn't much comfort, though. She probably wouldn't see him again.

She turned over, struggling to find a comfortable position while her thoughts raced.

It was of no use.

Quietly she got up to get some air.

"ONE OF OUR CANNONS ALONE can take out that ship," the first said. He had seen the *River Rat* once and knew that it could possibly be the least formidable ship on the river, if not in the entire zone.

"Yeah," someone else said, "but we're not going to let them have all the fun!"

The room erupted in laughter. When the merriment died down, the commander spoke. "Unfortunately, they are not going to have the chance."

The team looked at him with puzzlement. It was the second who finally asked the question. "I don't understand," she said. "I thought the orders were to take them out?"

"They are," he replied. "But there are rumors on the lattice that they took children as hostages." A silence filled the room as each officer thought about their own family. "If we have to, we'll follow our orders to the letter," the commander said, "but not before we attempt to extricate the hostages. If last reports are accurate they will be here in half a day's time. I want a plan to intercept them in half that time. Get to work, people."

DERRING LOOKED UP AT THE moon, bathed in the only natural light that her species could tolerate. "Hello, Tayshaw," she said as Lyrie stepped onto the deck. "Can't sleep?"

"No," the young woman replied with a sigh. "Derring," she asked, "have you ever fallen out of love?"

THE COMMANDER SAT AT HIS desk reviewing his orders. He wanted to relay the intel that he had received about the hostages to Central Command, but the weather grid was causing interference on the lattice. He was certain that they would not have ordered him to proceed with an all-out assault if they had been aware that there were children involved. His first knocked. "What have you got for me?"

"Sharv," the man replied. "It's only two hours from here and if we miss them we take them here."

He handed the plan to the commander, who reviewed it. "Do you think twenty can do it?" he asked.

"Absolutely. A ship that size can't hold more than ten, and even if only half that number are hostages, they're acceptably outgunned."

"What if they decide to kill the children?" the commander asked. "We'll have sharpshooters positioned in the trees. If it looks like it's going bad, we'll hit them with so much charge they won't have time to harm them." The commander shook his head as he signed off on the plan. "I hope so," he said.

"Sir?" the first asked. "I believe that this is the right course of action, but I would be more comfortable if we had one or two Seb-Ichi with us."

"No luck reaching Central, I take it?"

"No."

"Don't worry, sir," the first said, "we'll bring them in."

LYRIE AND DERRING STOOD DECK watch and talked while Hemingway steered the ship through one challenging pass after another. Their somber conversation was frequently punctuated by a string of curses that emanated from the pilot's berth each time the *River Rat* hit a particularly choppy patch of water. Around 3:00 a.m. the boat pitched hard to port, creating a splash that rolled high over the bow and completely soaked the pair. The aqueous assault was nothing compared with that which erupted from the android's mouth. So foul was the streak that it caused the young woman to blush and the Lokaryn to consider for a moment if what had been proposed was actually anatomically possible. She decided it was not. "Hemingway!" she scolded. "There are children on board."

"That can be remedied," he retorted. "Start with Timan."

"Is he always this colorful?" Lyrie asked.

"No," the Lokaryn answered, "he's usually worse."

No one knows where the tradition of not wearing red started, and it is, of course, absurd. However, always be mindful of it; myst-clipper crews are notoriously superstitious.

—Morgan Garand

CHAPTER 71

GEDRICK STOOD LOOKING INTO HISTORY.

Cade. Seyschell. The chief. Now Damien Cairo had joined those gathered around the massive bog-oak table. While he had never been a part of the crew, Cairo had attended more than one briefing on this ship. Soon enough, Derring, Hemingway, Hennix, Tarro, and of course Kisner would join them.

The chief spoke first. "Not another of these stare-off-into-space sessions, if you please. I have an engine room to run and more than a few additional engineering chores to finish up."

Gedrick looked at his chief engineer with a nod of understanding.

"We have approximately half a day of normal sailing ahead of us to enter the back channels of Ravensford."

"How do we know that they won't be closed off like the ones in Thieves'?" Seyschell asked.

"Thieves' acknowledges the problem and works to prevent it by sealing its borders where they can. Ravensford maintains such things aren't possible, so they don't move to fix what they don't admit exists."

"That's idiotic."

"I'll tell the tarran you feel like that when I see her next," Cairo said.

"Thanks," Seyschell replied with a smile and a nod. "Let me know how she reacts."

"For the love of…" the chief started growling before Gedrick pressed on.

"We'll harbor in one of the outer district diplomatic moorings. There aren't many places that allow technological ships, and the diplomatic zones have the most active ports, so they'll provide the best cover."

Chapman spoke next. "It would seem to afford reasonable access to the Winter Arc where Mr. Klemm's farm is. The question is, can you travel inland with that eye of yours?"

"It's surrounded in biological tissue, so unless I poke myself in the eye with a sensor crystal we should be OK. We can't carry anything technological with us, and portal crystals are far too risky."

"So if we get caught?" asked the sergeant from Cairo's team.

"We get out the old-fashioned way," Cairo replied.

"In other words, pray for rescue," Seyschell said with a smile and a tilt of her head.

"The teams will split up. Cairo and his team will head to an outer district toward a monastery where they may be holding the Kwynian soldier."

"What makes you think he'll be there?" Chapman asked.

"Reports tell us that he was severely wounded in the attack," Cairo said. "He was blown through the Lokaryn's escape portal and lost his legs as it collapsed, according to the telemetry that we deciphered from the helmet feeds. His wounds would have been mortal if not for the aid given to him by the Lokaryn they were pursuing. A female Lokaryn."

"Derring," Cade finished.

"Yes, and if it is Derring, then she maintains ambassadorial rank and—"

"Her presence in Kwyne is not a treaty violation," Gedrick finished.

"That's all well and good, but I think we…you've moved beyond that," Cairo said.

"How so?" Seyschell asked.

"In response to the execution of the Lokaryn, which you already know about, there was an attack on a Nehreton yacht returning home from the proceedings," Cairo explained. "So now we have hostages in Lokaryns'. If I can get to this soldier and he can confirm the story, I can present that information to the general population of Kwyne and deescalate this whole thing before it gets any more out of control."

"Why not just accompany us to Klemm's and get the source material—Derring. She admits to being in Kwyne, she has ambassadorial status, end of story," Cade responded.

"Not end of story. If we reveal her identity, she's a clan lord running an android through Kwyne. If, on the other hand, a decorated member of the Kwynian military tells the broadcast information bureaus that one, we executed the wrong Lokaryn, and two, the real Lokaryn we were 'after' saved his life, but can't be identified, my people will work to make amends. With Derring back in place in Lokaryns' and a contrite rohnin, we'll avert this thing and then move on to figure out who was pushing the buttons in the first place."

"So why go to the monastery?" the navigator asked.

"Sorry, got off track. The wounded soldier would need a level of healing that would be hard find. Seb-Ichi monks would be capable, but few would tolerate tech users. There is one who is in a remote monastery. He was exiled for just that tolerance of technology." Seyschell looked at Gedrick, who said nothing. "If the soldier is not there, perhaps the monk could offer some guidance on how to find him," Cairo finished.

"In the meantime, we find Derring and Hemingway and get out of the zone. We take the Klemms and whoever else with us. We meet up back at the ship and drop you off in Thieves' Zone, then recheck the Bitch for any other crew members," Gedrick said.

"I'll be truly amazed if it works out that way, but I don't see a better plan," Chapman said.

"OK, agreed then," said Gedrick. "We dock in Ravensford tonight after sunset. Rohnin Cairo and his team will head out first. An hour later, my team will head into the Winter Arc. McCormick will take the ship back out. Everyone is back here in three days. We sail with the morning tide on the fourth day. Otherwise you wade home through the myst. Agreed?"

Though there was consensus around the table, they all had their doubts.

As the group broke up to tend to their individual preparations, Chapman remained behind.

"What's on your mind, Nev?" Gedrick asked.

"Do you think McCormick is up to the task of commanding the ship?"

Gedrick looked up at him. "You selected her as your replacement."

"Yes."

"I selected you as my replacement, should it become necessary."

"Yes."

"Do I have any reason to start mistrusting your judgment?"

"No."

"Then what was your question?"

"She is young and this crew has not fully gelled. Besides, how do you know she won't just take off with your ship?"

"You never really know, but you're forgetting one thing."

"Sir?" Chapman said with no small indignation. "I doubt it, but what would that be?"

"The chief is remaining aboard."

There was a moment or two of silence.

"Captain, while I understand that the master of a ship is warranted to apportion any justice they see fit, would that constitute cruel and unusual punishment for McCormick?"

"Mr. Chapman? You may take that up with Merchants' Zone synod of trading houses. Until then, you're dismissed," Gedrick said, suppressing a smile.

"Very good, sir."

The hours turned quickly as the teams prepared to depart. Gedrick had readied his equipment days before and spent the remaining time resting.

A small knock came at his door, awakening him. It was Seyschell.

"Asleep?" she asked.

"Yes," he said in surprise. "For the first time in a long time, I find I can sleep. Even an hour is restful."

Seyschell smiled at that and handed him a cup of coffee she had brought from the galley.

"You used to be that way. When we were running 'droids, you could sleep on moment's notice and wake ready to fight the Grendel ten minutes later."

"I was younger then," Gedrick said, drinking from the mug, then placing it on his bunk side table.

"It's good to be alive again, isn't it?" Seyschell asked with a wicked glint in her eyes.

"And it would be good to remain so," came the voice of the first officer from behind her.

"Is Commander Chapman making a comment about my safety?"

"No, just wondering if you can manage not to have a weapon pointed at your head when we leave the ship this time." Chapman slid inside the room and presented the captain with a second cup of coffee. "We docked about twenty minutes ago, Captain, and the teams are assembling."

"I wasn't the only one staring down a barrel of a gun," Seyschell countered, looking at the two cups of coffee the captain now had.

"I would appreciate it if you would both avoid the experience," Gedrick said, stretching and gathering his gear. "Let's go." He stood up and looked at the second cup of coffee on the stand, still steaming hot. He handed his knapsack to Seyschell.

"Carry this, would you?" He then picked up the second cup and proceeded out the cabin door. He made his way with a cup of coffee in each hand, Chapman behind him and Seyschell bringing up the rear carrying both of their equipment. With her considerable strength, it was a negligible load.

Rohnin Cairo's team had gathered on the foredeck. Night had fallen now, and the stars looked down on them through the phobes' amazing shielding. Only out on the myst did they seem clearer.

Gedrick walked up to Cairo, who stood looking at the stars.

"One would think that you'd be checking your gear before a mission."

"Two rechecks are enough, if you were careful putting it together in the first place."

"Fair enough."

"Do you ever look at them, Ged?"

"What, the stars? We navigate by them sometimes when we don't want our navigational information available to the net rogues."

Cairo looked at him.

"I mean just look at them. Not use them, just watch 'em."

Gedrick smiled a little at that.

"You think someone is going to steal them from us?"

Cairo sighed. "You really are hopeless, you know that?"

"Opinions vary. Remember, if you get into trouble, you can still signal the ship for an early pickup."

"Risking the possibility that we then wouldn't be able to pick you up, Captain."

"You have the option, Damien, and let me tell you, if *I* need to call the ship back early, I won't hesitate."

"It's time," the boatswain called. From different areas of the ship the first team gathered. It included the major and the sergeant from Cairo's team and two sailors from the *Shicaine*.

Cairo shook hands in turn with Chapman and then Gedrick. After a bone-crushing hug from Seyschell, he turned to hear the chief say: "Try not to screw it up for the lot of us, Your Godship."

"Have you ever thought of putting him back in that garbage bin where you found him?" Cairo asked Gedrick.

"Daily. Good luck."

With that, Cairo's team was down the plank and across the dock. They were gone from sight within a minute.

Gedrick sat down and started to look through his own gear again. As he did, McCormick walked up.

"Any final orders, sir?"

"Don't sink the ship, don't be late, and don't sleep in my cabin."

"Aye, sir."

The hour turned and the boatswain again said, "It's time."

Gedrick, Cade, Seyschell, and Chapman headed for the gangway off the ship. Two midshipmen were to go with them. Gedrick stopped abruptly as he looked at one of them.

"Why in the world are you wearing a red shirt?" he asked.

"I didn't think about it. It's just a shirt."

"Would you take that damn thing off! You'll show up as bright as day in that thing. Someone give him a black shirt."

The man quickly stripped off his gear and vest, then the offending shirt, and grabbed a black one from a fellow crewmember.

"I never took you for superstitious, captain," Chapman said quietly.

"I'm not, but why tempt fate?" Gedrick replied with a smile.

Seyschell rolled her eyes, and they were soon down the gangway onto the dock.

Gedrick looked back at the *Shicaine* for only a moment as she slipped her moorings. He rarely got to see his ship from this perspective: He appreciated her graceful lines and power as she began to move. For a moment he remembered his first sight of her and the crazy old man who had faith that a young captain could handle a unique ship.

"Come on, let's go," Seyschell said softly as she tugged on Gedrick's arm.

The trip inland went quickly and without issue, though security in the zone was noticeable everywhere. The team was fortunate in that the governmental efforts were hampered by squabbles over jurisdiction between zone and arc forces. This left some areas double guarded while others were guarded only by local militia, or not at all.

After a days' travel by foot—and wagon, when they could beg a ride—they found themselves near the inner district barrier wall. They made a show of asking to pass through the checkpoint and were rebuffed like everyone else. Gedrick sat down under the shade of a nearby tree and drank from a waterskin.

Here, all the forces of the zones were mustered. Local militia, arc forces, and zone troops all arrayed around the entryway. This entry was closed, and except for a few persistent locals trying to bribe their way through, the militaries were here alone. Seyschell flirted with a few of the soldiers, which Chapman found oddly irksome.

"Now what?" Chapman asked as he sat down beside his captain. "Do we travel to the nearest open checkpoint, or did you have another plan?" He continued to watch Seyschell as she twirled her hair, tilted her head just so to look up at the men, and acted positively…feminine.

"It would take too long to go around. As near as I can tell from what I'm overhearing from the locals, the next checkpoint is almost a day's travel."

"I don't see an alternative, unless you have something up your sleeve."

"Just my arms, but that might do."

Seyschell wandered back over to where the rest were sitting and sat cross-legged in the sun.

"Enjoy your talk with the locals?" Chapman asked.

"Why yes, I did, First Officer," Seyschell said with exaggerated sweetness.

"Seyschell," Gedrick said somewhat impatiently.

"OK," she said. She was enjoying Chapman's reaction, but knew that time was short. "If we stand right in front of the third structural column from the left side of the checkpoint, there are about eight to ten meters between the tree line and the wall."

"About? This requires some precision," Gedrick said.

"What requires precision?" Chapman asked.

"It's hard to flirt and stare at the bushes at the same time, Captain."

"Excuse me?" Chapman asked, not fully understanding the exchange.

"I asked our copilot here to get me some coordinates for a line-of-sight portal and she comes up with a rougher than rough estimate. I hope you don't mind going though life with a thornbush sticking out of your…"

"Sir, I might suggest that we move on. Before we attract too much more attention." Chapman motioned toward the guards, who were starting to take notice of their bickering.

The group quickly gathered up their gear and headed to an area away from the roads and paths that circled the inner district wall.

Sitting down again, Gedrick placed his knapsack between his legs and started to open the top. Chapman sat nearby.

"Exactly how are we going to get across the inner wall? You mentioned a portal crystal?"

"Correct."

"I'm not an expert, but portals work relative to one another, correct?"

"Yes they do."

"So if I move the opening two feet forward, the exit moves two feet forward as well."

"Correct."

"Unless you knew ahead of time that we were going to need a crystal that would project an opening nine meters in front of us, how are we going to pull this off?"

"I'm going to make one."

"You never fail to amaze me with your hidden talents." Chapman said.

"My father was a crystalsmyth by trade. Like most master craftsmen, he taught his children the skill from an early age. Now, if you'll excuse me for a bit, I'll need to concentrate on this."

Gedrick manifested his bondling in his right hand and held a pure blue crystal in the other. He knelt and bowed his head and began a low-pitched hum. His breathing became rhythmic as he entered into a state of deep meditation. The bondling surrounded the crystal, providing the intense pressure needed to shape it to the proper structure. The whole process took perhaps three hours.

As the bondling retreated back inside of Gedrick's body, he opened his eyes and looked over the crystal, which now swam with multicolored hues in a shape like two pyramids connected at the bases.

"Do you need to rest?" Chapman asked, having sat through the whole thing in utter amazement.

"No, actually. The process is quite restorative. I feel better afterward. You draw in a lot of energy to infuse into the crystal, but whatever is left over stays with you."

He handed the crystal to Chapman and stood up. "It's just a suggestion, of course, but I'd let Miss 'About Eight to Ten Meters' go first," Gedrick said.

"Aye, sir," Chapman said, looking the crystal over.

Smything crystals is an honored, even exalted profession, and truly, all of Ravensford depends on the skill of the crystalsmyth.

—Magnus Dorn, Ravensford historian

CHAPTER 72

Ravensford Zone

IN AN ISOLATED AREA OF the garrison, the smyth had gotten the order and set to work.

He looked at the coordinates that he had written on a stained piece of paper and went into his storage closet to select the right materials. The closet was kept dark and the materials were kept in amber jars in order to minimize their exposure to light. Once mined and exposed to the elements they slowly began to dissipate energy, a process that the darkened conditions helped to keep to a minimum. A small spider dangled from a silver thread in the corner of the room, catching the smyth's attention. "Hello, Nash," he said in greeting.

"They always wait until last minute," he muttered as if he expected the small arachnid to empathize with his plight. "And a challenging one too." He deftly felt around the carefully arranged shelves, the contents of which he had memorized. His hand rested on a large jar, from which he extracted several gems with a set of tongs. "A tricky one this is going to be," he said. "Needs to be a very stable portal." His fingers tapped the tops of jars as he silently counted them out in his mind. He selected another and extracted two larger gems. A small amount of ambient light reflected off the crystal onto the spider, which ran up the strand in response to the stimulus. "It'll take more than a minute to move twenty men and all of their equipment through, and we wouldn't want anyone to get caught midway." He placed the last of the gems in a small black pouch. "A fusion job is always a bastard," he muttered.

"BETTER GET DOWN BELOW," HEMINGWAY said as the magenta glow of dawn began to peek over the hills that abutted the river.

Derring pulled her shroud tightly around her face and descended into the pilot's berth. Lyrie had stayed with her for most of the night, only recently returning to the cabin when she could no longer keep her eyes open. "Are you going to keep going?" the Lokaryn asked the android.

"No," he said. "Ren's done a good job with the day navigation and the more experience we can give him, the better. I'll have him check the dampening field and take watch on the deck."

Ren ran through the ruins of his family's farm, with a blaster in one hand and his bondling ready in the other. The bloodred sky was matched only by the crimson pools that stained the earth where he had been, and the staccato of the hard driving rain punctuated his fury. Movement to the left caught the attention of his cybernetic eye, and he broke into a dead run in the direction of the smoldering foundation of the farmhouse. "You will pay for what you have done!" he screamed at a solitary figure who was attempting to hide. His weapon barked loudly as blast after blast pummeled the figure.

Without warning, the scene shifted and he stood over the badly burned body of a Seb-Ichi warrior. The man's breathing was ragged and his voice raspy as he repeated one word over and over: "Heretic."

"Wake up!" the Lokaryn said, shaking the young man again. Ren was clearly in the throes of a nightmare and had been shouting, "I am not a heretic!"

"I am, and you should check out the clubhouse before you decide not to join the club," a voice called from the deck.

Derring rolled her eyes. The young man finally opened his and sat bolt upright in his cot, panting. "Are you all right, Ren?" she asked.

He looked around the room, struggling to clear his head and get his bearings. It finally registered. "Derring," he said sheepishly.

THE FIRST BARKED ORDERS TO the twenty members of the expedition team who had been charged with intercepting the *River Rat*. Given the speed of the river and the reputation of the vessel, he had estimated that it would arrive at Sharv in approximately five hours. He was not a man to take chances, however, and he had directed the team to have the equipment prepped and on the transport carts in one hour. Eager to see action, they had responded with enthusiasm and would likely complete the task in half the time. Now all he needed were the crystals.

STILL GROGGY FROM HIS DREAM, Ren double-checked each dampener to ensure that it was operating within correct parameters. Hemingway had shown him how to check the emitter flow and to calibrate the units if necessary. The young man had learned quickly and had soon gained the android's confidence. "All clear," he yelled into the berth.

"Aye, Captain," Hemingway said with a small measure of pride.

Belowdecks, Timan fumed. Lyrie's behavior had become increasingly distasteful to him, particularly the way she seemed so comfortably to embrace heresy. "I don't care," he said to her. "I still don't like it."

"We were only talking, Timan," the young woman replied, hands on hips and flipping her hair back in frustration.

"Lyrie," he said more calmly. "Don't be upset, I'm not blaming you. This is not your fault. Your father should never have put you in this position."

"My father," she hissed, "did not put us in this position any more than yours did." A look of horror crossed the young man's face. "That's right, Timan. You think you're the standard of piousness, but your family is just as much a part of this. Perhaps you should spend some time thinking about why that is." She turned on her heels and stormed out of the cabin.

THE SMYTH TOOK HIS TONGS and placed the larger of the two gems on a scale. Swiftly running the calculations through his head, he determined that he would need to decrease its mass by ten percent in order to maximize the energy flow. The key to keeping the portal open lay with the smaller of the two gems; the first served as its energy source. Too much power and it would burn out prematurely, snapping the portal closed. Too little and it would not function at all. He gently placed the crystal in a vice, tapping it with a small chisel using precise strokes. Bit by bit he created a small hollow into which he inserted the smaller gem. He then placed them in a small steam-powered tumbler, which would subject them to high pressure and ultimately fuse them, the last step toward readying them for activation. He set the timer on the unit and waited.

THE ABANDONED MINES OF SHARV were approximately halfway between the garrison and the *River Rat* at the moment that the air began to shimmer and a portal opened. The area was beginning to hum with residual energy as first light touched the millions of crystal chips that were strewn everywhere, causing them to vibrate. Rather than producing a dissonant sound, they produced a vibration that was remarkably soothing.

Vis-Shan was the first to emerge, with Peli Domar right behind him. Although the monk had assured him of the stability of the portal, the Kwynian soldier still wasn't taking any chances. He dove through, hitting the ground and tucking himself into a roll that brought him back to his feet. Vis-Shan came through quickly as well, his bondling manifested as an imposing sword.

As a military man, Peli Domar was used to moving fast and traveling light. To the amazement of Vis-Shan, the camp was set up in no time, giving them the opportunity to survey the immediate surroundings. They had chosen a spot that would afford them a long vantage point of the river and the only thing left to do now was to wait.

THE SMYTH REMOVED THE NEWLY minted portal crystal from the tumbler's compression chamber and examined it carefully with his loupe. Flawless, he thought. Such was his skill that, had he offered his talents on the open market instead of in the service of his government, he could have amassed enough riches to live handsomely in Merchants' Zone. He took out a polishing cloth and gave the crystal a vigorous rub. When he was finished, it shone intensely. Satisfied with his work, he placed it in a black pouch and called for a runner.

THE KWYNIAN AND THE SEB-ICHI spent the first few hours in relative silence, enjoying the stillness of the morning. A gentle breeze blew over the river, carrying the light scent of the surrounding aborra trees with it. Had they not been on a critical mission, either man could easily have been lulled into the cozy confines of a nap.

"Is all of your zone this beautiful?" Domar asked.

Vis-Shan thought for a moment. "Yes, most of it is. Why do you ask?"

"No reason in particular. It just feels really peaceful here. It's not something that I often experience."

"No?" Vis-Shan said with a note of small surprise.

"My life is good," Domar said. "I love my family and I am proud of the work that I do. But, I sometimes feel the weight of my responsibilities. Somehow here, they don't seem quite so heavy."

"Responsibilities have a way of doing that," Vis-Shan offered, feeling a small twinge of guilt for how he had handled his own. "Even here."

They returned to their silence, each enjoying a moment that he knew he might not see again anytime soon.

Why bother with freedom when the populace will settle for the appearance of freedom?

—Unattributed

CHAPTER 73

Ravensford Zone
Winter Arc, Inner District

THE AREA AROUND THE CHECKPOINT was quiet in the small hours of the morning. Soldiers talked amongst themselves, weapons were down, and the atmosphere was relaxed relative to the daylight hours, when travelers quarreled endlessly in vain attempts to gain access to the inner district. Gedrick set up the crystal quietly, and outside of a small popping sound when the portal opened and closed, they were silent.

Gedrick, of course, let Seyschell go first.

Once inside the inner wall, the group continued to move toward Klemm's farm. After another day of travel, the main roads gave way to smaller ones and they soon crested the range that created the outermost border of the valley that held Stannis Klemm's farm.

Gedrick looked down across the valley. His augmented vision felt very much like a curse at the moment he zoomed in on the farmhouse.

"Merciful…" he said quietly.

"What?" Seyschell asked, with some small alarm in her voice.

"The house is gone. Looks like it was burned. The barn as well. The crops are torched." Scanning across to the Josphers', he saw that it was the same story, and the Woodses' as well. "They torched them all. Stannis's land seems to have battle damage—I can see a burned-out mech in the kitchen garden behind the house."

"Do we go down?"

"Only way to find out if they were killed."

"We could go by the local pub and sit a spell. I'm sure it will be the talk of the town," Chapman suggested.

"Strangers in town so soon after something like this? I think we'd attract more attention than we'd like," Gedrick said.

"As opposed to poking around at the farm?" Cade asked. "If the fires are out, the bodies will have been removed by now. I'm surprised the mech is still there."

"They aren't all that easy to move, and people around here would likely treat them like toxic waste. All in all, I think we have all the information we're going to get from the farm."

"Well then. Who's buying the first round?" Gedrick said without much enthusiasm.

"You are, Captain," said Cade and Seyschell in unison.

"Old joke," Cade explained to Chapman as he headed down the slope into the small town that served the area farms.

The town was busy. Busier than Gedrick had ever seen it in the years that he had been with the underground. The recent events had spread though the area like wildfire, bringing bounty hunters and curiosity seekers from all over. There were several pubs in town. The group found their way into an out-of-the-way one that few non-locals knew about.

Gedrick opened the door. Once they stepped inside, all eyes were on the strangers.

"*Aki-ya-tie*," Gedrick said, by way of the local greeting.

"I don't know you," said the bartender. "Are you from around these parts?"

"No, I'm not," Gedrick responded. "I worked old man McCullough's farm for a few seasons. My friends and I are looking for work, thought we'd see if he needs a hand."

Chapman looked at Seyschell doubtfully.

Seyschell leaned over and whispered, "Neighbor of Klemm's, nice old guy passed away about six years ago."

"Sorry to be the one to tell you, McCullough passed away some years back now."

"I see. Well, he couldn't live forever, now, could he?"

"Suppose not."

"Could we get a draught and maybe some food?"

"Aye. We've one thing on the menu."

"Whatever you have, and five tankards."

"If you're looking for work, you got money to pay?"

Gedrick laid the money down for the drinks and food before the bartender pulled the first drink.

The hours passed slowly and Gedrick and his crew melted away into the crowd.

A good many customers came in as the evening progressed. The spirits flowed and loosened the tongues of many patrons. Piece by piece a picture emerged. By the end of the night they took their leave, heading again into an unpopulated area.

"Nera is dead," Cade began.

"I heard that as well," Seyschell said. "I think his son Ben is as well. The rest are unaccounted for."

"We have two days remaining," Gedrick said.

"That's not enough time to do any sort of search," Cade observed.

"We don't have to search. There are very few places that they could go."

"Again, the monk," Chapman said

"It seems so. We can travel the riverways and cut our time down significantly."

"There's a trading post called Satara over the valley's northern range. We could probably pick up transportation there. Then we could be near the extreme outer district in a fraction of the time of overland travel. From there, it's a short trip to the monk's."

"That still leaves us short time on getting back to the ship."

"Once we're in the outer district, the crystal grid gets pretty thin. We'll be able to send a short-burst transmission to notify Shicaine to pick us up without drawing much attention."

"Where?"

"While most of the water that flows down the river is reclaimed at the edge of the zone for purification, a small runoff exits the zone carrying effluent of no use or that can't be adequately purified."

"It's the zone's sewer, in other words."

"It's a way of venting unwanted material. There are some old docks just outside the zone wall that serve as a small smugglers' port. There should be tunnels leading from the outer district to the docks. If we can get out there, the *Shicaine* can pick us up and we'll be on our way."

"Why do the Ravensfordians allow this?"

"It's a big zone. A few black market types making a few caryns aren't going to be worth the bother. Besides, the local officials often avail themselves of the services.

"OK, any other thoughts?"

"Just one," Seyschell said. "I wanted to bust that drunk guy Fargus in the mouth back in the pub."

Nice thing about innocent bystanders, they're rarely armed.

—Thorpe's Corporation security forces training manual

CHAPTER 74

THE SILENCE OF THE SENGORAN River was broken by the unmistakable sound of an opening portal. The Kwynian whipped around and watched in amazement as soldier after soldier poured through. "Let me handle this," Vis-Shan said, as he manifested his bondling. Domar watched his new companion standing with the large broadsword his bondling had formed. He had always respected the Kuhbrik as the ultimate fighting force, but seeing this sight made him thankful that Ravensford was a traditional ally of Kwyne.

"I am Vis-Shan," he said to the team leader, "Seb-Ichi of the fourth order. What is the nature of your mission?"

"I am Tol-Sharra," the leader replied, "first from the Shavarra Garrison. They told us that Seb-Ichi assistance would not be possible. I am pleased to see you here."

Vis-Shan decided to play along, adding a touch of annoyance to his voice for effect. "I was dispatched while in *Val-cor-dora*," he said, naming a Seb-Ichi meditation practice that he knew would be familiar to the soldier. "So I would appreciate it if you would tell me what is of such critical importance that a Seb-Ichi centering ceremony would be disrupted."

"My apologies, Vis-Shan," the first said. "You know how things have been in-zone since the incursion," he added, by way of explanation.

"Yes, of course," Vis-Shan said graciously, knowing that he now had the man off-balance. "Please brief me on the specifics of your mission and how I can be of assistance to you."

TIMAN CAME TOPSIDE AND FOUND Lyrie standing alone by the bow. "I'm sorry," he said. "This is all so disorienting." He slipped his arms around her waist, and to his surprise she did not resist. "I don't know why my family was involved in this," he continued. "It goes against everything my parents ever taught me."

Lyrie remained silent, allowing Timan to hold her as she began to second-guess herself. Recent events had been hard on everyone. Perhaps Timan's parents had not prepared him for anything beyond the life of a farmer. Was that really his fault?

"Watch the current, Ren," Hemingway cautioned as the craft rocked violently. "You've never seen a Lokaryn vomit and I assure you it's not a pretty sight."

The young man screwed up his face at the mental image. "No worries, Hem, I've got it under control."

The android scanned the charts that he hoped were up to date. He had observed the previous captain briefly and was certain the only thing recent about the charts were the numerous food stains that adorned them.

"How much longer to the garrison, Hem?" Ren asked.

"Assuming our current rate, we would reach it in several hours, I'd say."

"Any plan for how we're going to get by it?"

Hemingway thought for a moment, and with a faint smile said, "None whatsoever."

"THIS IS SERGEANT PELI DOMAR of the Third Arc Special Operations Group," Vis-Shan said, feeling no need to embellish. Lies had the tendency to get complicated, and in this case the truth would fit the team leader's assumptions. "Sergeant Domar was in pursuit of a Lokaryn who portaled in-zone. As you can see, it cost him, but he has agreed to work with us as part of a joint operation."

"A pleasure to meet you," Tol-Sharra said, extending his hand. "I can see that the bravery of the Kwynian military is not understated.

"Thank you," Domar said, nodding.

"Let me bring you up to speed," the team leader said. "Our intelligence indicates that a craft was stolen from the Satara Trading Post. We are not certain as to the exact time, since it was widely assumed that the captain had simply not tended to his vessel." The pair looked at him with puzzled expressions. "The captain of the *River Rat* is something of a local legend," Tol-Sharra explained. "His exploits are well known and have made for many a good laugh over a pint. When the ship went missing, it was naturally assumed that its disappearance was merely the next chapter in his story."

"He must be something if it raised no alarm during current conditions."

"Yes," the first mused, "he is."

Vis-Shan only half listened as Tol-Sharra resumed his update. He knew that Peli Domar would soak up the information, which freed him up to figure out how they were going to intervene. Short of killing the expeditionary force, which he did not want to do, he had no answers. More than likely he was going to have to let the craft get captured and attempt to portal its occupants out under the cover of darkness. It would not have been his first choice, but he was fairly certain that it was the plan that would result in the least casualties for his charges.

HEMINGWAY SCANNED THE CHART AND said, "I think I may have a solution."

"Really?" Ren said brightly.

"Possibly," the android stressed, "but I want to run it by Derring before I get anyone's hopes up." He opened the cabin door and saw her shrouded figure deep in prayer. "*Tu'l shura, me gravi lunis,*" she intoned. "*Au l'orstra ne lantus b'duvi.*" Hemingway recognized the language as ancient Kwynian, something that his counterpart had spoken when it was considered a modern language. Though he had heard her pray often, he had never heard her use the ancient form of the tongue. It was the form closest to that actually spoken by Thecla, and it made him wonder if Derring thought it might somehow reach the Kwynian messiah more easily. Though often quick with a quip at less than appropriate times, he sat silently, listening to her words, a gesture of respect for the most selfless being he knew.

THE MORNING PASSED INTO MIDAFTERNOON with the expedition team largely unoccupied. Camp was established, the afternoon meal prepared and eaten, and the only thing left to do was to wait. A few men patrolled the camp perimeter, more out of routine than actual necessity, and the remainder either talked, rested, or engaged in card games. Vis-Shan and Peli Domar volunteered to keep watch on the river, which afforded them the opportunity to strategize.

"So you propose that we let them get captured?" Vis-Shan asked.

"Exactly," Domar replied. "The soldiers believe that the children are hostages. If they are anything like my comrades, they will be reluctant to engage in a fire fight that could harm them."

"I agree," the Seb-Ichi said, nodding.

"But," Domar emphasized, "I have seen situations where good men have lost control. In spite of honorable intentions, many innocents have been harmed. I've observed the team leader defer to you as Seb-Ichi. If we can bring the vessel to shore, with no shots fired, I believe that he will follow your lead as to how the 'prisoners' are treated."

The young Seb-Ichi considered the logic of the sergeant's argument. "I agree," he said finally. "But do you think that the Lokaryn will recognize you in time?"

"Yes," Domar answered, "I think that she will."

IN HER PRAYERS AND MEDIATIONS, Derring often found herself haunted by the faces of those from whom she had fed. She prayed for them, each and every one, the number growing with each passing year. Then she prayed for forgiveness. A forgiveness that she deeply doubted she would receive and one that she was even less sure she deserved. It was in this moment of prayer that she saw a new face. Not one from one from whom she had fed, but instead one whom she had spared. The Kwynian soldier, Peli Domar. Every fiber in her body had thirsted for the man, had screamed in hunger for her to taste his essence and slowly draw it in. The man had hunted her, and by every lokaric code he was rightfully hers. It had been all that she could do to resist the temptation.

Her invocations complete, she felt a gentle touch on her shoulder. "Derring," Hemingway said softly. "We need to talk." The slender Lokaryn slowly opened her eyes and turned to face the android. "What is it?" she asked.

"I think I have an exit plan," he replied, "but I'm going to need your help."

PELI DOMAR REACHED DOWN AND picked up a handful of crystal shards. "Do these things have any value?" he asked.

"Not really," Vis-Shan answered. "They do emit energy, but because they are fragments they don't resonate in the focused way that a well made crystal does. The area is something of an energy vortex, really. It sweeps around with a great deal of power, but it isn't well harnessed."

Domar examined the shards and thought for a moment. "I wonder if there is a way we can use that quality to our advantage."

THE AFTERNOON PASSED INTO EVENING as the sun began to set over the hills. Ren had piloted the ship most of the day as Hemingway discussed his exit plan with Derring. Chirra and Jarrel kept watch at the stern while Lyrie and Timan engaged in quiet détente on the bow.

About an hour from Sharv, Hemingway called everyone together. "As you know, there is a rather large garrison at the mouth of this river. It's likely that they don't see a great deal of action and they're probably more than happy to unload on our little boat." Heads nodded around the tight bridge. "About an hour from here the charts indicate that there is an abandoned mining area, which has the benefit of serving as a natural dampening field." Ren nodded enthusiastically, immediately grasping the concept as the android continued. "We're going to disembark there and rig the ship to autopilot down the river. If it works the way I intend, they'll blow it out of the water and presume us incinerated." Chirra and Jarrel grimaced at the image. It was not so long ago that they had seen their family's homestead in ashes.

VIS-SHAN RETURNED TO THE BANKS of the river with two plates of rations. "Anything yet?" he asked Domar.

"No," the Kwynian replied as he rearranged the food on his plate. "Is this standard military fare?" he asked with wrinkled nose.

"I honestly have no idea," Vis-Shan replied. "But it does look awful, doesn't it?"

Domar tried a forkful. "It tastes even worse," he said. The pair choked down as much as they could and cleaned their plates in the river. "I've been thinking," Domar said. "I don't like our odds with this much military around. Even if we can warn the ship off, the chances are good that someone will start a firefight."

Vis-Shan nodded. "I've been thinking the same thing," he said. "We've got to move down shore and wave them off."

The first watched the pair from a distance and considered his good fortune at having Seb-Ichi help.

"First?" a young man's voice said; it was his command sergeant.

"Yes?"

"Quite lucky that command could spare us a monk."

"I'm not so sure, Command Sergeant."

Making enemies is bad for business.

—Merchants' Zone second commandment

CHAPTER 75

THE SATARA TRADING POST WAS buzzing with energy.

As Gedrick and his shore party entered town, they could sense tension that was born of too many bounty hunters without a quarry and a local population who had had their fill of them. Gedrick knew where to find transport.

"Who's buying the first drink?" Gedrick said as the group surveyed the town.

"You are, Captain," they responded in unison, Chapman included.

The first officer and the navigator shared a smile at that.

The group again headed for a local pub. The town was a short stretch of buildings along one street. All were raised about two feet from the ground to allow for the floodwaters that punctuated the seasons in the zone. A small boardwalk ran along the entire stretch on either side. Steps down onto a dirt main road occurred at each storefront. Carts and wagons pulled by various beasts of burden kicked up a fair bit of mud as they slipped and plodded along. It was early evening as they headed into the pub.

They took a seat at an empty table toward the back of the establishment. Gedrick called to a man sweeping the floor.

"Excuse me, barkeep, could we get a round of ale here?"

The man looked glumly over at them.

"I'm sorry, is there something wrong?" Gedrick asked, not understanding the man's reluctance to do his job.

"I'm not a barkeeper, if you must know, I'm a riverboat captain."

"Of course you are," Gedrick replied, not knowing what else to say.

The man sighed deeply. "I'll get your drinks," he said, and he walked over to the bar.

The crew again fanned out to gather whatever information they could and to try to find a transport downriver. After an hour or so they reconvened.

"Not much to report," Seyschell began. "Locals have been getting into tangles with the bounty hunters who think there is still a chance the 'fugitives' are hiding in the local mines."

Chapman went next. "This might be of interest: The man that we first talked to may actually be a riverboat captain. He says his ship was stolen last week. He's trying to work up enough money to buy a new boat."

"Really?" Seyschell spoke for the group. "Did he happen to mention if it were a synthetic, a Lokaryn, and a bunch of phobes with their kids?"

"Curiously he didn't," Chapman deadpanned. "But he did get one piece of information from the harbormaster. There was a dockworker named 'Hem' on duty the night the boat disappeared. It was a man the master had never seen before. Or since."

"OK, so our group was probably through here. We're on the right track," Cade said.

"So now what?" Seyschell asked.

"You said the man you talked to was trying to work up the money for a new ship, right?" Gedrick asked.

"Yes, the bar owner has the rights to a ship docked in the harbor," Chapman said. "The owner of the ship died in the presence of one of the female 'employees' upstairs. He hasn't been able to sell the thing yet. The captain over there thinks that he can work up enough money to buy the boat, but he's drinking his wages every night. At the rate he's going the thing will be sold long before he gets close."

"We have enough in the way of gems with us so we should be able to cover the cost," Seyschell added.

"From what I've heard of these inland river systems, they aren't too forgiving. Shifting shoals and submerged hazards could make it a short trip," Cade said.

"Sounds like we have a solution to our problem," Chapman concluded. "We hire the 'captain' to guide us down the river. He takes the boat in payment."

"And in doing so we've repay the debt our team incurred in taking the boat in the first place," Gedrick said, and then, turning to Chapman, "Please don't misunderstand; they wouldn't have taken the boat had circumstances been different."

"I understand, Captain. They couldn't very well start wandering around the village asking for passage downriver without risking discovery. What I don't understand is why Hemingway gave his name, or part of it in any case."

"Bread crumbs. If someone like we were following them it would be recognized, otherwise a man with no description and a name like Hem? Wouldn't get anyone very far in an investigation. You start thinking that way after a while when you do this sort of work."

"I see. Are we doing 'the work' or gathering your crew back together for their combined safety, Captain Gedrick?" Chapman asked.

Gedrick said nothing in response. He offered only a tight smile. "Seyschell, are you in the mood to help with a negotiation?" he asked, still looking at Chapman.

"Aye, aye, Captain," Seyschell said. "Mr. Chapman, will you be my protection if that bad ole man gets rough, please," she said, feigning helplessness while shooting him a wicked smile.

Gedrick rolled his eyes and went to find the owner.

Seyschell turned around, looked over her shoulder in a very seductive way, and tripped on a drunk. Catching herself, she made her way over to the captain of the *River Rat*, not looking back at Chapman, who was busy stifling the urge to laugh. Among other urges.

Seyschell straightened herself as her mark looked up from sweeping the floor.

"Are you all right, miss?" he asked.

"Why yes, thank you for asking. Let me buy you a drink," Seyschell said.

In the beginning, the Maker used ACGT & U to create the DNA and RNA for all living things. We found these too limiting. Today we are introducing M, B, and R—the first of many planned improvements in the genetic code.

—McAllister's Ltd. media announcement

CHAPTER 76

Ravensford Zone
Upper Sengoran River

THERE WAS A FAMILIAR BOB and swell to the world as the captain of the *River Rat* awoke to the familiar sounds and smells of the riverbank. The air filled his nostrils like a cleansing wind. He smiled happily to be free of the smoke-encrusted stench of the dank broom closet that served as his room these last few days. He pulled a blanket up to his chin and shifted on a comfortable mattress laid out on the deck.

It was then that it hit him.

He slowly opened one eye. As he did he found six strangers gathered around him looking down. He had woken in some fairly unusual situations over the years, but this one was shaping up to be one of the worst.

"Good morning, Captain," Chapman began.

"Good morning," he replied, not knowing what else to say. "Where am I?"

"Aboard our ship heading downriver," Chapman responded.

"I see. Why?"

"You have agreed to be our guide," Chapman again responded truthfully.

"May I get up?" the hungover man asked.

"If you feel it will serve you better in guiding the ship, then by all means."

He wobbled to his feet.

"I agreed to guide you?" the hungover man asked.

"Yes," Chapman replied pleasantly.

"Did I ask for any payment?"

"No."

"I see. Is there anything to eat?"

Seyschell handed the man some bread and a warm mug of coffee.

"The deal is this: We need a guide to get downriver in the shortest time possible. We are on the ship that you wanted to buy from the owner of the pub where you were doing whatever it was you were doing. We now own it. We believe it may have been our friends who took your ship. If you get us downriver without issue, you will be given this ship in payment and you will forget this ever happened. You will count the loss of your old ship as part of the trade for this one, which from your description sounds like the best deal you'll ever get. Should you breathe a word of this to anyone, you forfeit the ship and will in all likelihood wind up in the lokaric feeding chambers. Do we have a deal?"

"Say the part about the lokaric feeding chamber again?"

"Do we have a deal?"

"If I say no?"

"Then you are welcome to leave the ship."

"You'll let me off at the next harbor? No hassle? No problem."

"No, I said you are welcome to leave the ship. You may swim to shore, or walk if you are able. We will not put in to shore for you to do so."

"You can't swim these currents. It would sweep me down the rapids."

"Shame, that."

"So I can guide you down the river and keep this ship or drown?"

"Yes. And remember, should you decide to share this situation with anyone, we will know."

"How?"

"The same way we knew how to find you in the first place."

"Which was?"

"None of your business. Do we have a deal or not?" Chapman said with finality. Seyschell snatched the bread from his hand and moved toward the mug.

"Yes, yes, we have a deal," he blurted out, reaching over slowly and taking the bread back from Seyschell. "Who the hell would believe me anyway?

"We're about two kilometers downriver from Satara."

"Yes, I know the river. Do you know how to handle the rigging of a ship?"

"We'll figure it out."

"You want the fastest route?"

"Yes."

"Very well. In a few kilometers there will be a fork in the river. Take the left."

According to the Merchants' Synod, making enemies is not profitable. Hell, not only is it profitable, it's a hell of a lot of fun.

—Arles Timmerson, captain of the myst-clipper *Impulse*

CHAPTER 77

Deep myst aboard the *Impulse*
Arles Timmerson, commanding

TIMMERSON GRASPED THE WHEEL WITH one hand and a bottle with the other as he cruised through the atmospheres. The floor was littered with empties. An organics storm raged around him, but he was not concerned. The *Impulse* had plenty of shielding, and he had piloted through worse storms while a lot more drunk. In truth, there were only a handful of pilots that would even dare to be out in such a storm, and fewer yet who could successfully navigate it.

He had just left Merchants' Zone having finished his delivery. It had been a good payday, though he had more than enough caryns to be comfortable. He did not need to work and he was not a man who sought comfort except, perhaps, in the arms of a woman with teeth. "Pour me some whiskey and lead me to bed," he sang in a grizzled and mostly off-key voice. "Lend me your sympathy and charms." He steered hard to port, narrowly avoiding a flare-up. "Give me the treasures for which other men would kill." The ship shuddered from another flare just a few feet ahead. "Then let me die happy in your arms."

He was almost out of the storm.

He turned around to the sound of applause. Before he could get his bearings, she grabbed him by the shoulders and threw him hard to the ground. The great ship began to come about without its pilot to guide it.

He squinted, trying to see his assailant.

"You don't recognize me?" Kell said, crestfallen. "I am disappoint-ed!" The voices complimented her sarcasm.

The *Impulse* was not a ship to be left to govern itself, and it spun to the current. Timmerson looked through his hazed vision and tried to clear his head. He did recognize her. It had to have been a good forty years, but she had not aged a day.

He had been a much younger man then, crewing on a merchant ship and carousing whenever they were in port. They met in a bar and he was at once enchanted. She had been singing torch songs, in an almost otherworldly voice, and had flashed him a fantastic smile from across the dimly lit room. On her break he bought her a drink, which she declined. She did not decline his company, however, and after the bar closed it took little coaxing to get her to come home with him. But as he reclined on the bed and watched her dance, something caught his attention. And though drunk, he knew he was in danger. It was a small thing, but significant. As she danced, she passed by the shiny brass knob of the closet door. Though the room was dimly lit he could see other images reflected in it. When she passed by it, however, he saw nothing. And then he knew.

The *Impulse* was beginning to heel over as it spun. She was losing her life's breath—the depth between her keel and the rocks below.

Timmerson had said nothing, knowing that she was stronger and could easily dispatch him. He had to go through with the act. She slowly danced, facing the music, ignoring him. In other circumstances he would have found this indifference immensely alluring. The games women play. But he was on to the dangerous game, and began to prepare. He made a great show of unbuckling his trousers in a drunken frenzy when in fact he was loosing an eight-inch blade. It was a blade that reflected a wisdom greater than his twenty-two years. He had purchased it some three months earlier and it had cost him a dear price. It was a unique item, a pressure-treated diamond blade with an adamantium hilt encased in siribium, and it fit his hand perfectly. A seam of silver ran through the blade. The seller promised it would be the ultimate blade: it would never break, it would never fail, and in a pinch it would stun even a Lokaryn.

He defined this situation as a pinch.

While making a great show of falling backward onto the bed, he in fact was stashing the blade under the pillow. Though ready, outmaneuvering a Lokaryn was still a slim hope at best. He struggled to his feet, half acting, half inebriated. Those were liberal estimates.

When she had whipped herself into a complete frenzy she threw him onto the bed and mounted him. It was an awesome display of power.

The *Impulse* rocked more violently.

But Timmerson was ready and anticipated her next move. As she ground her pelvis against him, she arched her back, closed her eyes, and stretched her arms high above her head. He knew the attack was coming and seized the moment. He reached under the pillow and found his knife. As her arms swung down toward his chest he attacked. The momentum of her movement drove the blade deeply into her chest. Her eyes flew open in shock. Then she screamed. Finally she collapsed. The last he saw of her face was when he finished sealing her into the wall. Sealed away for all eternity, or at least his lifetime, he had hoped.

The kick to the ribs focused him. "So you do remember me!" He nodded slowly and tried to get up. She smashed him down again. "Do you have any idea where a Lokaryn goes when they're staked?" she asked, but did not wait for his reply. "The need to feed never goes away, you know. You just simply exist in a state of slow starvation." She slowly twirled her long blond hair with a finger. "It can last for hundreds of years." The voices were growing restless. She got close to his face and whispered in his ear, "So tell me, Arles, what's the longest amount of time you've ever spent in agony?" He didn't answer. "Perhaps we'll find out tonight," she said.

It finally happened. The *Impulse* struck the shallows hard. She had been moving at a reckless pace when Timmerson was at the helm, avoiding danger only by the grace of design and his knowledge of flight. A clipper upon the jagged shores meant death to the ship and her crew. Fortunately for the crew of the *Impulse*, they were in-zone for shore leave and Timmerson took the ship out alone, as was his way.

With the quickest of movements, Kell sprang to her feet and toppled a bookcase of navigation manuals onto Timmerson's legs. As she did, she flashed him a sardonic smile. "No, no, my dear captain, it won't be so easy as acid dissolving your lungs."

Though his legs were not broken, he was now immobilized. "You bitch," he hissed, "leave me to die with my ship."

The *Impulse* slammed hard into the mountainside, impaling herself on an outcropping. The crash did not free Timmerson, and miraculously Kell maintained her balance.

"Oh I will, Arles. After I'm done with you, I'm going to have the *Impulse* melted down for cattle-gelding shears, or perhaps razors for the fine ladies of Merchants' Zone. I'll be sure to leave you in it when I do."

"I should have set you out in the sun when I had the chance."

Another kick to the ribs, and then she leaned in close again. "We'll continue this in a moment," she said, "but first I have some business to attend to."

She left the bridge, and Timmerson suspected that she was going to the shielding room to reconfigure the shields. This would keep the environment from entering the hull breach. It was clear that she intended his torment to last a very long while.

He worked at the case, but quickly surmised that he would not be able to free himself. His tools were three decks down, the case weighed a quarter of a ton, and he had to admit, her aim was excellent. There was only one tool left at his disposal: anesthesia in the form of a case of 180-proof alcohol. It was within reach and he silently said a prayer of thanks to the uncle who had given him his first taste of it. This same uncle had cautioned him that it was possible to drink oneself to death. Timmerson reasoned that now was as good a time as any to try. Stretching his arms to the near breaking point, he secured a bottle between the tips of his fingers and carefully pulled it toward him. He unscrewed the top, took a breath and began to ingest the fluid at as fast a rate as possible. Who knew, maybe what he had heard of lokaric physiology was true. In any case, if he couldn't die in the arms of a woman, at least he could die in the arms of Bacchus. Not nearly as alluring, but much more forgiving.

After an undetermined amount of time, he had opened his third bottle and was well involved with it when a sudden jolting move shook him to awareness. It seemed to be his visitor from before, but he could only smile. He only knew she couldn't have any of his whiskey.

Kell, enthralled by the fact that she had finally trapped the man who had staked her, missed the fact that Arles Timmerson, for the first time in many, many years, was as drunk as a first-time sailor.

She grabbed his arm, nearly yanking it from the socket. "One bite, old man, and I own you forever. But I won't risk your blade again. If I make you an undead, you could turn on me. No, my old friend," again the sardonic smile, "no immortality for you today. Just a slow death. One pint at a time." Her voices roared in anticipation.

She produced a diamond-tipped blade. "Look familiar?" she asked as she expertly sliced his radial vein with it. It began to slowly ooze. "Bleed me some vino from the veins in your arm!" She mimicked his song as the low-pressure vessel trickled blood into a clear drinking goblet she had retrieved on her way back to the bridge. "You've fallen victim to my charms." The voices sang with her, adding a discordant harmony to her words.

Once the goblet was full, she sealed the wound against a steam pipe, intending to cause him pain. But he only smiled. Pain would not be much of a concern to Arles Timmerson for a few hours yet. It was the best he could do given the circumstances.

Kell sang on. "I'll take your life force and slowly you'll die, then you'll pass unhappy in my arms." Well pleased with her parody, she failed to appreciate the danger she was in. In mock salute, she raised the goblet high and threw back the contents. Her smile widened with each sentence of the malevolent toast, but he could neither hear nor remotely comprehend what she was saying.

As he turned his head, he saw that his other arm was extended and spilling forth red life into the goblet. He smiled and wondered how long it would take until the full force of the alcohol in his stomach leached out into his system. He attempted to seem concerned. He attempted to seem worried and scared, but his mind was drifting to a brownie recipe that he had been discussing with a woman, postcoitus, just prior to her husband coming home and him diving out a window. Delicious brownies. He wondered if his guest enjoyed the red goblet as much as he had enjoyed the brownies.

She wobbled a bit and blinked as she righted herself, and then cut him a third time. He recognized that she was attempting to bleed him to near death before she bit him. Once he was bitten there were only two courses. Death, slow as it might be, or conversion to the undead. His mind wandered again, this time to an outer Merchants' Zone dish that was popular when he was a crewman. Known as Asayaron, it was cheap, filling, and tasted like feet. Caught up in the throes of this memory, Timmerson unexpectedly did something entirely in keeping with his character. He offered a very loud, very respectable, very forceful…

Fart.

Kell was halfway through her third goblet, deeply involved with her drink, when the eruption occurred. She stopped abruptly, and burst out laughing, spraying blood as she did. Timmerson smiled a proud smile and let loose a second course. It was not as impressive as the first, but it certainly made for a suitable encore.

Kell fell to the ground, laughing. "Arlzzzz," she slurred. "You ffffffffarted."

Timmerson could only smile and say, "Yez, I doo that," as a profound thought struck him. The Lokaryn finished the goblet and wrinkled her nose. "Do Lokaryns ffffffffart?" he asked. "I never got to know your name, whaz iz your name."

"Oh, iz Kell," she slurred again. "No, Lokaryns don't fart." She thought for a moment. "I misth that."

"I would too," Timmerson agreed somberly. He tried to look at her, focusing past the instruments and the wreckage. "Hey, it's almost dawn," he observed deliberately.

She stood on wobbly legs, unfocused, and looked at him. "OK," she slurred as she lurched out of the bridge, presumably into the Badlands.

"Hey! Get this off of me," he shouted, but she was too far gone both physically and otherwise to hear.

So there he remained, pinned under the case, in his wrecked myst-clipper. Alcohol at hand and three pints of blood gone. With the exception of the clipper, things, he thought, could be worse.

The fool may yet be the most powerful force in the universe to be reckoned with.

—General Igor Chumley, founder, Chumley's Zone

Chapter 78

Ravensford Zone
Lower Sengoran River

"It had the benefit of being fast," Seyschell said, nursing several bruises. She was glad to still be alive.

"I can't imagine the Sluice would be much worse than that," Chapman observed, nursing several more.

"It's really not difficult. If you stay in the center part of the rapids, the path is pretty clear," the captain of the newly named *River Rat II* said. He maneuvered the craft with some ability into a slip at the downriver trading village.

"We'll bear that in mind next time down," Gedrick said. "We need fast overland transport, where can we obtain horses?"

"You can get horses at two traders over on the west side of town, they're at the edge with the horse pastures beyond. But do you want really fast mounts?"

"We're listening."

"I know where you can find a man who sells McAllister steeds."

"What do you want in return for the information?"

"Only that you tell him that I sent you. I owe the man some money."

"Surprising," Chapman said.

"The finder's fee for sending you would cover it and then some."

"Done," Gedrick said, extending his hand to confirm the deal.

"Head straight north about two hours out of town on the main road.

You'll see a large old barn, blue. The only blue barn you'll see. The farm name is Brishta Khus. You'll know it, because there are trees there unlike anything in the zone. A man named Alden Tennist sells the mounts from McAllister's. He breeds powerful hybrids."

The harbormaster approached the ship, surprised to see this particular captain at the helm. "A new ship? Where did you steal this one from?" he asked. He didn't want an answer; he referenced the sheath of papers in his hand and looked down at the man. "One hundred to tie up and another three hundred in back fees or you can be on your way and take your crew with you," he said, noting that Gedrick and the others were assembling for departure.

Gedrick was bent over his gear and in the ensuing silence looked up at the captain of the *River Rat II*, who smiled back at him pleasantly. Gedrick then looked over to the harbormaster, who stood impassively, awaiting payment.

Sighing in exasperation, Gedrick climbed onto the dock with his gear and slapped a gem into the harbormaster's hand.

The crew made their way quickly out of town, stopping only briefly to reprovision for food. Several hours later they stood at the edge of a large expanse of farm with a blue barn. It took some time to realize what was so different about the plants in this area: As the group looked at the plants, the plants looked back. Some moved with the slow undulating movement of a snail, while others sniffed the air.

"This is going to be different," Seyschell said, as an evergreen bent over to see her a little better.

The team walked up to the front door of the farmhouse. As they did they became more and more aware that the plant life around them was anything but normal. There was grass along the main path to the porch of the house. Seyschell strayed onto the green innocuous-looking blades only to have them shatter beneath her foot. Looking more closely at the place she had set her foot, she commented, "It's crystal."

The group looked across the expanse of what they had previously thought was a field of grass, perhaps an acre or more surrounding the house.

"All this is crystal?" Chapman asked in amazement.

"I would assume so," Gedrick said, scanning the field. "It has strange properties, though. It's not entirely crystal; there is bioenergy here as well as crystal. It would seem to be a blend of plant and latticed mineral."

"It will grow like grass, but the different minerals in the latticework of the crystal element will conduct current." The speaker was an elderly man leaning against a post at the far side of the porch. He smoked an old pipe, the contents of which expelled a dying wisp of smoke.

"And the dead areas?" Gedrick asked, trying to seem nonplussed. "That run between the areas of..."

"I call it C-grass."

"The dead areas that run through the C-grass?"

"It's not dead, it's just normal grass."

"So you can walk and tend the C-grass without crushing it?"

"That's a benefit, yes, but not the primary purpose."

"Which is?"

"It's an insulator."

"I don't understand," Gedrick admitted. "Are you Tennist?"

"No, I am his son, Aien."

"Can we see your father, then?"

"I don't know, can you?"

"I'm not sure what you mean by that. Not to be impolite, but by the look of you, your father would have to be quite old. Is he still alive?"

"Very much so. You of all people should know that looks can be deceiving."

"Why is that?" Gedrick asked, suddenly very aware of his tactical disadvantage.

"Your eye, of course. It looks normal enough, but it's not, now, is it?"

"Circle!" Gedrick ordered. His crew immediately formed into a tight circle, their backs to one another.

"Relax, Captain," Aien said, walking down the porch stairs toward them. "You are among friends."

"How did you know?" Gedrick asked, scanning furiously for any sign of the power surge from a weapon.

"Seriously, Captain, you're in no danger, and not to be impolite to you but you look the fool right now doing that."

"Stay where you are, Aien. How did you know?" Gedrick repeated.

"Captain, your eye was easy enough to detect when you crossed onto our crystal grid. It's well protected, I must say, but you're in a field of sensors."

"I'm not the only person in the world with an artificial eye."

"True enough. The rest was a guess. Seyschell, I believe, is your name. Is that correct? A small blonde traveling with the one-eyed man. The others I can't quite place, but *you* are the master of the *Shicaine*, Captain Gedrick. You can relax; my father and I are members of the railroad. Though he was in a different cell than you, your exploits are legend. He told me the stories. *You* are supposed to be dead."

Gedrick came up slowly from the defensive position that he was in. "May we see your father?"

"Certainly, this way," Aien responded, and he walked into the farm-house.

The group followed the old man inside and up the main flight of stairs, then another flight and through a doorway into what seemed to be an attic stairway. While it was cramped, it was in no way dirty or dusty the way attics can be. Walking without saying a word, Aien led them to a turret room with windows in every direction.

"I don't believe it," Gedrick said.

"What, it looks like grass. What's so amazing?" Seyschell asked.

"The crystals and insulators are laid out like a circuit board."

"What the hell?" Seyschell thought out loud.

"Tennist is this circuit board?" Chapman asked.

"His consciousness is contained in there, yes," Aien responded.

"How do we talk to him?"

"Just as you are. He can hear you."

"And how does he respond?"

"Through me would be easiest."

"So you are a projection of him?"

"No, I am his son."

"I don't understand."

"You don't know where babies come from?"

"Yes I know where babies come from and they don't come from patches of grass."

"I didn't come from a patch of grass. I was born of a woman name Elena. She passed some years ago of cancer."

"Do you have children?"

"Not yet," said the old man.

"Captain, this is all very fascinating, but we're in a bit of a rush," Chapman noted.

"You're not the least bit curious as to how, and why, a giant organic computer is sitting in the middle of a zone that holds technology to be the embodiment of all evil?" Seyschell asked.

"Quite curious, but they will be here in a few weeks and we can come back. Your shipmates, however, are not so endowed."

"He has a point," Aien said. "I'm speaking for Alden Tennist now: We'll be here. Help your friends. Chances are that they'll have stayed on the river longer than you did. They'll need to get off at a less-populated area. Traveling with a sentient and all."

"How do you know about that?" Seyschell asked.

"All cells in the railroad were alerted that a sentient was being run. Possibly through Ravensford. The Lokaryn is not with you. Is she the one running the sentient?"

"We won't be sure until we meet up with them," Gedrick said.

"I'm to give you our fastest mounts. Be aware, they're violent creatures that require a rider that gives them no latitude for self-expression."

"Self-expression?" Chapman asked.

"If you don't show them who's boss from the beginning they sometimes try to eat you."

"Nice," Seyschell said.

"Let's go," said Gedrick.

The group headed to the stables to find the mounts. They were large animals that stood as tall as a horse, but looked more like a great cat. After a frighteningly brief explanation of the hazards of the cats, the mounts were saddled and the group headed out across the plains of the arc.

The cats proved reliable mounts as the group progressed steadily toward the monastery, and thankfully, no one was eaten.

They came upon the monastery by break of the second day. Sore and tired from the journey, they dismounted knowing that meager rest, at most, awaited them. Two crewmen still mounted were sent to survey the area. Gedrick walked toward the door of the main building with a reluctance that Neville didn't understand. Gedrick knocked. A moment passed without response.

"There are torches burning—a little strange in the daytime," Chapman observed.

"Perhaps they fell asleep with them burning?" Seyschell said.

"Not likely. Life in these places is all about routine. If the torches are still burning, there's a good reason,"

"Do you think Cairo made it?" Seyschell asked.

"I have no idea," Gedrick said as the two crewmen returned.

"Any sign of battle damage?"

"No, sir."

A crashing noise from within the building raised the alert level of the entire team.

The door splintered as Seyschell destroyed it. As they went through its shattered remains, they saw the first officer looking in at them in disbelief.

"You might have tried to open it normally!" Chapman said shaking his head.

"Old habits," Gedrick replied.

The rest of the crew moved quickly inside. They readied crystal weapons and Gedrick manifested his bondling. In a moment they found a man in monk's vestments writhing on the floor. Gedrick reabsorbed the bondling and rushed to the man's side. The man was bloodied and swollen in the face, the result of having repeated seizures on the tile floor. The violence and power of his movements warranted a more cautious approach, Chapman thought, as Gedrick rushed to assist the man. Moving to protect the stricken man's head from further damage, Gedrick called his name as he had from the first time he could talk:

"Uncle!"

There is no greater weapon than diversity. A diverse society blends your strengths and theirs. And all others they welcome. Consider carefully before provoking the pluralistic society.

—*Better Living Through Conflict: A Guide to War*
Chumley's Zone publication

CHAPTER 79

Ravensford Zone
Lower Sengoran River

PELI DOMAR STUDIED THE TWO senior soldiers, who were conferring intently.

"Do Ravensfordian soldiers usually confer this much?" he asked.

"How would I know," Vis-Shan replied. "I've been assigned to the monastery since I ascended to my junior rank. I haven't a clue how much they confer."

"Perhaps they're on to our little plan."

"Perhaps, but I don't see another way to deal with this, do you?"

"No. But if we're going to go, we better do so now," he said.

"Agreed," the Seb-Ichi monk replied. "But we better tell them where we're going."

Tol-Sharra and his second-in-command, Gho, watched as the pair approached. "I trust your meal was satisfactory?" the first asked with a mischievous look in his eye.

The Kwynian managed a weak smile. "It's certainly on par with what I am used to in my own unit," Domar said.

"Then I do feel sorry for the soldiers of Kwyne!" the first said, causing laughter to erupt within the group.

"What can we do for you, Vis-Shan?" Tol-Sharra asked.

"Sergeant Domar and I have been discussing strategies for apprehending our travelers with little or no bloodshed," he began.

"A goal we share," Tol-Sharra replied.

"We believe that should the ship get as far as here, the element of surprise would be lost."

"Unlikely," the first said. "We have sharpshooters in the trees. They would be able to provide adequate warning."

Peli Domar stepped in. "With no disrespect intended," he said, "I disagree. Your shooters would have two choices, shout alerts to the rest of your team or begin firing. Either outcome would alert the ship and likely result in casualties."

THOUGH THEY HAD WATCH ON the stern, Chirra and Jarrel noticed it first: a change in the energy of the area. "Lyrie, do you feel it?" Chirra shouted to the bow.

"Yes," she said.

"Feel what?" Timan asked.

"The energy in the area has changed. It's like looking into a fog bank," Lyrie said.

Timan concentrated. "You're right. Our range is diminishing."

"Chirra," Lyrie yelled back. "Go tell Hemingway we can no longer scout ahead." This had never happened to her, and the experience was disturbing.

"WHAT DO YOU PROPOSE?" THE team leader asked.

"I assume that the communications lattice is not well established in this area," Vis-Shan said, already knowing the answer.

It was Gho who replied, "No, it is not."

"Do any members of your team have the sensitivity?" Vis-Shan asked, hoping that the answer would be yes. While few Ravensfordians possessed the full psionic capabilities of the Seb-Ichi, a few did have lesser abilities and a slightly larger number than that had telepathic sensitivity.

"Yes," Tol-Sharra said. "We have two."

WITH DUSK UPON THE RIVER, Derring entered the pilot's berth, her shroud drawn tightly around her. "I'll take watch shortly," she said to Hemingway.

"Actually," he replied, "I think we should have the children stay out there a little longer. We should be getting close, and good as your night vision is, we'll need their abilities."

The Lokaryn concurred. It was at this moment that Chirra burst into the berth, clearly agitated. "What's wrong, Chirra?" Derring asked.

"I'm having trouble feeling things," she said as tears began to well in her eyes.

Hemingway considered her words for a moment. "We're closer than I thought then," he said. "Ren, cut our speed a little. Let's approach slowly."

Derring put a hand on the girl's shoulder. "Don't be afraid," she said to Chirra. "The area that we are seeking is going to make you feel different, but it will only be for a little while. Do you believe me?" Chirra looked the Lokaryn in the eyes, trying to be brave, and nodded. "Why don't we go up and watch together." The girl took the Lokaryn's hand.

OF THE TWO RAVENSFORDIAN SOLDIERS with telepathic sensitivity, ironically neither was tasked to communications. One was responsible for logistics, while the other was the cook. The latter, the brunt of many a well-deserved barb, was thrilled to be given a different assignment.

"Here's the plan," Vis-Shan said. "Sergeant Domar and I will go three kilometers downriver. Corporal Tam will position herself by the riverbank and while she's at it maybe catch dinner. Sergeant Ha' Lora will take up position at the halfway point to serve as the relay. Understood?"

Everyone nodded in agreement.

"Are you sure that you do not want to bring more with you?" the team leader asked.

"No," Domar replied. "If your goal is to protect the children, then it's imperative that we have the element of surprise."

"Very well," Tol-Sharra said.

When the party had left, Gho turned to his team leader and asked, "You are comfortable with this?"

"I am not, but his logic is excellent and to contest it would surrender a tactical advantage—surprise," Tol-Sharra replied.

"I find it hard to believe that the Seb-Ichi is providing aid to the fugitives," the junior soldier said. "It seems unthinkable."

"I find it a possibility that I must entertain. But let us hope it is you who are correct. In the meanwhile, take our three best soldiers and flank our Seb-Ichi friend. Position yourselves four kilometers downriver. As soon as you spot the ship, send the swiftest back to camp. The remainder of you are to head to Vis-Shan's position and observe."

Gho nodded. "And if they are up to something, as you suspect?" he asked.

"Kill them, then target your weapons on the boat. Do not sink it. Disable her and let the current carry her downriver."

Vis-Shan and Domar reached their destination quickly. The phobe was astonished by the Kwynian's agility on his prosthetic legs. "What do we do now?" Domar asked.

"We send out a little test message to our communications team and then we wait."

"Have you thought about what happens when we intercept the ship?" Domar asked.

"Yes," Vis-Shan said. "We activate our return crystal and get out of here as quickly as possible."

"Doesn't that put you in danger?" the Kwynian asked.

"Yes, it does, but it's the only option."

"Not necessarily," Domar replied.

CHIRRA LOOKED GRIEF-STRICKEN AS SHE was able to sense less and less. Jarell attempted to comfort her, but found his own senses beginning to diminish and was himself clearly rattled.

"Just stay sharp with your other senses," Derring said. "The other will return once we are past this area."

Chirra nodded bravely.

In the pilot's berth, Ren and Hemingway navigated the *River Rat* through the Sengoran's currents. "I think we are close," Ren said to the android. "I agree," he replied. "We're going to hit some shallows as we get nearer the mining area."

"Why would they mine in an area that wasn't easy to navigate by river?" Ren asked.

"You have to go where the resources are," Hemingway said by way of explanation. "They used flat-bottom barges. Harder to steer, but a lot less likely to ground and dump cargo into the river." Ren nodded. "Just remember that you are not captaining such a ship," Hemingway said with a smile.

"Aye, aye, sir," Ren replied with a smart salute.

VIS-SHAN SAT ON THE BANKS of the Sengoran River in a focused meditation. Within a few moments he began to emit a low hum, not unlike the mating call of insects that the soldier had heard around his childhood home. Domar watched in fascination as Vis-Shan sat perfectly still, almost statuesque in his bearing. Domar had seen many technological marvels in his life, but none had amazed him the way the phobes' use of energy did. From his crystalline prosthetics to telepathic communication and even the crystal portal that had cost him his own legs, he found himself filled with a sense of wonder.

While the Seb-Ichi monk sat in deep concentration, casting his aspect over the dampened area, Domar began to work on his part of the plan. He reached into his pack and removed two items from it: a small pouch of crystal shards that he had been collecting and a black egg-shaped device that fit neatly in the palm of the hand. The latter was a standard-issue Kwynian small impact explosive that could be easily thrown or planted. Though he had been in-zone a relatively short time he was surprised by how foreign the device felt to him. *Perhaps I have a phobe's soul,* he thought with a chuckle. Carefully, he twisted open the shell of the device and removed the explosive contents, a malleable puttylike compound, from the detonation wires. Screwing the device back together, he set it down and began to gently turn the explosive in his hands, warming it and making it pliable. As he turned the substance, he began to mix in crystal shards until most of the contents of the pouch were gone. He hoped he had collected enough—enough to cause the destruction of a small ship.

Vis-Shan's humming grew louder, and his body swayed a little. Suddenly his eyes popped open and he began to point. "Over there," he said. "Can you see it?"

Domar squinted and was able to make out a small shape in the distance.

From his position downriver, Gho also saw them, and began to move his team back within range of the Seb-Ichi.

Aboard the *River Rat*, it was Timan who saw the pair on the left bank of the river, and he shouted warning to the rest.

"Good job, Timan," Derring said, which caused the phobe to smile in spite of himself. He noticed out of the corner of his eye that Lyrie was also smiling at him.

"What do we do?" Lyrie turned to ask the Lokaryn, only to see her disappear right in front of her eyes. "Derring!" she exclaimed, not understanding.

"Over there," Timan said, pointing at the shore. To their amazement, Derring now stood on the shore poised to attack.

One moment Vis-Shan and Peli Domar were tracking the ship, the next there was a Lokaryn two feet in front of them about to strike. The Kwynian knew her at once, but realized he did not know her name. "*Trud' dara ma' vorta d'otovra!*" he shouted, repeating the words that she had prayed while ministering to his wounds.

It was enough. Derring snapped her head in Domar's direction, at once recognizing the soldier whom she had assumed had bled to death despite her efforts. "Peli Domar," she said.

He smiled at her, no longer afraid. "Thank you for what you did for me," he said, bowing slightly.

The Lokaryn returned the bow, then shifted her attention to Vis-Shan. "And you are Seb-Ichi, though I do not recognize your order."

"I am Vis-Shan," he said. "I serve the one who has been outcast."

"The monk!" she exclaimed. "Then it is indeed our good fortune to find you!"

From the shadows the team watched the exchange. They looked to Gho for the signal to intercept, but he held up a hand silently, then pointed to the boat. It would be easier if everyone disembarked. It was clear that the Seb-Ichi knew this Lokaryn, which meant that Tol-Sharra's suspicions had been correct. The question now was what to do about it. A Lokaryn and Seb-Ichi monk were formidable opponents. The children were hostages, so they would not hesitate to kill them. The Kwynian, however, was vulnerable.

"Steer to shore, Ren," Hemingway said. "Nice and slow. Do you see them?"

The young man saw three figures on the shore, the shrouded one whom he recognized as the Derring. "Huh?" he said.

"Didn't know about that little magic trick, did you?" Hemingway said.

"Nu-uh," Ren responded, finding himself at a loss for words. As interesting as he was finding technology to be, this was the most amazing thing that he had ever seen.

"Ren!" Hemingway yelled, grabbing the wheel to avoid a small out-cropping of rocks. "Pay attention!"

"Sorry, Hem."

"Ask her to show it to you another time, OK?"

Ren nodded.

From the shore, Vis-Shan attempted to guide the *River Rat* in. When the ship was a couple of feet from the river's edge, Ren quenched the crystals. Timan and Lyrie threw the mooring lines to Derring, and she and Peli Domar pulled the ship toward the riverbank like experienced dockhands. Aboard, Hemingway pried a deck plank loose to create a makeshift ramp to disembark.

Lyrie threw her arms around Derring and hugged her tight. "If you're going to just disappear like that, would you mind giving me a little warning," she admonished with a smile.

"Sorry," Derring said, returning it. "Instinct." Once introductions were proffered, Peli Domar began to explain the exit strategy to the group.

"Time is short, so please pay attention. There is a platoon of zone commandos just north of here awaiting our return," Peli Domar said.

"Really?" Derring said with a raised eyebrow.

"Before you get the wrong idea, we mean to disappoint them. Our rescue portal back to the monk's is in the vicinity of where they've set up camp, and the night won't last indefinitely."

"How do we draw them off?" Lyrie asked. The utility of her father's endless and inscrutable lessons was becoming clearer with each passing day.

It was Peli Domar's turn for a raised eyebrow. Rather than answer he held up an explosive device embedded with crystal shards.

"We bring them here by blowing up your ship," Vis-Shan interpreted.

"That much explosive is going to leave a divot in the riverbed and nothing but splinters," Derring observed.

"I didn't know how large your ship was and there's no time now to downsize the charge," Domar replied.

"We'll call ahead the next time," Hemingway said.

"Get any gear that you want off the ship. I'll set the charge amidships," Domar instructed. "We blow the ship and head south. We'll swing around, hopefully behind the troops, and once we get back to Sharv we'll activate the crystal. Once through the portal, I'll have a decent meal on the table back at the monks' before you've all finished taking much-needed baths."

Hemingway leaned over to Derring. "Sounds great—so how come it never works out that way?"

Domar set the charge as they quickly cleared the ship. The fuse set, they set out south, and minutes later an enormous flash of light was followed by the report of a huge explosion.

"Think you used enough explosive there?" Hemingway asked.

"Got the job done, didn't it?" Domar said.

"Old railroad joke," Derring explained. "Let's go."

A few minutes down the road Hemingway suddenly stopped. Derring sensed the synthetic's abrupt halt and went to mist immediately.

"Back to back," Hemingway commanded as the group formed a tight circle. With few weapons it was a futile gesture.

"Sharv is in the other direction," Gho said calmly as he walked toward them. "You are surrounded and we will fire on the entire group, children included, if the Lokaryn does not make herself known right now." Gho raised his hand as his men prepared to fire.

Derring immediately solidified between Lyrie and the outside threat. Gho motioned with his upraised hand to close the circle, then lowered it slowly.

"Dammit, Derring, you and Gedrick! Sometimes it's OK to take your chances in a fight," Hemingway said.

"Sometimes, but not this time," Derring replied.

"You will accompany us to the camp at Sharv," Gho continued. "Comply and no one needs be hurt." The tension in the air was palpable as the troops began to come out of the woods from their concealment. The prisoners knew that the soldiers were a breath away from firing.

"If you please." Gho motioned back toward Sharv.

"The Lokaryn will require shelter come dawn," Hemingway said.

"In what way is that my problem?" Gho answered without emotion. "Now, if you please, before one of my men gets the idea that you are resisting and starts shooting."

Tread lightly: The mind's eye is the most dangerous of all places. It can lead a faithful man to infidelity and it can lead a holy man to heresy. Unchecked, it can lead a sensible man to his death.

—Kuna Latte, first rohnin of Kwyne

CHAPTER 80

"UNCLE?" CHAPMAN ECHOED IN SURPRISE.

In his mind's eye, the monk could see a hazy moment of sound and light. The vision of his nephew, many years lost, shouting into the depths of this new vision. The monk reached up and grabbed his would-be savior. Instead of salvation, he pulled Gedrick into the depths of the chaos.

Seyschell and Chapman watched as Gedrick stiffened in the grip of the monk, who thrashed far less violently.

Seyschell tried separating the two, but soon stopped.

"You can break down the door, but you can't pull these two apart?"

"Not unless you want me to bust a few bones trying," she shot back.

"What now?" Cade asked.

"As long as they're still breathing, we wait," Chapman replied.

"And if they stop breathing?" Cade asked.

"If they stop breathing, they'll probably let go," Chapman said.

It was some thirty minutes before the monk's grip fell away from Gedrick's shoulders. The captain of the *Shicaine* fell to the ground.

As always after a vision, the monk concentrated on his breathing, unaware of anything else. Slowly the sound of pain filtered into his consciousness, as did the sounds of people tending a fallen man. Slowly he came to.

"Ga-darick? Is it you?" he said weakly.

"Yes, Uncle, it's me," Gedrick said, trying to massage blood back into his arms.

" 'Ga-darick'?" Chapman asked.

"The proper pronunciation of his name in these parts," Seyschell answered.

"You still have the visions, obviously. Thanks for bringing me along on that one. What the hell was it?"

"It's been a while, where have you been?"

"It's a long story. We're looking for friends of ours. Has anyone named Klemm, Jospher, or Woods made contact with you?"

"No. Help me to the chair. You," he said, motioning to Seyschell, "please make some tea."

Cade and Chapman helped the older man to a chair at a table in the kitchen. After a few minutes the tea was made and the monk had collected himself enough to continue.

"Your friends may be the subject of the vision I was having when you found me. My aide Vis-Shan left some hours ago with a Kwynian soldier to try and help them."

"What was in the vision?"

"The original vision had your friends on a boat under attack on the river."

"That wasn't what I just saw when you brought me into this one."

"No, it's changed. Every time we react to what the visions show us, there are alterations in the outcome. Some subtle, some drastic."

"What did this vision show you?" Seyschell asked Gedrick.

"I was too disoriented to know what I was looking at," he replied.

"You were looking at the crystal fields at Sharv," the monk said. "Your friends, my aide, and the soldier are all going to die there."

"How far is it?"

"About a day's ride."

"They only have a few hours on us and we're on mounts. We'll catch them."

"No, you won't. They portaled to the site. I have the coordinates to a clearing in the area. We still collect crystals there when we need them. I smythed a crystal to get them there."

"Any more portal crystals?"

"No. I made the one. I didn't anticipate needing another."

"Couldn't you smyth another one quickly?" Chapman asked Gedrick. "I saw you smyth the one to get past the wall in a few hours."

"That was a line-of-sight crystal, the simplest form of portal. This one would have to cover a lot more distance. It would take a couple of days to complete. We can cover the distance before that on the cats."

"You can still smyth crystals, Ga-darick? Your father would be proud."

"I doubt it, but this isn't the time for that conversation. We need provisions and a fast route to Sharv," Gedrick said.

The monk nodded.

"It's about time you got here," a voice called. The crew whipped around to find Damien Cairo and his team standing just outside the doorway.

"It's definitely her, Gedrick," the former rohnin said with a nod. "I'm sure of it."

"So am I," he replied. "As soon as we reprovision..."

"We ride," Cairo finished.

The explosion purged Turin Tan of the wicked and left the city a ruin. The Heart of Thecla, still aflame, was carried away by the young boy who, being pure of heart, was untouched by its fire. Know this: The heart shall redeem the worthy and destroy the wicked.

—Tor' Manat
Kwynian Sacred Writings

CHAPTER 81

Deep myst
Aboard the *Blackthorne*

"WHORE!"

"Sinner!"

Kell's head pounded with each shrill admonishment from her mother, while the other voices murmured their assent in the background.

Her stomach churned and rolled, like a clipper in rough myst.

"What have you done, Kell?" her mother asked.

"Nothing, Mommy," she heard herself replying. Only it was her childhood voice that she heard.

"You ruined it, Kell, you ruined it all! And what do you think is going to happen now?"

"Please, Mommy."

Her stomach did a summersault, causing her to retch, but it was the sound of a door opening that brought her back to the present.

The woman could shatter diamonds with that voice, Kell thought.

Slowly she opened her eyes and was greeted with a white spinning ceiling. Where the hell was she? Before she could get her bearings, she retched again as her churning stomach forced foul-tasting bile into the back of her throat. She hadn't eaten in years and was amazed that her organs were still capable of producing the vile stuff.

"Well, my dear. It appears that you have accomplished your task after all." The voice chuckled. "A pity you lost your quarry, though."

Kell rolled a bloodshot eye in the direction of the sound and saw the figure of T'Gareth standing just to the right of the feather bed on which she lay.

"What do you mean lost?" she croaked, as her head continued to pulse.

"Timmerson survives, Kell."

"What!" she exclaimed, immediately regretting her own volume. "That's not possible. I drained him a glass at a time."

"I see. And do you feel his force within you?"

Kell searched deep within herself for a moment. It was true that Lokaryns absorbed the life force of those they fed on. Timmerson should be pulsing through her body, and yet she did not feel him.

"I do not," she replied, her demeanor souring even more. For the first time in her life, Kell was puzzled. How could it be? She had boarded the *Impulse* and easily dispatched with the old man, pinning him beneath a bookcase. She had damaged the ship's engines. She was able to visualize piercing the vein in his arm and filling the goblet. But then it got strange. There was singing…and laughter. Laughter? Why would Timmerson have been laughing?

And then it hit her. The old bastard was drunk!

"I see you've figured it out. You never could hold your liquor, Kell!"

More chuckling.

She shot darts at him with her eyes.

"Well, if it makes you feel any better, it won't be for long. Timmerson is currently enjoying Captain Loh'l's hospitality aboard the *Blackthorne*."

With great effort, Kell raised herself up onto her elbows so that she was facing her clan lord.

"Timmerson is mine," she hissed.

"I'm afraid not, Kell. Things are progressing rapidly. I gave you Timmerson because it served my purposes. Now it does not."

"Timmerson is mine!" she shouted, raising her voice to her clan lord. It reverberated in her head.

It was risky behavior.

"And you are mine. Just as I made you, so can I unmake you Kell!" T'Gareth glared at her.

"I have served you well, and repaid you a thousandfold."

"Your abilities have always been an asset, but your independence is becoming a liability. When you came to me, Kell, you were fascinated by our history. You absorbed it like a sponge. We are standing at an historical crossroads. Will you waste the opportunity to write it, on a petty vengeance?"

Kell absorbed the words and opened her mouth to reply. It was at this moment that her body did something that it had not done in nearly ninety years. She pulled back her long blond hair and vomited.

"Wait," T'Gareth said sarcastically. "Don't answer yet."

When she was done spewing the black stuff, she wiped her mouth on the snow-white comforter.

"I can offer you so much more than Timmerson," he said.

"I'm listening," she groaned.

"You've spent a human lifetime chasing Timmerson. And for what, because he bested you? There's always that risk when dealing with humans."

"Because he sealed me in a wall!" Kell answered. "Do you have any idea what it's like to be imprisoned in a small space, T'Gareth? To get weaker with every passing second, with every passing year? Well I do. I spent thirty years doing just that, listening to *her* berate me every single second. Just like she did when she put me in that cursed closet!"

"Even after you killed her she remained with you," T'Gareth observed.

"She is always with me," Kell said.

T'Gareth paused, to give her the time to consider her own words.

"Then perhaps it is not Timmerson who is your enemy. Perhaps not even your mother."

"What do you mean?" Kell demanded.

"Did she not punish you in the ways that she was taught, in the ways that she herself was punished?"

"Yes," Kell conceded.

"Then perhaps, Kell, your enemy is not a person, but a culture."

"Kwyne?" Kell asked.

"You had not considered it?" T'Gareth said.

"I had not."

T'Gareth was truly surprised. Though it was his intention to manipulate her in order to draw her into his larger plans, he had not expected this response. Perhaps things would be easier than he had first believed.

As he looked at her, she took on a softer air, reminding him of how he had experienced her when her father had first been assigned to the ambassadorship in the Lokaryn Zone. He offered her a smile.

"What if I could provide you with something far greater than Timmerson. Something ultimately more—" He paused for effect. "—satisfying?"

Now it was Kell's turn to be surprised.

"More satisfying?" she asked.

"Yes, but not without its challenges. There is evidence to suggest that the location of Kwyne's most precious artifact has been determined."

"The heart," Kell said derisively. "I know *that* legend well. There was many a day where I was threatened by what it would do to me if I did not behave."

"I had cause to see it once, and I can assure you, Kell, it is no legend."

"You have seen it?"

"Yes," he lied. "And if we were to possess it, I can assure you that we would rain utter destruction down upon the streets of Kwyne. On all the streets of T'Amorach. Perhaps then that little vengeful appetite of yours would finally be satisfied?"

"Yes," said Kell. "I believe it would."

The voices agreed.

A drunken old man on his feathered death bed
Asked for the charms of a whore
To send him off rightly and give him some rest
But in the end all he asked for was more.

—Myst chantey attributed to Arles Timmerson

CHAPTER 82

Deep myst
Aboard the wreck of the *Impulse*

DEEP ON THE FOGGY MYSTS, a ship of considerable reputation lay wrecked. Her engines were dead and her crew of one was passed out on the floor of the bridge. It was not the first time this had happened.

No one was more surprised to wake up alive than Arles Timmerson himself. His head was pounding, it hurt to breathe, and the only recollection that he could immediately muster was that of some sort of party. His mouth tasted as though a mouse had sought refuge in it during the night and died. He gingerly opened one eye and winced as the light registered like a dagger somewhere within the deep recesses of his brain. He tried again, with slightly better results, groaned, and attempted to sit up. It was then that he realized his legs were pinned by the large bookcase that had once held his navigation manuals. The manuals were strewn about the cabin, as were several bottles.

Several empty bottles.

The room wobbled and spun around him, but he could not be certain if it was from the waves of the myst or his burgeoning hangover.

"Son of a bitch," he muttered, as he slipped back into unconsciousness.

He was awakened some time later to a noise that sounded vaguely like a wake-up alarm. With his eyes still closed, he slapped around with his free arms, hoping for a lucky hit that would shut it off. No such luck. He opened one eye and the light felt as though it had smacked him in the head. He groaned. "Will somebody please shut that thing off?" It continued, and seemed to get louder.

Hexa…

The alarm had a rhythm to it, and in spite of his annoyance he soon found it running through his head like an old familiar song.

Hexa…

His fingers tapped along as though they had a consciousness of their own. Soon he found himself humming an old sea shanty that fit the beat of the pattern.

"When I was a lad, I wanted her bad

With each day, I wanted her more.

But my love she dismissed, so I set out to myst,

To write my name in mystfaring lore."

He sang several more verses with the repeat of the alarm providing the foundation.

Hexa…

The pain in his head had subsided into a dull throb, and it occurred to him that a little more drink might set things right. He looked around, at first seeing only empty bottles. But then…

Hexa…

He resumed his song, rocking his body to the rhythm in an attempt to roll the bottle closer.

Success!

Hexa…

"Last verse," he yelled as if leading a chorus of drunken sailors. He took a satisfying swig.

"I returned from the myst, richer than rich

With my love for her stronger the more.

She offered her arms and I shared in her charms.

Like the others who'd purchased them before.

"Like the others who'd purchased them before!" he repeated with greater gusto.

The ship shuddered as the patterns of the waves changed. It was then that it struck him. The pattern was not an alarm, it was a repeater, and it was broadcasting his location. The change in the wave patterns could only be from another ship.

He pondered this for a moment, and could not come up with an answer that made sense. There was no doubt in his mind that the Lokaryn intended to kill him. So why had she bothered to put a repeater on his ship? Salvage? Why not just kill him and take the ship? Why bother to scuttle her? The *Impulse* rocked harder as the other ship grew closer.

Whatever the answer, he was certain that whoever was coming was not someone he was going to be happy to see.

He took a deep breath and an even deeper swig.

The breeding of old-world jungle cats into rideable mounts has a desirable side effect: It culls out careless riders, which in turn reduces the feeding costs of the animals, which can be considerable.

—McAllister's Ltd. brochure

CHAPTER 83

DERRING SAT CLOSE TO LYRIE as the minutes counted down. The light of the campfire played across the small group as the guards stood in concentric rings around them.

Timan stood near Gho, bargaining for any concession that would set his family and friends free. Domar and Vis-Shan talked with Hemingway quietly. Chirra was held by Jarrel, while Ren said nothing, but remained by Hemingway's side. Weapons were pointed at the Ravensfordians and the soldier from Kwyne. The troop commander continually stared at Derring while he toyed around with a coring device, repeatedly firing it into the air. The harsh snap of the metal teeth coming together to form a cup intended to remove a lokaric heart made Lyrie jump every time she heard it.

"Lyrie," Derring said softly. "Come dawn I want you to get as far away from me as you can. And promise me something."

Lyrie had been quietly leaning against Derring's shoulder, unwilling to contemplate what the morning would bring. "I don't want to talk about this, Derring."

"Lyrie, promise me you won't look when it happens," the Lokaryn pressed on.

"You can mist away, Derring. Please," Lyrie pleaded.

"No, Lyrie. I believe Gho when he says he'll kill each of you in turn and I'm not willing to have that on my conscience."

"So I have to have *your* death on *my* conscience."

"Tayshaw, I have prayed for this day since I was first converted. Now it is here and I can share my last hours with people I love. There are far worse ways to die."

Timan walked over and sat down heavily near Vis-Shan.

"How did the negotiations go?" Hemingway asked in a flat tone.

"Tol-Sharra has accused us of being traitors. As such, he won't come down to talk with me. Gho has told me that we are considered contaminated by exposure to technology and, until we can somehow prove our story, we are conspirators."

Domar spoke next.

"Tol-Sharra is a crafty one. He knows that he has Derring as long as he's willing to shoot his prisoners. He'd lose the fight ultimately, but not before one or all of the Ravensfordians were killed. In a few hours, the sun will take care of his Lokaryn problem and his odds will be all the better."

Hemingway straightened somewhat.

"Nice government you've got here," the android said, looking directly at Timan.

"They're doing what they have to do, not what they want to do," Timan shot back. "If you hadn't come here in the first place none of this would be happening."

Vis-Shan felt his bondling stir. It was bondling song—the music the bondlings sang to one another when they were close enough. He looked over at Hemingway, who returned the look with an almost imperceptible smile.

"In fairness, Hemingway was unconscious when he was carried though the portal. He did not make the decision," Domar countered.

"Don't throw facts at the boy," Hemingway said, "it just threatens his ignorance."

Derring whispered quietly into Lyrie's ear. "Prepare yourself."

"For what?" she whispered back. The anger that was always seething just below the surface in Timan rose into full bloom as he defended himself in the argument with the sentient.

"You know what? I've had about enough of your self-serving garbage."

The guards looked on somewhat amused at the exchange, but needed to keep control.

"Simmer down, we don't want to hurt anyone."

"Just trying to settle a disagreement. Maybe you can help me out here. I'm an artificial, so we don't do things this way, but if you wanted to win the heart of a woman, say young Lyrie over there, would you start singing songs about barnyard animals?" Hemingway asked.

Timan was on his feet. Weapons were immediately leveled at the irate Ravensfordian, but none fired. Hemingway ignored the young man's menacing stance.

"Shut up!" Timan shouted.

"And if so, which would you chose? I mean does a duck work better than a cow or a pig."

The guards were lulled by their superior numbers into a moment of laughter as the young man stood humiliated by the android.

Riding his mount full force into the brunt of the outermost ring of soldiers, Gedrick held the reins of the great cat in one hand and the reins of several more in the other. Seyschell, Chapman, Cairo, and Cade followed closely on his lead. The rest of the team struck from different angles. With a fierce battle cry he loosed the cats on the outer ring of soldiers. Freed, they savagely tore into their prey. The bondling deflected the few blows that managed to come close to him.

Gedrick drove his cat over the soldiers and the animal slid, coming to a stop. The cat struck several guards, sending two into the fire. Burning logs rolled across the ground, spreading flames as they did. The two men screamed and rolled on the ground trying to extinguish the flames, but in doing so spread the fires in new directions. Gedrick's mount regained its footing quickly. Its ears pinned and its teeth bared, it slashed the chest of Gho, who had charged Gedrick's position, missing narrowly with a crystal bolt. The man dropped, trying to hold his heart inside of his chest. Another soldier fell to the bondling, which Gedrick now wielded like a sword.

Seyschell reached down and grabbed by the leg a man who was leveling a crystal weapon at Chapman. She spurred the cat on into the crowd, swinging the man like a mace. Her cat slipped and slid in the blood flowing from the carnage, until she finally dropped the pulverized body to join back up with Gedrick. The flames were spreading quickly now, adding to the pandemonium of the situation.

Seyschell reached down and pulled Chirra and Jarrel onto her mount. Meanwhile, Ren, who stood openmouthed in the middle of the chaos, was scooped up by Chapman.

Peli Domar fought with astonishing agility but was stopped dead in his tracks by a vision he never in his life thought he would see: the rohnin of Kwyne atop a massive lion reaching down to give him a hand onto the mount.

The rohnin fired a crystal over Domar's shoulder, killing a would-be attacker.

"We really should go now," Damien Cairo said. Domar took his hand and swung up on the mount. The rohnin spurred the cat to a sprint. Vis-Shan brought a mental link to a riderless cat and jumped on it as it loped past him.

The troop commander moved quickly to take Lyrie hostage, but found her fist in his Adam's apple. Coughing and spitting up blood, he cursed. Derring tore the coring device from his hands, and before he knew what was happening, she had placed it to his temple and fired the mechanism.

She threw Lyrie on one of the mounts before the man's body had hit the ground. Timan jumped onto this mount as well.

"Go!" Derring commanded. She turned to see a soldier, who was about to attack her from behind, fall as he slid from Gedrick's sword. Derring looked up to see Gedrick, bloodied but alive, riding an enormous black jaguar that almost melded with the night. The flames played across the animal's sleek fur, making it seem as if he was atop fire itself. He held his hand out to pull her up. She looked to see that all the children were atop mounts and satisfied that they were, she took his hand.

"You know how to make an entrance, Captain," Derring said, trying to sound much calmer than she actually felt. She hadn't realized it until just his moment, but her heart had started pounding in her chest.

"In is the easy part. It's the exit that's always the problem," Gedrick replied, trying to hide his own exhilaration.

Hemingway continued to fight until he heard a whistle and he saw Cade motioning to him. With a final attack he launched himself onto Cade's mount.

"Hey, old man, think you can find your way out of this crap?" Hemingway asked Cade.

"Straight lines, bucket brain. Easy enough for even you," Cade shot back, urging his cat into the night.

"We've got them all," Derring said.

Gedrick surveyed the scene, and finding all his riders still mounted, sounded the retreat.

"Break!" he shouted.

Flames spread everywhere now, as the cats coursed through the mayhem granting death to anyone foolish enough to attempt an attack. They vanished into the night, leaving only the cries and moans of the injured and dying.

Sunrise

-Nathaniel Gedrick, captain of the Shicaine

CHAPTER 84

THE JOURNEY BACK TO THE *Shicaine* was a blur to everyone. The joy of being reunited, the horror of the battle that saved the lives of the captured, and the fear that they could be attacked at any moment erased all awareness of the time or distance that had passed.

Derring rode with her arms around Gedrick as he drove the massive jaguar forward. He knew she didn't need his body to steady herself as they rode, but prayed that she didn't release her grasp from around his waist.

They reached the smugglers' port exhausted but without further incident. The masts of the *Shicaine* were lit with watchmen's lanterns that twinkled from behind a tree line just outside the zone wall. With a final turn they were in the small village that adjoined the wharves.

The bloodstained group atop fearsome mounts drew stares from the locals, who were not generally easily impressed.

For the first time since she joined Gedrick on the jaguar, Derring released her grip and slid down to the ground. She stared up at the *Shicaine*. The light played across the spars and rigging, highlighting the ship's lines. The blackness of the night sky outside of the zone shielding made the ship seem as if it were floating free from the world below it.

Derring stood there with tears streaming down her face as Heming-way came up beside her and slide his hand into hers.

"Welcome home," the android said, squeezing her hand gently.

They started up the deck behind Gedrick.

"I am *not* getting on that thing," Timan announced loudly.

"A few more breaks like this and I might start believing in that god of yours, Derring," Hemingway said. Timan finally followed the group up the gangway with a sullen look.

"CAPTAIN ON THE DECK," CAME the voice of the command deck watch officer. It was minutes before dawn and the *Shicaine* was in a lightly running reach. She had half sail out and the ion skimmers worked, as always, at capacity.

"Report," Gedrick said.

"Making good time, sir, on half sail, ion skimmers to full, batteries at full charge across all banks and engines at the ready should we need them," said the deck watch officer, as if announcing a perfect report card.

"Half sail?" Gedrick asked. He allowed latitude for his officers to exercise individual style, but they had best be ready to have a good reason for anything that they did.

"Resting the crews for the heavy sailing during daylight, sir. We are still short on crew and the round-the-clock sailing could fatigue them," the officer responded.

Gedrick paused for a moment. "Good thought, but full sail at night gains us ten knots, whereas half sail during the day only loses us five knots. Keep the idea, but switch the schedule over the next few days." He walked over to a recess and found the last cup of coffee lurking at the bottom of an hours-old pot of nearly black liquid and quickly claimed it—with no challengers.

"Gentlemen." Gedrick drew the first sip of the murky stimulant. "The captain has the bridge." The crew knew immediately what their captain intended, and headed for the mess. Often Gedrick would relieve the night watch early, and for a brief while as the sun rose, he would be alone with his ship. The sailing master looked up at the captain from the work deck and nodded.

Finally alone, Gedrick set the forward watch ports to reflect the incoming light. In the darkness of the expanse, they remained perfectly clear, but soon they would filter all light that entered the cabin. Once the command deck was set, he assumed a position outside of the starboard hatchway with the door open about one-third.

He stood for several minutes looking down on the deck as the crews went about their business, oblivious of their singular audience. He leaned against the doorway and again took a sip of the strong coffee in his hand. He did not need to look into the command deck to know that she was there.

Derring sat on the floor with her back to the forward portlight. She could see Gedrick clearly though the partially open door. She drew her knees up to her chest, and for the first time in longer than she could remember, she felt safe.

"Come here often, sailor?" she asked without any warning.

Gedrick smiled at that. It was an old joke that they had once shared.

"Yes," he replied, in no way startled that she was there, while taking another sip of his coffee. He did not look down toward her; he dared not.

"You used to hate getting up before sunrise," Derring said with a slight smile, looking straight ahead. She did not look at him either. "What happened to that?"

Gedrick never took his eyes off the horizon. "I haven't missed a sunrise aboard the *Shicaine* in five years."

Derring's eyes took on a sadness that transcended the centuries of her life. She remembered back to the last night that they spent aboard the *Shicaine* together. It was the time just before dawn. They were alone that night: most of the crew was gone already and his ship was heading toward her safe haven. Though she would be protected in her zone, she felt as if she were being transported to a prison. Every mile, every swell of the myst brought her closer to a despair deeper than she had ever known. Yet in those few hours that they held the bridge, the ship seemed to be theirs alone. The world seemed to be theirs alone. The eternity that stretched out before her, seen by so many of her race as a blessing, she would thankfully have traded for just one more sunrise with this man.

It was to be the last dawn that she would have with the man who had given her back the sun.

Becoming Lokaryn was not a choice that Derring made, it had been forced upon her. Of all the reminders of her life lost, the most hurtful was the loss of the sunrise. How she loved the sunrise. She would rise with the missionaries and greet the day with thankful prayer. By the end of the day, exhausted, she would often be in bed by sundown. But each day the sun rose again, and with it she was renewed. During that brief time that she was mortal and worked toward being worthy of ministry, she saw the rising sun as God's daily call to her. After her conversion to Lokaryn she could never have the sun again. Should she willingly give herself to the light, it would be suicide and her soul would be forfeit. That she could never again see the sunrise weighed heavily on her. She could go for days without feeding, months without drinking, but each and every single day God called to her in the sunrise and she could not answer. The sun rose as it had without her for so many years.

Then came the Cataclysm, the brutal time afterward, the rise of the sentient androids, and then...the railroad. She met Hemingway and through him the *Shicaine* crew and...Gedrick.

She served aboard the *Shicaine*. At first for only a mission. Then two. Then without ceremony or notice she became a permanent, even indispensable, part of the crew. No one ever thought about it; it was just how things should be. One day, for no particular reason, she was on the bridge, *they* were on the bridge. Gedrick placed her with her back to the front viewports and began describing the rising sun to her. His tones, his inflections, even his breath changed with every new color. Soon the dawn became him. Colors could not have flight without his voice. Often, after a long a mission or a hard night's sailing, he would not be there for the dawn. He held the dawn in no particular esteem, and she never told him what it meant to her. The errors we make.

That last night aboard the *Shicaine* he described the sunrise one last time: The sky was black, with a crisp gentle breeze following the ship. The stars were bright. The constellations would make for easy sailing on a night like tonight. Hints of light, subtle and sublime, made their first reaches into the night sky. Lightly, the first grey was realized to silver as a hint along a cloud edge. The mighty stars succumbed one by one to the dawn's touch. Those silvers of intensifying tone, blossoming into deep purples, then into tendrils of blue, yellow, orange, red and then…the first rim of the sun. The blessed sun. Arising with that ever-present call to the Maker's work, Derring said a silent prayer of thanks. The sun continued on its ascent, making the black of the night and the white of the stars bow to the oranges and reds of the spreading day, then finally to the blue. Gentle soft deep blue. Those few moments of that last dawn replayed in her mind countless times. Every syllable, every nuance, every breath. For five years it was all that she had left.

A few short hours ago she was running. Scared and angry, trying to protect her family. Now she was here, no longer the protector. That burden was lifted. She breathed her first easy breaths in a long while. Here she sat, five years later, watching him. He carried the weight of many more than five years. But his eyes burned with that same intensity. More so. He looked at the horizon, seemingly to pull the sun over it. Then the blackness softened.

Derring watched the beginnings of the first dawn she had been able to experience in many years reflected in Gedrick's eyes and in the hues that bathed his face and body. Every movement, every moment of his experience she would etch on her memory.

"The western sky…" he began.

The past wasn't what you thought it was. The future may be what you hoped for, but not in the way you wanted. The present is delusion soon to be shattered.

—Badlands cleric

CHAPTER 85

Deep myst

Aboard the *Shicaine*

"YOU? FORBID? *ME?*" THE WORDS shot from Lyrie's mouth like an arrow aimed directly at Timan.

"Yes. I forbid. It is the man's place to safeguard the woman's well-being, both physical and spiritual."

"This is going to be good," Ren said to Chirra, and snickered. He looked on eagerly, as if watching a Maritano duel between two Seb-Ichi.

"Shut up, Ren!" Lyrie commanded. "Timan Jospher, I will not be herded around like property even after we've taken the vows. You had best get used to that notion now. If you want some subservient little mouse…"

"Lyrie. I am not treating you as property, but I simply cannot condone your attendance at this meeting."

"It's called a briefing, Timan. It's for all members of the crew."

"We are not members of the crew," Timan countered.

"Oh! Good point there," Ren said.

"Shut up, Ren," Timan ordered.

"We're going to the briefing, if for no other reason than to stay informed. They may have some idea on how to meet back up with our families. I don't see how hiding in our cabins benefits us."

"For starters, we have spent far too much time already in the presence of that artificial and now we're surrounded by machinery and metal. It's literally holding us above death from the myst below our feet."

"You'd rather try walking over the myst?" Lyrie asked, with no small degree of sarcasm.

"What good is being saved from the myst if the manner causes the desecration of our eternal souls by technology?"

"Wow, that was really bad," Ren commented.

"Shut up, Ren," both Lyrie and Timan said at the same time.

"You see, you *can* agree on something, now can we go before we're late for the briefing?" Ren asked.

"Yes," Lyrie said, standing up.

"No!" Timan said in a forceful voice. He reached for Lyrie's arm to restrain her, only to find his own forearm in Ren's grasp. Though impressed with technology, Ren was at heart a farm boy. He had worked from his earliest memories at demanding physical jobs, and his grip succeeded at getting Timan's attention.

Timan looked at Ren. Gone was the smart-aleck little brother and in its place he found himself staring into the eyes of a man ferociously protective of his family.

"Don't *ever* think to do that again, Timan," Ren said.

Timan pulled his arm away from Ren and stared at the younger man.

"This is a mistake," Timan said.

"Then it's ours to make," Lyrie said, and left the room with Ren close on her heels. Chirra and Jarrel followed.

Lyrie and Ren walked along silently until they got to the briefing room. She looked at her brother in a whole new light. They stopped outside the door and Lyrie kissed him on the cheek.

"My hero," she said.

Ren suddenly felt very uncomfortable outside of his role as the younger brother. Not knowing what else to say, he asked, "Do you think they even want us in there?"

"One way to find out."

They could hear conversation on the other side, some heated voices that were mostly responded to by a gravel-voiced man who used the word "impossible" quite a bit. Some were laughing; others were simply conversing. Lyrie knocked softly. Taking a deep breath, she opened the door into a new world.

"I see our newest crew members are here," Gedrick said. "Let's get started."

The room was beginning to look crowded to Gedrick's eyes, but he welcomed that development.

"Don't be late for briefings," Chapman said as he checked the companionway for stragglers. "One of your group is missing," he added.

"He won't be coming," Lyrie responded.

Chapman said nothing but left the door open for some air in the crowded space.

Gedrick looked around the room, surveying the group. He realized that the past and the future were merging. The old world was represented by the chief, Damien Cairo, Hemingway, Cade, Seyschell, and Derring. The new appeared in the persons of Chapman, Griz, Vis-Shan, and Peli Domar. He found himself captain of a formidable crew. The thoughts of escape dwindled in the face of the threats of which he was now becoming aware. Perhaps it was time to face them head-on. He locked eyes with Cairo for a moment, and Cairo smiled as if reading Gedrick's thoughts. He shifted to Derring, who did the same. Then Hemingway. And on and on until he reached the chief.

"For the love of cogs and pistons would you stop daydreaming. I have work to do," the chief growled.

"Does he do that at every meeting?" Chapman asked Seyschell, who stood right next to him.

"He usually finds something to complain about, but the captain has been pretty good about giving him ammunition lately," she replied.

"Distracted," Chapman observed as Gedrick collected his thoughts and the chief fumed.

"And he will be until every crew member is accounted for," Seyschell said.

"I have some ideas about that," Gedrick began. "Our next port of call needs to offer fast transport back to Kwyne for Rohnin Cairo and his team while providing us access to former crew members of the *Shicaine*."

"Thieves' Zone fits both criteria," Seyschell said. "Members of the crew would likely gravitate back to the Drunken Angry Bitch, the Ravensfordians would be trying to make their way there, and Thieves' Zone offers access to most of the other zones."

"The problem may be," Chapman said, "that those ports will be very closely watched now with so many other ports closing down."

"We've had business dealings with at least one discreet port master in Thieves," Seyschell said.

"But remember that discretion is a matter of the highest bidder," Griz said.

"As it's always been," Gedrick added.

"Thieves' Zone, then, is a reasonable next step," Chapman concluded.

"Captain!" came the voice of First Officer McCormick.

"Aye."

"We just received another of Mr. Chapman's myst phantoms. It reads 'Hexa—Tranti—Mala—Hexa.' "

"Kisner!" Gedrick exclaimed with a broad smile on his face.

Some grow up in a single moment.

—Ravensford proverb

CHAPTER 86

"CAPTAIN, WE'RE COMING UP ON the coordinates," Chapman called through the comm system. Gedrick lay awake in his bunk, unable to sleep from the anticipation.

"Very good, Mr. Chapman. I'll be right up."

Chapman nodded to the steward, and a new pot of thick coffee was started brewing.

A few minutes later, Gedrick arrived on the command deck. With a quick look over the railing at the sailing master, who signaled that all was well, he returned inside.

"Status?" he asked, through habit.

"We secured from powered sailing about two hours ago. A near contact brought us to conventional sail. It was a cargo ship headed to the far side of the central chasm. She didn't seem to pay us any attention, but…"

"I agree, better safe than sorry."

"We'll be at the pickup coordinates in less than an hour."

"Very good. You're going to like Kisner."

"You met on the *Shicaine*?"

"No, we met under Captain Timmerson. He left sometime after I did. When I got the *Shicaine*, he joined my crew, as did several of the others from the *Impulse*."

"That speaks highly of your service to that ship," Chapman said.

"*More* to the fact that Timmerson's recklessness could be a little nerve-racking at times," Gedrick replied. "When I got the *Shicaine*, I offered Kisner my old ship, but he declined. Instead, he joined me as the first officer. It just about killed us both when we had to split the crew up. But it was the only way."

"You don't sound convinced."

"I know my decision was right. It saved the lives of the crew, but not a day goes by when I don't wonder what would have happened had we stood our ground. They had Kisner and Cade and we had our backs to the Sluice. What would *you* have done?"

"Given the opportunity, I'd negotiate a deal that would save my crew," Chapman answered.

"Every time I replay that day in my head, I can't figure out where it went wrong. I can't see any other options: Either fight and die, or deal and lose my crew but spare their lives."

"It's a burden that I'm glad I don't carry, Gedrick," Chapman said, lost in thought.

Gedrick looked up at his first officer.

"Oh, I'm sorry, Captain."

"Don't be. That's the first time you've used my name without the title before it. I think you've earned the right."

"Thank you, sir."

"Don't let it go to your head," Gedrick said with a wry smile.

"Captain," Cade said. There was a pause.

"What's wrong, Cade?" Gedrick asked.

"There's a weak signal bearing true north from our position. Looks to be a wreck, but it must be recent, because there's still a power signature."

"Mr. Chapman, bring the crew to alert stations. Cade, plot a course. Helm, bring us to the new heading. Get senior crew up here."

The alarm went throughout the ship that a rescue might be on. Within minutes Seyschell and Hemingway were on the bridge, as were Derring and the chief. Ren was hot on their heels, but remained on the deck outside. As welcome as he had been made to feel, he was still hesitant about being in the presence of the Heretic of Ravensford. Moments later, he was joined by the rest of the Ravensfordians.

Gedrick leaned over to look at them collected in the companionway.

"You may enter the bridge," he said. "If for no other reason than to keep the companionway clear." They filed in and stood against a back wall like observers.

"Captain," Chapman said. "Forward lookout reports that the wreck is coming into view."

Gedrick picked up a spyglass and scanned the distance.

"Son of a bitch!" he exclaimed.

"What's wrong, Captain?"

"It's *Impulse*."

"Timmerson?" Derring said.

"Yes."

"Are you sure? It's been years since you've seen the ship," Seyschell said.

"That's *Impulse*, I'd know her if it had been a hundred years. Cade, take your soundings and get me in as close as you can, but allow the ship a few routes out of here. Commander McCormick, you have the conn."

"You're not going alone," Derring said.

"No, I'm not going alone, but I'm not taking any of you either."

"It could be a trap, you know," she cautioned.

"That thought had crossed my mind. That's why I need you here so that if things go wrong, I have a credible backup plan."

"Who do you propose goes with you then?" Derring asked.

"My bondling," he replied.

"I see that five years has not improved your decision making," Hemingway finally piped up. "So will you be swinging in on a rope, or swimming through the myst with a knife in your teeth?"

Gedrick ignored the android's barb.

"I'll go with you, Captain," Lyrie said. "Having a psionic with you would give you an advantage."

"Absolutely not," Timan replied. "If anyone has to fulfill that role I'll do it."

"Oh good. If a group of mercenary cows has taken over you can sing them to death," Hemingway said.

Gedrick looked the android square in the eye. "Enough, Hemingway," he said, "You may disagree with the decision that I made five years ago, but it was mine to make and everyone is alive because of it. Now if you don't have something meaningful to say, then either shut up or get off my bridge."

"You want something meaningful," the android replied, "then how 'bout this: Lyrie is right. A psionic would be of benefit, but you'll need three of them to form a good field."

"I scarcely think bringing children on a raid is prudent," Chapman said.

Timan bristled at that. "A child? In your culture, perhaps. In mine, men my age own farms and have families," he said.

"I mean you no offense, Timan, but think about this. Three of you would be required. Does your culture also consider Lyrie, Jarrel, and Chirra to be adults?" Chapman asked.

Timan saw the error of his logic. Should he be selected, Lyrie, arguably the strongest psionic of their group, would still need to go.

"I understand," Timan said. "I concede the point."

"No. It makes sense," Lyrie said. "Three of us could monitor the *Impulse* while you go aboard. It's a sensible move. We could spread an excellent sensing field."

There was a momentary pause as Gedrick collected his thoughts, readying to reject the notion diplomatically.

"She's right," Derring said quietly.

"You're taking her side?" Gedrick asked. "I don't believe this."

"Lyrie is an adult and can make her own decisions," Derring said, echoing Lyrie's statement from aboard the *River Rat*. "Timan, Jarrel, Chirra, and for that matter Ren have the right to make their own decisions. It's their lives too."

Lyrie turned to face the captain with a look of determination.

Gedrick had wished to avoid the situation of leading anyone else into danger, but the truth was a psionic field greatly increased the chances of success. If there were crew trapped in the wreck they could find them far more quickly. If someone approached closely, it would allow for at least some warning. It was at times such as this that he hated his duties as captain.

"Commander McCormick," Gedrick said, "select a security detail to go over. Tell the bosun to ready the captain's gig. Once I'm aboard *Impulse*, I'll determine a safe spot and signal back portal coordinates to the chief. Then I'll set an autopilot return for the gig. That should make it simple enough to recover. Our psionic team comes through the portal on the *Impulse* side and stays near the opening. The security detail stays with them. I go into the ship alone."

"Excuse me, but when did a portal come into the equation? For that matter where is it coming from? There's no one we can trust. Certainly not the zone-based portal companies," Seyschell said.

"I believe it will be coming from the *Shicaine*," Chapman answered.

"Mr. Chapman is correct," Gedrick said.

"What? How did you know that?" Seyschell asked, not quite grasping what was being said.

"The only way to set dynamic coordinates the way the captain is describing is by using a technologically based portal. Tech portals allow for great flexibility in creating entrances and exits on demand. We couldn't have known in advance what coordinates we'd need and the captain can't take a few hours once over there to fashion a line-of-sight crystal. A tech portal is the obvious answer."

"You figured that out just this moment?" the chief asked, with a suspicious look in his eye.

"Well, that, and the fact I've seen the units you've been prototyping. Two of them in fact. You drew power through a number of systems to keep your power consumption covered, but fractional increases in almost every system in the ship had to be going somewhere. It was like following a trail of breadcrumbs from there."

The chief mumbled some curses under his breath about which orifice of the Grendel might have begat the first officer, but he said nothing further.

"I still don't see how it's possible to generate one from a ship this size," Peli Domar said.

"The generators themselves aren't overly large. The targeting computer can be a fair size, but running it through the *Shicaine* mainframe would obviate that need," Cade offered.

Domar persisted. "I wasn't thinking about the size of the units. They move them from place to place aboard ships, so I assumed they would fit. But portal generators take far too much energy for a ship to support, even a portal small enough to permit the passage of crewmembers. They tried it for a number of years with rescue ships, but it always burned through the available energy supply too quickly to be of practical value."

"We have a power plant on the ship capable of sustaining the field," Gedrick answered with a glance over at Derring.

"We think," the chief said. "We've never tried it out."

"Kind of thin to be staking your life on isn't it, Captain?" Chapman ventured.

"We have experimented with the power usage on a limited scale. We should be able to sustain the portal with an acceptable margin of time."

"And if you can't?" Seyschell asked.

"If time allows, send the gig back. If it doesn't we'll see how it plays out."

"Back to plan B."

"It's settled then. Timan, Lyrie, and Jarrel will portal to the *Impulse*, but I will go into the ship alone. Security will stay with the Ravensfordians and the group will remain near the portal at all times. Listen to me now. I will have your word that at the first sign of trouble you will proceed through the portal back to the ship."

"Yes," they answered in turn.

A silence ensued. Few liked the plan, but there were no other options. Gedrick continued.

"Very well, then. We board *Impulse* find the survivors and get out of here."

"To where?" Chapman asked.

"Assuming nothing goes wrong, we reach the coordinates, pick up

Kisner, and then head to deep myst as fast as we can. We'll figure the rest out from there."

"Could you use the portal on the ship itself to get away if there's a problem?" Ren asked.

"No," Cade answered. "It's been tried in the past. The generator has to remain intact throughout the transit of the object. As the generator itself passes through the portal, it disrupts the field and destroys whatever is in it at the time. Nice idea, though."

Ren smiled at the compliment in equal measure to Timan's scowl.

"And the backup plan?" Chapman asked.

"That's your job. From my end I'll keep sending telemetry from my eye."

"Aye, sir," Chapman responded.

"Chief, since our cat is out of the bag, orient the senior crew on the use of the portal generator."

The chief nodded and drew close to the captain. "The kid almost had it," he said.

When the past arrives, be assured, it will want its pound of flesh.

—Merchants' Zone proverb

CHAPTER 87

"READY TO TAKE A DIP in the myst, Captain?" the boatswain asked.

"You have a unique way of putting things, Silas, you know that?" Gedrick said.

"A talent, to be sure, Captain," the boatswain responded. "Ready the deck?" he called to the crew standing nearby, including the first officer.

"Ready," the deckhands answered.

"We've established entrance coordinates," Chapman said. "We've tied the telemetry from your eye into the computer, so once you see the spot you want, lay down the transponder, and we'll have the portal up in less than a minute. Any other orders, sir?"

"Take care of my ship, Mr. Chapman," Gedrick said.

"Aye, aye, Captain. She'll be just as you left her," Chapman responded.

Gedrick went aboard the captain's gig. In a moment the hatch was sealed and the davits swung the small boat through the protective shielding of the *Shicaine* and out over the myst. A moment later it was lowered to the caustic sea below. Gedrick fired his engines and sprinted across the short expanse of myst between the *Shicaine* and the *Impulse*. Keeping the *Shicaine* at a good distance was a sound tactical move, but every moment he spent out in the open felt like a lifetime.

"Scans remain clear, Captain," Cade reported over the comm link. It was a small reassurance, but a welcome one.

Gedrick reached the *Impulse* after an eternity. His craft bumped its deck, which listed strongly to one side. He lifted the forward hatch of the gig and jumped the small distance to *Impulse*'s deck. The tide was low and the ship was high enough above the myst on the rocks to offer some small margin should he slip. He quickly found an unsecured hatch and moved inside. Finding an open bay midships, he scanned the area with his cybernetic eye, allowing the holographic generator on the *Shicaine* to paint a reasonable facsimile of the area on the targeting computer. Areas he could not see were left blackened out on the three-dimensional representation that now hovered over one of Cade's navigation tables. Gedrick dropped the transponder.

"Commence portal generation if you please, Mr. Chapman," Gedrick said quietly.

"Chief. Commence portal generation," Chapman relayed.

Lights dimmed as the energy was brought to bear on creating a portal from the *Shicaine* to the *Impulse*. On deck, a small black spot appeared, hovering in midair. It quickly grew in size until it was an oval six feet tall and three feet wide.

"Team ready?" the boatswain asked.

"Ready," they all responded.

Turning without further comment to the inky blackness of the portal, the security detail chief stepped though first and quickly cleared the exit for the others. In a few seconds they were all through. Gedrick stood on the other side to greet them.

"Set up a perimeter around the telepaths," Gedrick instructed the security detail. "You three, begin creating your field."

He scanned the area quickly. Little had changed since the last time he was aboard the *Impulse*. There was some reassurance in that. He made his way into the command deck without issue.

Once inside his skin began to crawl. He could sense a malevolent presence, though not strongly. He made his way forward, and there he saw ruins. The bridge was in disarray, with equipment smashed and nothing moving. In that moment he feared the worst.

He activated the scanning function of his eye and found a thermal signature under a heap of shelving. Manifesting his bondling, he moved them quickly to find Arles Timmerson, his former captain, still breathing.

"What the hell are you doing on my ship?" Timmerson said, very hungover. "Get the hell out of here."

"The *Impulse* was attacked. She's wrecked. I have to get you out of here," Gedrick said.

"I don't need your help," Timmerson slurred.

Before Gedrick could respond, the ship was rocked by a violent explosion.

"Get out," Gedrick called to the rest of the boarding party, but it was too late. The attack had created enough instability that the portal collapsed and they were all trapped aboard the *Impulse*.

Pulling his wrist controller up to his face, Gedrick whispered a command into the microphone. He looked out from the command deck and saw the *Shicaine* starting to move. He could hear the gunfire as forces boarded the *Impulse*. He assumed that the phobes and the security forces were dead as he watched a portal open in front of *Shicaine*. He smiled as she disappeared through the dark opening.

The last words Gedrick heard before a stun blast brought him into darkness were spoken by Timmerson, looking over Gedrick's shoulder:

"You again."

If it doesn't feel like the end of your days, it probably isn't.

—Ga'tomas, Seb-Ichi monk

CHAPTER 88

DARKNESS AND PAIN WERE THE first two sensations that Gedrick felt when he awoke. He was standing and tied to something. He felt the rise and fall that one only experiences during a myst swell. The right side of his chest ached, and in trying to move he found that his arms were tied behind his back. Any attempt to move them caused enormous pain from something stuck in the meat of his muscles there. He could not manifest his bondling.

Activating the thermal scan of his synthetic eye, he saw that people, mostly at a distance, surrounded him. As he looked left, he saw several images similarly bound, and to the right there were several more. By their sizes and number he surmised that the entire boarding party had been captured, as well as Timmerson.

His blood nearly froze solid in his veins when he first heard the voice.

"Good morning, Captain Gedrick." It was the last voice he wanted to hear under these circumstances.

"Kisner?" he said in a voice filled with despair.

Tearing the hood from Gedrick's head, his former first officer held the burlap cover aloft as if it were a beheading. It was a triumphant moment his captor meant to savor.

"Captain Kisner Loh'l, commander of the *Blackthorne*, at your service."

"Kisner, what..." Gedrick didn't get another word out before he felt an energy stick drawn across his neck. With Gedrick coughing and gagging, Kisner Loh'l went on.

"Captain Loh'l will do from you. And don't try to manifest that bondling of yours, I've taken the precaution of placing an inhibitor on your chest. If that thing tries to peek its head out, it will be electrocuted. Take off all their hoods," he directed nearby members of his crew.

The hoods were quickly removed. Timmerson seemed hungover. Timan looked as if he were about to chew through the ropes that held him. Lyrie stared off into space. Jarrel seemed frightened but looked Gedrick in the eyes to acknowledge that he was ready, as did the three members of the boarding party.

"You wrecked my ship to get at him?" Timmerson asked Loh'l.

"I wrecked your ship because I wanted to, it was fun. Because I was paid good money to deliver you up to Kell, and because it was excellent bait for my good friend Captain Gedrick here."

Kisner pulled a man from the ranks of his crew and placed him face-to-face with Gedrick.

Tarro looked at his old captain, at the angry red welt across his neck, the brutal treatment that he was sustaining. The former *Shicaine* intelligence officer wanted to shout out, but he held his calm.

"Well?" Kisner demanded.

"Captain, I don't know what you want of me," Tarro answered.

"Do you know this man, Jayesh?" Kisner asked Tarro.

"I know what I just heard you say, that he is Captain Gedrick of the *Shicaine*."

"Kisner, you really have lost you mind, you know that?" Timmerson said.

His latest ploy to uncover Tarro having failed, he turned back toward the elder captain. "You may actually get out of here alive, old man, if you play your cards right."

"So you can sell me back to the Lokaryn? No thanks."

"I don't see that you have much choice in the matter. Now, Captain Gedrick. You will get on the comm link and instruct *Shicaine* to return to these coordinates. At that point you will turn her over to me."

"Since you are going to execute me anyway, why would I do that?"

"Perhaps I will and perhaps I won't. It depends on if you maintain any worth to me. But since you are so keen on saving your crew, again," he added with sarcasm, "if you bring *Shicaine* to me, I will spare these lives. Except, of course, for Timmerson, who has some unfinished business with a Lokaryn." Loh'l offered his best serpentine smile. "And I guarantee that I will stop hunting *Shicaine* crew."

"Well, your guarantee isn't worth pig's dung!" Timan snarled.

"Excuse me one minute, Captain," Kisner said pleasantly. "I have to tend to a small disciplinary problem." He walked down the row of prisoners at a leisurely pace.

Arriving at Timan, he said, "You have a loud mouth, boy. But I admire your spirit. Tied up. About to watch a beheading, and, depending on Captain Gedrick's decision, maybe to experience your own. Who knows where this will take us, eh? Yet you speak up. Good for you, but a man has to live with his decisions. Right, Captain?" Kisner called over to Gedrick.

"Your business is with me," Gedrick shouted back. The telemetry relay of his eye could not reach the *Shicaine* wherever she was, though he continued to look around, logging distances and movements. If he could get the information to the *Shicaine*, the chief might be able to portal in troops.

"No, Captain, my business right now is with this young man who has made a decision to speak his mind." Without a moment's hesitation, Kisner pulled a nasty-looking pistol from his side holster and shot Jarrel in the leg, severing it below the knee. The young man screamed in pain. The only small favor was that the wound was cauterized by the blast.

"Bastard!" Timan shouted. He began to form a psionic assault. Perhaps he couldn't kill everyone on the ship, but he would kill this man.

Kisner then placed the pistol to Lyrie's temple.

"You're a Ravensfordian, correct? I so much as get a headache during these proceedings I will ventilate her brain. If I fall, my first officer will be happy to complete the task."

"Well, if I must," Ma'Goran said with mock reluctance and gave the phobe a slight bow.

"Got it?" Kisner said.

"Yes," Timan said through clinched teeth. He continued to gather his force.

"Captain," Ma'Goran said. "Perhaps we should proceed. Time may not be on our side."

Abruptly Lyrie began looking around quickly in every direction.

"Perhaps you're right," Kisner said. "But I've been looking forward to this for a long time and I intend to enjoy it."

Ma'Goran gave him a vicious kiss.

"What the hell happened to you?" Gedrick asked.

"I'm asking the questions, and you need only answer one. Will you surrender *Shicaine* to me? I'll spare the others' lives. I will spare the crew, current and former. I will."

"I doubt it. I don't know who you are or what you have become, but you'll kill everyone."

"Very well then. Perhaps your death will inspire your crew aboard *Shicaine* to negotiate. Killing the others leaves me no negotiating tools, and alive, you give the orders. Since you've decided to be as hardheaded as ever, you get to go first."

Kisner motioned to several crewmembers, who moved a heavy guillotine to the middle of the deck.

"Put him in." Kisner sneered. "I'm not kidding, Gedrick. This is larger than you and me, and I will kill you."

"You were going to kill me no matter what."

"Let him watch the blade the whole way down," Ma'Goran suggested.

"Sir?" a crewman asked.

"Put him in facing up so he can see the blade coming," Captain Loh'l affirmed.

An evil murmur arose from the crew.

Gedrick was grabbed roughly and slammed onto the boards, which had been cobbled together by the ship's carpenters. He looked up to see the angled blade with a keen metal edge dangling over his neck.

All things die. He recalled the teachings of his Seb-Ichi master. *To embrace death when it comes will give you peace.*

Yet he felt no peace. His mind turned to the one woman he had ever loved. It was good to have seen her again, and though it was an impossible situation, he would give much for another day. He looked over and saw Lyrie staring at his neck and up toward the blade again and again. Her lips formed the word "Ren" many times. He felt horrible that Stannis Klemm's daughter would have to witness such a thing. Still he could not bring himself to believe even now that this was to be his fate, not while the *Shicaine* sailed with an able crew.

If it doesn't feel like the end of your days, it probably isn't. The words his uncle had shared with him, when he was a boy, drifted through his mind.

"Look away" was all he said to the group, but they could not.

With a very subtle popping noise, a small circular device dropped from a portal that had manifested some ten feet above the deck and landed with a small thud. *One of the phobes must have made contact,* Gedrick thought. His eye sent out its accumulated information about the layout of the deck. The telemetry was picked up by the probe and relayed back to the *Shicaine*.

There was a pause in the activity of the execution. No one was sure what had just happened. It took a moment before Kisner shouted: "Probe! Prepare for boarders!"

The deck became alive with activity as men and women rushed to the munitions lockers and pulled personal weapons. Chaos erupted.

"Do it!" Ma'Goran shouted to the executioner, who was looking around frantically.

The executioner pulled the lever.

"No!" Kisner shouted a moment to late.

The blade accelerated toward Gedrick amid the chaos of the deck. A small popping noise announced the opening of a portal. Gedrick heard the noise but knew that any help would be too late. Salvation appeared in front of his eyes, as a portal manifested directly in the course of the blade. Kisner stood mere feet away from him and watched as the blade disappeared a few inches from the flesh. The blocks that supported the blade landed harmlessly on either side of Gedrick's neck.

Stunned, Kisner was standing there with his pistol drawn when he heard another popping sound over his head. He leaned back ever so slightly. It was the only thing that prevented a killing blow, as the blade dropped through the exit portal toward his head. Instead it sliced into his right shoulder before coming to rest in the deck and severing his foot in half in the process.

A portal opened beneath the guillotine and the whole apparatus disappeared through the darkness. Weapons fire erupted from the small portals that now seemed to open and close at random around the deck. Portals opened beneath each of the prisoners, and they quickly disappeared as well. Kisner shouted through his pain, attempting to arrange a defense. He started firing his pistol down into the portals as they closed. His crew followed suit. Ma'Goran finally restored some semblance of order by shooting two of her own crewmembers.

After the last of the portals had closed and the deck had quieted down, Kisner seethed. "What are our casualties?" he demanded.

Ma'Goran scanned the pockmarked deck. "Jayesh," she said. "Where the hell is Jayesh?"

Aboard the *Shicaine*, Gedrick still ached from the impact of hitting the deck of the cargo bay. Derring walked up to the guillotine and put a foot on it. Leaning in to Gedrick, she said, "I told you it was a trap."

"I told you plan B would work," he replied. "Now would you get me the hell out of here."

Derring reached down and removed the inhibitor with a quick pull that took a small amount of flesh with it. The bondling, unleashed, made short work of the ropes that held Gedrick, and soon he was on his feet.

Looking for all of the boarding party he counted two additional persons. One was Timmerson; the other he did not know.

"Who the hell are you?" he asked, drawing his bondling.

"Hexa—Veta—Greno—Hexa," the stranger replied.

"Tarro?" Gedrick asked, dumbfounded.

"Yes, Captain. Good to be aboard. Assuming we survive this, I have some intel for you."

Vis-Shan was already tending to Jarrel's wounds. "We have a good supply of crystals aboard. You should be able to find what you need to tend to the leg."

"Oh no," Gedrick heard Derring say.

Turning, he saw the rohnin propped up against a wall. He had a small smile on his face as he sat slumped over to one side. He had been shot in the center of his chest. He was still alive, but would not be for much longer.

Let the dead man stop the war.

—Unknown

CHAPTER 89

"THE CONDEMNED ARE ABOARD," GRIZ called up to the bridge.

"Go!" Chapman ordered Seyschell in the pilot's crib.

Seyschell swung the ship around in a tight arc, and slammed the thrusters forward. The *Shicaine* leapt to the power and surged above the myst. Cade's hands moved across the navigation grids as if a day hadn't passed since the last time he had done this.

"Threat bearing twenty degrees port, designate Threat Alpha," he called out.

"That didn't take long," Chapman noted. "Calculate new course and feed to the pilot."

"Done," Cade said.

"Identity of threat and do they see us?"

"Transponder is not transmitting, Commander. Size and general configuration would indicate a Chumley's Zone frigate. Direct intercept course."

"Great. Open a comm link to the engine room and get the captain up here. Instruct gunnery crews to get their stations hot, but wait for weapons-free command from me. Load those diamond-tipped ordinance that we picked up."

"You play rough. Do you think it will come to that?" McCormick asked.

Before Chapman could answer, Cade settled the question.

"Threat—correction. Threats, multiple. Bearing forty, sixty, and one directly astern."

"Astern is *Blackthorne*. The others?"

"The big one is a Mastiff. Designate Threat Delta. No doubt there, she's the one bearing at sixty degrees. The other looks to be a corporate cruiser, trifoil. She's fast. Designate Threat Epsilon. All on intercept courses."

"Even *Blackthorne*?"

"She's just getting underway, but yes, she's coming about."

"Not to state the obvious, but it would appear that your ex-shipmate has made some rather impressive friends," Chapman said.

"Time to intercept?" McCormick asked.

"The only ship with enough speed to intercept us is the trifoil and she probably couldn't sustain the closure speed near long enough to catch us. Plus we do have a few extra horses in the stable if we need them," Cade said.

"True, but our reserves are low after that last portal," Chapman said.

"Yeah, you still need to explain who teleported our ship," Cade said.

"Chief?" Chapman called on the comm link.

"Here, Commander."

"We're going to give your girlfriends a bit of a workout, you ready down there?"

"They're always ready. That's why they're my girlfriends."

"Keep the link open, Chief."

"Aye," the chief acknowledged.

"Captain on the bridge," the sergeant at arms announced.

"I have the conn, Mr. Chapman. Status?"

"Good to have you back, Captain. Four threats, frigate at zero-two-zero relative, Mastiff at sixty, both Chumley's Zone. The *Blackthorne* is behind us and we've got a Thorpe's trifoil at forty starboard."

"Nothing else?" Gedrick asked.

"New contacts," Cade replied.

"I was kidding," Gedrick said. "Same old luck."

There was a pause.

"Cade? Want to give us a number?"

"Still counting, Captain. The computer is up to twenty. Smaller ships but quite a few of them. Likely coming from the Mastiff battle platform. They're fanning out."

"What happens when he runs out of letters in the alphabet?" Chapman asked.

"We start using the names of your mother's old lovers. The ones she knows," Chief called though the open comm link.

"Don't you have an engine room to watch?" Chapman asked politely.

"Captain, we're fairly ringed to the starboard side, but the port is clear."

"Well. We've rated some of the line's finest ships. I'm honored," Gedrick said.

"THIS IS OUTRAGEOUS!" KISNER LOH'L screamed into the comm link at the commander of the *Glorion*, the Mastiff-class battle platform.

"Loh'l, my orders are clear. The *Shicaine* is not to escape. You had your chance and your need for theatrics squandered it. Now, I have broad latitude in how I execute my mission, but the *Shicaine* will not escape again."

Kisner recognized the hint and seized on the moment. "Then perhaps you could be of assistance to me in another way. *Shicaine* is known to carry large quantities of gems in her holds for trading purposes. I will need some of that space for my equipment once I have transferred my flag to her. I could use your assistance in storing those gems."

Kisner's mind screamed through the pain of the wounds he had just received, but he remained the captain, and he had a job to do. He looked on with some satisfaction as the *Glorion*'s commander allowed a small smile.

"For the moment my ships will not engage *Shicaine*. You may recommence your negotiation when the *Shicaine* is penned in. Make no mistake, though, I will destroy the ship should she seem ready to slip your tether again."

Kisner ended the conversation with a contemptuous thought that he kept to himself.

ACROSS THE MYSTS THE TRAP was evident.

"We're not in range yet, but from what I know those ships could be moving faster," Cade said.

"Would I be correct in assuming that the best open venue to us is due west across the top of the Sluice?"

"Yes, Captain."

"Any intel on the other side."

"No, sir."

"So if we go up there and there's another armada or even a Mastiff on the other side…"

"We're stuck."

"I see. Chief, how close to ready are we?" Gedrick called into the comm link.

"Sorry, Captain, not even near close. I'll need a much larger charge on those cells, several hours' worth at least, and you'll need to minimize the energy output of the ship at that."

"Very well, Chief, make ready."

"The ionization will be too heavy in the Sluice for portal formation. That's what happened with *Wiscott*."

"You don't worry about that, you just tell me when we're ready."

"Aye, Captain."

"Mr. Chapman. Make for conventional sail."

"Captain?" he asked.

"They have us, we know they have us, and to pretend otherwise is wasteful. Kisner is well aware that I know that there are more ships on the other side of the Sluice. So we sail up there, conserving our power. Let him pull his drawstrings tight. He knows we'll try to negotiate our way out."

"Captain, your little science project worked well, but with the ionization in the area, the chief is correct, it won't allow that scheme to work."

"Aces, Mr. Chapman. Always have an ace. Make for conventional sail."

"*Shicaine* is making for the head of the Sluice. Full sail," the nav officer of the *Glorion* reported.

"Poor *Shicaine*," the commander of the *Glorion* said. "No chance of escape. Conserving her energy for the last breakout. Maybe she'll wait for nightfall. I don't trust this, Captain. He's as slippery as a McAllister's prostitute."

"Sir? What about your arrangement with Captain Loh'l?" the executive officer asked his commander.

"I made no deal. The man is a pirate. He has no scruples, no discipline. I told him what he wanted to hear so that he would comply with our plan with a minimum of resistance. Captain Loh'l will walk away from today empty-handed, if at all. If we can take *Shicaine* whole, more's the prize, otherwise, when *Shicaine* comes into the optimal firing solution, destroy her. If *Blackthorne* thinks to object, destroy her as well. The commander in chief was clear in his orders."

DERRING MOPPED THE HEAD OF the rohnin of Kwyne. Pale and breathing with shallow breaths, he looked at her.

"Does it come down to us, Derring?"

"It may, Damien," Derring said with a sorrow on her face she had not known since she had lost her brother.

"What would the book counsel us, sister?"

"Damien."

"Let go of your facade and share your faith with me. Sister, help me, time is short."

Derring looked into Damien Cairo's eyes. He did not judge her. To his eyes she was not evil, but a fellow believer. He knew her faith. In this most desperate of moments the demigod of Kwyne lay dying asking the maligned embodiment of all evil for guidance in the scripture.

"Derring, help me," he implored.

"The book would say to put your faith in Thecla," she answered honestly.

"Perhaps we both should," he said quietly.

"CONTACT. THREAT DELTA HAS TURNED on her transponder."

"Identification?"

"It's the *Glorion*, sir."

"So we have the *Glorion* on our tail. Well, at least we rate the very best."

"We're receiving telemetry on the far side of the Sluice now, sir. No ships on the far side yet."

"Curious. We probably just haven't seen them. What do you think, Mr. Chap—"

"Weapons hot on the *Glorion*, sir!" Cade shouted.

Gedrick shared a look with his first officer that lasted a fraction of a second.

"Helm, hard a-port," Gedrick commanded as he made for the pilot's crib.

Chapman shouted, "Crash the sails. Pull in the foils. Countermeasures!"

"Torpedo—Torpedoes free, sir! They're trying to flush us out into the far side of the Sluice."

Gedrick dove into the pilot's crib, ignoring the harnesses and slamming the console down.

"Powered ops now!"

THE ROHNIN HELD HIS HOLY book in his hands. Images of his wife and children played around him. He knew he was losing his grasp of reality. Time was short.

"Derring, will you help me save T'Amorach?" he asked.

"Damien. Please, I swore never to do such a thing," she pleaded. He was white now. The color had even gone from the creases in the palms of his hands. His heart raced and he panted for words. They numbered so few now.

"*Arantago malinus acinus preto. Magn…Tu'l shura…*" His voice trailed off. He slurred a few more words as his life ebbed. The Kuhbrikian captain and sergeant leveled their weapons on the Lokaryn.

CHAPMAN AND SEYSCHELL MOVED ACROSS the bridge in a blur, setting for powered ops. Cade plotted the torpedo's course. The *Shicaine* fired to life in an instant, throwing many to the ground with her acceleration. Her sails ripped under the strain. The foils were pulled in as quickly as possible, but the damage to them was unknown.

A huge stone massif stood in front of the *Shicaine*, but she slid by it with the grace of a dancer.

"Full power," Chapman shouted.

"Full power aye, sir," the chief responded.

"Countermeasures free!" Cade reported.

Gedrick drove the *Shicaine* deep into the labyrinth of the Sluice.

"Massif, one-thirty-five relative!" Cade shouted. Gedrick had already adjusted.

"Massif, bearing zero-zero-five!" Cade shouted, but again Gedrick had already compensated. The navigator fell silent as Gedrick continued in his trance, avoiding one deadly stone outcropping after another.

Without warning, the *Shicaine* slowed and came about.

"Ready gun crews, anchoring charges!" Chapman shouted down to the boatswain.

"Port and starboard gun crews fire!" Chapman directed.

WITHOUT WARNING, DERRING DISARMED BOTH men. She was back to Cairo's side before either realized what had happened.

"Leave us," she said.

"No, ma'am," the sergeant said. "We protect the rohnin. We cannot leave his side. Kill us if you must."

"Only if you must," the captain added. "Clan Lord. He will die. The zones will fall upon each other. His intention was clear. You can buy him the time he needs to avert the war."

"You don't know what you are asking," she said.

"No, I don't. But the rohnin does."

"He will be an undead. Your demigod converted! Do you not think that will bring war?" Derring was desperate.

The sergeant spoke next.

"Dead, the war comes. Even undead, we have some options."

It was in this moment that Derring understood. She laid the rohnin on the floor in front of her, silently blessing herself in a prayer of forgiveness. Gently, she picked him up and drew his neck close. His heart was slowing now, his breaths were grasping for threads of life. She brought her teeth to his neck. She had never converted anyone to the body. It had been one of the few things that enabled her to hold on to an illusion of humanity.

Sinking her teeth into his carotid, she drew in a small bit of his blood. It was laced with death. The blood tasted bitter; drinking it was almost like drinking acid. It was not the warm, comforting fluid that she sustained herself on, but rather, a bilious noxious fluid that turned her stomach.

The connection made, she infused herself into Cairo's body. She repeated this process many more times. Each time the vile sensations repeated themselves until finally the initiation was complete. Exhausted, she fell backward. Tears streamed from her face.

THE HARPOONS FLEW OUT FROM the *Shicaine* and imbedded themselves in the wall of the Sluice.

Gedrick shook from the reverie of piloting. Standing from the crib he looked somewhat drunk.

"Chief?"

"We can use the increased ion flow from the Sluice to decrease the recharge time, but it's still too early to tell how long it'll take."

"Captain Gedrick," came the voice of Gedrick's once-brother, Kisner Loh'l.

The *Shicaine* crew looked at one another.

"Gedrick, answer. It is pointless not to. I can stop the attack, but you must answer me," Kisner said. "The situation aboard the *Blackthorne* is not what it seems. It was all for show. Gedrick I know how mad you are, I know I shot one of your crew, but these are desperate times. There is a war coming, and to stop it requires drastic measures. You know this. Talk to me."

"Let him eat static," Gedrick informed the communications officer.

"Options?" he asked the crew.

"Negotiate," Seyschell said. "The *Glorion* being here means that the governments of the zones have found out we were reunited. They will understand that we had no choice. We agree to the original deal."

"The problem is that Cairo isn't in the power structure of Kwyne to bargain for us," Gedrick replied. "He was key in those negotiations, and not to be harsh about it but he's a dead man who hasn't stopped breathing yet."

"And won't for some time yet," Derring said, walking in looking utterly defeated.

"What have you done?" Gedrick asked.

"Cairo asked to be converted to stave off death. His protectors made a convincing case."

"Dear Thecla! The rohnin of Kwyne is a Lokaryn?" Chapman said to no one in particular.

"No. He is not a Lokaryn, yet. He is an 'initiate.' He has not fed yet. He won't need to for some time, days, perhaps a couple of weeks. So he is not yet a Lokaryn, but he also won't die tonight," Derring said, sitting heavily in a chair.

"So we have two weeks," Seyschell said.

"Yes," Derring replied.

"To do what?" Chapman asked.

"Avert the war," Cade said.

"To find Thecla's Heart," Gedrick corrected. "Chief?"

"Not yet."

All is not as it seems.

—Kisner Loh'l, captain of the *Blackthorne*

CHAPTER 90

THE *SHICAINE* WAS TRAPPED.

Hours stretched out as charge after charge was released into the currents of the Sluice. The *Shicaine* remained safely hidden in the rock labyrinth, but the ship's crew heard the register of each charge as if it were right off their bow.

The senior crew, past and present, as well as the Ravensfordians, were assembled on the bridge. Damien Cairo, though lucid, looked worse than death.

"Their attack pattern indicates that they don't know where we are yet, but sooner or later they'll figure it out," Cade said.

"*Blackthorne* continues to send messages to Chumley's Zone and to the military ships demanding the cessation of hostilities. The corporate-zone ships are not engaging," the communications officer reported.

"Small favors," Chapman said. "Continue monitoring."

"We can't stay here forever," Seyschell observed. "So let me make sure I've got this. We're stuck here. The ionic interference is far too dense to form a rescue portal. We have no one to negotiate on our behalf, and eventually they'll figure out how to direct the charges and blow us out of the Sluice. In other words, things are back to normal."

"A half-lokaric rohnin qualifies as normal? You must tell me more about the old days," Chapman answered.

"The increased ion density works to our advantage," Gedrick noted.

"How?" Seyschell asked.

"We need to recharge our batteries. The increased ion flow over the collectors will shorten that process significantly."

"And then what?"

"We leave."

"They are mine!" Kisner screamed.

"Have they answered you?" the commander of the *Glorion* asked.

"Not yet, but they will!"

"If you get to them first, Captain, we can talk. Until then, any provocative move by *Blackthorne* against any ship except *Shicaine* will be viewed as a declaration of war by your crew on our entire zone and we will respond appropriately."

THE CHARGES CONTINUED TO EXPLODE in the myst. The sounds and energy echoed off the walls and mesas of the labyrinth.

Each explosion shook the *Shicaine*. Sometimes it seemed as if they were so close that the *Glorion* must have figured out how to penetrate the murk of the Sluice and were readying the killing blow. Each of the crew had long since fallen silent, left with their own thoughts.

Chapman stood up suddenly and walked over to the captain. Everyone on the bridge looked at the two.

"Yes, Mr. Chapman," Gedrick said as another explosion rocked the ship.

"Captain, you have not told us your intentions."

"My intentions, Mr. Chapman?" Gedrick looked around the bridge. "We've been here once before and negotiated our way out. I've spent the last five years regretting that decision. If we surrender to the military, they'll take *Shicaine* but we'll all survive. If, on the other hand, the chief calls up from the engine room with the word that we have enough power, we'll have a chance at escaping—though at odds anyone would not willingly take. If I transfer the rohnin, he lives, but the secret that he's undead won't last long. If I screw up and everyone dies…"

"Captain, what are your intentions?"

"My intentions? After five years of thinking about this every day, I know I would rather be doing this for the next few minutes and die, than spend the rest of my life wishing I had. Does that make my intentions clear, Mr. Chapman?"

"It does indeed, Captain. Very good," Chapman said, returning to his duty station.

"Aye, aye," the bridge crew said in unison.

"Aye, aye, Captain," Hemingway said.

"Gedrick to engine room. What's our status, Chief?"

"We have the power, Captain. But the ionization is still too heavy in the area."

"Program in these new coordinates, Mr. Cade. Bosun, check the drop package and confirm that it's operational-status."

"The drop package?" the boatswain asked.

"Yes. Do it now."

"Aye, sir," the boatswain replied.

"Communications Officer, open a channel to the *Blackthorne*," Gedrick instructed.

"*Shicaine* to *Blackthorne*."

"Loh'l here. Surrender the ship and I will allow the military to take your crew. You know that they will be safe that way. Gedrick, all is not as it seems. You must trust me."

"*Blackthorne*. *Shicaine* declines."

Almost as if on cue the depth charges intensified, exploding with an enormous ferocity.

Gedrick strapped himself into the pilot's crib.

"Set a starboard anchoring line from the stern cannons. Then cut the bowlines. Starboard first, then the port," Gedrick said.

The deck crew responded reflexively and the ship swung over in the current.

"Away missiles," he commanded, and the myst was set to blaze. It came roaring out of the labyrinth toward the waiting ships, engulfing them in a wave of burning myst. The crews aboard those ships now fought for survival.

The *Shicaine* righted herself and headed down the Sluice. She did not fight the current as so many had before her but instead rode the sweep, using it as a boon.

The burning myst cleared the ionization quickly.

"I have a firing solution," the weapons officer from the *Glorion* shouted.

"Make your target!" the captain ordered. "Full spread. Fire when ready!"

Chapman looked out from the command deck and saw Gabriel's Lantern at its base, burning beautifully.

"My God," a crewman murmured.

"Focus, people," Chapman said in a steady voice.

"Chief, are the generators online?" Gedrick asked.

"Hell of a time to ask, but yes."

"Do you have the new coordinates?"

"Yes, Captain. I hope you know what you're doing."

"Me too, Chief." Gedrick smiled. "Initiate sequence."

The crew of the *Shicaine* passed Gabriel's Lantern with their eyes clear.

"Sir. All firing solutions lost," the weapons officer of the *Glorion* reported, looking up to his captain. "*Shicaine* has gone over the Sluice."

www.ingramcontent.com/pod-product-compliance
Lightning Source LLC
Chambersburg PA
CBHW030742030726
47497CB00001B/92